PENG

PIECES (

G000088510

Bestselling author Sinéad Moriarty lives in Dublin with her husband and their three children. *Pieces of My Heart* is the sixth of her nine novels. Her other titles are: *The Baby Trail*, *A Perfect Match*, *From Here to Maternity*, *Keeping it in the Family* (also known as: *Whose Life Is It Anyway?*), *Me and My Sisters* and *This Child of Mine*. Her ninth novel, *Mad About You*, is published in summer 2013.

Pieces of My Heart

SINÉAD MORIARTY

PENGUIN BOOKS

PENGUIN BOOKS

Published by the Penguin Group

Penguin Books Ltd, 80 Strand, London WC2R 0RL, England

Penguin Group (USA), Inc., 375 Hudson Street, New York, New York 10014, USA

Penguin Group (Canada), 90 Eglinton Avenue East, Suite 700, Toronto, Ontario, Canada M4P 2Y3
(a division of Pearson Penguin Canada Inc.)

Penguin Ireland, 25 St Stephen's Green, Dublin 2, Ireland (a division of Penguin Books Ltd)

Penguin Group (Australia), 707 Collins Street, Melbourne, Victoria 3008, Australia
(a division of Pearson Australia Group Pty Ltd)

Penguin Books India Pvt Ltd, 11 Community Centre, Panchsheel Park, New Delhi – 110 017, India

Penguin Group (NZ), 67 Apollo Drive, Rosedale, Auckland 0632, New Zealand
(a division of Pearson New Zealand Ltd)

Penguin Books (South Africa) (Pty) Ltd, Block D, Rosebank Office Park, 181 Jan Smuts Avenue,
Parktown North, Gauteng 2193, South Africa

Penguin Books Ltd, Registered Offices: 80 Strand, London WC2R 0RL, England

www.penguin.com

First published by Penguin Ireland 2010
Published in Penguin Books 2011
This edition published 2013

001

Copyright © Sinéad Moriarty, 2010

The moral right of the author has been asserted

Typeset by TexTech International
Printed in Great Britain by Clays Ltd, St Ives plc

A CIP catalogue record for this book is available from the British Library

ISBN: 978-0-241-96740-9

www.greenpenguin.co.uk

Penguin Books is committed to a sustainable
future for our business, our readers and our planet.
This book is made from Forest Stewardship
Council™ certified paper.

ALWAYS LEARNING   **PEARSON**

For Amy

A smooth sea never made a skilful mariner

I

I examined myself in the mirror. I hadn't worn this black dress in years, but it still fitted, which was a relief. I moved closer and peered at my face – daylight was harsh: all I could see were lines everywhere, mapping out my life so far.

I decided to focus on the positive – the dress fitted. Having children young definitely helped you to maintain some kind of waistline.

Sally came up the stairs and walked into the room. She looked stunning in a black trouser suit. Not having children at all helped you to maintain a sensational waistline.

'Nice suit,' I said.

'Prada. My present to myself for my forty-third birthday,' said my best friend. 'New boobs for my fortieth, Botox for my forty-first, Restylane for my forty-second and now designer clothes.'

'Well, you look brilliant. I think I'll have to ask Paul for a full face-lift for my birthday.'

'Hey, you're the hottest mother I know. My sisters all look like old women.'

'I don't feel remotely hot. Look at all these wrinkles.'

'That's why they invented Botox.'

'I know, I know. I just hate needles.'

'Muuuuum!' yelled Sarah, storming into the bedroom. 'There is no way I'm wearing this nun's outfit.'

'I want you to look respectable. Just put it on.'

'If I have to wear it, I'm not going.' She threw the navy dress onto my bed and folded her arms.

'Sarah, I haven't got time for this.'

'Come on, I'll help you find something,' Sally said, ushering my bolshy sixteen-year-old out.

As they left, Alison walked in, wearing a simple but elegant beige shift dress. 'Is this OK?' she asked.

'It's perfect, Ali.' I smiled at my eldest daughter. 'You look lovely. Come on, let's go check on Charlie.'

My father was standing in the hall in his best suit, looking very pleased with himself.

'Are you feeling all right, Charlie?' Alison asked, laying a gentle hand on his arm.

'Never better. I've been waiting for this day for twenty-three and a half years,' he said, beaming.

'Charlie!' I scolded half-heartedly.

'This is the best day of my life.' He grinned. 'I'll celebrate the tenth of August every year.'

Sarah came strutting down the stairs in a black mini-skirt and a black top with *Babe* emblazoned across the front. I glanced at Sally, who threw her arms into the air. 'This is mild – you should have seen what she wanted to wear.'

'Sarah, you do know we're going to a funeral, not a nightclub,' I reminded her.

'Legs like this deserve to be shown off,' she said, flicking back her long dark hair.

'Sarah –'

Charlie put his hand on my shoulder. 'Leave her, Ava. She'll liven things up.'

'Where's Dad?' Alison asked.

I sighed. 'Stuck in work. He said he'd meet us out there. Come on, everyone, into my car.'

Paul was waiting for us at the church. 'Why is our sixteen-year-old daughter dressed like a hooker?' he asked.

'Talk to Sally. I left her in charge,' I replied.

'You should thank me.' Sally laughed. 'She wanted to wear hot pants, so we compromised.'

'Ava left *you* in charge of Sarah's wardrobe?'

'Are you implying that I dress inappropriately, too?' Sally said, playfully punching his arm.

'Did you forget your shirt?'

'Smartarse. Prada trouser suits don't require shirts,' she retorted. Then, turning to me, she asked, 'I'm not showing too much cleavage, am I, Ava?'

Before I had the chance to reassure her that she wasn't over-exposed, Charlie jumped in: 'I'd like to see a lot more,' he said. 'I've always been a boob man.'

Sally, Paul and Sarah tried not to laugh, while Ali looked embarrassed.

'Charlie!' I hissed. 'We're at your wife's funeral.'

'I can't help it. I haven't had sex in six years!'

'That is a serious famine,' Paul agreed.

'Ewww, Charlie, do old people still do it?' Sarah asked.

'Any chance they get,' Charlie assured her. 'And now that Catherine has finally died, I'm free.'

'Was she really that bad?' Ali asked.

'She was out of her mind with drink for twenty years. I've been cleaning up vomit for decades.'

'Were there no warning signs in the beginning, before you got married?' Sally wondered.

'I just thought she was good fun, lively. I didn't realize she drank half a bottle of vodka before every date.'

I patted his back. 'You've had a tough time, but it's over now.'

'Alleluia! I'm back on the market, so watch out, ladies.'

'You can come out with me and my single friends,' Sally offered.

I pinched her. Why was she encouraging him? He was like someone escaped from prison – he needed to calm down. I was worried he'd go out and shack up with the first woman he happened to bump into. After my mother died, Catherine was the first he'd met and look what a disaster that had turned out to be. Charlie had never been on his own. He liked being in relationships. I'd need to keep a close eye on him.

We headed inside and sat up at the front of the church. Sally was in the pew directly behind us. There were barely twenty people in all, including us. Catherine had clearly alienated almost everyone. The priest cleared his throat and began . . .

He talked about Catherine's 'fun-loving nature and her unfortunate decline in health'. He said she had been 'a loving wife to Charlie for over twenty years'.

'There was no loving,' Charlie grumbled, under his breath.

The priest noted what a wonderful carer Charlie had been, looking after Catherine through some very hard times. He then asked us to take a few moments to reflect on our own personal memories of Catherine.

After we had reflected, the altar boy carried the water and wine to the priest. As he approached the altar, he tripped on his vestment. The water and wine went flying, most of it spilling at the priest's feet. There was a deathly silence. Then Charlie began to laugh. Soon half of the mourners had joined in while the other half looked appalled.

The priest peeled the boy off the floor, muttered, 'I'm terribly sorry. If you'll excuse us a minute while we regroup. This is most unusual, never happened before,' and led him, red-faced, to the sacristy. Once they were out of earshot Charlie said loudly, 'I can tell you now it was Catherine who tripped that poor boy up. She doesn't want us having any wine without her.'

'Heaven must be a drink-free zone.' Sally grinned.

'Or else she's drunk it dry already.' Charlie and Sally erupted into a fresh fit of laughter.

'For God's sake, you two,' I hissed at them. 'We're supposed to be the chief mourners here. Everyone's staring.' They struggled to compose themselves.

Paul leaned across me and whispered to Charlie, 'You're a saint for staying with her all those years. Were you not tempted to do a runner?'

4

'I was, I was, but I'm an old-fashioned fellow,' Charlie admitted. 'Till death us do part and all that. That's why I'll never marry again. From now on I'm going to look after myself. No more lost causes.'

'Maybe you should breathalyse them on the first date,' Sally said, her shoulders shaking again.

I shot her a warning look. '*Stop* encouraging him.'

'Is it over yet?' Sarah yawned, thoroughly bored by the whole thing.

'Nearly,' Paul said. 'And don't even think about putting that iPod on. I can see it in your pocket.'

'But Ali's been texting David the whole time and you're not giving her grief.' Sarah pouted.

'Ali, put your phone away,' Paul told her. She finished a message quickly and stuck the phone in her pocket.

The priest returned, the altar boy following with replenished containers. 'I'm terribly sorry for that interruption,' the priest said. 'Fred here would like me to apologize to you all on his behalf, especially the grieving family.' I suppressed a smile. We couldn't have looked less like a grieving family.

After the final blessing, the undertakers moved in quietly to bring the coffin outside to the hearse. The congregation followed. People came up to Charlie and said they were sorry for his loss . . . She was better off now . . . At peace . . .

The rest of us stood apart, basking in the hot sun.

'Oh, my God,' Sarah squealed suddenly, 'he just pinched that woman's arse!'

We spun around to see Charlie groping someone's bum.

'That is truly the definition of mutton dressed as lamb,' Paul marvelled. We watched the woman kissing Charlie's cheek, leaving a bright red lipstick mark, then tottering away in six-inch heels and a very tight short dress, with a slit up the side.

'I can't believe he made a pass at someone at a funeral. At his *wife's* funeral,' Sally gasped. She grinned. 'Charlie's going to be so much fun now he's been set loose. I'm raging I'm going away. Ava, text me the juicy stuff.'

'I can't believe he's my new house-mate,' Paul said.

'Charlie's moving in?' Sally looked at me.

'It's only for a few months. He sold his house and bought an apartment, which isn't quite ready yet.'

Charlie bounded over, rubbing his hands together. 'Well, well, well, it looks as if I'm already in demand. Lily said she'd like to meet up for a drink some time to see if I'm doing OK.'

'Seriously, Charlie, Catherine hasn't even been buried yet.' I pointed to the coffin lying in the open hearse.

He put his hand in and patted it. 'Well, Catherine, I hope they've restocked the bar for you up there.'

'Hey, Charlie, you know what would have been hysterical? If you'd played "Another One Bites The Dust" in the church.' Sarah giggled.

'Or the Jam's "Going Underground".' Paul grinned.

'No, no, Elton John's "I'm Still Standing",' said Sally.

'"Always Look On The Bright Side Of Life"?' Ali piped up.

'I think Queen's "Don't Stop Me Now" is more apt.' I laughed.

'No,' said Charlie. 'There's only one song that sums up how I feel. It's Bachman-Turner Overdrive's "You Ain't Seen Nothing Yet".'

2

As the mourners began to take their leave, Charlie turned to us. 'I'd like to invite you all for lunch and some drinks. Let's give Catherine a good send-off.'

'Sounds good to me,' Sally said.

'I'm in.' Sarah tucked her iPod into her pocket.

'Ali?' he asked, as Ali sent her twentieth text of the day.

She smiled. 'Sorry, Charlie, yes, I'd love to come. I'm not meeting David until later.'

'Looks like you have a full house,' I said to Charlie.

'Uhm, I'm afraid I'll have to pass,' Paul said. 'I need to get back to work. Sorry, but lunch hour on a Saturday is manic. I'll see you all later.'

I bit my tongue and fixed a smile on my face as Paul strode towards his car.

'Right then, follow me,' Charlie said. 'It's a little Italian place just around the corner here.'

Sally linked my arm. 'You OK?'

'Yeah, fine. I really wasn't close to Catherine – I hardly knew her, to be honest.'

'I mean about Paul not coming with us,' she said gently.

I shrugged. 'His priority is work. We always come second.'

'Come on, Ava, you know he loves his family.'

'He's got a funny way of showing it,' I muttered.

Sally squeezed my arm. 'He'll come around.'

'Come on, you two,' Sarah called back to us. 'Get a move on – I'm starving.'

The little bistro proved to be very nice. We were seated at a cosy round table and Charlie ordered a bottle of Prosecco.

'Bubbles, fantastic!' Sally said, holding out her glass.

'Can I have some?' Sarah asked.

'Of course you can,' Charlie said, pouring her a large glass before I could object.

When we all had our glasses filled, Charlie raised his. 'I'd like to propose a toast. To new beginnings. After years of misery, Charlie Hayes is getting back in the saddle.'

'I'll drink to that,' Sally said. 'Here's to you meeting a sober sex-bomb and me meeting a gorgeous Spanish billionaire next week when I'm sunning myself in Marbella.'

'That Lily woman at the funeral looked like a sure thing, Charlie.' Sarah took a large gulp of her Prosecco. 'And I'd say you'll definitely get lucky in Spain, Sally. You're pretty hot for an oldie.'

'Oldie!' Sally exclaimed. 'I'm not old, thank you very much. Your mum and I are still young. We discovered leggings, micro-miniskirts, Madonna and Demi Moore long before you did.'

'Did you really wear micro-minis?' Sarah looked at me doubt-fully.

'Your mother had the best legs in college. How do you think she attracted your dad?' Sally laughed.

'You should show them off, Mum,' Ali said. 'They still look good.'

'No way!' Sarah chimed in. 'I do not want my mother walking around in minis up to her arse.'

'You don't need to worry,' I assured her. 'My legs only look good from the knee down now. Cellulite has taken over my thighs.'

'They're still bloody good.' Sally winked at me.

'I think you're both great for your age,' Ali said.

'Thanks, Ali,' I smiled at her, 'but everyone thinks Sally's younger than me.'

'But I've had a lot of work done.'

'You should have Botox, too, Mum. Your wrinkles are get-ting bad.' Sarah pointed to my forehead.

I put my hand up and felt the deep lines. Maybe she was right.

'Spanish ladies are very sexy. I might have to take a little holiday there myself,' Charlie mused.

'You should,' Sally enthused. 'I use a great company that does good packages for single people. They always recommend nice places that aren't full of families or loved-up couples. It makes going away on your own a lot easier.'

'I hear those 18–30 clubs are good.' He grinned.

'Groooosssssss!' Sarah squealed.

'I'm sorry to have to tell you this, Charlie, but you might be a year or two too old for that.' Ali giggled.

'I'll keep an eye out for some suitable *señoras* for you.' Sally patted his hand.

'*Señoritas*, please, Sally!' Charlie chuckled.

Ali's phone beeped. She started texting back immediately.

'Seriously, Ali, do you and David *ever* stop?' Sarah rolled her eyes. 'You must text each other, like, fifty times a day.'

'We like to keep in touch.'

'Ah, first love . . . I remember that. Enjoy every minute, Ali,' Sally said, while Sarah made vomiting noises.

'How long are you going to Spain for?' Charlie asked Sally.

'Two weeks. Fourteen glorious days of sun, sand and . . . who knows what else?'

'You're so lucky. I wish I was going away to the sun.' Sarah groaned. 'I can't bear the thought of going back to school.'

'You've still got two weeks' summer holidays left. Try to enjoy them instead of moaning all the time,' I said.

'I'll think of you getting your books and uniforms ready while I'm sipping *piña coladas* on the beach,' Sally goaded her.

'Catherine was fond of *piña coladas*. When we went on our first holiday together, she used to knock back four at breakfast,' Charlie said.

'Why was Catherine such an alco, Charlie?' Sarah asked.

'She was just an unhappy person,' I said quickly, trying to be kind to the memory of my recently deceased stepmother.

'That's Ava, always looking for the good,' Charlie said. 'The

9

truth is that Catherine was one of those people who think life owes them something. Her father walked out when she was a child and she felt hard done by because of that. But I couldn't see it as an excuse. I grew up in an orphanage and got the holy shit beaten out of me regularly by the older boys, but you don't see me crying into a bottle of vodka to drown my sorrows.'

I always felt so sorry for Charlie when he talked about his childhood, which he didn't often. It was heartbreaking to think of a little five-year-old boy losing both parents and then sent off to be raised in an orphanage. My mother always used to say that the experience had made him incredibly open-minded and generous to people from all walks of life. He knew what it was to be an outcast, to be at the bottom of the pile. He had faced loss and heartache at a very young age, but instead of making him bitter or hard it had left him with his love for life and people.

'If I'd known what Catherine was really like,' Charlie continued, 'I'd never have married her. She was nasty and bitter when she drank, which was all day.'

'You certainly rushed into it,' I said, remembering how he'd announced his engagement three months after my mother had died. I had been devastated to lose her so suddenly and when Charlie had got married so soon after, it had caused a rift between us. Luckily it hadn't lasted long, but I had been really upset for a while.

'With you off in college, I was lonely and desperate, Ava. I didn't know what I was doing. I was heartbroken when Moira died.' To the girls, Charlie added, 'Let me tell you something. Never make big decisions when you're unhappy. By God was it a mistake. I ended up being Catherine's nursemaid for years. I should never have married anyone. I should have gone to Hollywood when I was seventeen and pursued Ava Gardner or Marilyn Monroe instead.'

'But if you hadn't stayed here and married Granny Moira, you wouldn't have had Mum,' said Ali.

Charlie looked at his granddaughter, his face softening. 'You're absolutely right, Ali, as always.'

'Charlie!' a man called from across the restaurant.

'Bollox,' Charlie cursed. 'It's Billy Norman, Catherine's cousin. I'll have to go over and say hello. He's an almighty bore.'

While Charlie made polite – or, in his case, not so polite – conversation, Sally asked me how long he would be living with us.

'I don't know. Until he feels ready to leave, I suppose,' I said, trying to sound breezy.

I had asked him to move in two weeks ago, after Catherine was placed in a hospice. I wanted him to have his family around when she died. We had the space and I was worried about him getting depressed on his own. But he was like a man escaped from captivity. On the one hand I was delighted to see him so carefree after having been weighed down by her drinking for so many years, but on the other, he was becoming increasingly inappropriate and erratic and I was worried he'd get himself into trouble.

Still, it was a temporary arrangement. Charlie was only due to stay until the new apartment he had bought was ready. It was due for completion in a couple of months. The funny thing was, I liked having him around. Paul owned a gastro-pub, which meant that he worked irregular hours and was often out at night. I liked having Charlie's company – as an only child I'd always been close to him, and the girls adored him.

'I hope he stays for ever,' said Sarah. 'He's a riot. Was he always this much of a live-wire, Mum?'

'Not as bad as he is now. He always had a slightly mad streak in him, though. I think it comes from growing up in the orphanage where he really had to fight for attention. When I was young, he'd sometimes collect me from school dressed as Superman. He'd put on a pair of red Y-fronts over his suit trousers and a red towel on his shoulders. The other kids thought he was great, but I was mortified. Now that he doesn't have to look after Catherine, he's just letting go and enjoying his new-found freedom.'

'Did you have a hard time with her, too? I mean, I know we didn't see her much, but you must have had to deal with her?' Ali asked.

'It wasn't so bad. I was already in college and living on campus when he married her, and Charlie always made sure she was either sober or out of the way when I called in. Then I met your dad, got married at twenty-two and my own life took over.'

'There's no way I'd get married that young,' Sarah said. 'Didn't you want to travel and go wild in your twenties?'

'Not really. After my mum died and Charlie married Catherine, I felt a bit lost. I was angry with Charlie, and because I didn't have any brothers or sisters to talk to about it, I felt really lonely. I was desperate to create my own family unit and your dad was so solid and sane. I felt very safe with him. I couldn't wait to get married and have a family of my own. It was all I wanted.'

'I'm not going to have kids till I'm at least thirty,' Sarah said, reapplying lip gloss for the zillionth time that morning.

'Actually, that's a good idea. Sometimes I think I had you guys too young. I was clueless.'

'But, then, if you don't get married young and focus instead on your career, like me, you might never get married,' Sally mused.

'Did you ever come close?' Ali asked.

'Twice,' Sally admitted. 'But neither worked out for different reasons. It just wasn't meant to be.'

'Do you mind being on your own?' Sarah wanted to know.

'Most of the time it doesn't bother me.'

'I think I'd like to get married young,' Ali said. 'I'd like the security of it.'

'You're just nauseatingly in love,' Sarah said. Then, to me, she added, 'Although I'm glad you had us when you did. It's cool to have a young mum. Some of my friends' mothers are so old and frumpy.'

I was thrilled with this rare compliment from Sarah. 'Really? Do you?'

'Yeah, but it's time for Botox. It's all beginning to sag, Mum.'

'You look gorgeous, Ava.' Sally laughed, poking Sarah in the ribs. 'Don't mind this cheeky cow.'

As Ali's phone beeped yet again, Charlie arrived back at the table. 'What a boring old fart that fella is. I need a drink.' He grabbed a passing waiter and ordered another bottle of Prosecco.

3

I stirred the porridge and breathed a sigh of relief that school was starting again. It had been nice having the girls around all summer, but it had been difficult trying to juggle work with keeping them occupied and out of trouble.

I heard the kitchen door open and turned to see Ali, immaculately dressed in her uniform. Her blonde hair was perfectly blow-dried and I could see she had put on a little makeup. Her face was glowing with happiness. She looked beautiful.

'Big day!' I smiled. 'Everyone's going to see you and David together.'

She blushed. 'I'm a bit nervous. I think a lot of people'll be surprised that he's going out with me.'

'Ali, for the zillionth time, you're stunning and he's the lucky one.'

'I know, but everyone fancies him, so it's a really big deal.'

'I'm sure lots of the boys in your class fancy you, too.' I couldn't understand why Ali was unable to see how gorgeous she was. If I had been that good-looking at seventeen, I would have strutted around town like a peacock.

'They don't, Mum, but thanks anyway. Can I help with that?'

'No, thanks, it's nearly ready. Sit down and have some juice.'

Paul came in, reading the newspaper. 'Well, Ali, big day today, your final year in school. You'll be out in the big bad world soon.'

She groaned. 'Don't remind me, Dad. I'm not going to have a life this year. It's going to be non-stop studying.'

'Well, don't work too hard. Enjoy yourself as well, have fun with David,' I said, worried that Ali would wear herself out.

Most mums had to beg their kids to study, but I had to drag Ali away from her desk.

'No problem to a straight-A student like our Ali,' said Paul, patting his daughter's arm. 'I know she'll do brilliantly.'

'Ah, but all work and no play make for a very dull life,' said Charlie, shuffling through the door in his slippers and dressing-gown.

'Morning, Charlie,' said Ali.

'Hello, my angel,' he said, kissing his granddaughter on the forehead.

'Good morning, Charlie,' said Paul.

'What's good about it? It's lashing rain, I didn't sleep a wink last night and I haven't had sex in years.'

'Charlie! It's eight o'clock in the morning,' I said, glaring at him.

'Hey, Charlie, are you moaning about your love life, or lack of it, again?' asked Sarah, plonking herself down on the chair beside him.

'Yes, I bloody well am. It'll shrivel up and drop off if I don't get some action soon.'

'If you're really desperate, you could always pay someone?' Sarah suggested.

'Well, I must say this is lovely breakfast conversation,' said Paul.

'That's enough, thank you, Sarah,' I said curtly, 'and you need to take your makeup off. You look ridiculous.'

'Muuuuum, *everyone* wears makeup in school now. It's no big deal. Only total nerds don't. Do you want me to be a social outcast?'

'If it helps you focus more on your studies, then that would be fine,' said Paul. 'You should take a leaf out of your sister's book.'

'Newsflash! I'm going to be an actress, not a doctor, so I really don't need to get ten zillion points in my finals like brain-box Ali. Besides, in case you forgot, I'm on my transition year, which is all about exploring your creative side, so I don't need to study.'

'After your poor results last summer, you'll be studying extra hard this year,' I said. 'We've discussed this already, Sarah. There'll be less drama and more work from now on.'

'Ava Gardner – now, there was a dramatic actress. She had the best face in Hollywood,' said Charlie.

'Is that why you named Mum after her? Because she was your favourite actress?' Ali asked.

He shook his head. 'Not really. Your grandmother Moira wanted to call your mother Noreen. I said no way was a daughter of mine going around with a rotten name like Noreen. I wanted her to have a good strong name. Something different. Something people would remember.'

'Oh, they remembered all right. I was the only Ava in Ireland,' I said, laughing. 'But I am glad you saved me from being called Noreen – it would have been much worse.'

'So I did something right,' he grumbled.

'Yes, Charlie, you did,' I said, kissing his head.

'OK, come on, eat up, you lot – you don't want to be late on your first day,' said Paul.

'I'm knackered,' Sarah muttered, as she stood up to reach for the cereal. 'Getting up at half seven is obscene.'

'Pull your skirt down, for God's sake. It's school you're going to, not a disco,' said Paul, frowning at Sarah's hoisted-up uniform.

'Hellooo! How else am I going to show off my tan?'

'I'll tan your hide in a minute, missy,' said Paul.

'Dad, you know I don't understand when you talk like a bogman,' said Sarah.

'Don't be so cheeky,' Paul replied, trying to stifle a smile.

'I'm not being cheeky, I'm being honest. I don't know what you're talking about.'

'Well, that makes two of us, because half the time I've no idea what you're saying either,' said Paul, gulping down the last of his coffee and making for the door. 'I'm gone. See you all later.' The door slammed shut behind him. I tried to remember the last time I'd got a goodbye kiss.

'Get out there and sow your wild oats,' shouted Charlie, as the girls went to get their coats and bags. 'You're only young once.'

'Seriously, Charlie, can you please tone it down? Don't encourage Sarah – she's a handful as it is.'

'She's spirited.'

'High spirits can get you into trouble.'

'She's a grand girl. She's just different from Alison. It doesn't mean she's wild.'

'I know I shouldn't compare them, but Ali's been such a dream daughter. I've never had to worry about her.'

'She's a gem, all right, but sometimes I think she takes life too seriously,' said Charlie.

The kitchen door opened. 'Mum, we're going to be late,' said Ali, looking worried.

'Coming,' I said, grabbing my keys from the counter and heading for the door.

As we pulled up outside the school, Sarah snapped off her seat-belt. '*Oh*, my God, there's Bobby Masterson-Brown – how fit is he?'

Alison and I peered at a tall, broad boy with badly highlighted hair and saggy trousers, strutting across the grass.

'He looks ridiculous,' I said.

'Mum, you have no idea what's cool these days. Bobby's hot.'

'Where's David?' I asked. Ali blushed. She had now been going out with David for six weeks. He had called into the house the week before and seemed nice in that gawky teenage, monosyllabic way. He was very good-looking, like a young Johnny Depp. I could see why so many girls fancied him. Ali seemed almost in awe of him. I had to keep reminding her how lucky he was.

'I'm meeting him outside the gym in five minutes,' she said, beaming.

'There's Elaine,' squeaked Sarah. 'Oh, my God, she's, like, black. The bitch! I've got to find out what fake tan she's using. Later, Mum.'

'OK, 'bye,' I said, as the door slammed and I watched my younger child hiking up her skirt and screeching as she met her friends.

'I'd better go, too. I'll see you later,' said Ali, kissing me on the cheek. She walked over to greet her best friend, Donna, and they headed inside together, arms linked.

It never ceased to amaze me how two daughters born of the same parents could be so completely different. Ali was blonde, green-eyed, studious, shy, gentle, thoughtful and sensitive. Sarah was less conventionally pretty. She had long dark hair and nice blue eyes, but she had inherited her father's strong jaw, which looked good on a man but out of place on a girl. She had also been born with incredible self-confidence. She had a really bubbly, outgoing personality, a wide group of friends and a constant stream of admirers.

While Ali focused on studying, Sarah focused on her social life. Ali had one true best friend, Donna, while Sarah seemed to have a new best friend every week. They were like chalk and cheese, but they got on very well. As an only child I envied their closeness. I would have loved to have a sister to talk to growing up. I hoped that, despite their different personalities, they would always be close.

I turned the car around and headed to work. Sally was back from her holidays today and I was dying to catch up with her. Our children's party business, Happy Dayz – which we'd set up ten years ago as kind of a hobby on the side – was now really successful, which was fantastic, but I'd missed Sally when she was away. We had expanded from kids' events to sweet sixteens and even, sometimes, eighteenth and twenty-first birthdays. I had been swamped over the last few weeks and had been coming home late every night. I wanted to be around more for the girls now that they were back in school, so I'd be happy to share the workload again – and the gossip.

While I focused on the creative side, working with the parents on party themes, food, decoration, gifts and entertainment, Sally did the books, the website, organized suppliers and hired and fired all the part-time staff. In the ten years we had been up and running, we had seen parties go from fairly simple princess and pirate themes to wedding-like extravaganzas. It was never dull and I loved it.

I pulled into the office space Sally and I rented, which held our stock of basic party essentials – bouncy castles, little tables and chairs, boxes of balloons, banners, costumes, music, face paint, *piñatas*, gift bags, candles and industrial-size jars of sweets. We had found a wonderful chef, Helen, who made birthday cakes and did all of the food that was more complicated than sandwiches and sausages, which I managed. As I was getting out of my car, my mobile rang.

'Hello?'

'I not working in you house any more,' said Magda, our Polish cleaning lady.

'What's wrong? What happened?'

'You daddy is bad man. Very bad.'

'Oh, no, what did he do?'

'He is hiding and jumping out, like tiger. I very scared. My heart stop. I tell him he very bad man. He laugh and then he try to do kissy-kissy.'

'I'm so sorry, Magda. I promise I'll talk to him and he won't do it again. Please don't leave.' Magda had been with us for years. She was a life-saver – I'd die if she left.

'I have husband in Poland. I no kissy-kissy other man. You daddy old and ugly. I tell him. He say, "I pay you for the sex." I not prostitute. I good Catholic girl.'

Jesus, when had my father turned into a sexual predator?

'OK, Magda, the next time he tries to kiss you, just hit him over the head with the brush. You have my full permission to use violence.'

There was silence.

'Magda?'

'I am already using little bit of violence today.'

'Is he all right?' I asked, suddenly worried. Magda was built like a shot-putter. My father was five foot seven and wiry. My money was on Magda in a fight.

'Ya, he OK. He not jumping any more.'

'Put him on to me.'

'Hnnnlo?'

'Charlie? What the hell are you doing, sexually assaulting my cleaning lady?'

'Stupid cow doke my nobe.'

'What?'

'Stupid cow doke my nobe!'

I heard a scuffle and then Magda's voice came back on the phone: 'I think you come now. I give you daddy slap on nose. He not happy.'

'I'm on my way,' I said, sighing as I turned the car around.

4

I stormed into the house to find Charlie lying on the couch with a bloody towel held to his nose. Magda was sitting beside him, drinking a small glass of brandy. They were laughing.

'What the hell is going on?' I asked.

'Magda and I had a small misunderstanding,' said Charlie, sitting up to reveal his squashed nose.

'I can see that,' I snapped.

'You daddy give me this for shock,' said Magda, gulping the brandy.

'I see,' I said, trying to remain calm. 'Charlie, can I have a word in private, please?'

'Oh dear, Magda, I'm in trouble,' he said, winking at her as she giggled. What had happened to the furious phone call about sexual abuse?

I dragged Charlie into the kitchen, leaving Magda to finish her drink. 'What are you doing?' I hissed at him.

'I'm having a conversation with Magda. Did you know she comes from a small town two hundred miles north of Warsaw?'

'Yes, I did. Charlie, I don't want her ringing me in a state and breaking your nose.'

'I don't think it's actually broken. Magda just got the wrong end of the stick. I asked her for sex, offered to pay for her trouble, and she thought I was accusing her of being a prostitute. When I explained that I hadn't had sex in six years and was just desperate to get some action, she took pity on me.'

'She had sex with you?' I gasped.

'Sadly, no. But she said she has a friend who might oblige.'

'Charlie, you're sixty-eight years old. You can't go around propositioning women. You could get arrested.'

21

'I may be in my sixties, but there's life in the old dog yet,' he said.

'Look, I'm asking you as a favour to me – your daughter – to stay away from Magda and don't give her any more drink.' I looked at my watch. 'I have to go now. I'm late for work. Just behave yourself and don't grope Magda – or anyone else who happens to ring the doorbell for that matter.'

I went back to Magda, who was nestled into the couch with her feet up on the coffee-table, polishing off her brandy. 'I'm off now, Magda. My father won't bother you any more.'

'It OK now, Ava. I understand. Poor Daddy marry bad lady who always drunk. He don't have sex for long, long time. He is sad man. I help him.'

'No, Magda, honestly, he doesn't need to be encouraged. Thanks all the same, but please don't help him. Just . . . ignore him.'

'You daddy just lonely. I lonely, too. I not wanting the sex with you daddy, but I have friend who maybe have the sex. I ask.'

'Please don't ask your friend. My daddy needs to calm down. Look, I have to go. I'll talk to you next week,' I said, running out the door. 'Oh, and, Magda, no more violence. If he starts acting up again, just lock him in his room or something.'

I finally got into work. Sally was on the phone, her long brown legs on the desk, berating one of our suppliers. She waved at me as I came in.

'What do you mean you don't have thirty-four Spiderman chair covers? I need them for Saturday at two o'clock so you'd better bloody find them. Don't even think of calling me back. If you have to paint them yourself, just do it.'

'Welcome back!' I said, leaning over to hug her. 'You look amazing. You're as brown as a berry. God, I've missed you – I'm no good at doing the books and dealing with grumpy suppliers. Besides which, Charlie's lost the plot completely.'

'Tell me all!'

'He just sexually assaulted Magda.'

'Jesus Christ! My money's on Magda. I bet he didn't get very far.'

'He got a bloody nose for himself.'

Sally threw her head back and whooped. 'Good old Magda.'

'What am I going to do with him? I found Viagra in his bedroom.'

'Come on, Ava, he's had a miserable twenty years. He needs to let loose for a while.'

'I'm all for him enjoying life, but he has to calm down a bit. I don't want him rushing into another relationship, like he did with Catherine.'

'He's nearly seventy, I doubt he's looking to fall in love. He just needs to get laid. How does Paul feel about Charlie living with you?'

I sank back into my chair. If I was to be honest, I didn't know. Paul and I never seemed to chat any more. It was always just swapping information about the girls or work or who was picking up the dry-cleaning/dinner/weed-killer/light bulbs . . . We needed some time to ourselves, but there never was any.

'He seems OK about it. Since they added the fancy beer garden in May, the pub's been getting busier and busier, which is great, but it means he's always at work. He's very tolerant of Charlie – they've always got on well – and it's only for a couple of months.'

'And the girls?'

'They adore him, of course, but I'm not sure he's a very good influence on them. He's constantly complaining about not having any sex.'

Sally sighed knowingly. 'Well, that's what happens when you don't get any action. It starts to consume you.'

'What about Spain? Did you meet some hunky Spaniard to share your sangria with?'

'No, no hunky men for me, I'm afraid. I did meet a lot of

short, sunburnt Irish and Englishmen, most of whom were married and those few who weren't were far more interested in their golf game than dating a woman. I'm telling you, Ava, if I don't meet someone soon, I may end up in bed with your dad.'

'Oh, God, don't even joke about it.' I giggled.

'Needs must!'

'So, no action?'

'If they're not freaks, they're married. I'm telling you, it's slim pickings out there for a forty-three-year-old woman. I should have got married young like you. I've missed the bloody boat, train and bus. My smugly married sisters helpfully remind me on a regular basis that it's my own fault because apparently I was too picky and fussy when I was younger and now all the good guys are gone.'

'They don't really say that, do they?' I asked, pouring us both a cup of coffee.

'Thanks.' Sally helped herself to some milk. 'I swear, Ava, they're so smug with their husbands and their two-point-four children and their ridiculous four-by-four jeeps that they insist on driving to ferry their kids down the road to school and back. All I ever hear about are little Johnny's ear infections, or the hilarious thing he said to his teacher, or the fact that Philip's mother looks like she's had Botox. Jesus, they're so insular and boring.'

'Maybe it's because they don't work. When the girls were small I didn't work and I was terrified of becoming boring. The kids do become your sole focus and it's scary. You talk about your children all the time because they're both your job and your personal life. That's what drove me back to work!'

'I don't go out and bore people about my job or my personal life.'

'I know, but I think sometimes it's insecurity that does it – a lot of full-time mothers feel undervalued and unappreciated.' I took a bite of my chocolate biscuit.

'Bullshit. It's smugness. They don't like successful single women. They think we all want to shag their husbands.'

'Because they're insecure!'

Sally threw her hands up in the air, knocking some files off the table. 'About *what*? I'd love to be married to a millionaire and swan around all day having facials and playing tennis.'

'No, you wouldn't, you'd be bored silly, and you don't like children.'

'Whoever said anything about children? I just want the man and the money.' She chuckled.

'Ninety-nine per cent of women are not married to millionaires, Sally. And stay-at-home mothers do not have an easy time of it. They spend all day cooking, cleaning, washing and dealing with tantrums and melt-downs. No one ever tells them they're doing a good job. There are no promotions, no wage hikes, no union rules. I have to be honest, as jobs go I found it thankless drudgery.'

'Fine, but why bore everyone to death about it when they go out?'

'Because they're trying to justify their existence.'

'What about single women's existence? How do we justify ours? Apart from work, we have a pretty thankless life, too – no one to share good or bad news with, no one to snuggle up with on rainy Monday nights when we're feeling miserable, no one to rely on financially. If we lose our jobs or get sick, we're screwed. And as for holidays, they're a minefield. You either go on your own or with a single friend who may be fine to go out with on a Saturday night, but not to spend two weeks sharing a hotel room with. Or your third choice, which is to latch on to one of your siblings' family holidays where you have to be "fun" Aunt Sally and end up looking after the kids while the parents just "pop out" and come back four hours later reeking of wine.'

I sighed. There was no easy answer. 'You're right, that is awful. I just don't think anyone has it easy. Please feel free to call over to me any Monday night. You can snuggle on the couch with me and Charlie. Paul's always out, so we'd welcome the company.' I fiddled with a paperclip.

'So Paul hasn't cut back on his hours, then?' Sally asked.

'If anything, he's working more. But I've got Charlie so life is never dull.'

'And how are the gorgeous girls?'

'Are you sure you want to know about my kids?'

'Come on, you know I love them. Toddlers I don't do, but teenagers I can at least relate to. Let's face it, I'm a teenager in an old woman's body.'

'Remind me again why you co-own a children's-party-planning business?' I laughed.

'Because my wonderful partner deals with the children and their neurotic mothers while I deal with the money and the fathers.'

'How come I get lumped with the kids and their psychotic mothers?'

'Because you can handle them. I'd just be rude and that wouldn't be good for business. So, how are the girls?'

'Ali's in amazing form – she's totally in love. It's still going strong with David.'

'Good for Ali. Oh, to be seventeen again!' Sally stood up to pour herself more coffee – she always drank at least four cups in the morning while I could only ever manage one.

'I know. I'm a bit worried, though. It's only been eight weeks and she's completely besotted with him. You know Ali, she wears her heart on her sleeve. I just hope she doesn't get hurt.'

'It'll do her the world of good to focus on men rather than school books for a while. She should be having more fun.'

'Yeah, you're right. When I think of myself at seventeen, sneaking out the bedroom window and cycling off to parties, I can't believe I have a daughter who is so well behaved. Mind you, Sarah's the other extreme.'

'She's not really that bad. She just likes to push the boundaries.'

'And my buttons. She really knows how to wind me up.'

'That might have something to do with the fact that you're very alike.'

'Me and Sarah?'

'Come on, Ava, you've mellowed a bit over the years, but you were a live-wire in your day.'

'I never spoke to my mother the way she speaks to me.'

'That's because you were too busy sneaking around behind her back. At least Sarah talks to you and tells you what she wants.'

'I suppose that's something. All the parenting experts say that communication with your kids is vital and she's certainly good at communicating. Sometimes, though, I wish she'd put a sock in it.'

'She'll be fine, she's just lively.'

'That's one way of putting it.'

'So, what's been happening since I've been away?'

'The Brown-Kennedy party went well, but they haven't paid the bill, so I need you to call the dad and sweet-talk the money from him.' I handed her a Post-it with his number on it.

'No problem, leave it to me. He'll have a cheque in the post today.'

'Great.' I opened one of the files on my desk. 'Now, we've got the Mallow twins' seventh-birthday party in two weeks. They want a crocodile cake that spurts blood when you cut it. Helen reckons she can work something out with raspberry coulis for the blood. They want a small marquee decked out in jungle style. The mother wants safari outfits for the twins and their dad. She also wants an outfit for herself, but not shorts and a jacket. She wants us to source a sexy safari dress.'

'Which is what, exactly?'

'She's thinking tight leopard-print minidress with a sun-visor to match.'

Sally stared at me open-mouthed. 'But she's fifty . . . and fat.'

'Harsh.' Mrs Mallow was actually forty-seven, and while she

wasn't fat, she definitely didn't have the figure required for tight minidresses.

'She looks like a transvestite,' Sally said. 'Look, I'm no one to slag off someone for getting work done, but she needs to stop the Botox – her eyebrows are disappearing into her hairline. If I ever get like that, tell me.'

'OK, I will, and you must tell me when I look like a hag and need to have something done. Now, I've actually sourced the dress already on the Internet. There are – would you believe? – ninety-five thousand nine hundred Google results for sexy safari dresses. The one I've gone with is very revealing so I think she'll like it. I've worked out the costs for the party, but Helen reckons the price of making the cake and the hundred chocolate snakes, lizards, scorpions and terrapins could be higher. She'll give us a final price tomorrow.'

Sally looked at the numbers. 'Thank God for parents with too much money and no sense! Now, show me this dress.'

I pulled it out of the bag and Sally screeched, 'You cannot be serious – it's obscene!'

I grinned. 'Sally, may I remind you that the client gets whatever the client wants and this little number is what Nancy Mallow is looking for.'

'All that money and no taste, it's a travesty.'

I glanced at my watch. 'I've got to run. I'm going to drop into Nancy later on my way to collect the girls from school.'

'OK, see you tomorrow. I hope she likes her stripper dress.'

5

Unfortunately, Nancy Mallow didn't like the dress I'd found because it wasn't short enough, apparently.

'Come on, Ava, I'm in my forties, not sixties. My legs are still in good shape so let's show them off.'

I tried not to look as shocked as I felt. 'OK, Nancy. I'll try to get something shorter for you.'

'Good. Now, about the food for the adults. I think sushi and some nice canapés will do. We'll be spending the afternoon in the house and popping down to see how the boys are getting on every now and then. I don't want them in my house, so please make sure they're contained in the marquee and the garden. I've just had new carpets put down and I don't want twenty-five mucky boys running about.'

'In that case, maybe having it outside the home would be easier?' I suggested. 'We could hire somewhere for you.' Clearly this woman didn't want any children within a mile radius of her house. I was surprised her own kids were allowed to live in it.

'I wish I could, Ava, but Dan said, "What's the bloody point in having a big house if you can't have a party in it?"' She rolled her eyes. 'Men just don't seem to mind mess and dirt. Now, regarding toilets, they can use the one at the back of the garage.'

I was surprised she wasn't going to make them pee in the bushes – it would have been in keeping with the jungle theme.

'I hope you have lots of activities planned for them. I want them kept busy so we adults can have a few drinks in peace.'

Why do people like this have children? I wondered. As if on cue, the twins came charging into the kitchen and proceeded to have a wrestling match.

'Stop it, you two, you're going to break something,' Nancy snapped.

They stuck their tongues out at her and continued to beat each other up until one of them fell against the dresser, knocking over a large bowl that smashed on the floor.

'GET OUT!' screamed Nancy, and the boys fled. I bent down to help her clear up the mess. 'That was a wedding present from my godmother.' She shook her head. 'Do you have children, Ava?'

'Two girls, but they're teenagers now.'

'God, I wish I'd had girls. Boys are a nightmare – I just can't understand them. I had three sisters and we never behaved like that. All they do is fight and break things. I have no control over them at all. They never listen to me and their father is away all week. When he gets back he just wants to be a "fun" dad so he wrestles with them. Honestly, I feel as if I have three sons, not two.'

'As the saying goes, girls wreck your head and boys wreck your house.'

'Well, I can tell you, Ava, boys wreck your house *and* your head.'

'They'll probably calm down soon. I think seven is supposed to be a turning-point,' I lied.

'The day they leave home will be a turning-point,' she said wearily. She shook the remnants of her wedding bowl into the bin.

Her desire not to have the party inside the house now seemed wise and sensible.

On my way to pick up the girls from school, Paul rang. 'How did today go? Good to have Sally back?' he asked.

'Brilliant. I appreciate her more every time she takes a holiday.'

'You make a good team.'

'You're not going to believe what Charlie did.'

'Nothing would surprise me.'

'He sexually assaulted Magda and she broke his nose.'

'Jesus Christ! He must be desperate – Magda looks like a bloke.'

'Don't be mean about her. She's wonderful.'

'Poor old Charlie just needs a good shag. He's got six years of pent-up sexual frustration, and that's not healthy.'

'OK, OK, let's stop talking about my father's sexual needs, please.'

'Fair enough. Listen, I'm going to be late tonight. We're installing the new surveillance equipment – apparently it takes a while – so don't wait up for me.'

'Do you really think you need it?'

'These cameras are top of the range. They'll give me a crystal-clear picture of the cash register from twenty feet away so none of the staff can steal from me.'

'I don't understand why people would steal from their employers.'

'Everyone wants more, especially when things are good and our figures are up twenty per cent. This is exactly the time when staff get greedy. Anyway, don't you worry about it – that's my job. Sorry to miss dinner.'

'Again.'

'Come on, Ava, don't start.'

'Paul, you haven't been home before midnight in two weeks. I'm fed up.'

'The business is going well, you should be happy. Besides, once this security equipment is in place, I'll be able to watch everything from my laptop, so I can be home more.'

Great, I thought. When he can access the pub from home, he'll never switch off and unwind. He'll be glued to the bloody laptop. I didn't feel like a fight right now, though. 'I'm pleased that things are going well, but I'd like to see you once in a while, and so would the girls.'

'I'll be home for dinner tomorrow. Besides, I see the girls every morning at breakfast. I don't see why –' A female voice called him in the background. 'Look, I'm sorry, I have to go, Ava, I'll see you later.' He hung up.

I flung my mobile onto the passenger seat. Of course I was pleased the pub was doing so well, but with both of us working long hours and looking after the girls and now Charlie, Paul and I hardly had any quality time together any more. What was the point in working so hard and making money if we never got to enjoy it?

When the girls were small and we were living in a sleep-deprived haze, we used to fantasize about the trips we'd take when they were older – long weekends in Berlin, New York, Barcelona, Milan . . . Then when we'd had that scare eight years ago, we reiterated our commitment to living more and working less. But instead of doing things with me, Paul had taken up surfing, become completely obsessed with it, and spent all his spare time chasing waves. And then Happy Dayz had taken off and suddenly here we were, still working hard and too busy to enjoy it all. We hadn't done any of the things we'd planned. In fact, we saw less of each other now than we had when the girls were babies.

Sarah and Ali came out of the school gate together. They were both full of chat.

'Honestly, Mum, you should see the amount of homework we got – our first day!' Ali said. 'It'll take hours to finish.'

'How's David?' I asked.

She beamed. 'He's just great.'

'You should see them, Mum,' said Sarah. 'It's sickening. They go around holding hands all day long and Ali stares at him with these big moo eyes.'

'Ah, young love.' I smiled.

'Hey, Ali, who's that new girl in your class?' Sarah asked. 'Everyone was talking about her today. She looks like a super-model.'

'Her name's Tracy. She's been expelled from three schools. She's good-looking, but I don't think she's very clever. She thought Aung San Suu Kyi was a form of martial arts.'

Ali and I giggled. Sarah looked at us blankly. 'What's so funny?'

'Come on, you must know who Aung San Suu Kyi is?' Ali said.

'I've no idea what you're talking about. Does that make me thick, too?'

'No, it makes you uninformed,' I said. 'You should pay attention to current affairs.'

'*Booooring*. Besides, that Tracy girl doesn't need to know about current affairs – she's going to make millions as a model. Everyone was talking about her. *And* all the guys were drooling over her.'

'She wants to go to New York and model,' said Ali.

'Is she really that good-looking?' I asked.

'Yes, and she's stick-thin,' said Sarah. 'I bet she eats nothing. Did you see what she had for lunch?' she asked Ali.

'No, Sarah, I don't go around staring at people's lunch boxes.'

'You were just too busy staring at David. I'd say she lives on rice cakes,' Sarah said.

'How could anyone live on those? They're like cardboard,' said Ali.

'Nobody's that thin naturally so she must starve herself,' said Sarah. 'All models do.'

'That's ridiculous,' I said. 'Being too thin is awful.'

'Are you mad?' Sarah said. 'I'd much rather be too skinny than fat. I think Tracy looks amazing.'

'There's nothing attractive about matchstick legs and sunken cheeks. Victoria Beckham is much prettier when she has some flesh on her bones.'

'She always looks great, even when she's really skinny, and her clothes are so cool,' Sarah disagreed with me.

'Victoria's a bit scrawny, but Tracy's taller so she looks more like a model, kind of like Keira Knightley, naturally slim,' Ali said.

'What does David think of her?' Sarah asked.

'He said he thought she was pretty, but he didn't see what the fuss was about.'

'He's got very good taste.' I smiled at Ali. 'Now, how do you fancy going to Carluccio's for dinner to celebrate or commiserate your first day back at school?'

'Brilliant, I'm starving,' Ali said.

'Sounds good to me,' Sarah agreed.

'OK so. We'll just swing by and pick up Charlie.'

'Will Dad be coming?' Ali asked.

'Not tonight. He's tied up.'

I texted Charlie to let him know to be ready, and he was waiting outside when we reached the house. He climbed into the car with his red nose and black eyes.

'Charlie! What happened to you?' Ali gasped.

'I fell over getting out of the bath,' he said, looking at me.

'Really?' said Sarah. 'It looks like someone boxed you in the face.'

'Yes, well, they didn't. He just fell,' I said firmly. The last thing I wanted was for the girls to find out that their grandfather was a molester.

6

The day of the Mallow twins' party quickly turned into a night-mare. I had a hysterical phone call from Nancy at nine in the morning to say that because of the weather the night before the marquee was now flying in circles around the garden.

I called Barry, the supplier, and arranged to meet him there at ten o'clock. He held up the filthy, ripped tent and cursed. 'I don't believe this. It's wrecked. The bloody thing is in tatters. I pegged that down last night and there's no way it should have come up, regardless of the weather. Look – there's big holes here where I planted the pegs. It looks like someone dug them up.'

'Jesus Christ, I'll kill them,' Nancy huffed.

The twins were frog-marched down to explain what they had done. 'It was only a joke,' Ryan said.

'It was just for fun, to see if it would fall down,' Harry added.

'Well, it's not very funny, lads. My tent is ruined and it's going to cost a lot to replace it,' Barry said. 'And before you ask, no, I don't have another for you. They're all booked up today.'

'What are we going to do? I have twenty-five boys and their parents arriving in four hours,' wailed Nancy.

'It looks like the party is going to have to be in the house,' I said.

'Over my dead body,' Nancy said, through gritted teeth. 'Right, there's nothing else for it. They'll have to be in the garage.'

'I don't want to have a party in the garage,' Ryan whined. 'It's smelly and dark.'

'Yeah, Mum, the garage is crap,' moaned his twin, Harry.

'It'll be fine, boys. Ava will make it nice, won't you?'

'I'll do my very best for you.' Not having seen the garage, I wasn't going to promise a miracle.

'You're so mean, Mum. Dad would *never* make us have our party in the garage.' Ryan threw himself on the ground and began to wail. This kid was really beginning to get on my nerves.

'Well, your father's not here, as usual, so you can stop that whingeing.'

'When is he coming?' Harry asked.

'Whenever he bloody feels like it,' she muttered, under her breath.

'Will he be here for the party?' Ryan asked.

'Who knows? Daddy does what Daddy wants and to hell with everyone else.'

Clearly all was not well with the Mallows. I felt sorry for Nancy, who was completely strung out, but I felt even sorrier for the boys. They might be annoying, but they were genuinely upset that their dad wouldn't be there for their birthday.

'I'll tell you what,' I said, in super-enthusiastic mode, 'let's go and take a look at the garage and we'll see what we can do to make it like a really cool jungle.'

'It's this way,' Nancy said.

I followed her and the twins through her huge kitchen, living room and hall, and out into the dark, damp, cobweb-infested garage. I had four hours to clear it, clean it and transform it into a jungle. How the hell was I going to manage that?

'Can you really make it into a jungle?' Harry asked.

'Sure, no problem. I'll call a few friends to come and help.'

'I have to go, Ava. I've a hair and makeup appointment and the boys are getting their hair cut, too. We'll be back around twelve,' Nancy said. Then, fighting back tears, she whispered, 'Please don't let me down. They need to have a nice time. Their arsehole of a father isn't going to be here.'

I put my arm around her. 'Don't worry about anything. I promise they'll have a great birthday.'

As soon as they left, I called Sally, Charlie and the girls.

36

I needed all hands on deck. They arrived over – Sally had a boot-load of emergency equipment from the office – and we set to transforming the gloomy garage into a jungle.

'It's disgusting in here,' Sarah complained, as she carried a bin out.

'It's not exactly a party room,' Ali agreed, as she dragged an old carpet across the floor.

'Remind me why the hell she can't have the party in a wing of her mansion?' Sally grumbled.

'Because she's a bit neurotic and, to be fair, twenty-five seven-year-old boys would probably trash the house.'

'Well, I'll be charging a lot extra for this,' Sally said. 'I had a massage booked for this morning.'

'How much are we getting paid for working today?' Sarah demanded. 'We've been in school all week and it's supposed to be our time to relax, so we should get paid double what you were thinking of giving us.'

'You'll get nothing if you don't start working,' I said. 'Now, come on, we need to get a move on. The best thing to do is push all the junk to one side, cover it with a black sheet and work with the rest of the room.'

We used blow heaters to warm it up and get rid of the damp, then set up the trestle table and covered it with a bamboo-effect cloth, leopard- and zebra-print plates and cups. We covered the walls with black sheets and stuck life-size photos of animals to them. We set up potted palm trees in each corner. We rolled out large grass mats on the floor and placed slimy plastic creepy-crawlies all around. We put huge cut-outs of lions, giraffes and zebras all around the room. Then we hung a mosquito net across the ceiling and suspended spiders, bats and snakes from it, with balloons in zebra- and leopard-print. Finally, we stuck lion paw prints all the way up the drive to the door.

'Am I in Africa?' Helen asked, coming through the doorway bearing a very large birthday cake. 'Good job, guys, it's very jungle-esque.'

'And well done to you,' Sally said, nodding at the cake. 'It really does look like a crocodile. How did you do it?'

'Years of practice . . . and buckets of green icing.'

'The detail is amazing.' Ali came over for a closer look. 'What are the claws made of?'

'The claws are liquorice, the teeth are cut-up marshmallows, the eyes are whole marshmallows with black jellybeans for pupils and when you cut the cake, raspberry coulis will flow out like blood, just as they requested.'

'Little boys are freaks,' Sally said.

I showed Helen into the kitchen and she put the cake and chocolate animals in the fridge and left the canapés for the adults, plus the kids' lion- and zebra-face pizzas, elephant-shaped sandwiches and sausage rolls on the counter-top. We also had doughnuts, jelly snakes, spiders and dinosaurs and a fruit platter – which the parents always ordered but none of the kids ever ate.

'You know the score – pizzas and sausage rolls on medium heat for twenty minutes,' she said.

'Thanks, Helen. You've really outdone yourself with the cake.'

'You're welcome. I've got to run – I'm catering a dinner party for forty tonight.'

'Talk to you on Monday,' I said, as she left.

Just when things were looking up my phone rang. It was Toby, the owner of Clowning Around, which did the entertaining for us. He was twenty-seven and had started the company five years ago, after leaving college. He had a staff of ten and had been working with us for the past two years and so far had only let me down once . . .

'Listen, Ava, I'm really sorry about this but two of our guys have rung in sick and I don't have anyone for you until four o'clock.'

'Jesus, Toby, the party starts at two. How the hell am I supposed to keep twenty-five kids entertained for two hours? That's your job. That's what I pay you for.'

'I know, I know – look, this never happens but there's some weird Chinese flu going around. I gave them grief on the phone, but they're really sick.'

'Well, you have to find me someone else.'

'All of my guys are at the Festival of Culture in town today. I'm so sorry – I know I've left you stuck.'

'Bloody right you have. What about you? Why can't you do it?'

'I have to go to my cousin's wedding.'

'To hell with your cousin.'

'Ava, we're really close. I can't let him down.'

'You don't need to go to the church. You can go to the reception after you've finished here.'

'I'm a groomsman.'

'All they do is walk up and down the aisle with the bridesmaids – any fool can do that.'

'My mother would kill me, not to mention my aunt – she'd skin me alive.'

'Christ, Toby, you've completely landed me in it.'

'I know, and I feel really bad. Look, you have all the stuff for the games that I dropped in yesterday so all you need are the instructions, which I'll email to your phone now. It's all very straightforward. I promise to make this up to you – I'll take you and Sally out for drinks.'

'It'll have to be Dom bloody Pérignon.' I snapped my phone shut.

'I take it the entertainer isn't coming,' Sally said.

'What the hell are we going to do? I promised them Indiana Jones was coming to do the games and play with them.'

'Any chance we could rope Paul in?' Sally asked. 'Pun completely intended.'

I shook my head. 'He's gone to chase waves miles away. He'll be surfing all day.'

'Isn't Harrison Ford, like, ancient?' Sarah asked.

'He was a bit past his prime in the last film,' I admitted. Paul had insisted on seeing it and I'd spent the whole time worried that Harrison was going to have a heart-attack.

'Well, don't we all know someone who's old and mad?' Sarah grinned.

While I stayed to finish the decorating and set up the games Toby had sent over, Sally took the girls home to dress Charlie up as Indiana Jones.

Meanwhile Nancy and the boys came back. Nancy had big hair and heavy makeup. The twins ran straight into the garage and stopped dead in their tracks.

'*Cooooooooooooooooooool!*'

Thank God for that. At least the birthday boys were happy. 'Hold on, listen to this.' I played the safari soundtrack.

'*Cooooooooooooooooooool!*' they shouted, jumping up and down.

'Well done, Ava. It looks great,' Nancy said. 'Come on, boys, we'll go and get dressed – the guests will be here soon.'

As I was putting wild animal stickers onto white cards, I heard Sally's car pulling up. I hurried outside, praying this would work. Sarah and Ali hopped from the back seat, giggling uncontrollably. Then Sally jumped out and announced, 'I give you . . . Indiana Jones!' Charlie stepped out of the car. He was wearing the trousers of his good navy suit and one of Paul's shirts, which was too big for him and open to his belly-button. Hanging down from the side of his belt were a few of his ties, knotted together to look like rope, but they were all different colours so the effect was very odd. He had a black canvas camera cover looped into the other side of his belt like a holster, with a banana sticking out of it. He carried Ali's turquoise and white flower-print Roxy rucksack on his back and wore my wide-brimmed straw sunhat on his head with a piece of paper stuck to the front that had *Indiana Jones* written on it.

I didn't know whether to laugh or cry.

'It was the best we could manage in twenty minutes,' Sally said, trying not to laugh.

'What exactly am I supposed to do?' Charlie asked. 'I've never seen the movies so you'll need to fill me in.'

'He's like a modern-day Tarzan,' Sally said.

'That's right up my alley. I'll –' Charlie's jaw dropped. Nancy Mallow had just walked in wearing her very short leopard-print dress with plunging neckline.

'Me Tarzan, you Jane!' Charlie hurried over to introduce himself.

Nancy looked confused.

'Nancy, this is my father. He'll be helping out today,' I explained, hoping against hope that Charlie wouldn't pinch her bum.

'Nice to meet you.' She offered her hand for him to shake.

'The pleasure is *all* mine,' Charlie said, kissing it as Sarah and Ali made sick noises in the background. 'May I say you're a knock-out in that dress?'

'Oh, well, thank you.' Nancy looked pleased.

The twins came hurtling around the corner in their safari suits, but stopped dead when they saw Charlie. 'You're not Indiana Jones,' Harry shouted.

'Yes, I am.' Charlie puffed out his chest.

'No, you're not. You're old and you're wearing a girl's hat,' Ryan said cheekily.

'*Mum*, we told everyone that Indiana Jones was coming to our party,' Harry wailed. 'This is a granddad. I don't want him. I hate him – I hate you! I hate this party in the smelly garage.' With that, Harry and Ryan began to kick over the chairs and pull down the posters.

'Boys, stop,' Nancy said feebly, but they ignored her. 'Please, boys, if you're good I'll buy you a –'

'HOLD IT RIGHT THERE!' Sally roared. We all stopped dead in our tracks. I knew what was coming. I took Nancy firmly by the arm and said, 'Tell you what, Nancy, why don't you let us deal with this? You go and pour yourself a nice glass of wine and relax before your guests arrive.'

She looked at me uncertainly for a moment, but the thought of not having to deal with yet another tantrum won the day and she left, teetering across to the house on her dangerously high heels.

Sally bent down and grabbed the boys by the arm. 'Now, you listen to me, you little brats. We've just spent hours turning this dump into a jungle for you, so don't you dare knock things down. If I see you being rude or misbehaving again, I'll get Indiana here to tie you upside-down from the top of that tree and you'll miss the whole party. Let's be clear. I don't like kids, I think you're all little horrors, so I'll have no problem making you suffer.'

The boys looked shocked, but before they could run in and tell their mother that the party-planner had threatened them with violence, their first friend arrived.

Sally very rarely had to help out at the parties – only in emergencies like this – and it really was for the best.

'Why don't you head home? We'll be fine now,' I suggested.

'This is why I stick to the office. I just don't like them.'

'I know, and it's safer that way! Can you drop the girls home?'

'Sure.'

'Can you promise us she won't try to mow down any kids on the way?' Ali giggled.

'My God, Sally,' Sarah laughed, 'are you the Wicked Witch of the West or what? I'm glad you didn't babysit us very often when we were kids.'

Sally burst out laughing. 'You're still not too big for me to have a go at you so watch out.'

'Seriously,' Ali said, grinning widely, 'between you manhandling the kids and Mum bellowing at the clowns, I'm amazed you two ever got this business off the ground.' We all cracked up, laughing.

'Right, you lot, off you go. I'll see you later, girls – thanks for helping.'

'Aren't you forgetting something, Mum? Where's our money?' Sarah demanded. 'I'm exhausted.'

'I'll tell you what, I'll take you for lunch and we can discuss your wages,' Sally said.

'Cool! Can we go to the Asian Kitchen? They do the best dumplings ever,' Sarah said.

'That suit you, Ali?' Sally asked.

'I'm going to meet David.'

'Oh, to be in love.' Sally smiled. To Sarah, she said, 'OK, big mouth, it's just you and me.'

I waved them off, then turned to Charlie – there was another threat to be dealt with. 'Listen to me, Charlie. This is my job. I work very hard and I make a good living from it because my clients are always happy. You cannot under any circumstances grope any of the mothers here today.'

'But that Nancy one was giving me the eye.'

'Charlie, I don't care if she begs you for sex. You do not touch her. She is a client, OK?'

'OK, OK, I promise. But if she gives me her number, I'll take it.'

'You can do whatever you want with her once we get paid. For now, less focus on the mothers and more on the kids.'

When the other boys saw 'Indiana Jones' they all started jeering, calling him 'old' and 'crap' and 'a big girl'. That was until he started chasing them around, lassoing them with his 'rope' and tying them up against the trees, which they loved. The rougher the better with these kids.

After that, we played Giraffe, which involved tying twenty-five doughnuts from the trees and each boy had to eat one with his hands tied behind his back. The first to finish won a prize. We played Ostrich relay racing, where you had to run with a balloon 'egg' between your legs, and then we had jungle charades, where they had to act out wild animals.

When it was time for the cake I called in the parents. The

twins looked around for their dad. 'He got stuck in the airport.' Nancy shrugged.

They looked upset. 'Hey, come on, guys, I need you to cut the crocodile and see if he bleeds.' I tried to distract them.

They stabbed the cake aggressively with the knife and raspberry coulis flooded out.

'*Cooooooooooooooool!*' all the boys shrieked in unison. The twins smiled and I breathed a sigh of relief.

After eating, the boys were calmer, so Indiana Jones decided to tell them a story about his adventures in Africa.

While he was doing that, I packed the tables, chairs and partyware into my car. As I was coming back in to get the potted palm trees, I saw that all the little guests were mesmerized by the story. I leant in to hear Indiana say, '. . . she had the biggest boobies I'd ever seen . . .'

7

I looked at my watch – six fifty. Damn, he was cutting it fine. I swore under my breath. This debate meant a lot to Ali and I wanted us all to be there, cheering her on. Finally, he rang.

'Where the hell are you?' I snapped.

'I'm going to be late. We've had a crisis here. The back freezer defrosted and all the meat's off. I'm trying to source some before the dinner orders start coming in.'

'For God's sake, Paul, it's her first debate as captain of the team. It's a really big deal.'

Paul sighed. 'I'm not doing this to piss you off. I didn't defrost the bloody freezer – but it's a mess and I have to deal with it. I'll get there as soon as I can.'

'Fine.' I hung up and flung my mobile onto my bed. Typical! There was always some stupid crisis to be fixed and Paul seemed incapable of delegating. Having built the pub up from crumbling mess to success, he was a complete control freak. Last year it had won Dublin Pub of the Year, and while I was delighted that his work was being recognized, it had actually made him even more obsessed with the place. Running a successful pub and a kitchen serving high-quality food meant there was always a crisis – highly strung chefs walking out, staff calling in sick, kegs leaking, food deliveries not turning up . . . There was always something.

I changed out of the jeans and jumper I'd worn to the office and put on black trousers and a cream cardigan with black velvet trim.

'Is that what you're wearing?' Sarah asked, coming into my bedroom and flopping onto the bed.

'Yes, why?'

45

'It's a bit conservative.'

'I'm going to a school debate. What did you think I'd wear? A mini?'

'No, but you've got a good figure. You should dress a bit funkier. More edgy.'

'I don't even know what dressing edgy means.'

'Think Madonna meets Kate Moss.'

'Think mother of two not making a show of herself at her daughters' school.'

'Madonna has four kids.'

'She's a pop star who wears corsets and thigh-high leather boots. I run a kids'-party-planning company. Sorry to disappoint you, but I'm never going to look like Madonna. Now, come on, let's go or we'll be late.'

Ali was the captain of the debating team this year. She had been on the team the year before when they won the all-Ireland championship, so she really wanted to do well again. That night the team's first debate was against Brookfield College and she was very nervous.

When Sarah, Charlie and I arrived, Sally was already there waiting for us. She waved us to the front row, where she had saved us four seats. 'Where's Paul?' she asked.

'Some drama in work.' Sarah rolled her eyes. 'Mum's furious – don't get her started.'

'Thank you, Sarah,' I said. 'He's going to try to make it later.'

I smiled at Ali, who was busy talking to her team-mates. I gave her the thumbs-up. She smiled back, nervous but excited.

'So, is David the one in the middle?' Sally asked, looking at the debating team.

'He's not a debater!' Sarah squealed. 'He's way too cool for that.'

'There's nothing wrong with debating.' I didn't like her slagging Ali's hobby.

'There.' Sarah pointed to David, who was sitting in the back row with his feet dangling over the chair in front.

'Wow, he's gorgeous,' Sally approved. 'Very Johnny Depp *circa* 1989.'

'Yeah, he's cute,' I agreed.

'And cool,' Sarah added.

'Who's that sitting beside him?' Charlie asked.

'That's Tracy, the new girl I was telling you about, Mum.'

'The one who looks like a model?' I asked, turning around.

'Yes, isn't she fab?'

Tracy was tall and very thin, with high cheekbones, long, poker-straight black hair and almond-shaped blue eyes. She was very striking and angular, but not soft and pretty like Ali.

'She's all right, but she's not as gorgeous as Ali,' I said.

'She's a matchstick and no man wants that,' Charlie assured us.

'She seems a bit flirty,' Sally noted. 'We'll have to keep an eye on her.'

Tracy was leaning over, whispering something into David's ear.

'She flirts with everyone,' Sarah explained. 'The guys all love her.'

There was a clink of a glass and the chair of the debate stood up to introduce the two teams. 'Welcome, everyone, to this evening's debate between Brookfield College and Hodder College. The motion this evening is "Should minorities be treated differently?" Brookfield is for and Hodder against. The winners of this evening's debate will be chosen by their oratory style and their ability to convince the audience that they are right and not simply by their statistical analysis of the problem. Hodder will begin. Each speaker has fifteen minutes to put their point across.'

Ali went first. She was wonderful. I had goosebumps of pride. She held very good eye contact with the audience and her opposition, used her hands to emphasize key points and spoke clearly and very convincingly. She barely glanced at her notes and used humour to keep the audience engaged. It was perfect. We clapped and cheered loudly.

'Bloody hell, she's good,' Sally whispered.

'I know.' I beamed, unable to hide my pride.

'She gets it from me,' Charlie announced. 'I was always able to persuade people that black was white. It's how I survived in the orphanage.'

'Pity you couldn't have persuaded Catherine that water was vodka.' Sally giggled.

'You cheeky devil.'

'Can I go now, Mum? I've seen Ali,' Sarah said. 'Do I have to stay for all the others?'

'Yes, you do.' I laid my hand on her arm to stop her getting up.

'Come on! There's five more geeks to speak – it'll be so boring.'

'It'll do you good to listen. It's educational.'

'I get it – we shouldn't treat minorities differently because it doesn't do them any favours and it just pisses everyone else off. Can I go now?'

Sally shook with laughter beside me. 'If Ali's ever stuck for a team member, you should offer your services. You're very succinct and convincing.'

'Sit back down and be quiet,' I warned her.

Sarah crossed her arms and sulked for the next hour and a half.

Ali's team won and she was singled out for special praise as the best speaker. We all gathered around to congratulate her.

'I'm seriously impressed. Brains and beauty, you'll go far,' Sally said, hugging her.

'Thanks for coming,' Ali said. 'I'm glad it's over. I was so nervous that we'd lose in the first round.'

David came up with Tracy. 'You totally nailed it, babe. Well done.'

'Thanks.' Ali glowed.

'Yeah, congrats,' Tracy said.

Ali smiled politely and then, turning to David, said, 'The team's going for a drink to celebrate. Are you keen?'

'Actually, I'm kind of wrecked. I think I'll head home. I'll catch you tomorrow.'

Ali's face dropped.

'Hey, I'm driving if you want a lift,' Tracy offered, while I tried to resist the urge to elbow her out of the way.

'That'd be great. See you, Ali, have a good time.' David leant over and gave Ali a peck on the lips.

We all watched him leave with Tracy.

'Debating's not really his scene,' Ali explained.

'What is?' I asked, aiming for breezy but sounding angry.

'Going to gigs and playing guitar in his band.'

'Oh, God, gorgeous and a guitar player . . . if only I was twenty years younger.' Sally groaned.

'Twenty-five.' Charlie grinned.

'Steady on, he's taken,' Ali reminded us.

'Sorry I'm late,' Paul said, arriving in as the chairs were being stacked.

'It's OK, Dad. Mum said you had a crisis in the kitchen.'

'How did you do, Ali?'

'She was amazing,' I said coldly.

'The star of the night,' Charlie agreed.

'A credit to her parents.' Sally smiled at me.

'I'm sorry I missed you, Ali. I promise to be here early for the next one,' Paul said.

'Fat chance,' I mumbled.

'Ava!' Sally whispered. 'Be nice, he's trying.'

'Dad, you missed David. He's gone home with Tracy,' Sarah said. 'I'd watch her, Ali, she definitely fancies him.'

'He has the best-looking and smartest girl in the school,' Paul said, 'why would he go for second-best?'

'Oh, *puuuurlease*, Dad, that's *so* corny.' Sarah made vomiting noises.

'It's true, though.' Paul winked at Ali.

'Sarah has a point,' Sally said. 'I'd keep an eye on that Tracy. I didn't like her.'

49

Ali frowned.

'Hey, don't worry,' I said. 'David came here to support you.'

'And he sat through some really boring speeches, so he must be mad about you,' Sarah added. 'Seriously, Ali, I can't believe you choose to do this as a hobby. If it wasn't for Charlie's DNA, I'd think I was adopted. Now, can we please get out of here? My head hurts from all that talk about minorities.'

'Did you learn anything?' Paul asked.

'Yeah, just treat them the same! I do that anyway. I'm nice to everyone, even Doreen Nifel, and she's got really bad BO.'

'Our very own Mother Teresa,' Sally said, as we all laughed.

8

A few days later I arrived home from work to find Sarah pacing the hall.

'Thank God you're home.'

'What's wrong, pet?'

'It's Ali.'

'Oh, my God, what happened?'

'The stupid prick David dumped her for Tracy.'

'Don't say "prick".'

'Mum!'

'It's crass.'

'Can you focus on the situation, please?'

'So the little shit broke up with Ali to go out with that tooth-pick?'

'She looks like a model.'

'Ali's beautiful.'

'I know, she's really pretty, but Tracy's really confident and cool.'

'Oh, God, poor Ali. How is she?'

'Well, she's a mess, obviously. It's bad enough getting dumped, but for someone else in your class is the worst ever.'

'I'll go up to her.'

'Wait for a bit. She's on the phone to Donna now.'

'How dare he? I could kill him.'

'I know, but she needs to, like, get a grip. She was bawling crying in school today – everyone saw her. I told her she needed to pretend she didn't care.'

'Give her a break – it's just happened and she really liked him.'

'I'm aware of that, but you can't go around freaking out in school. Everyone was talking about it – how poor Ali was so in love with David and he was never really that into her and how mad he is about Tracy. It's embarrassing for Ali. She needs to go in tomorrow and act like she couldn't give a toss about him.'

'You're right. She should go in looking stunning and completely ignore him.'

'Exactly, and she should flirt with other guys and then the vultures like Jane Collins – who's just a fat jealous cow – will stop gossiping.'

'What did Jane do?'

'She was like the *News of the* bloody *World* – she told everyone as soon as it happened. She fancies David, too.'

'Is there anyone who doesn't?'

'Me! I wouldn't touch him with a barge pole. Besides, I've got a new boyfriend.'

'Who and since when?'

She beamed. 'Bobby! He asked me to go out with him this morning.'

'Oh.'

'*Oh?* Mum, it's the most amazing news ever. He said I'm the coolest chick in transition year, which coming from a jock is, like, major!'

'Well, I'm delighted to hear it. Is he a nice boy? Is he bright?'

She shrieked. 'He's the youngest guy ever to play winger on the senior rugby team. He is God.'

'Yes, but is he clever?'

'I dunno. He's not super-bright like Ali, but he's not thick. He's normal, like me.'

'OK. Well, just make sure you don't get too distracted with your boyfriend and neglect your studies. And be nice to your sister. The poor thing's had a very tough time.'

'I am being nice to her. I've given her my ten-step programme to get David to fancy her again. It's foolproof. It's never let me down.'

'I don't think that's a good idea. I think she should forget about him and move on to someone the whole school doesn't want to go out with.'

'The whole point is that she gets him to fancy her again and then she can dump and humiliate him. So, do you want to hear my ten steps?'

'Go on then.' I sat back, prepared to be entertained.

Sarah reeled them off. 'Step One: Always look your best, but don't look like you're trying too hard. Step Two: Whenever the guy you fancy is around, look like you're having the best time ever. Start laughing and smiling. Step Three: Flirt with everyone else when he's around, but not with him. Step Four: If it's Valentine's Day, send yourself cards to the school. Step Five: When you know you're looking really hot, roll your skirt right up and bump into him on purpose and drop your books. He'll help you pick them up and you can flirt just a little bit. Step Six: Find out what he's interested in and read up on it – I'm now an expert on rugby. I know all the names of the wingers on the other schools' teams. Step Seven: If he's really thick, you'll have to pretend you're not intelligent. If he's really clever, you'll have to study harder or maybe decide to fancy someone else. Step Eight: If he has brothers or sisters in the school, make sure you become friendly with them. Step Nine: If he's playing a match – rugby, hockey, tennis, whatever – turn up and pretend you're supporting someone else on the team. Obviously make sure you look amazing. Finally, Step Ten: Move in for the kill. Look all sad and pretend your dog just got run over. It has to be a dog because guys don't care about cats. Don't actually cry, because your mascara will run, but just be all down and "I loved Scooby so much", blah, blah, blah. He should put his arm around you and then you can tilt your head and – *voilà* – snog.' She took a bow.

I couldn't help but laugh. 'You're something else, Sarah Mullen. If you put as much effort into your school work as you did into your ten-step plan, you'd be a straight-A student.'

'All work and no play . . .'

'And all play and no work . . .' I replied. 'Now, go upstairs and finish your homework.'

She left the room, dragging her feet as she went. I went up to see Ali with a bowl of her favourite ice cream – Häagen Dazs strawberry cheesecake. I opened the door to her room and she looked up from her book. Her eyes were puffy from crying.

'Oh, Ali,' I kissed her, 'I'm so sorry. What a crappy thing to happen. Are you OK?'

She covered her face with her hands and sobbed. I wrapped my arms around her and tried not to cry. I wanted to call over to David's house and smash his face in.

'I just – uh-uh-uh – I just don't understand, Mum,' she sobbed. 'We were getting on really well and then in the last few days he started being all weird and kept saying he was too busy to hang out with me and then today he said he didn't think it was working out and he wanted to break up and then I saw him snogging Tracy.'

'Bastard! He's clearly an idiot if he can't see what an amazing girlfriend you were. He doesn't deserve you.'

'I'm not amazing, I'm crap. And I have to go to school and face everyone tomorrow and I can't bear it. Everyone will be talking about how I got dumped for Tracy. It's so humiliating.'

'No, they won't. People are far too wrapped up in themselves to care about anyone else. It'll blow over.'

'How am I going to cope? I have to see David and Tracy every day. It's going to be torture.'

'Oh, Ali, I know it seems like the end of the world now, but you'll get over this and find a new boyfriend who appreciates you.'

'But I love David!' She began to wail again.

I tried to think of something reassuring to say. What words would make a seventeen-year-old girl whose heart was broken feel better? I had no idea.

When I first got my heart broken my mother was dead. Char-

He found me sobbing into my pillow and when I told him what had happened he threw his hands up in the air and said he didn't know what to say, he had no idea how to make me feel better, that this was a job for Mum and he wished she was here, and we both cried.

I racked my brains, but all I came up with was, 'He's a loser and you're better off without him.'

'He's not a loser. I'd give anything to go out with him again. Maybe it's just a phase. Maybe he'll get bored with Tracy soon.'

'Ali,' I said as gently as I could, 'you need to let him go. Let him and Tracy have their silly relationship and just ignore him. Pretend you don't give a damn about him and his stupid new girlfriend. Go into that school tomorrow with your head held high and a smile on your face and pretend he doesn't exist.'

'That's what Sarah said – but I can't bear to see them,' she said, welling up again.

'If you really want you can stay at home tomorrow, but you'll have to face it the next day and I think it's better if you get it over with.'

She sighed. 'I'd rather do that.'

I hugged her and then, kissing her forehead, I said, 'I'll get you some cucumber for those poor puffy eyes and we'll make you up so you look incredible tomorrow. He'll be kicking himself when he sees what a mistake he's made.'

'Mum, Tracy's like a model. I'm nothing compared to her.'

'You're a super-model to me. You're beautiful and sweet and smart –'

'Muuuum,' she said, pushing me gently away.

'All right, I won't smother you,' I said, reluctantly letting go of her. 'I'll get you that cucumber, and if you want to come down and cry all night, I'm here for you. Or, if you like, we can watch a movie and order a take-out or go for a walk, whatever you want, pet.'

'I just want to be miserable up here.'

'Well, I'm here for anything you need.'

I went back down and met Paul coming in the door. 'Ali got dumped.'

'Oh, Jesus.'

'It's awful.'

'That little fucker.'

'My sentiments exactly. But the worst of it is, he broke up with her to go out with Tracy in her class who looks like a model.'

'No girl could be more gorgeous than Ali.'

'I agree, but now she has to face the happy couple every day. It's so humiliating for her.'

'Is she really upset?'

'Devastated.'

'Will I go up to her?'

'Yeah, do.' I went into the kitchen, Paul following me. 'Here, bring her up these cucumber slices.'

'Cucumber?' he said, staring at me as if I'd lost my mind.

'For her eyes. They'll help with the puffiness.'

'I'll kill that little shit.'

He was back down a minute later.

'Long chat, then?' I smiled.

'I had no idea what to say. You know what I'm like when they cry, I just panic.'

'So, what did you say?'

'I just said I was sorry and that she's wonderful and he's an arsehole.'

'You covered all the angles, then.'

'Women are better at this stuff.'

'Not really. I didn't know what to say either. I just listened to her and said pretty much exactly the same things you did.'

'Where's Sarah?'

'Supposedly doing her homework, but I'd say she's texting everyone she's ever met to tell them she's going out with Bobby.'

'What?'

'Sarah is, as of this morning, going out with Bobby Masterson-Brown, who apparently is a total stud.'

'Is he?'

'Nope, he looks ridiculous – badly highlighted hair and his jeans hanging down around his knees, but she seems very excited.'

'The last thing that girl needs is a boyfriend.'

'It might not be such a bad thing. It might settle her down a bit. Apparently he's not super-smart but not thick either.'

'I don't see anyone from Mensa going out with Sarah.' We laughed. 'Where's Charlie?'

I rolled my eyes. 'He's gone to meet that woman Lily from the funeral.'

'The one whose bum he pinched?'

'The very same.'

'Way to go, Charlie.'

'Apparently she's fifty-four, which is borderline. He won't go out with anyone over fifty-five. It's too old, despite the fact that he's sixty-eight.'

'He's right. You don't want them too wrinkly.' Paul laughed.

'I just hope he doesn't attack her in the car or something. He's like a teenager with raging hormones.'

'I admire his –' Paul was stopped short by the sight of my father strolling into the kitchen with a stumbling Lily in tow.

'Evening, all,' Charlie said, grinning from ear to ear.

'Well, hello there, Charlie,' said Paul, grinning back.

'I'd like you to meet the lovely Lily.'

''S lovely to meesh you,' slurred Lily.

She looked a lot worse than she had at Catherine's funeral. Her skirt was askew, her lipstick was all over her teeth and the middle two buttons on her blouse had come undone so we had a bird's-eye view of her bra. She was absolutely legless and it wasn't a pretty sight.

Paul guided her to a chair. 'Can I get you a drink or some coffee?' he asked.

Charlie stepped in, grabbed her by the hand and hoisted her back up. 'She's had enough drink. I just forked out for a bottle of wine that cost thirty-five euros. I didn't think I was going to have to take out a bank loan to get laid. Come on, Lily, the bedroom's this way.'

I looked at Paul. 'Should I stop them?'

'He's sixty-eight.'

'But she's a total stranger. What if she gives him a disease or robs him or something? I'll have to give him protection. Get me some of your condoms.'

And so it was that a forty-two-year-old mother of two found herself knocking on her father's bedroom door at midnight.

'I'm busy,' he roared.

'Charlie! Open the bloody door.'

'What?' A grumpy red face appeared.

'Here.'

'What's this?'

'It's a condom.'

'Lily might be a bit old to bear me children, Ava.'

'It's to protect you from other things,' I whispered.

'Like what?'

'*Venereal disease*,' I hissed, pushing the condom into his hand.

'Have you only one?' he asked.

'Jesus, Charlie.'

'I've taken some of that Viagra so I'm feeling good.'

'For goodness' sake,' I muttered, as I stomped down the corridor to get my father some more condoms.

I knocked on the door again. This time he opened it immediately.

'Here you go,' I said, handing him the box.

'I'd put ear-plugs in if I was you.' He grinned. 'I think Lily might be a screamer.'

9

Over coffee in the office Sally asked me how Ali was coping with her new single status.

'She's very subdued. I wish I knew what to say to make her feel better. I keep telling her she's gorgeous and there are lots of fish in the sea.'

'STOP! Don't say another word. That's the kind of stuff my mother is *still* saying to me and, believe me, it does not make me feel better. You mothers need to come up with some new material.'

'Like what?'

'I suppose telling her that copious amounts of alcohol help numb the pain is out of the question?'

'It most certainly is.'

'Honestly, there's nothing you can say. Some other drama is bound to happen in school and everyone will forget about it, although Ali never will. I still cringe when I think of Rozzer Dickson asking me to his end-of-school dance and standing me up. I waited for two hours, looking out the window in my midnight-blue satin meringue dress, while my parents kept trying to make up excuses as to why Rozzer was late. The best was when Mum suggested that maybe he'd tripped up on the way over, got concussed and was suffering from amnesia. At which point Dad muttered that if Rozzer ever darkened our door he'd know all about amnesia. I didn't leave the house for two weeks.'

'Oh, Sally, that's terrible.'

'It's probably the reason I'm still single. I wonder if you can sue someone for standing you up at seventeen thereby ruining your chances of getting married?'

'Do you think it'll take her ages to get over it?'

'Who knows? She seemed really into him. It's a hard knock.'

'According to Sarah, David's now in a "super-intense" relationship with Tracy. I don't know if that'll help Ali get over him faster or make it worse.'

'Worse, believe me. How's Sarah faring in her new romance?'

'You know Sarah – her relationships are always completely over the top. Bobby is in our house all the time and they're permanently wrapped around each other. I'm sure it's not easy on Ali.'

'What's Bobby like?'

'He seems nice enough. Paul's not keen on him because he talks like Sarah – in that California-airhead way – and he dyes his hair, which Paul thinks is very gay.'

'What I don't understand about teenage boys dyeing their hair is that they do it so badly. It looks orange. Why don't they get it done properly so it looks good?'

'Come on, Sally, we all dyed our hair with Sun-in and those other bleaches. You have to get it wrong before you get it right. Actually, Bobby's isn't that bad – I think he gets it done in a salon.'

'How's Charlie? Any sign of Lily?'

'Thankfully, no, it seems to have fizzled out. He's been relatively calm recently, which is a relief. I always imagined worrying about the girls sneaking people home at night, not my father.'

'He probably got rid of all those years of pent-up sexual frustration with Lily.'

'I hope so. He seems happier. But you never know with Charlie. How was your family lunch?'

'You mean my pity lunch.'

'Was it that bad?'

'Worse. Both my sisters were there so it was a full onslaught.'

Sally had two sisters, one older (Samantha) and one younger

(Hilary), who were both married with children. They couldn't understand why she wasn't and were always trying to fix her up.

After college Sally qualified as an accountant, then headed off on a trip around the world. She had met Stuart in Australia. He owned a bar on a beach in the middle of nowhere and offered her a job and to share his bed. She stayed for a year – it was the opposite of anything she'd ever experienced before: carefree, laid-back, no responsibilities, no exams, no suits – she went to work in a bikini. It was exactly what she needed. But after a year her mother flew over and told her, 'The holiday is over. You need to get back to reality.' So Sally moved to London, worked and played hard for ten years, got involved with her married boss, Jeremy, and when that went sour, she moved home to lick her wounds.

I had known her vaguely in college, but it was only when she came back from London and we met up at a mutual friend's house that we really clicked. A few months later, over drinks in a wine bar, we'd decided to set up Happy Dayz. She wanted out of corporate life and I wanted out of domestic life. Since then she'd never really gone out with anyone for more than a few months at most. She hadn't admitted it, but I think she'd really believed Jeremy would leave his wife. When he didn't, she was devastated and hardened her heart to protect herself.

'Tell me all,' I said, settling in my chair.

'It's the same old story,' Sally said, 'Samantha and Hilary trying to find me a husband . . .'

'Hi, Sally, any nice men on the scene?' Samantha asked.

'Nope,' Sally said, popping an olive into her mouth.

'Well, my friend Suzie's cousin met this guy on a blind date and she didn't find him attractive and they didn't even get on that well, but he asked her out again and they got on a bit better that time and then they went out again, and three months later they're engaged.'

'I see. So you're suggesting that if I go on a blind date with a bald, overweight loser I could fall madly in love and marry him?'

'There's no need to be snippy. I'm just saying you should give it a go. You never know, Sally, you might meet someone you like.'

'It's worth a try,' Hilary agreed. 'You're not having much luck on your own, so let us help you.'

'I'll think about it,' Sally said, to get them off her back.

'I don't understand what the problem is. You're an attractive woman with a good job,' Martin, Sally's brother-in-law, put in.

'She's too independent – it scares men off,' her other brother-in-law, Philip, helpfully explained.

'Excuse me, I'm in the room,' Sally fumed. 'Please don't talk about me in the third person and, besides, that's crap. If a man can't appreciate a woman who has her own life and her own career, then he's the one with the insecurities and the problem, not her.'

'You could try to soften up a bit,' Samantha said. 'Even women find you a bit prickly. My friends are always commenting on how cynical you are. They're afraid to bring up any topical issues with you because you just shoot them down.'

'That's because they don't have a clue what they're talking about. Come on, Samantha, even you can't defend that idiot friend of yours who thought a *hijab* was an Indian curry.'

'She's a busy mum of three. She hasn't got time to read up on current affairs.'

'That is such a lame excuse. Having children doesn't make you brain dead – look at Cherie Blair and Hillary Clinton, for God's sake.'

Martin choked on his drink. 'Get real, Sally. They're not the type of women that men want to shag. You don't have to dumb down, but maybe a less confrontational approach would work. Think less Hillary Clinton and more Carla Bruni.'

'So what are you saying? That a woman can't challenge a man if he says something she disagrees with in case he gets scared off? What are you, men or mice? Why do I have to pretend to be something I'm not?'

'You don't,' Hilary said. 'But it might help if you tone it down in the beginning. When the man gets to know you and falls for you, then you can challenge him on anything you want.'

'I'm forty-bloody-three. I'm too old to play games.'

'When was the last time you got laid?' Martin asked.

'None of your business.'

'Maybe you're too fussy,' Samantha suggested. 'Everyone compromises.'

'I'm not fussy. I'm actually very low maintenance. I don't want children; I don't need money, I have my own; I'm not expecting gorgeous looks, but I would like an independent man who enjoys a lively debate and makes me laugh.'

'What do you mean, "everyone compromises"?' Philip asked his wife.

'Philip, do you honestly believe I thought I'd end up with someone who's obsessed with collecting stamps?' Samantha snapped.

'There are a lot worse hobbies he could have,' Hilary said.

'He spends hours locked in his study staring at stamps through a magnifying-glass. It's not normal.'

'Would you rather he was in the pub drinking?' Martin asked.

'At least it's sociable and I could join in.'

'I've met some very interesting people through my stamp collecting. In fact, quite a few of the men are single and I was thinking of fixing Sally up with one of them,' Philip said.

'Is this what I've been reduced to, blind dates with stamp nerds? Someone shoot me now.' Sally covered her face with her hands.

'Don't be ridiculous, Philip. Sally needs someone who can challenge her, not some mousy stamp collector she can walk all over,' Samantha said.

'Are you sure you don't want children?' Hilary asked, looking lovingly at her two sons, who were busy shoving peanuts up their noses. 'They really are such a blessing.'

'I honestly think I can live without it, although it does look tempting.' Sally suppressed a smile.

'There's no greater love than –'

'A mother has for her child,' Sally cut her sister short. 'Yes, I know, Hilary, you've told me a million times. But everyone is different and children are not for me. I'd just like to meet a nice man and have fun. It would be lovely to have someone to go to the cinema with. Someone to go to dinner parties with. Someone to talk to when I get home after a shitty day in work. Someone to share good news with. Someone to spend Sundays with . . .'

'There's a bloke in my office who's just divorced his wife. Nice guy, not bad-looking, successful, top squash player. I could see if he's up for a night out?' Martin suggested.

'Why did he break up with his wife?' Sally asked.

'Caught shagging the au pair.'

'He sounds like a great catch, Martin, but I'll pass.'

'So, as you can see, it was another fun family lunch,' Sally said, pulling at the button on her jacket.

'It sounds awful. But, you know, although they go about it the wrong way, they are just trying to help,' I noted.

'I just wish they'd stop obsessing about me meeting someone because it makes me feel like shit. It's as if I'm not a whole person because I'm single. Of course I'd like to meet someone, but sometimes I'm happy being on my own. Why can't they just leave it?'

'Because when you love someone, you want them to have it all.'

'Yes, but your definition of having it all is not necessarily the same as the other person's.'

'That's true – I never thought of it like that.'

'I don't want children, but everyone thinks I'm saying that

because I'm forty-three and single. But that's not it. I just don't want kids. I never did. But Hilary can't accept this because her children define who she is. She has nothing else in her life. She barely leaves the house unless it's to ferry the boys to soccer or swimming. I think her life looks like hell and she thinks the same of mine.'

'I know what you mean, actually. When I met Paul and decided to get married, all my friends thought I was making the biggest mistake of my life. They tried to talk me out of it. They said I was going to miss out on my youth, I'd never travel and see the world, and I'd be a boring housewife in my twenties.'

'I remember when you got engaged – I hardly knew you but everyone who did was totally shocked.'

'They thought I was mad. But the point was that I needed stability. I craved structure and security. After Mum died and Charlie married Catherine, I moved out. I didn't have a family. I felt completely lost. I was living in an apartment alone at seventeen. So when I met Paul, I dived head first into the relationship. He was so strong and reliable and sure of himself and where he was going in life. I wanted to be part of that. He made me feel safe.'

'Did you ever feel you missed out on your twenties?'

'When I was stuck at home with the two girls and all my friends were travelling or partying all night I wondered if I'd made a mistake. That was a hard time. Paul had just bought the pub and was working day and night to make it a success, so once again I found myself alone. No one else had young kids and I had to make a new set of friends. But, I must say, Charlie was great. He used to babysit whenever I needed a night off, or just to go out for an hour. We got very close when I had the girls. I think in a way he saw it as a chance to make it up to me for marrying Catherine and leaving me on my own after Mum died.'

'I think being a young mum is cool. I see my sisters and they're going to be sixty when their kids are in college.'

'Paul and I always planned to do our travelling when the girls were finished college. We said we'd sell up and head off into the sunset. Do all the fun things our friends were doing while we were having kids and building a life together.'

'You should do it.'

'I hope we will. It would do us good.'

'Well, that's all you need – the desire to do it.'

I smiled. '*I* want to, but I'm not so sure Paul does any more.'

She looked at me as if she was about to ask something, but then changed her mind. I started to busy myself with some files. If she was nice to me right now, I'd burst into tears, and that was the last thing I wanted to do.

10

Ali continued to be quieter than usual for the rest of the week and moped around the house, sighing a lot. But on Sunday morning, she came into the kitchen, where I was sitting with Sarah, having tea and chocolate biscuits, and said she had an announcement.

'What is it?' I asked.

'I've made a decision. There's going to be a new me,' Ali said.

'Alleluia. All that misery was becoming a pain.' Sarah stuffed another biscuit into her mouth.

Ignoring her sister, Ali continued, 'I've decided I'm going to get fit and healthy. I'm cutting out all junk food from now on.'

She seemed extremely enthusiastic about her new plan and I was delighted to see her snapping out of her gloom. 'Why did you decide this?' I asked.

'I just think that if I eat a healthier diet it'll give me more energy and help me feel better, look better and study better. There's so much more work this year, I need to be fit and healthy. So, from now on, no more crisps, chocolate or biscuits for me.'

'To be honest, I think that's a great idea. I could do with it myself. I always seem to put on weight in the autumn,' I said, pinching the layer of flesh overhanging my jeans. 'I'll stock up on fruit this week.'

'OK, great.'

I was pleased that Ali was taking an interest in something. And she was right: we did always have biscuits, chocolate and crisps in the house. Both Paul and I had a weakness for sweet things and we had been indulging it more than normal lately because the weather had turned so cold and a cup of tea is miserable without a chocolate biscuit to go with it. But I didn't worry about it. I always put on weight in the winter and lost it in the spring. And the girls ate well: I cooked dinner, if I wasn't working late, and it was always relatively healthy – and they were both slim, so I never worried about the odd bit of junk food.

'Hold on a minute,' Sarah said. 'There are two children in this family and I don't want to cut out all junk. I need something nice to eat when I'm watching TV. I need my mini-Crunchies, so don't even think of not buying them.'

'Fair enough. I'll get you those, but I'll cut out the crisps – you don't need both.'

'OK. Bobby's actually really health-conscious, so I don't mind eating more fruit. He said we should eat blueberries in the morning because they're a super-fruit.'

'I'll put them on the list.'

'I also want to cycle to school,' Ali said.

'Are you insane?' Sarah stared at her sister. 'It's four miles uphill.'

'I know, but it'll help keep me fit.'

'But you get plenty of exercise in school, don't you?' I asked.

'I just think it would help wake me up in the mornings. It's no big deal.'

'Don't even think about asking me to cycle,' Sarah said. 'My hair would be a mess by the time I got in.'

'Sorry, Ali, but there's no point me driving Sarah to school while you cycle. Besides, the weather's really bad at the moment – you'd catch your death of cold on a bike. If you want to go cycling at the weekend, that's fine.'

'I don't want to go at the weekends. I want to cycle to school.'

'Why the sudden interest?' I asked.

'Oh, forget it,' Ali said, and stormed up the stairs.

I turned to Sarah, surprised at Ali's outburst. It was unlike her to snap. 'What's wrong with your sister?'

'Dunno. I suppose she's just pissed off about David and his new super-model girlfriend being all over each other,' said Sarah.

'Don't say "pissed off".'

'OK, fed up, then. I don't hear you correcting Charlie when he curses like a drunken sailor.'

'That's because he's sixty-eight and it's too late to change him.'

I went upstairs to Ali's bedroom. She was sitting at her desk, which was covered with textbooks. I sat down on her bed. 'Ali, sweetheart, I know it must be really hard for you seeing David with someone else. Are you all right? Do you want to talk about it?'

'No, Mum, I really don't.'

'Are you sure? I'm happy to sit and listen if you want to rant and cry and get it off your chest.'

'I'm fine. I really need to work now.' She picked up her pen and began to write.

I patted her shoulder. 'OK. Well, just make sure you don't overdo it.'

I came back downstairs and went into the lounge, where Paul was reading the Sunday papers. He looked up. 'Is everything all right? I heard doors slamming.'

'Ali's just upset about David.'

'Arsehole.'

'I agree. It must be awful having to see him all over the new girlfriend.'

'Well, the best way to get over a guy is to get under a new one.'

'Paul!'

'I'm not suggesting she goes out and shags the whole football team, but a new boyfriend might cheer her up.'

'True, but you can't go out with someone you don't like.'

'He might grow on her.'

'It's a bit soon. Let her wallow for a bit, it's what girls do – part of the healing process. First you're devastated, then you're furious and then you move on.'

'I'm not looking forward to the furious phase.' He smiled.

I picked up the travel section and flicked through it. There were lots of city-break autumn offers. One to Paris caught my eye. On our third wedding anniversary, Paul had taken me to Paris for a romantic weekend. We didn't have much money, but we stayed in the Hôtel de Verger, a small hotel in a converted abbey near the Luxembourg Gardens. Our room had a tiny balcony where we had breakfast every morning, looking over the rooftops. It was one of my favourite memories and it was where Ali had been conceived.

I looked at Paul, who was engrossed in the sports section. Maybe if we both got away from work, the girls, Charlie and all of our responsibilities here, we could rekindle our romance and get our spark back. Paris would be perfect. 'Paul, look at –'

His phone rang. 'Hiya, Gary. Oh . . . I see . . . Right . . . Is he there with you now? OK . . . Thanks for that . . . I'll be right down . . . I owe you,' he said, and hung up.

'What's happened?' I asked.

'Charlie's been arrested.'

My hand flew up to my mouth. 'Why?'

'Drunk and disorderly. He was arrested at the Sunshine Home.'

'Oh, my God, he was drunk in the nursing home?' I was genuinely shocked. 'But how? He didn't have any drink with him.'

'I don't have the details. Gary's one of the policemen who drinks in the pub. He just did me a favour by calling. He said if we can pick Charlie up now they won't press charges.'

Cursing my father under my breath, I grabbed my coat and we headed out.

When we arrived at the police station, Gary was waiting for us.

'Thanks for this,' said Paul, shaking his hand. 'Drinks are on me the next time you're in the pub.'

'For nothing,' said Gary, grinning. 'He's kept us all amused for the past hour with his stories. He's a gas, man.'

'Where is he?' I asked. 'Can I see him?'

'Sure, Niall will take you down. I just need Paul to fill out a few forms.'

'Thank you, Gary. I'm sorry my father's caused so much trouble,' I said, attempting a smile.

The junior policeman, Niall, showed me to the room where they had put Charlie. He was sitting on the table swinging his legs like a little boy and holding a handkerchief to his bloody lip.

'Charlie!'

'Now, I know what you're going to say, but hear me out first.'

'This'd better be good. Paul had to call in favours to get you out of this mess.'

Charlie began to explain. He had gone to visit his sister, my aunt Daisy, in her nursing home. She had Alzheimer's, so he found visiting her difficult . . . 'When I walked into her room, poor Daisy was all scrunched up in her bed, looking miserable. She's got much worse. She hadn't a clue who I was. She kept introducing herself – "Hello, my name's Daisy" – over and over again. Then she'd ask me who I was. I'd say, "It's Charlie here, your brother. D'you remember me?" and she'd lean over, stick out her hand and say, "Hello, my name's Daisy." It was ridiculous. I'd introduced myself to my own sister twenty times. I was going mad. I looked around for something to distract her and saw a bottle of sherry on her shelf so I poured us both a drink, for medicinal purposes. Anyway, she seemed to perk up a bit, so I poured us another . . . and so on.

'I decided she needed a change of scenery, so I threw her in the wheelchair and took her down the lounge with all the other nutters and started talking about old times, thinking maybe she'd remember our childhood. "Daisy, do you remember when we used to go dancing on a Friday night after work? You were going with my best friend, Frankie. We'd go to the dance halls and jive to Elvis, Little Richard and Bill Haley. And remember how you loved Doris Day. Remember you used to sing '*Que Sera, Sera*'?"

'Suddenly this ancient dinosaur of a woman comes charging over – well, she's going pretty fast for a two-hundred-year-old on a zimmer frame – and she starts howling, "*Que sera, sera, whatever will be will be* . . . " And Daisy joins in. The next thing I know, half the room is singing and it's great. At least the poor eejits remember something.

'So I'm singing along and encouraging them, but then the dinosaur starts bawling. She's howling, "Oh, boo-hoo, my boy-friend used to sing that to me."

'"When – in the eighteenth century?" I asked.

'Then I hear a voice behind me. "Are you taking the piss out of my granny?"

'I turn around to see a big tall fella giving me the evil eye. "No, I'm just trying to cheer her up. It's like a fecking morgue in here."

'The big lad leans in closer. "Have you been drinking?"

'"Yes, myself and Daisy here have just had a few sherries," I said.

'"You're a disgrace," he says.

'"Who are you calling a disgrace?" I replied. "Before I came in your granny was sitting in the corner like a dead person. Now at least she's singing and crying. Better to feel something than nothing."

'He pokes me in the chest. "I don't need you upsetting my granny. Now, go back to your wife and stop causing havoc."

'"She's not my wife, she's my sister."

'"No wonder she's mad," he says.

'There was no way I was letting that go. I know Daisy's off her rocker, but no one else is allowed insult her. So I punched him, but I was a bit unsteady on my feet, what with the bottle of sherry inside me and all, so I missed and he boxed me in the face.'

'How old was he?'

'Fifty?'

'You're certifiable. Why would you pick a fight with someone thirty years your junior? No, scratch that, why would you pick a fight with anyone in an old folks' home?'

'You haven't been listening. I didn't pick any fight. He started it.'

'You were drunk, Charlie! Aren't you a bit old for public brawls?'

'No, I just need to get fit and then I'll go back and knock him to the ground.'

'You will do no such thing. From now on you're going to behave like a normal almost-seventy-year-old man and not a fifteen-year-old boy. How did the police get involved?'

'When I fell down, all the nutters started shouting and roaring and a nurse came in, saw me on the ground with blood spurting out of my mouth and called the police. I presumed they were going to arrest your man for punching me. While we were waiting for the police to arrive, another nurse came in and helped wipe the blood off my face and gave me some ice. She happened to be very attractive.'

I shook my head. 'Please tell me you didn't.'

'She had the best backside I've seen in twenty years so I just gave it a little pinch and she started hollering.'

'What a surprise.'

'In the old days women would have been flattered by the attention. It's all so bloody serious now. If you look at someone sideways, you get arrested.'

'It's called sexual harassment. I wouldn't take kindly to a dirty old man pinching my bum in work.'

'Ah, it was only a bit of fun,' he grumbled.

'Fun that almost landed you in jail! If it wasn't for Paul you could have been charged. Why can't you get a pipe and slippers, do crosswords and bird-watch?' I was utterly exasperated.

'Ava, I'm never going to be the type of father who bird-watches or train-watches. Maybe I was born with a screw loose, but I'm not going to change now. Conforming is like dying. You lose your individuality. I learnt that in the orphanage. Even at the age of five I could see how most of the lads in there were institutionalized. There was no way in hell I was going to turn out like some robot. I fought very hard not to let the orphanage break my spirit and I'm sure as hell not going to let old age do it. I saw all those poor sods in that old folks' home, and I want to enjoy what time I have left with my mind intact. I'd rather die dancing than of boredom.'

I looked at him. My father. Charlie. The sixty-eight-year-old prize fighter. An eccentric. An original. His parents had died within six months of each other and his maiden aunt had taken in Daisy, but he'd been sent to the orphanage when he was just five years old. He'd run away at sixteen and joined a circus. But after a few years on the road he decided to get a more stable job and had started working as a runner in a factory that assembled televisions while going to bookkeeping classes at night. Within five years he was the floor manager and ten years later was promoted to general manager of the factory, a job he had held for thirty years until his retirement at sixty-five.

How was I going to get him to calm down? Could I? Should I? Would it be better to let him be the free spirit he was? Surely not if it meant ending up in prison.

'Charlie, I understand that you want to enjoy yourself, but while you're living under my roof you'll have to toe the line. I have two young daughters to worry about. No more sexual harassment and fighting and no more one-night stands either. When you're in your own apartment you can do what you like.'

He sighed. 'You're a tyrant.'

'Tyrants don't love their subjects.'

'I might as well be in jail.'

'I don't think the beds are as comfortable.'

Paul popped his head round the door. 'All clear. We can go now.'

'Thanks for that,' I said.

'Yes, thanks for bailing me out,' Charlie said.

'Pleasure. How's the lip?' Paul asked.

'I'll survive.'

'How does the other guy look?'

'Unfortunately I missed him.'

'I can show you a few moves,' said Paul.

'Thanks, but Mike Tyson here is retiring. For good,' I said, leading my father out to the car.

When we got home, Sarah and Bobby were kissing on the couch.

'SARAH!' Paul roared, as the two kids jumped up. 'What the hell is going on?'

'Nothing, I swear,' said a red-faced Bobby.

'We were just snogging. It's no big deal,' Sarah said.

'I'll be the one who decides what is and is not appropriate behaviour,' Paul snapped.

'Hey, Mr Hayes, what happened to your lip?' Bobby asked, clearly keen to distract us, having been found with his tongue halfway down our daughter's throat.

'Don't call me "Mr Hayes". It's Charlie. I was in a fight.'

'In the old folks' home?' Sarah asked.

Charlie nodded.

'Charlie, you're mad. How did it start?'

'It's a long story,' I jumped in. 'Now, Bobby, it's time you were heading home.'

'And next time you come here, keep your hands to yourself,' Paul added.

'Ah, he's only normal. Have you forgotten what it feels like to be sixteen?' Charlie remonstrated.

'I remember it only too well, which is why I want him to know I'll be keeping a very close eye on him.'

'Relax, Dad,' said Sarah. 'It's not like we were having sex.'

'I'll have less cheek from you,' said Paul, then turned to Bobby. 'OK, son, sling your hook.'

Bobby stared at him blankly.

'Dad's a bogger. He's from Galway. Half the time I don't understand him either,' said Sarah. 'He means you have to leave.'

'Oh, right. Cool. I thought he wanted to go fishing or something.'

'No, he's kicking you out. I was going to ask you to stay for dinner, but I wouldn't inflict this hostile environment on you,' said Sarah.

'It's OK, babe. I just need to get my bag.'

'Where is it?' I inquired.

'In my bedroom,' Sarah said.

'Go and get it. Your boyfriend can wait here,' said Paul.

While Sarah fetched the bag, Bobby shuffled uncomfortably from one foot to the other.

'So, are you still playing rugby?' Charlie asked him.

'Totally. I spend all of my spare time training, doing weights and generally trying to make my body a temple. I need to be in the best shape possible so I can become a professional.'

'Is that your career aspiration? To be a professional rugby player?' Paul wanted to know.

'Totally.'

'What about your studies? What about college?'

'Hello! Can you not give my boyfriend the third degree?' Sarah walked back into the room with Bobby's bag slung over her shoulder.

'You'd want to mind the roaming hands, Bobby. My son-in-law keeps a gun in the house. He might shoot you next time,' Charlie said, chuckling to himself.

'Charlie!' I said, furious that he'd mentioned the gun.

76

'Seriously, guys, I've known about the gun for ever,' Sarah said.

Bobby looked terrified. 'I just want you to know, Mr Mullen, that I, like, totally respect your daughter and would never do anything out of order. Sarah is in safe hands.'

'Well, you just make sure to keep those safe hands in your pockets or on a rugby ball,' said Paul.

Sarah walked Bobby to the door, then came back in and rounded on us. 'Why did you have to be so rude? He's, like, the coolest boyfriend ever and now he'll probably dump me because you threatened to, like, assassinate him if he looked at me sideways.'

'I've had enough of your cheek,' Paul told her. 'Go to your room, you're grounded.'

'What? You can't do this to me,' she screeched.

'Go now before I send you to a convent boarding school that'll put manners on you.'

'Muuuuum, do something,' my younger daughter pleaded.

'You were very rude to your father. I agree with his decision.'

'Grounded for how long?'

Paul thought about it. 'Until Christmas.'

Sarah gasped. 'That's a couple of months away. Charlie, help me!'

'Sorry, pet, they've grounded me too,' he said, going into the kitchen.

Sarah stomped up the stairs, muttering under her breath.

Paul sank down into the couch. 'Interesting day.'

'Never a dull moment in this house.' I sat down beside him. 'I don't like that fella.'

'I think he's OK, actually. He was mortified when he was caught and you scared the life out of him.'

'Good, because sixteen-year-old boys think of nothing but sex and how to get it.'

'All the time?'

'Every minute of every day.'

'Well, I know she's not having sex with him.'

'How?'

'Because I read her emails and she told her latest best friend Alex that she was going to make him wait at least six months.'

'Why?'

'So she could be sure he really loved and respected her.'

'Good for her.'

'She has incredible self-confidence. I wish Ali had more of it.'

'She seems a bit happier, these days.'

'A little, but she's still pretty down. Mind you, having to see the guy you're mad about all over someone else every day must be awful.'

'The year will fly and she'll be in college soon, surrounded by new fellas.'

'It's mad to think I met you in my first term in college.'

'Who'd have thought we'd still be here twenty-four years later?'

'No one.' I laughed. 'They all thought it was a fling.'

'We haven't done too badly.' Paul put his arm around me. 'Two lovely girls, a nice house, jobs we enjoy . . . I think we've done well.'

'Me too.' I smiled and as I turned to kiss him, he leant down and pulled out his laptop. 'That reminds me, I need to check how that new barman's working out on his first night.'

I was clearing up after dinner when my phone rang. It was Sally. 'I've just been on the date from hell. Can you meet me for a drink? I'm desperate.'

'You poor thing. I'll see you in the pub in twenty minutes.'

'Thanks, Ava.'

'What's up?' Sarah was painting her nails at the kitchen table.

'Sally's had a really bad date.'

'God, I'm so glad I'm out of the dating scene.' Sarah rolled her eyes. 'It's a jungle out there.'

I suppressed the urge to laugh. 'So it's still going well with Bobby, in spite of your father threatening him?'

'I have to be honest, Mum, we're the coolest couple in school.'

'How exactly do you know this?'

'Duh, because everyone keeps saying how amazing we are together and how we're made for each other.'

'You haven't been seeing each other very long. Take it slowly. Don't jump in head first – look at poor Ali.'

'You cannot compare us. David was never in love with Ali. She was totally obsessed with him and he really liked her, but she was always way more into him. Bobby thinks I rock. Seriously, Mum, you don't need to worry about me.'

'I'm glad you're happy. I wish Ali could meet someone nice.'

'Me too! She's no fun any more. All she does is work.'

'It takes time to get over a broken heart. We need to be patient and kind to her.'

'I am. I just wish she'd liven up a bit. She's got really quiet.'

'Hopefully she'll perk up soon. Maybe some other boy will catch her eye.'

'Not if she continues to walk around like a zombie.'

'Come on now, she's had a very public break-up. It's not easy for her.'

'She didn't even try my ten-step plan. She should listen to me – I know guys.'

'You do seem to have it all worked out. Maybe I should give your ten-step plan to Sally. I'd better go, pet. I'll see you later.'

'Say hi to Sally – poor her, he must have been horrendous.'

'Who's horrendous?' Charlie walked into the kitchen.

'Sally's just run away from a bad date. I'm going to meet her for a drink.'

'Enjoy yourself. I'll hold the fort – and be sure to tell her I'm always available.'

When I arrived at the Drift Inn – Paul and I had thought up the name one drunken night and loved it – Sally was sitting at the bar talking to Paul.

He looked up and smiled at me. Sometimes I forgot how handsome he was. The surfing had given him a rugged tan and kept him very fit. He had that strong jaw, which on a man was very sexy, and dark brown eyes, and although his black hair was thinning a little at the back, he still had most of it.

'Sally's having a double vodka. Apparently it was very bad.'

'I'll have a –'

'Mojito?'

'I was going to say white wine but, yeah, a mojito would be great.'

'Coming right up.' He winked at me. I watched him walk away, admiring his bum. It was nice – I hadn't felt so attracted to him in ages. Maybe I should hang around the bar more often.

I sat up beside Sally. 'If it's any consolation you look gorgeous,' I said. She was wearing a midnight-blue wrap dress, which showed off her tiny, gym-toned waist, with killer heels. I felt a bit frumpy in my jeans and flat boots.

'It's a waste of a good dress and makeup,' she said. 'Honestly, Ava, I'm too old for shitty blind dates.'

'I thought you were being a bit shifty today in work. Why didn't you tell me?'

'Because I didn't want you getting your hopes up and I didn't want me getting my hopes up and I knew deep down it would be a bloody disaster,' she said.

I could see she was fighting back tears. I took her hand in mine. 'I'm sorry it was bad. You poor thing. It's such bad luck.'

'Well, that's it. I'll never go on a date again. I'm hanging up my boots and dusting off my place on the shelf. If my sisters ever mention another blind date, I'll slap them.'

'I know this sounds like a silly platitude but I really believe you'll meet someone. You're such a brilliant person, funny, feisty, beautiful, clever –'

Sally put her hand up. 'Stop! Thanks for the ego boost but I'm swearing off men.'

'So what exactly happened?'

'My brother-in-law Martin set me up on a blind date with a new client of his called Jake. He's recently moved back to Dublin after twenty years in New York and wanted to meet someone.'

'Very promising,' I said.

'I thought so too. When Martin rang I asked him the usual questions – is he married? Recently divorced? Gay? Scarred by a fire that left him with only half a face? Ugly? Bad breath? Et cetera.'

'So, you covered your angles.'

'You have to, believe me. I've met enough freaks. It turned out that Jake had never been married, is not gay and has normal-smelling breath. So I decided to throw caution to the wind and go for it.'

'I'm not surprised. He sounded good on paper.'

'Exactly!' Sally thumped her fist on the bar. 'So then I Googled him and he's also really good-looking, so I started to get my hopes up, which is a really bad idea. He's handsome and he's lived away for years so he was new and interesting.'

'Seemed perfect.'

'That's what I thought. So I emailed him, keeping it light and breezy, and he emailed straight back, and he was funny and flirty. We had some banter back and forth. At this stage I'm thinking, He's too good to be true – which, of course, he was.'

'But how could you know? It was all looking so positive.'

'I know, and I spent a bloody fortune getting my legs and bikini-line waxed – there's the definition of hope – my hair blow-dried, a manicure and a pedicure. I put on my sexiest underwear and this dress, which you always say brings out my eyes.'

'It does. You look drop-dead gorgeous.'

'Waste of bloody money . . .'

Sally explained that when she went to meet Jake in Brooks, a wine bar, she'd had butterflies in her stomach for the first time in ages.

'There she is!' an American voice boomed.

Jake was swaying on a bar stool. He had clearly been there a while. Maybe he was just nervous. She walked over and shook his hand.

'Come on, babe, you can do better than that,' he said, kissing her on the lips. The alcohol fumes nearly knocked her out.

'Relax there, Jake. It's only seven o'clock,' she said, pulling back.

'What'll you have? Gin? Wine? Whiskey?'

'A glass of white wine would be great.' Sally sat up beside him and crossed her legs.

'Nice pins.' Jake grinned. 'You're in good shape for an older woman.'

'I'm forty-three, not sixty,' Sally retorted.

'My last girlfriend was twenty-two.'

'Bully for you.' Sally took a large sip of wine.

'Did Martin tell you I lived in New York for twenty years?'

'Yes, but I think I would have guessed from your strong American accent.'

'It's the best goddamn city in the world.'

'So how are you finding being back?'

'The weather's shit, the women are dogs – present company excluded – and the service is crap.'

'You're settling in well, then.'

Oblivious to her comment, Jake summoned the barman. 'Hey, buddy, I'm waiting on a Jack Daniel's and Coke. Are you fucking brewing the stuff out back or what?'

Sally was mortified. Everyone was looking at them and she could see people shaking their heads and whispering, 'Ignorant American.'

'Why don't you tone it down a bit? The whole angry-New-York thing is a bit over to the top.'

Jake thumped the bar with his fist. 'That's the problem with Irish people. You're all so fucking meek and mild. Bad service is not accepted in the US. If you order a drink, it comes right up. Here, you could be waiting all day while the barman chats to his friend or disappears for a fucking cigarette. If you don't complain, you'll never change it.'

'I think you're wrong. Irish people – of which you are one, in case you forgot – aren't meek and mild. We're just not aggressive and belligerent. To us, meeting someone for a drink is more about the conversation you're having than the speed at which the drink is served.'

'Why can't you have both – good service and good conversation?'

'You can. The service here is fine. You ordered the drink two minutes ago and it's on its way. How thirsty can you be?'

'It's Friday night, baby, so I'm very thirsty. Did Martin tell you what I do?'

'Something with hedge funds?'

'I was head-hunted to come and run one here for Cooks Brokers. These guys haven't a fucking clue how to run a fund. They're trading Mickey Mouse sums. If you want big returns, you've got to take risks, invest big and short sell.'

'Isn't it hard to find investors in the downturn?'

'Honey, no one says no to Jake Doran. I'm a fucking legend in this business. My reputation precedes me. I've made millions for all my clients and myself. They used to call me the Terminator because I had nerves of fucking steel.'

'I see. How does working here compare with New York? I remember when I first came back from London –'

'There is no comparison,' Jake cut across her. 'People here have no idea what real pressure is. They think working until eight is late. I pulled all-nighters two, three times a week. I was on Tokyo, New York and London time. People here think they work hard – they have no fucking idea.'

'That's very unfair –' Sally tried to get her point across, but was shot down again. The Terminator was on a roll.

'It's like the healthcare system here. Everyone pisses and moans about it, but no one does anything.'

'More than fifteen per cent of Americans don't have healthcare. That's almost forty-six million people. I hardly think that's a shining example of efficiency or equality.'

For once Jake didn't have an answer. Clearly he was not as *au fait* with politics as he was with his own ego. Sally sat back and enjoyed the moment.

'I need to take a leak. Order us another drink – it might just be here by the time I get back.'

Sally politely ordered another drink from the barman. Although Jake was clearly a tosser, he was drunk, which might explain some of his behaviour, and he was very good-looking. She decided to give him one final chance to redeem himself. Maybe hiding deep underneath the bluster was a nice man. Besides, she was all dressed up and had nowhere else to go.

Jake was striding back. He seemed more together. Maybe he'd sobered up a bit in the Gents. But as he got closer she saw white powder on the end of his left nostril.

'For an older woman you're hot,' he said, at the top of his voice as he groped her leg. 'I'd say you're great in the sack.'

Sally pushed his hand away and climbed down from her stool. 'Well, Terminator, that's something you'll just have to imagine. I'm leaving now before my eardrums burst and you bore me into an early grave. And you've got cocaine all over your face, which is both sad and pathetic.'

'. . . and that concludes yet another disastrous blind date.' Sally waved her glass in the air and knocked back her third double gin.

'What a jerk. I can't believe Martin thought he'd be right for you.'

'Listen, Ava, every blind date I've been on has been crap. People either think I'm a freak who likes other freaks or they think I'm so desperate that I'd settle for anything. Honestly, there's not one guy I've been set up with that I would entertain going out with. And don't tell me I'm fussy.'

'I wasn't going to, I promise.'

'Because,' Sally continued, slurring slightly, 'I'm not fussy. I'm just not prepared to settle for some arsehole who snorts his wages up his nose. I'd rather be on my own.'

'Who's snorting his wages up his nose?' Paul asked, coming over with two more drinks.

'Sally's blind date.'

'Mr New York himself,' she said, taking a large sip of her gin.

'What you need is a nice guy like me to look after you.' Paul leant over the mahogany bar. 'Good-looking, reliable, trustworthy, funny, bright –'

'Modest,' I added.

'Honest.' He scanned the bar to make sure no one was waiting to be served. When you were in the pub with Paul, you only ever had half his attention. 'Excuse me, ladies, one of our regulars is calling me over. Back in a minute.'

'Yeah, right,' I muttered. The reason the Drift Inn did so well was because Paul made his customers feel like his personal friends. They came to drink in the bar because it was lovely – he had based the décor on a Manhattan-style lounge. It had mood lighting, low chill-out music playing in the background, the floor was covered with deep red carpet and it had individual booths along one wall. It had lots of smoking chairs and book-shelves, big comfy sofas and open fireplaces that kept the place cosy in winter. The bar stools were covered with calfskin and had high backs – but customers came to drink here because they liked hanging out with Paul.

Sally looked over at him – he was laughing at something the regular had said. 'You're lucky, Ava. Paul's great.'

'Everyone's always telling me that. Whenever I come into the pub all the staff go on and on about what a genius he is at busi-ness and what a great boss he is. Of course he's good at his job – he spends his life here. The pub always comes first,' I said, the mojitos loosening my tongue.

'But he's mad about you.'

'If he's so mad about me, why is he never home? I'm not even competing with another woman! I'm competing with the pub. He never puts me or our relationship first any more. He's always working. We never go out together on our own. He works most nights. He takes Sundays and Mondays off. We usually take the girls out on Sundays for dinner or a movie, which leaves Mondays when I'm working and he goes surfing, and by the time we get home we're both too tired to bother. We're in a rut, Sally, which at forty-two is a bit scary.'

'At least you've got someone not to go out with.' Sally swayed a little on her stool.

'I'm sorry. I shouldn't be giving out, especially not tonight after your crappy date.'

'It's just too much hard work. I don't have the energy.' She stood up and made a toast. 'To a happy, peaceful life on the shelf.'

I finished my drink and watched Paul laughing and joking with his customers. He didn't look over at me once.

12

I was worried about Ali. She still wasn't back to herself. She seemed very down and she never talked to me. Autumn was always a really busy time for Happy Dayz, with birthday parties, Hallowe'en and Christmas events, so I was often late home and working at weekends. She was always in her room studying when I got in. I decided to make a conscious effort to be back in time to cook dinner and try to draw Ali out. I spent ages making her favourite dessert – profiteroles and hot chocolate sauce. I wanted to cheer her up any way I could. But when I produced it, she refused to eat it.

'It's your favourite. You always have seconds.'

'I'm not hungry.'

'You haven't eaten much at all.'

'I have. I ate chicken and vegetables and I'm full.'

'You're a bit peaky. I'm worried about you, pet.'

'No self-respecting man likes a skinny girl,' said Charlie. 'You need something to hold on to, something to cuddle up to.'

'Thank you, Charlie,' I said, before he could go into further detail. 'Come on, Ali, eat some dessert.'

'What's the big deal? I'm just not hungry.'

'I'll have her profiteroles if she doesn't want them,' Sarah piped up.

I ignored her. 'Just have one, Ali. I'll leave you alone then.'

'Come on, Ali, your mum spent ages making them for you,' Paul said.

'OK, OK, I'll have some.'

'There – isn't that delicious?' I encouraged her.

She nodded.

'Have another.' I spooned more onto her plate.

'No, thanks, I'm really full now. I need to go and finish my homework – I've got a history essay to hand in tomorrow,' she said, rushing up the stairs.

I looked at Paul. He shrugged. 'She's obviously still upset about your man.'

'She seems to be getting worse not better,' I fretted.

'Don't freak out, Mum,' Sarah reassured me. 'David and Tracy are all over each other in school, totally in Ali's face. Even I'd find it stressful. She might as well study twenty hours a day. At least it'll keep her mind off it.'

'I suppose you're right. It's just awful to see her so down.'

'In case anyone's interested, my relationship is going brilliantly,' Sarah announced.

'I'm delighted to hear it. Try talking to Ali, will you?' I asked. 'If anyone can cheer her up, it's you.'

'I have, Mum. I've tried a million times, but she doesn't want to talk about it or anything else. She's not interested. All she wants to do is study.'

'She'll have no problem getting the points to study medicine at this rate. The first doctor in the Mullen family! That'll be a proud day,' Paul said, as he got up to go to work.

'How come Dad always goes on about how proud he is of Ali and never says it about me?' Sarah complained.

'Don't be silly. He's proud of you both.' I began to clear the table.

'But he never says it to me. All he ever does is give out. Ali's always been his favourite. The perfect Ali. Saint Ali.'

'Don't be so ridiculous. Your father adores you. But if you want to make him really happy, concentrate on your studies this year and get good results in your exams. You know how important education is to him.'

'Why?'

'Because he was the first person in his family to go to college. It was a huge deal and he wants his children to have the same opportunities.'

'But what if I don't want to go to college? Will I be excommunicated?'

'Probably,' I said, smiling at her. 'So you'd better go up and do your homework.'

'But I'm exhausted from school – I need some time to unwind.'

'OK, Drama Queen. If you do an hour's work you can watch *Desperate Housewives* with me later.'

'Deal,' she said, and dragged her bag up the stairs.

The next day, I took Charlie to his apartment so we could see how the building work was coming along. He had calmed down a bit since his arrest – I think he felt bad about Paul having to get involved in bailing him out. He didn't mind me helping him out of the situations he got himself into, but he seemed a bit sheepish about his son-in-law having to save him.

Ali was very much on my mind. She didn't seem to be getting over the break-up with David at all.

'You're worried about Ali, aren't you?' Charlie said, as we drove over to his new home.

'Yes, I am. She seems so stressed all the time. And she's lost her appetite. All she does these days is study.'

'And cycle. She's never off that bike – she'll win the bloody Tour de France if she keeps it up.'

'Is she cycling that much? I hadn't noticed.'

'You've been busy working. Every Saturday afternoon she goes off on her bike for hours.'

'Really? Well, I suppose it's getting her away from her desk and out into the fresh air. Has she said anything to you about it?' I asked.

He shook his head. 'No, pet, she hasn't. Maybe she has a boyfriend she cycles over to see.'

'I wish she did have a boyfriend, but I know she doesn't. I got Sarah to check it out for me – my very own Columbo. I just wish she wasn't so distant. Where's the happy, chatty, sweet Ali of old?'

'Heartbreak doesn't heal overnight,' Charlie said. 'It took me years to get over your mother dying. I still miss her.'

'Me too.' I squeezed his hand.

'Ali will be fine. She just needs time.'

'I'd like to smack that stupid little shit for breaking her heart,' I fumed.

'I could have a word with him, if you like. Or we could get Paul to threaten him with his gun.'

'No, thanks, Charlie. You've been involved in enough fights already – and may I remind you that no one is supposed to know about Paul's gun. It's totally illegal.'

Charlie changed the subject. 'Did I tell you Magda's set me up on a blind date with her friend Agata?'

'No.'

'She's forty-one!' he said, beaming.

'That's a year younger than me!'

'I know. I've a good feeling about this one. Magda said she's a cracker.'

'Charlie, aren't you a bit old for all this?'

'No, I'm not. I'm lonely, Ava. I miss female company. Catherine could barely get out of bed for the last few years of her life so I was stuck in that bloody house day and night cleaning, cooking, washing and nursing her. When she died I felt as if I'd been given another chance at life. I want someone to have fun with. I want a companion. I want to live life to the full while I still can. Is that so strange?'

I reached over and kissed him. 'No, Charlie, it isn't. I'm sorry.' Maybe a girlfriend would be a good thing. It might calm him down. 'Where is Agata from?'

'Poland.'

'Does she speak English?'

'I don't know, I never asked. But sure we can speak the language of love.'

'OK, but just take it slowly this time. Don't sleep with her on the first date. Get to know her first. Let's not have another Lily.'

'I'm sixty-eight. I don't care what her favourite film is, what music she likes or what her hobbies are. I haven't time to be wasting.'

We pulled up outside the apartment block and headed in the main door. Except that it wasn't a door, just a hole in a wall. The building was a long way from completion. We found the man in charge.

'I thought the apartments were supposed to be ready soon?' I asked.

'Ah, well, now, missus, we've had a few setbacks with the bad weather and all.'

'What does that mean?'

'It means we're running a bit behind schedule.'

'How far behind?'

'I'd say about three months, maybe four,' he said, and walked back into the building site.

I tried not to look disappointed. It was nice having Charlie around, and I enjoyed his company, but I wasn't sure how many more girlfriends I could take. We had converted the playroom into the spare bedroom and put a couch and a TV in there for him too. The downstairs toilet had a shower and that was now his bathroom. But it was a bit crowded and I was worried about Ali and wanted to keep an eye on her without Charlie distracting me by getting arrested. Still, it was only a few months.

'Well, it looks like I'll be staying a while longer,' Charlie said. 'Can you put up with me? I promise to behave and not get arrested any more.'

I smiled at him. 'We'll manage. Come on, I'll buy you a coffee.'

Later that day I called into the pub to tell Paul that my father would be staying a while longer.

'How much longer?'

'A few months.'

'That's OK.'

'Really?' I asked, surprised he was being so calm about it.

'Yeah, Charlie's good for a laugh. I've no problem with it.'

'Great, thanks. Actually, there's something else I wanted to talk to you about. I'm worried about Ali.'

'Why?'

'She's studying too hard and not eating properly, and apparently while we're at work on the weekends she's cycling for hours.'

'Well, I can understand that. Exercise helps clear your head. Surfing always makes me feel better if I'm worried about something. It's a great switch-off. It's a good thing she's cycling. You're always worrying about Ali. She'll be fine. It's a tough year and she wants to do well in her exams. She'll never have to work this hard again. It's Sarah I'd be worried about. We need to keep an eye on that relationship. I don't want any teenage pregnancies in my house.'

'Sarah's well able to look after herself, and Bobby seems like a nice boy. A bit of an airhead but decent. Besides, he's terrified of you.'

'Good, because I want him to keep his hands to himself. Sixteen-year-old boys have one-track minds.'

'What is it with you men? Charlie's obsessed with having sex and you'd think he'd be past it.'

'What can I say? It's the way we're made.'

I cringed inwardly. Paul and I hadn't had sex in weeks. He had made advances a few nights ago, but I'd been tired and not in the mood. I'd have to make more of an effort. 'Will you be home for dinner?'

'Yes – see you about six.'

'Great. Charlie's going out on a date so we'll have the place to ourselves.'

'Who's his date?'

'A forty-one-year-old Pole called Agata.'

'That's younger than you.'

'Only just. Besides, I'm a young forty-two.'

'You look good to me.'

'Glad to hear it. I don't want you running off with Agata's younger sister.'

'Is there one?'

'I don't know.'

'She could be tasty. Eastern European women are easy on the eye.'

One of the bar-girls came over to ask Paul a question. She was wearing a fitted black shirt, a short black skirt and high heels. I looked down at my jeans, flat pumps and pink shirt and decided that my wardrobe was in desperate need of an overhaul. Maybe if I felt sexier I'd be more up for having sex.

Paul turned back to me. 'Where were we? Oh, yeah, tasty Eastern European women.' He grinned.

'Do you think Magda's good-looking?' I asked.

'She's like a weight-lifter.'

'Harsh,' I said, feeling bad for poor Magda.

'But true.'

'She's just muscly from hard work.'

'She's four feet high and five feet wide, and it's got nothing to do with muscle.'

'You're very critical,' I said, aware of my stomach protruding over my jeans. I'd have to start doing sit-ups again.

'I compare all women to you and they fall short.'

I pulled my stomach in. 'Even the hot girl behind the bar?'

'Yes, even her.'

Later that evening, when Charlie had gone out on his date and the girls were doing their homework, Paul and I snuggled up on the couch with a glass of wine and watched a movie for the first time in ages. It felt really nice. I nestled my head into his shoulder and felt myself relaxing.

The doorbell rang. Sarah came thundering down the stairs to answer it. It was Bobby. He walked in carrying a large sports bag and they headed up the stairs to her room.

'Where are you two off to?' Paul demanded.

'Hello, Mr Mullen, how are you?' Bobby was obviously on his best behaviour.

'We're just going to study in my room,' Sarah said. 'We're helping each other with our history project.'

'All right, but you'll leave here no later than nine thirty, Bobby, and you're to behave yourselves. Do I make myself clear?' Paul growled.

'Yes, sir, absolutely,' said Bobby.

It was a disaster. Our night was ruined because Paul couldn't relax. He kept thinking they were up to no good. Every ten minutes he'd jump up and creep upstairs to listen outside Sarah's bedroom door. 'I can hear a lot of laughing and shuffling about,' he huffed.

'They're sixteen. They should be laughing and having fun.'

'They're supposed to be studying.'

'Come on, Paul, they're not stupid. They're hardly going to be misbehaving with us sitting directly underneath them.'

He sat down, took a sip of his wine, then heard movement again and flew back up the stairs. 'He's telling her to "Take it easy, don't overdo it,"' he reported. 'What does that mean? It sounds very suspicious to me.'

'He's probably talking about research for the project or something,' I said, leaning back into the couch, trying to focus on the movie. 'Come on, sit down. We never get time together any more and the pre-Christmas season will kick in soon – you'll be manic in the pub working every night. Let's enjoy this.'

'You're right. OK, press play.'

I turned the film back on and we watched in peace for ten minutes, but Paul just couldn't sit still. Eventually, on the fifth go, he came running downstairs and hissed at me to follow him up. 'They're up to something in there.'

'This is ridiculous,' I snapped, as I climbed the stairs. 'We're supposed to be having a rare night in without my dad or one of the girls on top of us.'

But Paul wasn't listening to me. He had his ear glued to the doorframe. He stuck out a hand and dragged me over. 'Listen to this,' he whispered. 'I told you that fella would try it on.'

I leant forward and heard Bobby say, 'No, dude, not like that, like this.'

'OK, I'm trying. It's my first time so I'm not very good at it,' said Sarah.

'I'll spread my legs wider so it's easier for you,' Bobby offered.

'Jesus Christ, the little pervert! I'll kill him,' Paul raged.

I grabbed his arm to stop him barging in. 'Hold on,' I hissed. 'Don't jump to conclusions.'

'Yeah, that's much better, let me get down lower,' Sarah said.

'I need more pressure here,' said Bobby.

'Like this?'

'Oh, yeah, that's it, you've got it. Come on, don't be afraid. Give me more.'

Paul's face turned an alarming shade of purple and, despite my best efforts to hold him back by grabbing onto his legs, he still managed to barge through the door, dragging me behind him. 'What the hell is going on?' he roared.

Bobby was standing on a black towel in a pair of tight black jocks. His legs were spread wide apart and Sarah, fully clothed, was on her knees in front of him.

Paul grabbed Sarah – and cursed. She was holding a spray gun full of a brown fluid and had squirted him in the face.

I started to laugh.

'This is no laughing matter!' Paul barked, as he tried to wipe the liquid off his cheek.

'What are you doing?' Sarah shouted.

Paul reached over to grab Bobby but I stopped him. 'Paul!' I said, trying not to laugh. 'It's not what you think.'

'My daughter's in her bedroom with a naked boy. What exactly am I supposed to think? That they're playing chess?'

'Seriously, Mr Mullen,' Bobby said, 'it's totally cool. There's no inappropriate behaviour going down here.'

'Well, do you mind telling me what you're doing in your underpants?'

'Sarah's giving Bobby a spray tan,' I said.

'A what?' Paul was clearly confused.

'Spray tan, Dad,' Sarah said. 'If you'd stop breaking down doors and listen for a minute I can explain.'

'It'd better be good.'

'Bobby's got a really important game on Saturday so we want him to look his best. I'm spraying him today and then again tomorrow so that he looks really tanned and hot in his white shorts.'

'Do you mean to tell me you're putting spray makeup on this fella to make him look like he has a tan for a rugby match?' Paul was incredulous.

'Yes.'

'Are you gay?' he asked Bobby.

'Oh, my God, like, absolutely not. As straight as an arrow, thank you very much,' said Bobby, highly insulted as he stood in his black jocks flapping his arms around to dry them.

'What self-respecting lad would put makeup on to play sport?' Paul shook his head.

'For God's sake, Dad, it's not the dark ages. Everyone does it now, except the bogger teams who don't seem to mind being white. What's wrong with wanting to look your best?'

Paul turned to me. 'Ava, help me.'

'It seems a bit extreme to be putting false tan on for a rugby match where you're going to spend most of the time covered with mud,' I said.

'I hear you, Mrs M,' said Bobby, nodding sagely, 'but the way I see it is like this – if I feel really good about the way I look, I'll play my best rugby. If I think I look crap, I'll just get down on myself and not play to my full potential.'

'I see. Well, that's an interesting point of view,' I said, to the boy who was turning brown before my eyes.

'For God's sake, son, put some clothes on,' said Paul.

'No way!' Sarah squealed. 'He's not totally dry yet. He'll streak.'

'I'm going downstairs now. In five minutes I want you dressed and on your way home. Sarah needs to spend more time on her schoolwork and less on painting her boyfriend,' said Paul, and stomped down the stairs.

'Put those towels in the wash,' I said to Sarah.

'Oh, they're my towels, Mrs M. I would never use yours. That would be totally disrespectful. The spray tan really stains.'

'OK. I'll see you in a few minutes,' I said, leaving before I started laughing again.

Downstairs, Paul was pacing the floor. 'What has the world come to? Fellas putting on false tan to play *rugby*!'

'I guess times have changed.'

'He must be gay.'

'Sssh. He isn't. Boys now are much more into their appearance than your generation was. They often spend more time and money on their clothes than girls do. It's harmless stuff.'

'It's not normal. Men don't wear makeup.'

Before Paul could cast any more aspersions on poor Bobby, the man with the tan and our younger daughter came down the stairs.

Glaring at us as she walked by, Sarah showed Bobby to the door. 'I'll see you tomorrow and we'll give it a top-up.'

'OK, babe, good job.'

As she walked past the sitting-room door on her way back upstairs, Paul called her in.

'I've nothing to say to you,' she said, arms crossed. 'You just totally humiliated me in front of my boyfriend.'

'Your father was concerned.'

'Next time I'd appreciate it if you knocked. Bobby is mortified.'

'So he should be. Are you sure that lad isn't a poof?'

'Believe me, Dad, Bobby is all man. The hits he takes on the pitch are unbelievable. He's a legend. All the other girls in school wish they were IMS.'

'Jesus, can you please speak English?' Paul was exasperated.

'In my shoes,' said Sarah, and flounced out of the room.

13

Ali had taken to having breakfast at six thirty and then doing an hour of study before school. I decided to set my alarm and join her to see if I could get her to talk to me. I was worried she was getting depressed.

I got to the kitchen before her and put on a pot of coffee. Ten minutes later I heard her coming down the stairs. When she saw me she frowned. Maybe this hadn't been such a good idea. She looked as if she'd prefer to be alone.

I jumped up and offered to make her breakfast.

'I'm not a child, I can make my own.' She poured herself a coffee.

I watched her slice a grapefruit into ten small pieces and then slowly eat them. She looked exhausted.

'Did you finish your essay?'

'Eventually.'

'Well, that's good. You should be able to take it a bit easier now.'

'Hardly.'

I tried to think of something to say, a topic that would interest her, but all I came up with was 'Are you OK about Charlie staying for a few more months?'

'It's fine.'

'Would you like some toast?'

'No, thanks.' She stood up and went to pack her lunch.

'Actually, Ali, I've made it already.' I handed her a bag of food.

'I can do it.'

'I know, but I think you need to eat more carbohydrates to give you energy. Look at you, you're exhausted.'

'I'm seventeen! I don't need my mother making me breakfast and lunch. Can you please stop fussing?' Ali shoved the lunch bag into her backpack and stalked out into the hall.

I watched her fidgeting impatiently, pacing up and down. I missed the old Ali – the one who chatted to me in the mornings, the one with the sunny disposition and the optimistic outlook.

'Earth to Mum.' Sarah waved her hands in front of my face. 'Where's my breakfast – or am I expected to starve?'

When I got to work, Noelle Halloran called to talk about her daughter's fifth-birthday party. 'I just want to go over some details.'

'Sure, no problem, how can I help?' I said, putting her on loudspeaker so Sally could listen in.

'As I explained, Jessica-Anne suffers from food allergies and intolerances, so we need to be clear about the food: no wheat, no gluten, no dairy, no sugar, no peanuts or nuts of any kind – as you know, she has a tree-nut allergy – no seafood or shellfish, no eggs, no soya, no red meat, no kiwi, no berries of any kind, no caffeine and no yeast.'

'What are we making the cake of? Cardboard?' Sally whispered.

'Yes, Noelle, you faxed them to me last week, and Helen, our chef, is working away to come up with suitable party food.'

'Now Jessica-Anne wants Belle from *Beauty and the Beast* to come to her party and hand out presents to her guests, as we discussed. But she told me last night that she hates yellow so make sure the lady doesn't come in the yellow dress from the film. She wants her to wear the exact same dress in gold.'

'Aren't yellow and gold kind of similar?' I pointed out.

'Yellow makes her want to throw up, gold makes her happy.'

'She needs a good slap,' Sally mouthed.

'I'll do my best, Noelle, but they are similar colours so I just hope there isn't a bad reaction. How about changing it to a pink dress?'

'Ava, we had a two-and-a-half-hour melt-down last night over the colour. She wants gold. Please get me gold.'

'OK, Noelle, leave it with me.'

'Thanks.'

I hung up.

Sally was incredulous. 'Where do these kids get off? My mother would have slapped me black and blue if I'd had a tantrum over a dress colour.'

'I'd never have let the girls get away with that either. But a lot of it has to do with working mother's guilt. It is hard to juggle. Remember when I gave Sarah a mobile phone when she was eleven because I just couldn't listen to her whining any more? I was busy in work and tired and, to be honest, her having a mobile made my life easier.'

'OK – but come on, where does this kid get off demanding gold over yellow and *what* is going on with all those allergies?'

'The poor girl is probably just looking for attention.'

'Well, she's getting it, along with the vilest party cake ever seen. What food is left after that list – nettles and turnip? I know Helen's a miracle worker, but you can't make party food with no ingredients.'

'Helen's suggestions have included buckwheat cookies, sprouted quinoa and buckwheat millet sourdough bread and lentil burgers.'

'With a side order of cow dung, I presume,' Sally said, as we roared laughing.

Later that day, when I picked up the girls from school, I checked that Ali had eaten all her lunch. There was nothing left. I was relieved. At least if she was eating properly she'd be less tired and better able to cope with everything, and hopefully be less snappy with me.

While Ali looked out of the window, in a world of her own, Sarah asked me what was for tea.

'We're having stew tonight. Actually, Charlie's invited a guest.'

'Who?'

'Her name is Nadia. He's been on a few dates with her and he wants us to meet her.'

'What happened to the other one?'

'According to Charlie, poor Agata was too fat and boring for him.'

'Where's this new one from?'

'Poland. Apparently she's Agata's cousin.'

'Is she old and wrinkly like Lily?'

'I don't think so – she's four years younger than me.'

'What? That's gross. How could someone that age sleep with an old man like Charlie?'

'Who said anything about sleeping together?'

'Come on, Mum, Charlie isn't looking for a chess partner.' Sarah rolled her eyes.

'Your grandfather is lonely. He wants a bit of companionship, that's all.'

'So you don't mind that she's younger than you?'

'I'm not thrilled about it, but she seems to make him happy and so far she's kept him out of trouble.'

When we arrived home, Charlie was dressed in his best suit and sitting beside him on the couch was a woman who appeared a lot younger than me. She was very pretty, but she was wearing really bright pink lipstick and a lot of blue eye-liner, even though her eyes were brown, which gave her a very seventies look. She was dressed in what should have been a conservative navy skirt suit, but it was exceedingly tight and, with no shirt underneath the jacket, her bra was on view and her boobs were popping out. I tried not to look as shocked as I felt. Where did Charlie find these women? Why couldn't he just meet a nice little old lady, who liked needlework and knitting, and stop bringing home these younger women who looked like they'd rather go clubbing than knit jumpers?

Charlie jumped up and introduced us. Nadia stood up and shook our hands. She was tall and slim. I held my stomach in and vowed to make more of an effort with my appearance. I was wearing jeans and a jumper of Paul's that made me look bigger than I was, although on the upside, it hid my winter tummy.

'It's nice to meet you,' I said.

'I am happy to be here. You daddy fery nice man,' said Nadia, winking at Charlie.

'Yes, he is.'

'You have fery nice house.'

'Thank you. And where do you live?'

'In bad house with bad peoples.' She looked sad.

'Don't worry, pet, we'll soon sort that out,' said Charlie, handing her a tissue. Then, gazing at me, he said, 'Poor Nadia has ended up in a house with a group of thugs. She's only been here a few weeks and yesterday she woke up and all her savings were gone. Robbed.'

'Who are these people? Did you go to the police?' I asked.

Nadia's head snapped up. 'No police. They hate Polish peoples. Police no help me.'

'Well, could you move in with Agata? Isn't she your cousin?'

'Agata haff no rooms. She haff six peoples living in her house. I all alone. So, so lonely.'

'Now, now, it's all going to be fine,' said Charlie, as Nadia sobbed into his shoulder. His face only reached her boobs: she was at least a foot taller than him and she was wearing really high heels. 'You can move in here until you get sorted out.'

What the hell was he saying? Had he completely lost his marbles?

'Hold on, Charlie, that's not really an option. I'm sure Nadia has other friends she can stay with.' The house was crowded enough as it was. I had to stop this.

Nadia threw her arms around me. 'Oh, Ava, you such good woman. You safe me.'

I peeled myself away. 'No, Nadia, I'm sorry, I really can't have you to stay.'

'It's only for a little while,' Charlie said. 'Come on, Ava, a few days, a week at the most, just until the poor girl gets sorted.'

Paul arrived home. 'Hello,' he said, extending a hand to Nadia.

'Nadia, this is Paul, my son-in-law,' Charlie said. 'Nadia here is homeless and I told her she could stay for a few days, if it's all right with you.'

Seeing easier prey, Nadia pushed me aside and flung herself into Paul's arms. 'Thank you so much, Paul. You safe my life,' she said, kissing his face as Paul looked at me with an expression that said, 'What the hell is going on?'

'I go to toilet. I back in minute,' Nadia said, and rushed out of the room before I could retract Charlie's offer.

'Jesus, Charlie, have you lost your mind? Inviting a stranger to live in our house without even discussing it with me?' I was furious.

'She's a wonderful lady,' Charlie said. 'And she needs our help.'

'There is no way she's moving in here.'

Charlie looked to Paul for help. 'Paul, you're not going to leave poor Nadia on the streets. You of all people know how dangerous it is out there.'

Paul shuffled from one foot to the other. 'Well, Charlie, it does seem a bit impulsive. How long have you known her?'

'Three weeks.'

'Has she nowhere else she can stay?'

'No. All her money was stolen and she's only been in Ireland a few weeks so she hasn't any friends.'

'I see,' Paul said.

'She could be a psychopath, murderer, con-woman,' I said, and wanted to add 'prostitute' but held back in front of the girls.

'She's a beautiful person,' Charlie said. 'Not just a cracker to look at, she has a big heart.'

'She is very good-looking,' Sarah agreed.

'Great figure,' Ali added.

'I'm sorry, she can't stay and that's final.' I was fed up with Charlie turning the house into a circus.

'I think I'm in love,' Charlie announced.

'*What?*'

'You heard me. And she'll only be here until she gets back on her feet.'

'Paul, talk sense into him.'

'Well, now, Charlie, Ava has a point. This woman is a virtual stranger. There are lots of women who come to Ireland looking to prey on vulnerable older men. You need to be careful.'

Charlie's face got very flushed. 'Nadia is a good person who's down on her luck. What happened to the Irish being a welcoming nation? What happened to A Hundred Thousand Welcomes to All who Come to Our Shores?'

'We're not the bloody tourist board,' I hissed. Before I could vent any more of my anger, Nadia rushed back into the room.

'Oh, Charlie, you are hero for me.' She kissed him passionately in front of all of us.

I spun around to get Paul to help remove this woman from our house and found him staring at her legs. I thumped him on the shoulder.

'What?'

'Do something.'

'What do you suggest?'

'Call the police and have her arrested instead of staring at her legs.'

'On what charges?'

'I don't know – breaking and entering.'

'Your father invited her here.'

'Coercion.'

'He doesn't look intimidated to me,' Paul said, as he watched Charlie kissing this stranger.

'Seducing him under false pretences.'

'That's not actually against the law.'

I sat down in the chair beside the door and buried my head in my hands.

'This is cool.' Sarah giggled. 'Charlie's girlfriend is younger than Mum. We're like those people on *Ricki Lake*.'

14

Nadia moved in the next day with all her possessions. Three large suitcases were dragged through the house into Charlie's room. He swore to me that it was only a short-term solution and he'd find her a new place to live as soon as possible. Clearly the suit she'd worn the day before was a disguise because, from the moment she officially moved in, the miniskirts and boob tubes were out in abundance. I caught Paul staring at her cleavage on several occasions.

She was overtly sexy and it made me very uncomfortable.

'You'd think she'd put a shirt on,' I huffed, as she strutted about the house in a denim miniskirt and a vest top that left little to the imagination.

Paul shrugged. 'I dunno, looks fine to me.'

'She's like mutton dressed up as lamb.'

'If the mutton has the body of a lamb she can get away with it.'

'Shouldn't something be left to the imagination?'

'It's not as if she's walking around in her underwear.'

I looked down at my black polo neck and black trousers. Was I a frump? Had I let myself go? I was in pretty good shape – sure I had a bit of a flabby stomach and chunky thighs, but what mother didn't?

'What do you think of what I'm wearing?' I asked my husband.

'Very smart,' he answered.

'What exactly does "smart" mean?'

'It means smart.'

'But not sexy?'

'It's a jumper and trousers,' he retorted.

'Do you think Nadia looks sexy?'

'Uhm . . . no.' He hesitated. 'I think she looks available.'

'What do I look?'

'Married.'

'Frumpy.'

'That's not what I said.'

'Yeah, but it's what you meant.'

'No, it isn't. I wouldn't want you walking around in mini-skirts.'

'Why? Do you think my legs are too chunky?'

'No. You're a bit old for them.'

'I'm forty-two, not seventy.'

'You're the one who said Nadia looked cheap.'

'And you said she had a great body and looked fine. Obviously I'm too fat to wear short skirts.'

'Ava, you're not fat.'

'That's it. No more desserts for me.'

'You're not fat.'

'I've put on a few pounds.'

'You look good to me.'

'She's only four years younger than me and has no lumps and bumps. She's so toned,' I complained.

'You've had two children.'

'Aha, so you do think I'm lumpy.'

'I never said that!'

'Do you think she's a prostitute?' I asked, deciding to get off the subject of toned bodies as I munched a KitKat.

'No. But I wouldn't be surprised if she starts asking Charlie to "lend" her money.'

'So you don't think she's in love.'

Paul laughed. 'I give it a month. She'll try to get as much money as she can out of him and then leave.'

'Jesus, Paul, this is really serious. What if Charlie starts giving her his savings? He has quite a bit of money left from the sale of the house, but it's his pension.'

'We have to make sure that doesn't happen. The good thing about having Nadia living here is that we can keep an eye on the situation. Don't worry, I'm watching her.'

'Is that why you stare at her boobs all the time?'

'They're hard to miss.'

'Try looking up.'

I wasn't sure how Nadia stayed so slim: she quite literally ate us out of house and home. Every time I walked into the kitchen she was eating. I was complaining about it one day when Ali said she'd like to start cooking.

I was pleased that she wanted to do something other than study and that she was showing an interest in food, so I encouraged her. The next thing I knew, Ali was spending hours going through all my cookbooks looking for recipes to try out. I came home one evening to find she had made creamy chicken korma and chocolate brownies for dinner.

'Wow, Ali, this is a fantastic spread. Put your feet up and enjoy it,' I said.

'Actually I had a bowl of the chicken while the brownies were in the oven. I need to catch up on my homework now – the cooking took longer than I thought. I'll take a brownie up with me.'

'Can you not sit with us for even twenty minutes?' I pleaded. This was the most animated I'd seen her in ages.

'No, Mum, I have to work.'

'Well, thank you fery much for this luffly food,' Nadia said.

'Yes, pet, it smells wonderful,' Charlie added.

'Yum!' Sarah said, her mouth full of korma.

Ali smiled. 'Enjoy!'

Maybe things were looking up.

That Saturday I had a big party to organize so I asked Charlie if he'd do the grocery shopping for me. Ali said she wanted to go with him because she had some new recipes she wanted to try out and needed ingredients. Sarah was tagging along too because Bobby was rugby training and she was bored. Paul was working and Nadia was at a job interview.

'What's her interview for, Charlie?' I asked, wondering what kind of job Nadia was aiming for.

'A nightclub.'

'Doing what?'

'Dancing.'

'They're going to pay her to dance?'

'She's very agile,' Charlie said, grinning.

'Oh, my God, Charlie's girlfriend's a pole dancer!' shrieked Sarah. 'Can this family get any weirder?'

'Is that true?' I asked, horrified.

Charlie, looking as proud as he had on my wedding day, nodded. 'Yes, it is.'

'But that's practically prostitution,' I gasped.

'Don't be so ridiculous. The girls nowadays just swing about on the pole and make up to five hundred euros a night. The men aren't allowed touch them. It's all very proper.'

'How do you know this? Please tell me you don't hang out in pole-dancing clubs.'

'Nadia told me. She said if she gets the job, she'll be a millionaire in no time.'

'Is it legal?'

'Of course it is.'

'Pole dancing is cool now, Mum,' Sarah piped up. 'All the celebrities do it to keep fit.'

'Do you burn loads of calories?' Ali asked.

'Loads. Maybe we could get a pole in the house,' Sarah suggested. 'Nadia could give us lessons.'

'Has everyone gone mad?' I shouted. 'There will be no poles or dancing or any of that carry-on in my house.'

I gave Charlie the shopping list and stormed out the door. For the zillionth time in my life I wished I had a sibling to help me look after him. My mother had begun to haemorrhage shortly after she had given birth to me and had to have a hysterectomy. With Charlie's only living relative, Daisy, stuck in an old folks' home suffering from Alzheimer's, I was all he had. I would have given anything for a sibling to share the madness with. I had been determined when Ali was born that I'd have one for her. I envied the girls sometimes. They had each other to talk to when Paul and I drove them mad.

When I got home later, Sarah was lying on the couch watching TV.

'Hi,' I said, flopping down in the armchair beside her.

'God, Mum, you look wrecked. Tough day at the office?'

'You could say that,' I said, smiling. 'Thirty over-excited seven-year-old girls at a *Hannah Montana* theme party. I'm badly in need of a glass of wine. Where is everyone else?'

'Charlie and Nadia have gone for a drink and Ali went off on her bike. She should be back soon. She was a total pain in the supermarket. Even Charlie nearly lost it with her.'

'Why? What happened?'

Sarah filled me in . . .

Charlie parked in the disabled drivers' section and got out of the car with a fake limp. Ali said she didn't think it was fair to take up a handicapped space, but Charlie pointed out that there were twelve handicapped spaces and only two cars in them. 'How many cripples can there be, wanting to do their shopping at twelve o'clock on a Saturday? Now, let's divide this list up so we can get out of here as quickly as possible.'

They each went their separate ways and agreed to meet at the checkout in twenty minutes.

Sarah got the items Charlie had given her from my list and a few of her favourite things – hot chocolate drinks, smoothies, granola bars and Ben & Jerry's ice cream. She then went to meet Charlie.

He was looking around impatiently. 'I hate supermarkets.

They're full of grumpy old people and screaming kids. Have you seen Ali?' he asked.

'No. You wait here, I'll go and find her.'

Sarah found Ali sitting on the floor surrounded by packets of food. She was reading the labels on them and taking notes on a little pad. 'What are you doing?' she asked her sister.

Ali looked annoyed at being found. 'I'm just checking to see what additives are in all these foods. Some of them are really bad for you.'

'Why are you writing it in a notebook? Are you doing a project for school?'

'No, I'm just making sure I don't eat any crap.'

Sarah looked into her sister's basket – low-fat cheese, low-fat yogurts, rice cakes, two chicken breasts and a box of Special K. 'Is that what you got? It's all gross.'

'No, it's healthy.'

'Rice cakes? Come on, they're like cardboard,' Sarah said.

'I like them.'

'Since when?'

'Since I decided to give up bad carbs.'

'Well, you look like shit – like you have the flu. Maybe you should try eating some of the "bad" carbs.'

'Go away. I need to concentrate.'

'Charlie's doing his nut. He wants to go.'

'I need more time.'

Charlie came around the corner, furious. 'What the hell are you two doing? Why are you sitting around writing in a book?'

'Ali wants to write down the content of everything in the shop.'

'I just want to read the labels,' she fumed.

'Read the labels?' Charlie was incredulous. 'In my day we ate pigs' trotters. Now come on, before I get really annoyed.'

Ali glared at them both and stormed to the checkout.

'She's always narky these days, Mum. I'm sick of her snapping at me,' Sarah said. 'And what's with all the sudden interest in cooking and food content? Why does she always have to be so intense about everything? When we got back she spent two hours in the kitchen making chocolate chip muffins and meringues.'

I rubbed my forehead. I had a splitting headache from the kids' party. All I wanted to do was put my feet up and drink a glass of wine in peace. But every time I came through the front door there was always something to be done or fixed or dealt with. It was relentless. 'Ali's a perfectionist. She can't do things in half-measures. It's just her personality.'

'I wish she'd chill the hell out. She's so serious about everything, it's a pain.'

'I know, but be patient with her. It's been a difficult few months.'

'Yeah, well, I'm not going to be her punch-bag any more. The next time she snaps at me I'm going to tell her what a pain in the arse she's become.'

I let my head sink back into the cushion and stared at the ceiling. When had we all become so stressed out? We always seemed to be fighting or snapping at each other now. I was sick of it. I wanted some peace. I closed my eyes and pictured waves gently lapping on a sandy beach. 'Maybe we all need a change of scenery. Why don't we go away for a week?'

'Yes! Let's go somewhere really hot.'

'Hot and sunny it is. I think it would do Ali the world of good and I wouldn't mind getting Charlie out of Nadia's clutches for a bit. It might get him to see sense.'

'He's happy – what's the big deal?'

'She's obviously after his money and I don't want to see him get hurt again.'

'OK, fair enough. Why don't we go just after Christmas? It's so boring here between Christmas and New Year. Can we go to Morocco? I'll get a brilliant tan. Everyone will be so jealous.'

'That would be the best time to go, but then Dad might not be able to come. It's a busy time in the pub.'

'We can't go without Dad. It wouldn't be a family holiday. And we can't wait and go after New Year because Ali and me will be back in school. Just tell him to leave the pub for once – it won't fall apart if he's not there for a few days.'

'I'll talk to him. In the meantime why don't I go and check what deals are available?' I said, and went upstairs to hide out in my bedroom for some peace and quiet.

But as soon as I had sat down on my bed, Sarah barged in. 'Mum, you forgot your laptop,' she said, sitting beside me. 'Come on, chop chop, let's see what's on offer.'

15

Nadia got the job at the pole-dancing club and Charlie kept saying how proud he was of her. You'd think she'd won a bloody gold medal at the Olympics, climbed Mount Everest and found a cure for cancer, the way he was going on. I know I was being childish, but he was praising her more than he ever praised me, and it got up my nose. Not only was I housing and feeding his latest girlfriend, but I now had to listen to how incredible she was.

Charlie insisted on following me around the house, going on and on about her. I'd just come in from work and tripped over a box of Nadia's belongings that had been thrown down haphazardly in the hall. I was feeling claustrophobic anyway and I was also annoyed that Nadia had never thanked me for allowing her to live in my house with my family. She seemed to take it completely for granted.

Eventually I snapped: 'What is so great about flinging yourself around on a pole? It's not exactly rocket science.'

'It requires extreme control and suppleness. She's like a gymnast.'

'It's called stripping, Charlie.'

'I don't know why you feel the need to put down Nadia's chosen career. She doesn't belittle yours.'

'There's nothing to belittle. I run my own company. I don't take my clothes off. And I certainly hope your girlfriend isn't saying negative things about me, considering the fact that I'm housing her and funding her insatiable appetite.'

'I never said she didn't say anything bad about you.'

'What exactly do you mean by that?'

'She thinks you're quite rude about her clothes.'

'Because I asked her to put a dressing-gown on at breakfast, instead of having to eat with her boobs in my family's face?'

'Among other things, yes.'

'It's not healthy for my children and husband to have that woman prancing about in skimpy underwear all day long.'

'They don't seem to mind.'

'I mind! It puts me off my food.'

'She's got a beautiful body – why should she cover it up? We're all too repressed.'

'Is that what she says?'

'Yes – and you know what? She's right. We're far too uptight in this country. Nadia says that Irish people have no sex appeal. We're too self-conscious. We're always hiding our bodies instead of celebrating them. Look at Ali, always huddled up in big baggy sweatshirts. It's ridiculous.'

'Please tell me you're not going to start parading around in your underpants.'

'I'm too old, but you should get out of those thick polo necks.'

'It's December. It's zero degrees outside. What should I be wearing? A bikini?'

'If you're going to be childish about it . . .'

'Why eferybody is shouting? I am sleeping,' Nadia complained, coming out of the bedroom in a tiny T-shirt.

'Oh, I'm sorry, Nadia, it's half past six in the evening and I thought you might be awake,' I snarled.

'She's tired from last night's work,' Charlie growled.

'Yes, I fery tired from dancing. It fery hard work.'

'I'm sure it is. Maybe you should consider some other form of employment that doesn't require gymnastics or taking your clothes off.'

'I like job. I fery good at it. I making good money last night.'

'Great – so you'll be able to find your own place, then.'

'Now, now. There's no need to hustle the poor girl out the door.'

'I see few apartments yesterday, but they horrible. I waiting for nice one.'

'Well, don't be too fussy, will you?'

Ali came into the lounge.

'Sorry, Ali, did we disturb your study?' I asked.

'No, it's OK, I was just going to get some tea. Congratulations on your new job, Nadia. Are all the girls as toned as you? It must keep them really fit.'

'Most girls are skinny but one girl not so skinny. She haff problems pulling herself up on pole.'

'You must burn loads of calories – it looks really physical.'

'Yes, it is. It like running marathon efery night.'

'But a lot more fun, I'm sure.'

'Ali, will you come help me get the dinner ready?' I ushered her towards the door. I didn't want her getting any ideas about taking up pole dancing as a hobby.

'Why don't I bake a cake to celebrate Nadia's job?' Ali offered.

'That would be lovely, pet,' Charlie said.

'I luff chocolate cake,' Nadia said. 'You fery nice girl, Aleeson, just like you granddaddy.'

I went into the kitchen with Ali. 'Does having Nadia here bother you, Ali?'

'No, she's OK and she seems to make Charlie happy, so it's fine with me.'

'If it ever does get too much, let me know and I'll have them both move out. You and Sarah are my priority. OK?'

But Ali wasn't listening. She was poring over my cookbooks, staring at the pictures of the chocolate cakes.

'It's really nice of you to offer to bake a cake.' I went over to stand beside her.

'I love cooking.'

'I'm delighted you've got a new hobby.'

She moved away from me and started opening and closing cupboards to get the ingredients she needed.

I stared at her. She was washed out and frail. Her sweatshirt seemed far too big for her and she had on the baggy black tracksuit bottoms she had taken to wearing every day after school. Despite the big lunches I was making for her, she was thin.

'Ali, is everything OK in school? Is David still going out with Tracy?'

She tensed. 'Yes, he is. Look, Mum, can you please forget about David? He's in the past now so stop bringing him up.'

'Sorry. You just don't seem yourself, that's all.'

'I'm fine – everything's fine. Please stop asking me how I am. It's driving me mad.'

'All right, but just promise me that if you're worried about anything you'll come and talk to me? OK?'

'Fine. Now, can you just let me get on with making my cake?'

I wanted to say more, but I knew I needed to leave her alone. If I pushed her too hard, she'd totally clam up on me. I bit back all the questions I wanted to ask her – why do you seem so unhappy? Why are you so tense all the time? Why don't you smile any more? Why are you so tired and listless? Why don't you see how wonderful you are? How beautiful? Clever? Kind? Lovely?

The problem with teenagers is that you lose them. Gone were the days of sitting my little girls on my knee to hug and kiss away their pain. Then, if they fell down, I'd given them a cuddle, a princess plaster and a sweet and all was well with the world. But now when they fell down, they didn't want my help. They didn't even want me to know about it. Everything was secretive – whispered phone calls to friends, hidden diaries, monosyllabic answers, locked bedroom doors . . .

Gone were the days when the girls bounded in from school full of stories of fighting in the playground, bold girls getting into trouble, the teacher giving them a gold star for work well done, new songs to sing for me, poems to recite for me, drawings to give to me . . . With teenagers you got shrugged shoulders, sullen faces and raging hormones.

I wanted the girls to be well prepared for life because you never know what's around the corner. I had been shocked when my mother died. It had been so sudden: one day she had a headache, the next she was dead of a brain tumour. I felt lost for years afterwards. I wanted to stay close to my girls: I knew what it was like to have no mother – lonely and frightening. They might think they didn't need me any more, but I knew they did. When my mother died a huge gap opened up in my life that no one could ever fill. Ali was now the same age I was when Mum died and I wanted to protect her for as long as I could. It was hard out in the world.

There were so many times over the years when I'd just wanted to pick up the phone and talk to my mother. To ask her advice, or cry about something or just tell her that I loved her and she had two beautiful granddaughters whom she would have doted on. To tell her that Ali looked just like her but Sarah had her eyes. To tell her that I'd set up my own business and was doing well. To tell her that I'd married a good man. To tell her that I was doing the best I could but that some days were really tough. That I wasn't managing to juggle it all. I wasn't a great mum, great wife and great businesswoman, but I tried – I really tried. I wanted to tell her that sometimes when I was giving the girls advice I used her exact phrases. I wanted to tell her that I was looking after Charlie for her.

I wanted to tell her that I appreciated everything she did for me growing up and that she was the best mum in the world and I was really trying to be like her, but I was struggling at the moment. That I felt overwhelmed with everything that was going on. That I felt I was losing control and didn't know how to handle it.

I wanted to tell her that I still missed her every single day . . .

16

The next day, Sally arrived in work wearing black leggings with a short-sleeved black woollen mini-dress over them and high black wedge-heel boots. She looked cool, stylish and gorgeous. 'Morning,' she said, putting her bag down and heading over to the coffee machine.

'Hi,' I replied.

'Coffee?'

'No, thanks.'

'So, what's on the agenda today?' she asked, sitting down at her desk, opposite me.

'Honesty.'

She raised an eyebrow. 'What's up? You look miserable.'

'I'm a middle-aged frump.'

'No, you are not.'

'I said you had to be honest.'

'I am being honest. You are no such thing. What's going on? Is Nadia still parading around in her skimpies?'

'Yes, she bloody well is, and it's driving me nuts. I know it's ridiculous. I have two daughters to worry about, one of whom is completely stressed out, and I have a job I need to focus on, but I'm getting into a rage about my father's girlfriend and her sexy body. What's wrong with me?'

'There's nothing wrong with you. It's normal to feel the way you do when you have a semi-naked body thrust in your face every day.'

'She looks so good and I feel so mumsy when she's around. I'm sure Paul is lusting after her. I can't believe my father's girl-friend is younger, prettier and in much better shape than me. It's crazy. But it's made me realize that I've got lazy.'

'You always look really smart.'

'Exactly. Smart. What is smart? Smart is safe, sensible, square.'

'No, it's appropriate, classy and subtle.'

'Nice try, Sally. Let's be honest as we agreed. I've got lazy about how I look. You, on the other hand, look fantastic and wear great clothes. I wear crap clothes that do nothing for me.'

Sally sighed and sat down. 'I have to make an effort because I'm still trying to meet someone. I'm getting older and competing with much younger women – it's boring and exhausting. I would *love* to wear a tracksuit every day and eat cream cakes. If I ever do meet a man, I'll hang up my high heels, put on five stone and only wear elasticated waists.'

'No, you won't. You're naturally stylish and always look brilliant. Having Nadia parading around the house has made me realize I need to make more of an effort. So I've decided to update my wardrobe and my underwear, but I need you to help me. Poor Paul has been looking at my off-white knickers and bras for far too long. I need to spice things up a bit. My clothes are boring and so is our sex life. It's almost non-existent. It's a sad day when your father's having more sex than you.'

'Well, I can help with the clothes, the sex life you'll have to sort out on your own, although I did read an article in *Glamour* last month that suggested spraying your partner with whipped cream and licking it off.'

I giggled. 'I can just picture Paul's face as I attack him with the can.'

'Tell you what, why don't we give ourselves the morning off and go shopping?'

'I'd love it. Make me into a goddess.'

Sally took me to boutiques I'd always been too intimidated to go into. They were the type of places where the staff pounced on you as soon as you walked in the door. They'd look you up and down with disdain while asking if they could be of any assistance. Then they'd follow you around asking if you were searching for something in particular. If you were brave enough to try on some clothes, they stood outside the changing room, shouting, 'Does everything fit? Do you need a bigger size?' And when you ventured out to look in the mirror they'd tell you it was 'just fabulous' and that there was a coat/bag/jacket/shoes to match.

Having arrived home from one of these places a few years ago with a hideous shapeless purple dress that made my pale skin seem washed out and did nothing for my green eyes – although the shop assistant had assured me that purple really drew out the colour – I swore never to go there again. Ever since I'd shopped in high-street chains or big department stores like House of Fraser where no one bothered you and you could sneak into the changing room with twenty items and not be harassed.

But going to the boutiques with Sally was a completely different experience because she took charge. All the assistants knew her and she handled them expertly.

She marched in and explained that her friend wanted some new clothes. 'We're talking smart casual. Everyday stuff for work and weekends, but something with a twist. Nothing too conservative.'

It was fantastic. I didn't have to say or do anything. I just stayed in the changing room while Sally made the assistants scurry around and she only let me try on what she knew would suit me.

'Pale-skinned girls with blonde hair need warm colours,' she assured me.

I tried on dresses, tailored trousers and skirts in grey, black, navy, aubergine, dark green, brown, red and cream. If something didn't suit me, Sally would shake her head and I'd take it off immediately.

She was a total pro. Nothing I bought would be wasted. Everything could be mixed and matched. I ended up buying four pairs of trousers, three skirts, four shirts, five tops, two jackets and two pairs of boots. Each item was more expensive than the last, but they were all gorgeous. I couldn't wait to wear them. I felt like an excited kid.

'Thank you, Sally.' I hugged her. 'I never thought shopping could be done so efficiently and that you could get so many things to match. I have a wardrobe full of clothes at home, but nothing goes with anything else.'

'The key to good shopping is thinking about it. You should never go on a whim. Always have in mind what you want to buy, and when you try it on, think very carefully about what you already have that you could wear with it. I honestly don't have that much stuff, but I can mix it all up.'

'And the quality!' I gushed. 'They were a bit pricy, but the way they hang and feel is amazing. I'm always looking for a quick fix. I never think of quality.'

'It's so important. My mother always told us "quality over quantity" and she was right. I have jackets I bought ten years ago that still look brand new.'

'I can't believe I've never asked you to come shopping with me before. You're a pro. If Happy Dayz ever shuts down, you could become a stylist.'

'We haven't finished yet. We still need to get you some decent underwear.'

Sally took me to a lingerie shop I'd never even heard of called Madame Sophie.

'You're going to love Sophie,' Sally assured me. 'She's brilliant. She's incredibly sexy in that understated French way and eats men for breakfast. She's currently on her third marriage.'

The little shop was tucked away behind the main shopping streets. When we walked in a little bell rang. Sophie came out and greeted Sally like an old friend. 'Darling, 'ow are you?'

'Good, thanks. I want to introduce you to my friend Ava. She needs a full overhaul.'

Sophie shook my hand and appraised me. She was small,

blonde and very petite. She had the tiniest waist I'd ever seen. She was wearing a grey trouser suit with a gorgeous cream lace camisole underneath. Sexy, but subtle.

'Ava, you do not feel sexy any more. You 'ave lost your sexuality – I can see eet in your heyes. But don't worry, I can 'elp you. Sexy is from ze hinside hout. Now go in zere and strip down to your hunderwear.' She pulled a black velvet curtain around me while I took my clothes off.

'Ah, *non, non, non*,' she said, shaking her head when she saw my grey underwear. 'You cannot keep a man 'appy with zees underwear. Your bosom is falling down to your knees. You are wearing ze totally wrong size. 'Ow many childrens do you 'ave?'

'Two.'

'When women 'ave children zey need even more 'elp to keep ze bosom hup. I will show you. Put zis on.'

I tried on bras that literally had scaffolding in them. My boobs went from droopy to pert. All the bras had wonderful frilly silk knickers to go with them.

'Do you get all your underwear here?' I asked Sally.

She nodded. 'I get some basics in M&S, but mostly I come here. As you can see, a good bra instantly transforms your cleavage.'

Sophie pulled back the changing-room curtain, exposing me in my new underwear. 'Now, zat is very nice, but you halso need ze corset hunderwear to pull in ze waist.' She handed me a sexy, lace-trimmed corset that tied at the front with a long line of little hooks. I couldn't believe the difference it made. I went from having no waist to a small, defined one, and I could still breathe.

'Wow,' Sally said.

'It's miraculous,' I gushed.

'Ze magic of proper lingerie.' Sophie smiled. 'Now, Sally, I want you to go and sit down. I 'ave one more zing I want Ava to try. Somezing only ze 'usband should see.'

Sally sat down and took out her BlackBerry.

Sophie came into the changing room with me. "Ow often are you 'aving ze sex?' she asked quietly.

'Not very often,' I said, squirming to admit it aloud.

'I can see zis. You 'ave no colour in ze face.'

I looked at myself in the mirror. Could everyone tell by looking at me that I was neglecting my marital duties?

'If zere is one zing ze French know, eet ees sex. You cannot let eet disappear. You 'ave to keep eet alive and you 'ave to work at eet. Sometimes I would much razer 'ave a glass of wine and read my book, but if a week 'as gone by, I know I need to 'ave sex. Never let eet go for more zan one week. Ozerwise 'e will start looking at ozer women.'

'I'm just tired at the moment. There's lots of stuff going on at home and I'm worried all the time and I'm just not in the mood for sex.'

'Ava, I know ze stress. I know ze feeling of wanting to sleep and not 'ave sex. But, actually, sex ees very good for ze stress. Ze orgasm release ze stress and you feel much better hafterwards.'

She handed me a black Lycra and satin-lined lace baby-doll with a ruffle hem and garter straps with a matching see-through thong and stockings. It was skin tight and quite uncomfortable, but it looked fantastic.

'Now you are feeling sexy, no?'

I laughed. 'Yes, I am.'

'Now you want to 'ave sex?'

'Actually, yes, I do.'

'*Et voilà*. You 'ave to feel sexy to want sex. Ze hunderwear ees vital. You Irish women don't hunderstand thees.'

'Well, this has been a very enlightening experience. Thank you, Sophie.'

'My pleasure. Your 'usband will be very 'appy tonight and so will you. Let you hin'ibitions go, 'ave sex like a tigress. Not like a missionary woman.'

'I'll take it all. And thanks for the advice,' I said, deciding it was time to go before Sophie started demonstrating positions she thought might spice up my marriage.

'Good luck,' she said, winking at me. 'Don't forget – like a tigress. *Grrrr*.'

I took Sally for lunch. 'Thank you so much for transforming me in one morning. I'd forgotten that great underwear and clothes could make you feel so good about yourself. I feel like a new person.'

'Any time, I enjoyed it. And I hope you're planning to wear some of that new gear tonight.'

'Absolutely. Sophie's put the fear of God into me. Not only did she say everyone could tell I wasn't having regular sex by my pasty complexion, but that if I wasn't having sex at least once a week my husband would stray.'

'In that case every married man I know must be shagging other women.'

'I was getting a bit freaked out in there.'

'Well, being on her third, she should have a few tips on marriage.'

'I wonder did number one and two only get sex once a fortnight.' We giggled and ordered more wine.

'So, what's your plan of action – or should I say seduction?'

'I'll text him later and tell him to come home because I need to talk to him urgently and then surprise him.'

'Why don't you leave a note in the kitchen, saying, "Come up and see me in the bedroom" or something? And have candles lit and sexy music playing.'

'You're good at this.'

'I watch a lot of movies.'

'I'll get some candles on the way home and download some mood music. Any idea what songs are good to have sex to?' I laughed. I was like a teenager about to lose her virginity.

'"I Want To Sex You Up".' Sally giggled.

'"Sexual Healing".'

'Anything by Barry White.'

'"I'm A Slave For You".'

'Oh, I know – Seal's "Kiss From A Rose". I've had sex to that, very effective.'

'Tried and tested! Wish me luck.'

17

When everyone had gone to bed, I wrote Paul a note and left it on the kitchen table under a bottle of wine. 'I need you upstairs now! Bring the bottle.'

Then I lit candles all over the bedroom, set up the iPod, drank a large glass of wine to get me in the mood and put on my new lingerie. I examined myself in the mirror. The very short nightdress was completely see-through and the thong almost non-existent. It made my bum look bigger than it was. I twisted and turned, peering at myself from every angle. In daylight, I'd have been arrested, but in the flattering glow of candlelight I didn't look too bad for a forty-two-year-old mother of two.

The wine began to take effect and I started dancing in front of the mirror to 'I Want To Sex You Up' . . .

'*Oh*, my God! What are you wearing?'

I jumped. Sarah was standing behind me in her pyjamas, looking horrified.

'Put your dressing-gown on, Mum. That's obscene.'

'Can you please knock before you come barging into my bedroom?' I snapped.

'I can see everything – it's *way* too much information.' She covered her eyes.

I grabbed my dressing-gown and put it on.

She noticed the candles. 'Oh, God, are you and Dad having sex tonight?'

'None of your business.'

'I'm going to be sick. You're not supposed to think of your parents doing it. It's gross.'

'It's not gross. How do you think you were conceived?'

'I don't think about it – ever. Is it like a special occasion or something?'

'No.'

'Do you dress up like this every night when we go to bed?'

'No.'

'Does Dad know you're doing all this?'

'No.'

'I'd say he'll be thrilled – you look very hot.'

'Do I?'

'Yes, but it's not something I ever want to see again. Mothers are supposed to wear aprons and bake cakes, not dance around in G-strings and suspenders.'

'Next time knock.'

'Next time I'll give you a week's notice.'

'That would be perfect.'

'Did you get the gear from Nadia?'

'No, I did not. It's mine. It's new.'

'Well, just don't start screaming or making embarrassing noises – my bedroom's only two doors away, remember.'

'That's enough, you cheeky thing. Off to bed with you. What are you doing up anyway? It's past midnight.'

'I just remembered that I'm supposed to bring in old books tomorrow to send to the poor in Africa. Personally I don't think a starving kid is going to be too thrilled with a book – I'm sure he'd prefer a steak dinner – but Mrs Regan said she wants books and you have loads of them. Can you leave a pile out for me?'

'Fine, goodnight.' I frog-marched her to the door and shut it firmly behind her. I turned back to the mirror and smiled. So I looked 'very hot'!

Ten minutes later I heard Paul coming in the front door. I suddenly felt really nervous. I knocked back another glass of wine. This was ridiculous: why was I nervous about having sex with my husband of twenty years?

I lay back on the bed, took a deep breath and waited. I could hear him on the phone in the hall, talking to the bar manager. I took another deep breath and tried to stay calm. Ten minutes and four sexy songs later he came into the bedroom, carrying the wine. 'What's going on?'

'I'm seducing you.'

'Really?'

'Yes.'

'Fantastic.' He took his jacket off and walked over to the bed. Suddenly he stopped. 'Hold on a minute. Did you crash the car?'

'No.'

'Is Charlie moving in permanently?'

'No.'

'Did you lose your engagement ring?'

'No, I bloody didn't. I didn't do anything, except spend a ton of money on underwear. I'm trying to be more *femme fatale* and less frumpy mother.'

'I'm all for that,' he said, kicking his shoes off. 'Would this have anything to do with a certain Polish pole dancer who parades around half naked?'

'No.'

'Well, whatever the reason, I'm a happy man,' he said, whipping the rest of his clothes off and hopping into bed. He reached over to kiss me.

'Hold on!' I stopped him.

'What's wrong?'

'I need you to lie back and close your eyes.'

'Kinky?'

'No, more sensual.'

'Bring it on.'

While he lay there, eyes closed and a very large grin on his face, I shook the can and then sprayed it all over his chest.

'WHAT THE HELL?' He sat bolt upright.

'Stop! You're spilling cream all over the duvet.'

'Cream?'

'Yes, you idiot. I'm supposed to lick it off now.'

'But it feels rotten. It's all wet and slimy.'

'It's supposed to be sensual.'

'Says who?'

'*Glamour.*'

'Who?'

'*Glamour* magazine. It said that lots of married couples needed to spice up their sex lives and this was one way to do it.'

'You read this in a magazine?'

'Well, I thought that maybe we'd got a bit stale lately, and with my father downstairs getting lots of action and you permanently staring at Nadia's boobs, I thought it was time to do something different.'

'Nadia's knockers are far too big and I don't need props in bed.'

'So you're not fantasizing about having sex with her?'

'Strange though this may seem, I am not in fact lusting after my father-in-law's girlfriend.'

'She's very sexy.'

'I don't happen to think so.'

'So you're not dreaming about her swinging around a pole in front of you.'

'No, Ava, I'm not. But if you fancied taking it up, I'd be happy to watch.'

'I can barely do a forward roll. I somehow doubt I'd be too hot at pole dancing.'

'That's fine with me. I'd rather keep it simple.'

'Really? You're not bored with our sex life?'

'To be honest, I think we could do with a bit more action, but I find you as gorgeous now as I did when I first met you. I'm a simple man. I don't need whipped cream or pole dancers. I just need you, naked. I'm going to wipe this stuff off, but don't move. I'll be right back.'

I lay down and smiled. Paul liked me just the way I was. He still fancied me. He didn't want to sleep with Nadia. He wasn't looking for kinky sex. All I had to do now was remember

Sophie's advice about weekly sessions and hopefully he wouldn't run off with one of the bar girls.

The next morning Magda arrived in to clean the house and I took her aside to talk about Nadia. Magda had been with us for years and we were very fond of her. She was kind, honest, lovely to the girls, loyal and generous. I was puzzled by her friendship with Nadia. They seemed so different.

'How long have you and Nadia been friends?' I asked her.

She was shocked. 'Nadia no my friend.'

'But you introduced her to Charlie.'

'I no introduce Nadia. I introduce Agata. You daddy no like Agata. He say she too old and fat. He like Agata cousin, Nadia.'

'So Nadia isn't your friend?'

Magda crossed her arms and shook her head. 'That girl no my friend.'

'Do you know her?'

'I meet three times.'

'And what do you think of her?'

Magda's mouth formed a tight line. 'She like the money.'

'Yes, I've noticed. Is she a good person?'

'I don't think she good person. I think she happy when she having money. You daddy silly man. Agata good person, she want luff. Nadia not good person, she wanting the money.'

'My father's vulnerable. He falls in love very easily. This is just like what happened with Catherine. When my mother died he jumped into a relationship with a completely unsuitable woman.'

'Nadia no luff him.'

'I know. I'm worried about him.'

'You no worry. I watching Nadia. You good family. You nice to Magda. If Nadia do bad thing, you tell Magda and I come with Polish friends and Nadia no problem any more.'

I was relieved to hear that. It was nice to know that the Polish community was on my side. Although I didn't want any actual harm to come to Nadia, the thought of her being carted out of my house by big strong Polish men was quite appealing. 'Thank you, Magda.'

'No problem. I like you family fery much,' she said staunchly, adding with a smile, 'even you crazy daddy.'

Later that day when the girls were doing their homework and the dinner was in the oven, I sat down in the TV room to go over some menus for a fourth-birthday party we had coming up – they had requested a Scooby Doo Adventure theme. While I was reading through Helen's suggestions for food – biscuits in the shape of bones to look like Scooby Doo snacks, mini hot-dogs and hamburgers and a cake in the shape of Scooby Doo's head with a bubble coming out of his mouth saying, 'Yikes' – I heard raised voices from Charlie's room.

'I want to get a booby job,' Nadia demanded.

'But your breasts are perfect,' Charlie said.

'No, they falling down now. The other girls are young and haff boobies that are sitting up, not falling down.'

'Did someone at the club tell you your breasts weren't perfect?'

'Nobody say nothing. Me, Nadia, want sitting-up boobies. But I need money. I no haff enough. You giff me money, please, Charlie. I pay you back.'

The cheek of her asking my poor father to pay for her boob job! How was she going to pay him back if she was in bed recuperating from breast surgery instead of swinging around a pole making money? And, besides, her boobs were enormous. They'd be pornographic if she got them enhanced.

'Of course I'll give you the money, but I don't want you to have the operation. It's dangerous. What if it went wrong?'

'You silly man, it no go wrong. I haff name of good doctor. He do Latvian girl and she haff beautiful boobies. With bigger boobies I make more money from customer.'

133

'But I think you're beautiful just the way you are,' Charlie insisted.

'You not listen to me, Charlie. I want new boobies. You no help me, I go to customer. He say he help.'

She was a real pro. Kick him where it hurts. She knew Charlie would freak at the thought of another man paying for her boob job.

'Who the hell is this customer? What's his name? I'll kick his arse. You're my girl, and I'll be paying for any plastic surgery you have.'

'Thank you, Charlie, I luff you. You good man.'

How could men be so stupid? She had him wrapped around her finger. I had to do something. I needed to make him see he was being completely manipulated.

18

The next evening, Sally came for dinner. We were planning to run through the details for the Scooby Doo party. When she saw Ali, she looked shocked. She gave her a kiss and asked her how she was.

Ali shrugged. 'OK, I guess.'

'You look tired and thin. Are you sure you're all right?'

'I'm fine – I've just got a lot on this year with exams and stuff.'

'Well, don't overdo it. It's not supposed to make you ill,' Sally said.

'I've been trying to get her to take it easy, but she won't listen,' I said.

'Please stop fussing. I'm fine.' Ali sat down.

Paul, Charlie and Sarah came into the kitchen. Thankfully Nadia had gone to work so we wouldn't have to hear her going on about her boobs.

'What do you think of boob jobs?' Charlie asked Sally.

Sally pointed to hers. 'These babies are not what God gave me, so I'm all for it.'

'Nadia wants to get hers done.' Charlie explained his sudden interest in breast enhancement.

'Oh, my God, they're huge already,' Sarah said, piling chicken and roast potatoes onto her plate.

'Charlie, I really don't think she needs to get them done, and if she goes ahead with it, you shouldn't be paying for it,' I said.

'I paid for these myself,' Sally admitted. 'It's a bit creepy when a man pays for a woman's plastic surgery – it's as if they're admitting they think she needs work.'

'I'm against it,' Charlie assured her. 'Nadia's perfect as she is.'

'Well, then, why would you pay for it?' Sarah asked.

'Because I want her to be happy.'

'If getting it done makes her feel good about the way she looks, she should do it,' Ali piped up.

'I agree with you, Ali,' Sally said, 'but Nadia should pay for it herself. Then, if something goes wrong or she decides she doesn't like them, she can't blame Charlie.'

'She doesn't have the money,' Charlie said.

'Then she should wait until she's earned it.' I wanted Charlie to see sense for once.

'Ah, but that's just it. She says she'll earn more if she gets them done.'

'She seems to be doing just fine,' Paul commented. 'I met her coming in from work the other night and she had a wad of cash in her hand.'

'She's only starting out. Why wouldn't I help her when I can?'

'You haven't been together very long. You should wait before forking out thousands for plastic surgery,' Paul advised.

'I agree,' I said.

'When you love someone you just want to make them happy,' Charlie declared. He was so maddening when he was totally love-blinded.

'If Bobby offered to pay for me to have my chin done, I would so take the money,' Sarah announced. 'I saw it on TV – they operate on your lower jaw and move it slightly back. The woman who had it done looked amazing.'

'What are you talking about?' I was horrified. 'You don't need surgery, you're perfect.'

'Come on, Mum, I have Dad's chin.' She pointed to it, then turned to Paul. 'Thanks a lot for that by the way. Anyway, I just think that if I had my chin pushed back a bit I'd be super-model gorgeous. As it is, I'm an eight-and-a-half out of ten, but if I didn't have the jaw, I'd be a ten.'

'You should be proud to have the Mullen jaw.' Paul rubbed his chin.

'Well, it sucks. I wish I had Ali's little chin, but I'm not, like, losing sleep over it or anything. Besides, now that I've found out you can have it operated on, I know I have options.'

'I'd like to get off the subject of plastic surgery,' I said. 'Both of you girls are gorgeous just the way you are.' I glanced at Ali, who was being very quiet. She was playing with her food. 'Ali, you're very pale tonight.'

'I'm fine.'

'Well, eat your dinner – it'll make you feel better.'

'Jesus, Mum, can you give it a rest for once? Stop trying to force me to eat. I'm sick of it.'

There was a shocked silence. We all looked at each other.

'Calm down, Ali,' Paul said.

'I'm sorry, but she's always nagging me.'

'Ava's just worried about you.' Sally defended me.

'Look, I don't feel very well. I'm going upstairs.' Ali stood up and left the room.

'She's very thin.' Sally broke the silence. 'I got a bit of a fright when I saw her. It's only been a month, but she's shrunk.'

'That's why I'm trying to get her to eat more.' I was upset. Ali looked really awful tonight. I'd been getting her to eat a proper breakfast in the mornings and making her a big lunch to take to school, but she still seemed to be losing weight.

'She's very thin at the moment,' Paul agreed.

'She looks like crap,' Sarah said. 'Maybe she's sick.'

I went up to check on her. She was lying in bed, under the duvet, fully clothed but shivering. 'Oh, Ali, pet, do you have a fever?' I asked, going over to feel her forehead.

She began to cry. 'I feel awful, Mum,' she said. 'I'm freezing.'

I went to get her an extra duvet and the thermometer. Her temperature was normal, but she was still shaking. I tucked her in and hugged her. She sobbed into my shoulder.

'What is it, sweetheart? Do you feel fluey? Is it your exams? Is it David? What's wrong, Ali? You can talk to me. Whatever it is, I'll do everything I can to make it better.'

She shook her head. 'It's nothing. I just feel really shivery and tired. There's some kind of flu going round at school. I'll be fine in the morning.'

'If you're not better tomorrow I'll take you to the doctor. I'm worried about you, Ali. You really don't look well.'

'It's OK, Mum – I feel a bit better already. I just need a good night's sleep.'

'I'll bring you up some Nurofen and a hot drink. It'll help you sleep.'

As I got up to leave the room, I caught an unpleasant whiff. 'What's that smell?' I asked. 'It's like gone-off cheese or something.'

'I don't smell anything,' she said.

'It's quite strong.'

'It's just you and your bionic nose,' Ali said, giving me a watery smile. 'Can you get me the Nurofen, Mum? I need it to help me sleep.'

She closed her eyes and I left the room. If she wasn't better in the morning, I'd take her to Dr Garner. She must have been coming down with this bug over the last week or so. That would explain why she'd been so snappy.

'Is Ali all right?' Paul asked, as I came in.

'No. Her temperature is normal, but she's shivering and seems exhausted so maybe she's picked up a virus. I'm going to get her a hot drink and some Nurofen.'

'That explains why she's been off her food,' Charlie said.

'She looks awful and she's upset. I'm really worried about her. I think she's over-stressed. Maybe she should take a few days off school. She seems overwhelmed with everything. I think she's getting depressed.'

'Did anything bad happen to her at school?' Sally asked Sarah.

'Not that I know of, but she does seem to be on her own a lot.'

'Where's Donna?' I asked.

'She seems to be friendly with Julie now.'

'I hope Ali hasn't fallen out with her. Maybe you could talk to Donna tomorrow and ask her,' I suggested.

'OK – but I have problems too.'

'Why? What's going on?' I asked.

'Rachel Black is, like, so trying to get into Bobby's pants.'

'The bitch,' Sally said.

'I sincerely hope that nobody is getting into Bobby's pants,' Paul exclaimed.

'Hello! It's an expression. Anyway, she says she can do perfect spray tans. Mine are still a bit streaky. Bobby was embarrassed last week playing the match against St Gabriel's because the back of his right leg had a big white patch where I'd missed, but I'm getting better. Besides, Rachel is, like, a total bitch – she's always trying to put me down. She made this big fuss about how I thought the Dalai Lama was an animal.'

'Sarah!'

'Well, Mum, a llama is an animal, isn't it?' she countered.

'She has a point there.' Sally giggled.

'What am I paying for?' Paul wondered. 'Thousands of pounds spent on a private education and you come out with that.'

'You don't have to rub it in. I've already been made a fool of. But it actually backfired on her because Bobby thought it was an animal, too. So now everyone knows that we're, like, a perfect match.'

'Just like Nadia and me.' Charlie beamed.

'How is your romance going?' Sally asked.

'Fantastic. I've been given a new lease of life. I feel young again and the sex is great. I'll tell you, Sally, I'm a different man.'

'Good for you. I need some of that. Maybe I should look at dating older men.'

'With Viagra, we're as good as the young fellas.'

'I'll keep that in mind.'

'Well, I hope you can tear yourself away from Nadia for New Year, because I've got some exciting news,' I announced.

'What?' Sarah asked.

'Remember we talked about getting away?'

'Oh, my God, Mum, did you book it?'

'Yes, I did. I've booked a family holiday to Tenerife.'

'Brilliant! Are you coming, Dad?'

'Yes, he is,' I said firmly. 'He's not happy about leaving the pub, but he's coming.'

'It's one of the busiest times of the year for me, but your mother put her foot down and said we all needed a change of scenery, especially Ali.'

'Cool. I can't wait.' Sarah's enthusiasm was infectious.

'I'm glad you're pleased. Hopefully, it'll do us good. I really want to get Ali away from her books and David and all the hassles of the last few months.'

'When are we going?' Sarah wanted to know.

'We fly out on the twenty-sixth of December for a week. I've run it by my business partner here and she's OK with it. In fact, she said she might come out for a few days.'

'Cool! We'll have great fun and I'll have a tan going back to school.' Sarah beamed.

'Nadia'll be delighted – she loves the sun,' said Charlie.

'I didn't book a ticket for Nadia. I presumed she'd be going home to Poland for Christmas.'

'Not at all, she's staying here with me.'

'I was thinking it'd be a nice *family* holiday,' I emphasized.

'Nadia is family.'

'No, Charlie, she isn't.'

'Actually, Ava, I've a bit of news myself.'

I put down the Nurofen, and the tea that I'd made for Ali, and sat down.

'As you know, I've grown very fond of Nadia. She has come into my life and brought a spring back into my step.'

'Good for you,' Sally said.

'She makes me very happy and I've fallen in love with her. I believe she feels the same way too, which is why . . .' he paused for effect '. . . I'm going to ask her to marry me.'

'*What?*' Sarah looked shocked.

'You hardly know her,' Paul said, incredulous.

'Maybe you should think about it a little longer.' Sally tried to be diplomatic.

'ARE YOU OUT OF YOUR MIND?' I roared. 'Did you learn nothing from the Catherine fiasco?'

'Nadia is nothing like Catherine. She hardly drinks.'

'That's not the point.'

'What is?'

'You jumping into marriage with women you barely know!'

Paul took the tea and Nurofen for Ali and ushered Sally and Sarah out of the room.

'I made a mistake with Catherine and I paid for it. Nadia is not a mistake. I love her. She makes me feel young again and she makes me laugh.'

'Fine, so live with her for a while. Why do you have to bloody marry everyone? You swore you'd never marry again after Catherine.'

'I didn't think I'd fall in love again, but I have. I'm old-fashioned. I like being married.'

'Jesus Christ, Charlie, when are you going to grow up? Marrying Nadia is the stupidest thing you could possibly do. She's a gold-digger. I can't protect you if you keep ignoring my advice. I told you not to marry Catherine and now I'm begging you not to marry Nadia.'

His face reddened. 'And when are you going to forgive me for marrying Catherine? I've paid my dues, Ava. I'm sixty-eight years old, I don't have a lot of time left and I've been lucky enough to meet someone I'm mad about. I'm not going to let this opportunity go by because you don't approve. Why can't you just be happy for me?'

'Because I know this is a huge mistake.'

'Didn't a lot of your friends think you marrying Paul at twenty-two was a mistake?'

'Yes.'

'And it turned out to be the best decision you ever made. Love defies logic.'

19

The next morning I was relieved to see Ali looking a bit better. She was up and dressed before me and was eating a bowl of cereal when I came down. She seemed perkier, but I still thought she should stay at home for the day. Charlie had offered to look after her while I was at work, but she insisted that she wanted to go to school.

'I feel much better. Please, Mum, I want to go.'

I checked her temperature. It was normal. 'OK, you can go to school, but if you feel like coming home at any time, call me. I've packed you a big lunch today. You need to build yourself up, pet.'

Ali put the Tupperware box into her bag and went to get her coat. While she was out of earshot, I reminded Sarah to keep a close eye on her and talk to Donna to see if she could shed some light on Ali's behaviour. I was worried that we were missing the big picture. Maybe something had happened in class that none of us knew about.

When I got to work, Sally was waiting for me. She handed me a coffee.

'Thanks. I need that. I was up all night worrying about Ali and Charlie.'

'You've a lot on your plate at the moment.' Sally stirred her coffee. 'How was Ali this morning?'

'Better. She's still peaky, but she seemed OK and insisted on going to school. I think she might be depressed.'

'She's very thin.'

'I know. I try to make sure she has a big breakfast every morning and I've been making her lunches lately to try to get her to eat more.'

Sally went to take a sip of her coffee, changed her mind and put her mug down. 'Ava, has Ali been doing anything out of character or strange in the last few weeks?'

'To be honest, she's been like a different person lately. Sometimes I don't recognize her. I keep asking her if anything is wrong, but she won't talk to me.'

'I suppose what I mean is, has Ali started exercising more or talking about weight all the time?'

'She doesn't really talk about weight, but then she doesn't talk to me about anything any more. She's taken up cycling and the other thing she's doing a lot of is cooking. She spends hours reading cookbooks and insists on baking chocolate cakes and brownies and muffins almost every day.'

'Does she cycle much?'

'She only goes on Saturdays when I'm at work, but Charlie said she's gone for ages sometimes.'

'Does she eat the cakes she cooks?'

'She usually takes them up to her room because she only allows herself a thirty-minute study break for dinner.'

'Ava,' Sally said, fidgeting with a paperclip, 'while you were having it out with Charlie, I went upstairs to talk to Ali. I got a fright when I saw how thin she was and she seemed depressed, as you said, so I wanted to check on her.'

'Did she talk to you?'

'No, she said she wanted to go to sleep but I noticed the smell of rotting food in her room. I think she might be hiding food under her bed.'

'I got that smell too. Ali said I was imagining things. I meant to go back up and investigate, but then I was distracted by Charlie's bombshell, and when I went up, she was fast asleep so I left her.'

'Ava,' Sally said gently, 'have you considered that Ali might have an eating disorder?'

'No . . . not really, because she eats a proper breakfast and lunch – although she has cut back on her dinner. I do think she's depressed, though.' I began to shake. I suddenly felt sick.

'Do you actually sit down and watch her eating breakfast?' Sally persisted.

'Well, I don't stare at her while she chews every bite. I'm up and down a bit getting things for the others, but I'm in the kitchen with her.' I was beginning to feel defensive and uncomfortable.

Sally stood up and began pacing the room. 'Ava, when I first moved to London I had a flatmate who had anorexia. She used to pretend to eat breakfast, but one day I saw her hiding her toast in her napkin when she thought I wasn't looking. She was also obsessed with cookbooks and cooking, but never ate what she made and she exercised non-stop. She used to do star jumps in her bedroom until two in the morning. She wore oversized baggy clothes all the time and she was permanently cold.'

My chest tightened. Ali was always cold and insisted on wearing that awful baggy tracksuit after school. My hand flew up to my mouth. 'Oh, Jesus, Sally.'

'Ava? Are you OK?' Sally asked, as I turned green. 'Look, it's just a thought. I could be totally wrong. I just felt I had to mention it.'

I tried to stand up, but fell back into my chair, my legs like jelly. How had I missed the signs? They were all there. How could I have been so blind?

Sally came around and knelt beside me.

'How could I have been so stupid?'

'Hold on,' she said. 'I'm sorry for giving you a fright. Let's take this one step at a time. It could be a phase. She might just be losing weight because she got her heart broken.'

I looked at my best friend. 'We both know it's not a phase. What am I going to do? How do I stop it?'

'Would you consider calling one of the help-lines to see what they have to say? I actually looked up a number this morning. They're supposed to be very good.' She handed me a piece of paper with a number on it.

My hands were shaking so much I couldn't dial it. Sally touched my arm. 'Would you like me to do that?'

I nodded. She punched in the numbers.

'Hello, Eating Disorder Help-line, can I help you?'

I cleared my throat. 'Yes, hello, I'm calling because I think . . . I think . . .'

'Take your time.'

'I think my daughter may have a problem.'

'How old is she?'

'Seventeen.'

'Why don't you tell me what she's doing that is causing you concern?'

The words tumbled out of my mouth: 'She's suddenly cooking all the time and cycling for miles and she only eats small meals in the evening and she's angry all the time and she seems depressed and she's constantly freezing and I thought she was eating breakfast and lunch, but now I don't know – I think maybe she's been hiding food when I'm not looking. She's really thin.'

'Is she tired all the time?'

'Yes.'

'Is the cycling a new hobby?'

'Yes.'

'Does she cut her food up into very small portions?'

'Yes.'

'Does she seem withdrawn and uncommunicative?'

'Yes.'

'When you try talking to her, how does she react?'

'She tells me she's fine and asks me to go away.'

'How long has she been behaving out of character?'

'About two and a half months but it's got much worse recently.'

'Did something happen to upset her?'

'Her boyfriend broke up with her a couple of months ago and she was devastated.'

'I see. It does sound like she might be developing an eating disorder. My advice would be that you take her to a doctor to be properly assessed. Your GP will be able to diagnose her and help you decide on an action plan. And I know how hard it must be, but please try not to panic – you're aware of it now and it's still in the early stages, so there's every chance you can help her to change her behaviour.'

The woman's voice was very soothing and comforting.

I began to sob. 'She used to be such a happy, lovely girl.'

'She still is. It's just hidden under all this stress and hunger.'

'Why am I so stupid? How did I not see it earlier?'

'This is not your fault. It's obvious that you care very much for your daughter and want to do everything to make her better, so don't be hard on yourself. We can't watch them twenty-four hours a day. Now, why don't you put down the phone and ring your GP immediately? You'll feel stronger when you know exactly what you're dealing with. And we're always here to talk to, whenever you need us.'

'OK, thank you.'

I hung up, put my head in my hands and bawled. Sally wrapped her arms tightly around me. 'What did she say?'

'She thinks Ali does have an eating disorder and I need to take her to the doctor immediately. Oh, God, Sally, how could I be such an idiot? How did I not pick this up? A mother is supposed to know when something is wrong with her child.'

'You knew there was something wrong with her, Ava, you just didn't know what it was.'

'But I should have seen this coming. I was so busy working and trying to save Charlie from himself that I haven't been concentrating properly on Ali. She should have been my priority.' I wiped my eyes with the tissue Sally handed me.

'She *is* your priority. You've been telling me for weeks that you're worried about her and you kept trying to talk to her but she blocked you out.'

'I should have tried harder. I should have kept a closer eye on her.'

'Ava, you did your best.'

147

'That's just it, Sally. My best isn't nearly good enough.'

'Come on, don't beat yourself up. You're a great mum.'

'Am I? Do great mums often miss the fact that their daughters are starving themselves? Do great mums need their best friends to point it out?'

'Ava, stop. It's not going to do you or Ali any good if you berate yourself.'

I took a deep breath. 'You're right. I need to focus on sorting this out.' I stood up and dropped my tissue into the wastepaper basket. 'I'm sorry about this, Sally. I know we're busy today but I need to go home. I want to call Dr Garner and get my head straight.'

'Why don't I drive you?'

'No, thanks. I'll be fine. I just need to process all of this and start figuring out how to fix it.'

'Are you sure? I'd be happy to help.'

'You've helped so much already. If it wasn't for you –' I began to cry again.

'Stop it. You knew something was wrong all along.'

I took a deep breath and composed myself. 'Thanks for everything. I'll call you later.'

'Good luck – and let me know if you need anything.'

I don't remember the journey home. I flung open the front door, ran upstairs to Ali's bedroom and looked around. There was a rotten smell coming from under the bed. I crouched down and gagged. Hidden there I found mounds of mouldering chocolate cake, slices of toast, mashed potato, steak . . . at least three days' worth of uneaten food. Covering my mouth, I piled it into her bin and looked at her desk. There were pictures of models pinned to the noticeboard above it. They were all painfully thin. How had I not noticed this before? I found the bathroom scales under her desk.

I turned her computer on and went into her Internet history. I felt physically ill when I saw the long list of sites that came up: thinnestofthemall, pro-anorexia, prettythin.com, ana'sthinspiration . . .

I logged on to a few and couldn't believe what I was reading. They encouraged you to starve yourself with advice like: 'Starving is an example of excellent willpower' and 'Bones are clean and pure. Fat is dirty and hangs on your bones like a parasite.'

It told you how to survive on one apple a day, recommending you cut it into eight slices – two for breakfast, two for lunch, two for dinner, and you still had two left for a snack. Apparently this way your body thinks it's eaten four times that day, but you've actually only eaten one apple.

They recommended not swallowing, just chew and spit the food out. And they said it was important to keep very busy, almost to the point of being completely stressed out, because then you can go for hours without being hungry or wanting to eat.

I put my head into my hands and sobbed. My daughter was anorexic and I'd missed all the signs. How bad was she? Why was she doing this to herself?

Charlie must have heard me crying, because he came up to me. 'Is this about Nadia?' he asked, sitting beside me.

'I don't give a shit about Nadia. Ali's got an eating disorder.'

Charlie stared at me. 'Now hold on a minute. I know she's got a bit thin, but that doesn't mean she's anorexic.'

I showed him the rotting food, the pictures and the websites. Charlie shook his head. 'I can't believe it. Ali's so sensible. It's so unlike her to do something so stupid.'

'What am I going to do, Charlie? You can die from anorexia. I have to stop it before it gets worse.'

'Don't go getting yourself into a state. No one is dying here. We'll sort this out. We need to talk to Ali first and see what she has to say.'

'I should have seen it. I should have stopped it. Mothers are supposed to protect their children. I just thought she was a bit down in the dumps. I missed it, Charlie. I completely missed it.'

'We all did, pet. We're all to blame. Now, come on, dry your eyes and take a deep breath. We'll get her better in no time.'

'Why you crying?' Nadia asked, standing in the doorway.

'We think Alison is anorexic,' Charlie explained.

'What this?'

'When someone stops eating and gets very sick,' Charlie said.

'Why she stop eating?'

'I don't know. Probably because that stupid little fucker broke her heart,' I raged.

'Aleeson is sad girl.'

'No, she isn't. She's a warm, loving, happy girl.' I didn't want Nadia commenting on Ali. I wanted her to go away.

'Since I living in you house, Aleeson is sad. She fery serious, all the time with the books, never smiling. All the time on her own. No boyfriend, no girlfriend. Nobody.'

'She has lots of friends,' I retorted. But Nadia had a point. Nobody called over to see Ali any more. Donna used to be on the phone all the time, or popping over to watch DVDs and swap clothes. That had all stopped. I'd just presumed it was because they were studying so hard for their finals. But now it seemed odd.

'Don't worry, love,' Charlie said, giving me a bear-hug. 'We'll get to the bottom of this. She'll be back to normal in no time. It's bound to be just a phase.'

'I hope so,' I said, crying into his shoulder.

20

I tried to make myself look as if I hadn't been crying all afternoon and went to collect the girls. On the drive over to the
school, I tried to work out what I was going to say, how I was
going to confront Ali. Part of me was desperately sad and guilty
but another part was angry with her. Why was she doing this to
herself? Was it all because of that stupid boy? Was she trying to
be as thin as Tracy? Maybe she thought that if she was thinner
David would fancy her again. She could die of anorexia – didn't
she understand that?

But as they walked towards the car my anger faded. Ali was
hugging her school coat around her, shivering. Her hair was
lank and lifeless. Her face was pale and pinched. I wanted to
wrap her up and take all the pain away.

'Hi, girls, how was school?' I asked, deciding to wait until we
got home to talk to her.

'Fine,' they both muttered. I looked at Sarah, who normally
jumped into the car full of dramatic stories about her day. She
seemed upset.

'Is everything OK?' I asked her.

She glanced at Ali. 'Yeah,' she said unconvincingly.

We drove home in silence. When we got in, Ali went straight
upstairs. As I moved to follow her, Sarah pulled me into the
lounge and closed the door.

'Mum,' she whispered, 'I have to talk to you.'

'What's wrong?'

'Ali's acting really weird.'

'What do you mean?' I asked, catching my breath.

'Well, you told me to keep an eye on her, so I did. I was a total
detective – Dad would have been really proud. First I caught

her flushing her lunch down the loo. She got really pissed off with me and said if I told you she'd say I was having sex with Bobby, which I'm not by the way. Then I talked to Donna, who said that Ali hardly ever speaks to her now. She said Ali's become a real loner. She spends every lunchtime running laps of the football pitches. She told Donna she's training for the marathon. The reason I didn't know this is because I spend all my lunchtimes with Bobby. Donna said she'd asked Ali if everything was all right and told her she was way too thin, but Ali just brushed her off.'

'Did anything happen in school to upset her?'

'I asked Donna that, but she said nothing's happened since David broke it off with her. David's still going out with Tracy, but nothing else bad has happened.'

'Thanks for doing all that, pet. I've been doing some detective work, too, and I think Ali's quite sick.'

'What do you mean sick? Like depressed?'

'No, I think she might be suffering from anorexia.'

'Anorexia? But that's really serious. Are you sure?'

'Yes, but I don't want you to worry.'

'How am I supposed to do that exactly?'

I put my arm around her shoulders. 'Sarah, Ali's going to be fine. I'll get her all the help she needs. Now, I need to go up and talk to her. Why don't you go in and help Nadia cook dinner? She's making some special Polish dish for us all.'

'Can't I just watch TV?'

'No.'

Sarah got up from the couch and grudgingly went off to help Nadia. I walked upstairs to talk to Ali. I was nervous about what to say, but I just took a deep breath and opened her bedroom door.

She was in the middle of getting changed. I screamed – before me stood a skeleton.

'Why the hell didn't you knock?' she shouted, grabbing her duvet to cover herself.

'Jesus Christ, Ali, what have you done to yourself?' I cried. She was so much thinner than I could ever have imagined, her ribs and hip bones jutting out.

'Get out!' she demanded, as she pulled a baggy tracksuit over her bones.

'You're a —'

'Fat cow? Yes, I know.'

'*No!* You're painfully thin. You're nothing but bones. Oh, God, Ali, how did I not see this? I'm sorry, pet, I've let you down.'

'Please go. Stop staring at me,' she begged.

I willed myself to be strong. I desperately wanted to pull her to me and hug her better. But she was standing as far away from me as she could get, her arms wrapped protectively around her tiny frame.

'I'm not going anywhere. We need to talk.'

'I don't want to talk,' she said.

'Ali, this has gone too far. I found the food under your bed. I know you've been flushing your lunches down the toilet in school, I know you've been running every day at lunchtime and I've seen those sick websites you've been on.'

'How dare you break into my computer?'

'Ali, I think you've got an eating disorder and we need to get you some help.'

'Go away, Mum. You're making a drama out of nothing.'

'Have you seen yourself? Have you seen how thin you've got?'

'Stop zoning on me. Stop spying on me.'

'Ali, please talk to me. I want to help you. Why are you doing this to yourself? Is it because of David?'

'WILL YOU SHUT UP ABOUT DAVID!' she roared.

'Something is making you starve yourself. I want to find out what it is and help you,' I pleaded.

'The only way you can help right now is by leaving me alone. Get out.'

I could see I was wasting my time. She was like a cornered

cat, lashing out. I stood up and willed myself to be calm. 'I'm going downstairs now. In ten minutes I want you in the kitchen, at the table. Nadia has cooked a special meal and you're going to sit down and eat it. This has got to *stop*.'

'Just go,' she said, turning away from me.

Paul had arrived home while I was upstairs with Ali, and Sarah had filled him in. 'What's going on? Sarah told me you think Ali's anorexic. Is that true?' he asked, as he closed the lounge door so we could have some privacy.

'Yes.'

'Are you sure you're not jumping to conclusions?'

'I've just seen her without her clothes on, Paul – she's skin and bone.' I began to get upset again.

'I know she's lost weight, but don't all teenagers go on stupid diets at some point?'

'This isn't a diet. She's starving herself. She's been lying to us and throwing her lunch out and pretending she's training for a marathon. I was talking to Sally and she said she got a fright when she saw Ali last night and that maybe she had a problem, and then I rang a help-line and they said it sounded like she had an eating disorder. When I looked in her bedroom I found lots of rotting food under her bed and horrible anorexic websites on her computer.'

'You and Sally rang a help-line?'

'Yes. I was worried and I wanted advice.'

'Come on, Ava, this is what you always do.'

'What is?'

'Panic.'

'What the hell is that supposed to mean?'

'Remember when Sarah had the measles and you thought it was meningitis? And when Ali had a cold and you thought it was swine flu?'

I gritted my teeth. 'I am *not* overreacting. Ali is really sick and we need to get her help or it will get worse and she could die.'

'Dinner's ready!' Sarah bellowed from the kitchen.

Paul moved to the door. 'Let's see how she gets on at dinner before we start talking about her funeral.' He walked out the door and an almost uncontrollable anger welled up inside me. It took all my willpower to take a deep breath and walk to the kitchen.

We all sat around the table and Nadia served us up a delicious stew.

'Bigos,' she announced. 'Traditional Polish stew. It make you big and strong.'

Ali was staring in horror at the plate of food. Her hands shook as her fork hovered above it.

'You eating up, Aleeson. You skinny. Men no like skinny, men like strong woman. You eat my grandmother stew, you have all the men in luff with you.'

'Get that into you. You'll feel better with some food in your stomach,' Charlie encouraged her.

'Go on, Ali, eat up. Your mother's worried about you,' Paul told her.

'It's OK, pet, take your time,' I said, as she chewed a piece of cabbage.

She continued to eat tiny mouthfuls of cabbage for the next ten minutes.

'Eat some meat. The iron will do you good,' Charlie suggested.

Ali picked up a piece of pork and put it into her mouth. We all pretended not to stare as she chewed. But when it came to swallowing, she couldn't. She began to gag on it.

'Just swallow it and stop making such a song and dance about it,' Paul scolded. 'It's only a piece of meat.'

Ali began to cry. 'I can't, Dad. I'm sorry.'

Nadia broke the silence. 'I tell you story about my granny dying of starfation in the war. This will helps you eat. My grandmother –'

'Thank you, Nadia, I'll deal with this,' Paul interrupted. 'Alison, eat your dinner.'

Ali tried to swallow another piece of meat, but ended up spitting it into her napkin.

I put my hand on Ali's arm. 'Come on, love, just eat small bits.'

'I can't,' she whispered.

'Just eat the bloody meat,' Paul snapped.

'I can't eat it. It's full of *fat*,' she screamed, and ran upstairs to her bedroom.

We all stood up to follow her. 'STOP!' Sarah shouted. 'I'll go. You're freaking her out. Let me talk to her.'

I crept up after my daughters. I had to find out what the hell was going on in Ali's head and I was determined not to let any opportunity to do so pass me by. I sat in the corridor outside her bedroom, with my ear pressed to the door.

'Ali, are you OK?' Sarah asked.

'You're a bitch. I can't believe you told Mum you saw me throwing out my lunch.'

'I had to. After Donna told me you've been doing a Forrest Gump impression every lunchtime, pretending to train for a marathon, I knew you'd lost the plot.'

'It's none of your business, you meddling two-faced bitch.'

'Jesus, Ali, why are you being so horrible? What's wrong with you?' Sarah sounded really hurt – I'd never heard Ali speak to her like that before.

'Stop making such a big deal out of nothing. I'm just trying to be healthy.'

'Starving yourself is not healthy. You're skinnier than Tracy and she's way too thin.'

'Am I really thinner than Tracy?'

I felt sick: Ali sounded thrilled.

'Oh, my God, you're actually happy about that? Are you nuts? She looks like crap.'

'No, she doesn't. You said yourself you thought she was like a model.'

'That was before she lost more weight – she looks like a skeleton now. Which, by the way, is what you look like.'

'I wish.'

'Mum thinks you're anorexic. Are you?'

'Of course not. She's just a drama queen. I'm absolutely fine.'

'Do you think you look good?'

'I'm a fat pig. My thighs are like tree trunks.'

'Seriously, Ali, if you believe that, you really do have a problem.'

'My only problem is my interfering mother.'

'She's just worried about you. Please, Ali, are you going to stop this now and start eating?'

'Why does everyone have to go on about food all the time? I am eating. I just don't want to be a big fat whale.'

'Look in the frigging mirror, Ali! You're a walking stick.'

'Get out. I don't want you in here,' Ali snapped.

'Fine, I'm going, but I really wish you'd stop this. Why can't you just be normal again? I can't talk to you any more. You're like a different person. You're always in a bad mood. I miss the old Ali.'

Sarah came out, upset. Seeing me hovering she said, 'There's nothing to hear, Mum. She's lost the plot. She thinks she's fat. She definitely needs help.'

I put my arm around her. 'It's OK, pet. Thanks for trying.'

'She's really bad, Mum.' Sarah's eyes welled up. I hugged her and tried my best not to join in. 'She just won't listen. I don't know what to say to her – she's like a stranger.'

'I don't want you worrying about it. Your dad and I will sort it out. Come back down and finish your dinner.'

Sarah shook her head. 'I'm not hungry. I'm going to my room.'

I stared at the two doors behind which my daughters were hiding, both upset, both confused, both unhappy. It seemed like only yesterday when we'd all cuddle up under a duvet on the couch on rainy Sunday afternoons and watch Disney movies together. I'd make a big bowl of popcorn and we'd eat and chat and sing along. I loved those days. I treasured those days. I missed those days.

Paul came up behind me. 'How is she?'

'Not good. She's in denial. She thinks she's fat. This is really serious, Paul. I'm scared.' I began to cry.

'Hey there, don't get yourself all upset. Let me try talking to her.'

He knocked on the door and walked into Ali's room. 'Hi, Ali. Listen, I'm sorry for shouting at you downstairs. I just got frustrated when you wouldn't eat.'

'It's no big deal.'

'Your mother is very worried about you. She's outside crying and blaming herself. She thinks you've got an eating disorder.'

'God, I wish she'd stop going on about it. She always has to make a huge deal out of everything. I just wanted to lose a few pounds and get fit.'

'Then why couldn't you eat your dinner tonight?'

'Because you were all staring at me, watching everything I put into my mouth. It totally freaked me out.'

'So you weren't refusing to eat, you just felt under pressure?'

'Exactly.'

'From now on, will you promise to eat proper meals with us and not leave half of it?'

'Yes, of course, no problem.'

'And you'll stop throwing your lunch out and hiding food under your bed?'

'For God's sake, I only did that once or twice because I didn't like what Mum had made for me.'

I couldn't believe how easily the lies were slipping off her tongue and how gullible Paul was being.

'Well, from now on you have to eat whatever she gives you. You do need to put on some weight.'

'OK, I will.'

'I'm serious now, Ali. You must get some flesh on those bones.'

'I said I would.'

'Right, well, that's sorted, then. Your mother will be relieved to hear it.'

Paul came out and closed the door behind him, looking pleased. 'She said she'd eat properly from now on. Come downstairs and have a glass of wine. It'll make you feel better. You've had a bad day.'

I was too shocked to speak. How could he be so naïve? Ali had been lying to us for months. We couldn't take her word for anything. She needed proper help. I was taking her to the doctor first thing in the morning. I was furious with Paul for letting her away so lightly and with Ali for lying again. His inability to see what was happening made me feel even more alone – I was up against this illness with no back-up.

While Paul went down to pour the wine I marched into Ali's room. She was sitting at her desk.

'For God's sake, it's like a bloody revolving door,' she grumbled. 'Can I please get some peace? I have work to do.'

I stood beside her desk. 'You may think you're fooling your father, but you're not fooling me, Ali. You have a serious problem and we're going to see Dr Garner first thing in the morning. I'm not letting this go on for one more day. I've already let it go too far.'

'I'm not going to see any doctor. I'm fine.'

'This is not up for negotiation. I'm going to make you better and nothing is going to stand in my way. I've been negligent and blind and I'm sorry for that. I should have seen the signs earlier. Now, I want you to put those books away and get into bed. You're exhausted.'

'I have an essay to do.'

'Not tonight. I'll talk to your teacher. Tonight you're to sleep. I want you fresh in the morning so we can work out the best way to get you well again.'

'Stop fussing.'

'Ali,' I said, putting my hands on her shoulders and forcing her to look at me, 'I love you and all I want is for you to be happy and healthy and I'm going to do everything I can to make that happen. We'll have you back to yourself in no time. Trust me, pet, I'm going to help you get better. Now, get some rest.'

She reluctantly turned off her desk lamp and put her books into her bag. 'Can you go now? I have to get changed and I could do without an audience.'

'Fine, but I'll be back up to check on you in ten minutes and you'd better be in bed resting or sleeping.'

She turned her back on me. 'Just close the door, will you?'

When I got downstairs Paul was on his way out to work. 'Where are you going? I need to talk to you about Ali.'

He looked at me, surprised. 'But I just spoke to her and she promised to stop all this mad dieting and eat.'

'Jesus, Paul, how can you be so naïve?'

He sighed. 'Don't you think you're overreacting a little? I know she's been hiding some of her food, but she told me she's going to stop all that and start eating now.'

'Will you get your bloody head out of the sand? She has an eating disorder, all the symptoms are there. Come in here and look at the websites she's been on.' I dragged him into the lounge and logged on to the pro-anorexia websites I had found on Ali's computer. 'Does this seem normal to you?'

He flinched when he saw some of the pictures of the girls being promoted as beautiful – they were emaciated skeletons.

'You see, this is really serious. She's not going to wake up tomorrow and be cured.'

'All I'm saying is, let's not jump to any conclusions. Let's see how the next few days go,' he said.

'Fine. Well, then, why don't you have breakfast with her tomorrow and see how much she eats?'

'OK, I will. I have to go now.' With that, he walked out of the door and went to work.

I spent most of the night on the computer looking up those evil pro-anorexia sites and then the best ways to cure the eating disorder. I learnt that anorexia is curable in 80 per cent of cases that are detected early and treated effectively. I tried to remember when I had first noticed Ali cutting down on her food. It was a couple of weeks after David had broken up with her, so two and a half months ago at the most. They all said that professional help was essential because it was a complex illness that affected a person's physical and emotional sides.

I read that people with anorexia were often perfectionists and overachievers, the 'good' child in the family who tries to please everyone. It was as if they were describing Ali.

A lot of the websites gave different advice, but they agreed that it was vital to get proper medical help and to get to the bottom of the psychological issues underlying the illness. They advised a patient and gentle approach and said it was important never to make negative comments about your own body.

As I lay in bed, I went over the last few months in my head. How had I missed the signs? They seemed obvious now. But how had things spiralled out of control so quickly? I kept seeing the vision of Ali in her underwear. It was heartbreaking. What mother would let her daughter get so thin without noticing? Was I so wrapped up in my own life? Was I selfish or just plain stupid? I tossed and turned, berating myself, until daylight finally broke.

21

When I walked into the kitchen the next morning, I found Paul and Ali sitting in silence. Ali had an untouched bowl of cereal in front of her.

Paul shook his head. Maybe now he'd realize how serious things were.

'Can you drive Sarah to school? I'm taking Ali to see Dr Garner,' I said.

'Sure. Is she up?'

'Yes, she's nearly ready.'

He looked relieved to be leaving the kitchen and Ali.

'Ali,' I said, 'I've rung the school and they know you're not coming in.'

'I don't want to go to the doctor. I'm not sick.'

I looked her in the eye. 'Ali, get your coat.'

Half an hour later we were in Dr Garner's surgery. She'd been our family doctor since the girls were toddlers. She was about fifty, tall, slim, and wore her hair up in a chignon. She was always impeccably dressed in a black, navy or grey suit. She had a kind but efficient bedside manner and, most importantly, I trusted her.

'Hello, Ava, hi, Alison. I haven't seen you in a while,' she said, shaking our hands.

'Hello, Judith, nice to see you again,' I said, sitting down.

'What can I do for you?'

'It's Alison. She's lost a lot of weight lately and she's refusing to eat. I've just found out that she's been hiding food under her bed, throwing out her school lunch every day and exercising obsessively. I'm really worried about her.' I tried to control the tremor in my voice.

Dr Garner gave my arm a reassuring pat. Then she looked at Ali. 'You do look very thin, Alison. Have you been trying to lose weight?'

'I'm just trying to be healthy. Everyone's making a fuss about nothing.'

'Do you think you've lost any weight recently?'

'Maybe a tiny bit, but not much. Nothing to make a big deal about.'

'How's everything at school? Is anything happening that's upsetting you? Are any of your classmates making you feel uncomfortable about the way you look?'

'Nothing's going on in school. Everything is fine.'

'Well, there was an incident in school,' I said. 'Alison broke up with her boyfriend a few months ago and he's now going out with another girl in her class who's very thin. It's been very difficult for her.'

'For God's sake, Mum, would you stop going on about David? It happened months ago, and I'm totally over it.'

'It must have been hard for you, though,' Dr Garner said gently.

Ali shrugged her thin shoulders. 'At the time it was, but it was ages ago.'

'Do you think his new girlfriend has a nice figure?' Dr Garner asked.

'Yeah, she does – she's a part-time model so she has to be thin.'

'Is that why you're throwing out your school lunches? Because you want to look like this model?'

'No, that's not it at all. I just threw a few of the lunches out because I didn't like what Mum put in on those days. I'm seventeen, for God's sake. I don't need my mother to make my lunch. It's embarrassing.'

'She was exhausted all the time and losing weight, so I was trying to get her to eat something more substantial,' I explained.

'That seems reasonable to me,' said the doctor. 'Alison, are you worried about your exams? You're in final year, aren't you?'

'I suppose I am a bit stressed about doing well, but nothing major.' She shivered and huddled even further under her coat.

'Are you cold all the time?'

'Yes – she's constantly freezing and wears layers of clothes even when the house is like a furnace.' I was determined that Dr Garner was going to have all the facts so she could make a proper diagnosis.

'Have your periods stopped?'

Ali's head snapped up. 'How did you know?'

'It tends to happen when girls lose a lot of weight.'

'Well, they only stopped this month. In fact, it's probably just a bit late because I'm tired.'

'Alison, are you happy with the way you look?' Dr Garner asked.

'Not really.'

'Would you like to put on weight?'

'God, no!' Ali's hands flew up to her mouth.

'Right. Let's weigh you and take it from there,' Dr Garner suggested. She pulled out a big set of scales, told Ali to take off her coat and step up on it. 'Six stone twelve pounds.'

Jesus Christ!

'You're very underweight for your height, Alison. A healthy weight for a girl of five foot eight would be ten stone or nine and a half at the least. You can sit down now. I'm going to take your blood pressure.'

Ali was three stone underweight. This was worse than I'd thought.

'Your blood pressure is low. Alison, for the next while I'd like you to cut out all exercise and have lots of rest. Maybe even take a break from the books for a few days and just build up your strength. Put your feet up and watch movies. I'd also like you to try to eat lots of little meals instead of three big ones. How does that sound?'

'It sounds fine, but I can't take a break from studying. I have Christmas exams coming up.'

'Well, don't overdo it. You need to rest. Now if you wouldn't mind stepping out for a minute I'd like to have a quick chat with your mum.' Dr Garner showed Ali out to the waiting room and closed the door.

'How bad is it?' I asked.

Dr Garner sat down beside me. 'Alison is very underweight and her blood pressure is low. Her symptoms would suggest that she has an eating disorder.'

'Anorexia?'

She nodded. 'How long has she been dieting?'

'About two and a half months, but it only got really bad in the last few weeks.'

'Well, that's very positive. Early detection is key to curing anorexia.'

'It still took me two months to find out. How did I not see what was going on?'

'Don't beat yourself up, Ava. It's extremely hard to tell when a child is just dieting or when it becomes more than that. Anorexics are very clever at hiding their illness, which is why so many aren't diagnosed for years. You did the right thing by bringing her to see me immediately.'

'Is she going to be OK? Don't some people die of this?'

'Yes, they do, but the majority get better, especially teenage sufferers. However, you'll need to watch her like a hawk and encourage her to eat little and often. She mustn't exercise at all. I'd also like her to see Mary Boland. She's a psychologist who specializes in treating teenage girls with eating disorders.'

'Do you think this is all because of that boy breaking up with her?'

'That certainly could have been the catalyst. Mary will help us get to the bottom of the problem, which will be a key factor in Alison's recovery.'

'Does she have a good success rate?'

'She's the best around. I think you'll really like her. In the meantime, someone will need to supervise Alison's meals and sit down with her while she eats. Gently encourage her to eat five or six small meals a day.'

'Is there anything else I can do to help her get better?'

'Just be there for her. Try to get her to talk to you and maybe do some fun things as a family. Make her feel as secure as possible.'

'I've booked a holiday to the sun at Christmas.'

Dr Garner smiled. 'That sounds perfect. A change of scenery will do her the world of good and the sun will help build up her immune system.'

'What if she refuses to eat?'

'If that happens, we'll have to look at more in-depth treatments. But remember, Ava, Alison's chances of full recovery are very high. You've sought professional help and are committed to helping her get better. These are all vital ingredients to her getting well quickly.'

'Thank you, Judith. Thanks so much,' I said, trying not to get emotional.

'If you're worried at all in the next ten days, call me and bring Alison back for a check-up before Christmas. In the meantime, book her in with Mary Boland and enjoy a nice family break.'

Ali and I walked to the car in silence. I was trying to figure out the best thing to say to her. But I was in shock. It had been confirmed: Ali had anorexia. She was sick. She could die. A mother's job is to fix things. I had to make this better. I had to save her. I concentrated on driving and took deep breaths. I was no good to anyone if I was hysterical. I needed a calm head.

'Ali, you heard the doctor. You're very thin and you need to rest and eat, so that's what we're going to do. I'll keep you at home for a few days.'

'No, Mum, you can't. I don't want to stay at home. I need to go to school and keep up with work. I'll just get bored at home. I'll eat.'

'Yesterday you promised Dad you'd eat but you had nothing for breakfast.'

'I was just stressed about going to the doctor. I'll have some cereal now. Don't keep me at home, Mum. Let me go to school.'

'Why are you doing this?'

'What?'

'Starving yourself. Why do you want to be so thin?'

'I just decided to be healthier, that's all. I don't have anorexia. I was just a bit too strict on my diet, but I'll stop now. It's all fine, Mum.'

'It's not all fine, Ali. Dr Garner told me to take you to see a psychologist.'

'*What?* I don't need to see a psychologist, I'm not mad. Jesus, Mum, why do you have to overreact to everything? I've lost weight, not my mind.'

'She thinks this woman will help you figure out why you're not eating.'

'Are you deaf? I'm not going to see a shrink.'

I parked the car in front of the house. 'Yes, Ali, you are.'

She followed me into the kitchen. 'Why are you trying to make me out to be crazy? OK, maybe my diet was too extreme, so I'll stop now. Just leave it alone, Mum. Don't start freaking out and sending me to see psychologists.'

'You've been lying to us for months, Ali. I don't know how to make you better, so I'm going to get help from people who can. I am not letting this go any further or get any worse. Don't you get it? I'm trying to help you.'

'I'm going to call Dad. He won't let you send me to a shrink, I know he won't.'

'Go ahead.' I handed her the phone. She knew she'd lost this battle.

'I'll talk to him when he gets home. I'm going to tell him what a psycho you're being. I need to go to school now.'

Ali went to change into her uniform and I made her lunch. When she came back in, I handed her the food. She rolled her eyes and threw it into her rucksack.

'Please eat it. Please don't throw it away. You need to work with me, not against me, Ali.'

'Whatever. Can we go now?' She avoided eye contact.

We drove in silence to the school. Ali refused to talk to me, so I gave up. She sat with her arms crossed, looking furious. I had no idea how to get through to her. I dropped her at the front gate and watched her walk across the lawn into the school. Who was this stranger who had taken over my Ali?

22

I drove to work in a daze and sat in the car park, leaning back into the headrest. I tried to breathe in and out slowly to calm down. I felt as if my head was going to explode.

Sally came out of the office and knocked on my car window. 'Are you OK? I've called you a million times. How's Ali?'

I got out and she hugged me. 'Let's go inside. I need a drink and a cigarette.' I hadn't smoked since I found out I was pregnant with Ali seventeen years ago, but I needed one now.

Sally lit me a cigarette and opened a bottle of wine that we kept in a little fridge in the office. In between gulps, puffs and sobs, I filled her in on the last twenty-four hours.

'Oh, Ava, I'm so sorry. Poor you. Poor Ali.'

'When you started talking about your flatmate it was like a light bulb went on in my head. All of Ali's weird behaviour suddenly made sense. How could I have been so stupid, Sally? I just thought she was a bit depressed because of David, but she was actually starving herself.'

'Don't blame yourself,' Sally said. 'Teenagers are always losing weight and being moody and Ali had a reason to be depressed – her first love broke up with her. How were you to know she was throwing out her lunch and running for miles every day at school? You can't watch her all the time.'

'She must have been hiding food in her napkin every time I turned my head, because I thought she was eating two slices of toast every morning as well as cereal. She's been deceiving us for weeks . . . It's so unlike her to be sneaky and manipulative.'

'The important thing is that you've found out what's wrong and you're doing something about it. How's Paul taking it?'

'Last night he told me I was overreacting, but when Ali

refused to eat this morning, he *finally* realized we have a problem. I'm raging with him for being so unsupportive.'

'It's harder for men to understand. They don't obsess about weight the way we do.'

'Do I talk about weight a lot?'

'No, you don't.'

'Sometimes I squeeze my stomach and say I need to cut down on bread or start walking again. Do you think I could have given Ali a bad body image? She's so bright and smart and beautiful I never worried about her, only ever about Sarah.'

Sally put her hand on my shoulder. 'Ava, you are one of the sanest women I know. You very rarely talk about weight and then it's only in a lighthearted way. This is not your fault. You can't control what teenage girls think. You're a great mother.'

'But that's just it, Sally, I'm not. I let this go way too far. The signs were there, right under my nose, but I was so busy with work and then Charlie and Nadia that I didn't see what was happening to my own daughter. I should have been more vigilant after she broke up with David. I should have seen this.'

Sally came over and put a comforting arm around my shoulder. 'No one saw the signs. Not you or Paul or Charlie or even Sarah. This is not your fault. You have to stop blaming yourself. You need to be strong and positive. You'll get through this.'

'She's changed so much, Sally, that I don't recognize her any more. She's so secretive and unhappy and short-tempered.'

'Of course she's grumpy – she's hungry all the time. Once she starts eating, she'll go back to being her old self. Just take it one day at a time and don't panic. Now, I want you to go home and focus on making Ali better. I'll hold the fort here. If I need you urgently, I know where to find you.'

'Thanks, Sally. I honestly don't know what I'd do without you.'

'If only some tall, dark and handsome man would say that to me.'

I called into the pub to tell Paul what the doctor had said.

'So she is anorexic? Are we talking life-threatening here?' he asked.

'It only gets really dangerous if she continues with it. So we all have to keep an eye on her and encourage her to eat to make sure she puts back on the weight she's lost.'

'I couldn't believe her at breakfast – she just refused to eat. I didn't think she was that bad,' he said, upset. Alison was his pride and joy. From the moment she had been born and he had held her for the first time, I was relegated to second position. They had had an immediate bond. He literally fell in love at first sight.

When Ali turned out to be the sweetest child, who never gave us a day's trouble and always did well in school, Paul became even prouder and more besotted with her. She was such a serious little girl, always trying to please everyone, always doing her very best at everything. Paul, coming from an all-boys family, couldn't believe that we had been blessed with such an angelic child.

When we went to parent–teacher meetings and the teachers praised her, Paul would lean over and say, 'She's a really special girl, isn't she?' and they'd smile and agree with him. Ali could do no wrong, and never did. Sarah, on the other hand, had ruffled his feathers from the day she was born. He adored her too, but they clashed a lot. I had to get him to stop saying, 'Why can't you be more like Ali?' I was afraid it would cause a rift between the sisters. But Sarah was so confident and self-assured that she'd never been remotely jealous of Ali's academic achievements, so it hadn't been a problem. The two had always been close – until now.

'Why don't we go out for dinner tonight to that place Ali loves – Carluccio's? I'll get Johnny to cover for me here,' Paul suggested.

'Great idea. I'll tell her when I pick her up from school.'

When I got home I called Mary Boland, the psychologist. Unfortunately she couldn't see Ali until after Christmas. I was disappointed, but at least I had an appointment for the first Monday morning in January. I then made an appointment with Mrs Wilkins, Ali and Sarah's headmistress. I wanted to make sure that everyone at school was on high alert. I locked Ali's bicycle in the shed and hid the key. I felt better already, less weepy and overwhelmed. I was dealing with the situation. I was back in control. I would fix my daughter. Everything was going to be fine.

When I picked the girls up from school, Sarah bounded over to the car while Ali trailed behind. 'Guess what?' she said.

'What?'

'You are looking at the new Juliet Capulet.'

'Who?' I asked, watching Ali as she climbed silently into the car. My heart sank. It was a lot easier to imagine her getting better quickly when I wasn't looking at her emaciated body.

'Hello! Earth to Mother. What do you mean "who"? Juliet Capulet – as in *Romeo and Juliet*. As in William Shakespeare's, like, most famous play ever. As in, like, Leonardo DiCaprio and Claire Danes in the movie? I've just landed the main part, and guess who's playing Romeo?'

I looked at her blankly.

'Bobby, of course! It's total fate. We're really into each other and Romeo and Juliet were, like, star-crossed lovers. It's the same story – except obviously me and Bobby aren't going to kill ourselves because our families hate each other. In fact, our families don't even know each other and you'll probably never meet Mr Masterson-Brown because he spends most of his time in Spain. He's so loaded he's, like, a tax exile or something. How cool is that?'

'Sarah, can you please speak in English? I have no idea what you're talking about.'

'She got the part of Juliet in the school play,' Ali translated.

'Well, that's great. Good for you. Are you doing the whole thing?'

'Yeah, right! *Hello*, do I look like I can swallow a book? We're

172

writing a summarized version in our own words. So it'll be modern English not all that olde-worlde crap that no one understands.'

'How eloquently put,' I said, winking at Ali, who would normally have laughed with me, but she was just staring out the window.

'We'll be performing on the twenty-ninth of January, so can you keep it free? It's at four o'clock, so make sure Dad is there too.'

'I can't wait,' I assured her.

When we got home, Paul and Charlie were talking in the kitchen. They stopped as soon as we walked in.

'There they are, my two beautiful daughters,' Paul said. 'How would you like to go out for dinner? Carluccio's sound good?'

'On a school night? Cool,' said Sarah.

'No, thanks. I've got way too much work to do,' Ali said, heading for the stairs.

'Hold on there.' Paul went after her. 'Since when do you pass up an opportunity to go to your favourite restaurant?'

'I'm too busy, Dad. I'm trying to study to do well in my exams so I can get into medicine, like you want me to. Get off my back.'

'Ali,' he said, reaching out to her, 'you can leave the books for one night. I thought we could have a nice family dinner.'

'I just told you. I don't want to go. Why don't you go without me?' she suggested.

'I want to go,' Sarah said.

'No. It was supposed to be a family meal. If Ali doesn't want to go, then we'll stay in,' said Paul, looking hurt at his eldest daughter's rebuttal.

'There's a nice bit of steak in the fridge – we can have that with some roast potatoes.' Charlie filled the silence.

'Good idea, Charlie,' I said. 'Dinner will be at seven. I want everyone downstairs on time and hungry,' I added, as Ali ignored me and rushed up the stairs.

While Ali did her homework, Sarah sat in the kitchen with

me and talked about the play and school and Bobby. I remembered Ali used to do that, come in and tell me about her day. But she hadn't in a long time. I missed her company.

'Sarah,' I cut across her story about how fit Bobby looked in training today. 'I need to talk to you.'

Her face fell. 'Is it bad news about Ali? I asked her how it went in the doctor's and she just said, "Fine."'

'Yes, it is about Ali. She's anorexic and it's very serious. She needs to start eating properly and put back on all the weight she's lost. We have to encourage her to eat. We must also be vigilant and keep an eye out for any signs of her hiding food or throwing it out. You'll have to watch her in school for me. I'm seeing Mrs Wilkins and I'm going to make sure all the teachers keep track of her too. We all need to work together to help her get better.'

'What happens if she doesn't want to eat?'

'She'll die.'

'Jesus, Mum!'

'What?'

'I'm sixteen – you're supposed to protect me from scary, nightmarish information, not blast it in my face.'

'I want you to know how dangerous anorexia is. I want to make damn sure you don't go and do something stupid like this. You're a beautiful girl with a lovely figure. Don't ever change it by going on some ridiculous diet and starving yourself.'

'Hello! Do you honestly think I want to look like a skeleton? No, thanks.'

'Maybe I should have told Ali she was gorgeous more often. Have I not complimented you both enough? Did I ever make you feel insecure about your bodies? Tell me what I did wrong.'

Sarah came over and hugged me. I was shocked: she never hugged – Ali used to, but Sarah didn't: it was 'lame'. 'Mum, chill. You always told us we looked great. Don't beat yourself up about Ali – she's too smart to continue with this crap. And as for me, there's no way I'm giving up my grub. It's my second love after Bobby. Besides, I know I'm hot, why would I want to mess with perfection?'

'Sometimes, Sarah Mullen, you are a rock of sense. Now, can you call everyone in for dinner, please?'

Sarah stuck her head out the kitchen door and screeched, 'DINNER'S READY. IT'S NOT EXACTLY CARLUC-CIO'S BUT IT DOESN'T LOOK TOO BAD.'

Ali came into the kitchen and stared at her plate. I had given her half the portion everyone else had.

'*Bon appétit*,' Charlie said.

'I luff steak,' said Nadia, shovelling a large piece into her mouth.

'Yum,' said Sarah.

'Mm, delicious,' said Paul.

'Come on, Ali, eat up,' I said, looking at her fork, hanging in the air.

'I'm sorry, I'm not very hungry. I might have a stomach bug.'

'Ali, I want you to get well. You heard the doctor. You need to put on the weight you've lost. Now, come on, eat up.'

She scooped up a few peas and chewed them slowly.

'So, Mum, I'm going to need a fabulous costume for the play. Juliet is, like, a total babe, so I need to look stunning,' Sarah announced.

'We'll see if we can get something on the Internet.'

'I help you. I sewing fery good. I sometimes make own cos-tumes,' Nadia piped up.

'Well, this one will require more material than a thong,' Sarah said.

'No problem – you give me material, I make dress. You pay me one hundred euros.'

'OK, but if I don't like it I'm not going to pay you.'

'It will be beautiful. You will pay me. I'm collecting money for my boobie job. Charlie no want to pay.'

'I thought he'd said yes,' Sarah said.

'He changing his mind efery day.'

'I just think she should give it some more thought,' Charlie said. 'It's a serious operation. I've been reading about it on the Internet – a lot can go wrong.'

While the others kept the conversation going, I watched Ali. She put a small piece of steak into her mouth. I smiled at her. At least she was trying.

'What are you planning on paying Nadia with?' Paul asked Sarah.

'It's a school project so you and Mum have to pay her.'

'You can pay her yourself out of your savings.'

'Hello! It's my English class play. It's William freaking Shakespeare. Like, seriously, it's not as if I'm asking her to make me a dress for a party.'

Paul put his hands in the air. 'OK, I'll pay for it if you'll please stop talking like a brainless American teenager.'

'Whatever, Dad.'

'Have some potato, Ali.' I pointed to the three untouched spuds still sitting on her plate.

She managed two small forkfuls. 'I'm full. I really need to get started on my homework.'

'Not yet, pet. I have your favourite ice cream for dessert.'

'Honestly, Mum, I really can't eat any more,' Ali said, panic-stricken now.

'A small bowl of ice cream will do you the world of good,' Paul told her.

Ignoring her, I put two scoops into a bowl.

'OK, then. I'll take it upstairs and eat it at my desk,' Ali said.

'No, you won't,' I said, leaving no room for debate. 'You'll be eating all your meals, including dessert, with us from now on.'

Ali picked up her spoon and mashed the ice cream up, playing with it until she saw me glaring at her and eventually ate a few small spoonfuls.

'So, Dad, the play is on the twenty-ninth of January and you have to be there,' Sarah said. 'Even if it's the busiest day ever in the pub.'

'I'll do my best.'

'You have to be there – it's my début as an actress and Bobby's mum will be there. You're to be nice to her and try not to talk about Gaelic football and bogger sports. She's really sophisticated.'

'This is the woman whose husband evades paying tax in his own country?'

'I'd appreciate it if you didn't actually say things like that to her. I don't want Bobby to dump me, thank you very much!'

'Are you writing the play yourselves?' I asked.

'Totally. We're making it way shorter. I mean, come on – who can remember five zillion lines? So we're doing a mini version in our own language, which is really cool.'

'Does your teacher approve of you rewriting Shakespeare?' Paul asked.

'Yeah, Mr Goggin's totally cool. He's new. He's only just qualified as a teacher so he's only, like, about twenty-two and he knows we all find Shakespeare a total snoozefest, so he suggested that we rewrite it in our own words so that we'd get a proper handle on the story. It's actually pretty cool because now everyone is really into the play and all the characters and we know what's going on and who betrays who and all that stuff. Our version is going to be so much better than the original.'

'Well, it'll be entertaining anyway.' Paul grinned.

'I really need to start studying now,' Ali said.

'Just one more spoon,' I told her.

'No. I've had enough. I'm going upstairs.' She hurried out of the kitchen and locked herself into the bathroom she shared with Sarah. I followed her up to make sure she wasn't making herself sick.

'Ali, are you all right?'

She opened the door. 'I'm fine. Please stop following me around. You're making me feel like a prisoner.'

'I'm just worried about you.'

'I ate my bloody dinner,' she shouted. 'Now can I be left alone to get on with my homework?'

'There's no need to be so rude. I just want you to get well again.'

'For the zillionth time, I'm fine. Now I have to study for my Christmas exams, so please leave me in peace.' She pushed past me to get to her bedroom and slammed the door in my face.

23

The next morning as I was sitting in work, sipping my coffee, looking over our upcoming events, desperately trying to distract myself from thinking about Ali for five whole minutes, Sally stormed into the office and flung her bag down. 'I hate my stupid family and I am never, ever going to one of their moronic parties again.'

'And a very good morning to you too.' I stood up and poured her a cup of coffee.

'Honestly, Ava, I've had it up to here with them all.' She sank into her chair.

'I take it last night wasn't a barrel of laughs.' She had been forced to go to her sister's house where a surprise party was thrown for her brother-in-law, Martin.

'It was a nightmare. Hilary should never have organized a surprise – it was a crap idea.'

'Was Martin surprised?'

'Hell, yeah!' Sally set the scene for me. 'So we were all hiding in the lounge when Martin came home. The first thing he said as he walked in the door was, "I have had the worst fucking day of my life. I had to lay off fifteen people. I don't want to speak to anyone. Take the phone off the hook. I need a bath."

'"Come in and have a drink and a chat," Hilary said, pulling him towards the lounge.

'"I don't want to sit down and talk, I want to soak in a hot bath and wash the day off me."

'"Just come in for a minute. A drink will do you good."

'"Jesus, Hilary, are you deaf? I've just had a fucking horrendous day and I want to be left alone for a while."

'Then there was some urgent whispering – "I don't fucking

believe this"; "Stop cursing, you're making a show of me"; "I told you I hate surprise parties, they're fucking ridiculous at my age"; "Everyone is here now, so just belt up and go in there with a smile on your face!"; "Oh, for fuck's sake".

'The door opened and everyone dutifully shouted, "Surprise!" Martin looked decidedly pissed off and Hilary was bright red with embarrassment.'

'Oh, the poor woman,' I said. I couldn't help laughing. 'That's a complete nightmare.'

'Well, a few drinks later and Martin was the happiest man there. He was going around slapping everyone on the back, thanking them for coming and cracking jokes. Meanwhile, I spent the night being introduced to the guests – all couples – explaining that, no, I didn't have children and I wasn't married.

'I'm telling you, Ava, as soon as I admitted to being single at a party full of couples, the women treated me differently. I went from being another wife and mother to a potential threat. Suddenly I was a single huntress who wanted to get into their husbands' pants at all costs. The fact that I wouldn't touch their husbands with a ten-foot pole was irrelevant to them.

'As for the men, some behaved normally and treated me like a regular human being, but most became overtly flirty and some tried it on. It was kind of like – I know you're a sad old spinster, but I'll grope your arse to make you feel a bit better about yourself, because being felt by me is such an honour.

'After two hours of this torture, I couldn't take another second of it. I headed home, where I curled up in front of reruns of *Sex and the City* and thanked God I wasn't married to some arsehole who went around groping single women. Maybe being on your own isn't so bad.'

'Where do these tossers get off groping you like that?' I fumed. 'As if they're doing you a favour!'

'It's so lame. They're such saddos. But the women are worse. They treat you like a leper.'

'I don't understand why they would do that. I'd never treat a single woman differently.'

'Hold on, if you were at a party with Paul and there was a single woman there who he was laughing and joking with for ages, are you telling me you wouldn't mind at all?'

'I might be curious as to who she was and what they were talking about, but I wouldn't make her feel bad.'

'After a while would you interrupt them?'

'I might go and say hi.' I began to smile.

'And would you leave them to it or would you stay and chat?'

'If she was attractive, I'd probably hang around for a bit.'

'You see?' Sally poked me in the shoulder. 'Even you would feel threatened. I know some of the wives don't mean to make me feel bad, but you constantly feel you're being watched and monitored because you are.'

'Yes, but I wouldn't go over and put my arm around Paul and stare the woman out of it. I'd just join in the conversation.'

'Yes, but you would feel threatened by the single woman, right?'

'Maybe a bit.'

'But why are you assuming she wants to sleep with your husband?'

'Because unfortunately I've seen single women coming on to Paul in the pub when I'm there. So it does happen and single women are more of a threat because they're looking for a man and some are very forward.'

'Fair enough, some single women are sluts, but take me, for example. Just because I'm looking to meet someone doesn't mean I want to sleep with every man I talk to. I like male company, and sometimes when you're single it's nice to go out and have fun with men. There's no ulterior motive, you just want to have a laugh. When you're single, you're with women all the time and it's nice to talk to guys too.'

'I can see that. I hate those parties where all the women end up at one end and the guys at the other. I always think they look like they're having more fun.'

'That's because most of the time they are. I've been stuck talking to married mothers about washing-machines, schools for kids and swimming lessons . . . It's so boring! You can be sure the guys are talking about fun things like sport, sex and cars.'

'I'd happily skip the car chat. But I have to say it really bugs me when single women come on to married men. It's disloyal to your own sex.'

'Well, I think both married women and single women can be equally horrible to each other.'

'Maybe we should write a book showing both points of view,' I said. 'It'd probably be a bestseller. We could call it *She-said, She-said*.'

'I'll drink to that,' Sally joked, holding up her coffee cup.

Later that day, when I got home, Charlie and Nadia were standing in the hall. Charlie had his car keys in his hand and Nadia was carrying a suitcase. Finally, she was going back to Poland. Fantastic.

'So you're off?' I said, proffering a hand.

'Yes. I am needing to do this before it too late.'

'Good idea. Well, good luck with it all.'

'Thanks you, Afa. I thinking you no approfe.'

'You're a bit young, that's all.'

'I thirty-eight. No so young.'

'You look a lot younger.'

'That because I am dancing efery night.'

'It does seem to keep you trim. Anyway, I hope everything turns out well for you.'

'I not afraid. I know this make my life better.'

'You're absolutely right. Best decision you've ever made.'

Nadia and Charlie looked at me quizzically.

'You're very positive all of a sudden. What's got into you?' Charlie wondered.

'Nothing. I just think that Nadia is doing the right thing. You seem to be taking it well.'

Charlie shrugged. 'She desperately wants to do it, so I'm trying to be supportive. As she said herself, it's her life. Who am I to stop her?'

'You're dead right. Let her go. It's best for everyone.'

'Come on, Charlie, I don't want to be late,' Nadia said.

'Goodbye, then,' I said, smiling at her. 'It's been nice knowing you. I hope you have a wonderful life.'

They both seemed taken aback. 'Why are you behaving so strangely?' Charlie asked.

'I'm just being nice. What's the big deal?'

'You're behaving as if you'll never see Nadia again.'

'Well, I probably won't.'

'Jesus, Ava, that's a terrible thing to say.'

'I'm sorry, but I'm just being honest.'

'You think she won't make it?'

'On the contrary, I think she'll do just fine.'

'Well, then, why did you say you wouldn't see her again?'

'Because I'm not planning any trips to Poland in the near future.'

'Poland?' Charlie exclaimed.

Nadia started to screech laughing. 'I understanding now. You think I leafing Eyerland. You see my bag and you think Nadia going back to Poland. Poor Afa, she thinks I not coming back.'

As Charlie realized the misunderstanding, he began to laugh too.

'What's so hilarious?' I demanded. 'Where are you going, if not back home?'

'I going for my boobie job,' Nadia announced.

My heart sank. So she wasn't leaving. I'd still have to face her every day until Charlie's new apartment was ready. I sighed. I could really do without Nadia parading her new boobs around my house.

'I decided to let her have her way and support her with the surgery,' Charlie explained. 'When I saw how unhappy Alison was with her mad dieting, trying to be thinner, I realized it was important for women to be happy with their bodies.'

'Come on, Charlie, I not being late.' Nadia tugged at my father's arm. Then turning to me she said, 'When I coming back, I looking like Pamela Anderson.'

'Oh, I've no doubt you will,' I muttered, under my breath.

'I'll be back later,' Charlie said, as Nadia walked out the door. Then, leaning over, he whispered in my ear, 'And I'd appreciate it if you were a bit more enthusiastic about the woman I love not emigrating back to Poland. What happened to the Irish being a welcoming nation?'

'May I remind you once again that it's my house she's been staying in, my food she's been eating and my hospitality she's been enjoying,' I hissed.

'It'd be nice if you could smile at her from time to time. She's a very sensitive soul. The Polish people have suffered a lot throughout the ages.'

'So I'm supposed to make up for centuries of injustice?'

'They had a very hard time with the Russians and the Germans.'

'I'm not Russian or German so why do I have to feel guilty about it? Or make up for it? Is she being nice to me because of the Famine?'

'Ireland remained neutral during the war and I think we have to make up for that.'

'I was born in 1966!'

'Charlie, mofe you arse,' Nadia roared from the car.

'I see what you mean about her sensitivity.'

'Everyone has their moments.' Charlie sprinted out of the door.

24

I took Sarah and Ali shopping to get some new clothes for the holidays. Sally said she'd come and help. Everything Ali tried on was too big for her.

'She's thrilled they're all too big. Did you see her smile? She hasn't smiled in months. She's actually getting a kick out of being so thin,' I whispered.

'That's the disease. The thinner you are the happier you are,' Sally said.

'I thought she was getting better. The sooner she sees the psychologist the better. Hopefully she can make her see how awful she looks.' I began to get upset.

'It'll be OK, Ava – you said she's eating more than before, which is great. It's slow but sure progress.'

'I know, but I think she looks worse. Then again, maybe that's because I'm now obsessed with her weight too.'

'Too big,' Ali called, from behind her dressing-room curtain.

'Let's see if these fit.' Sally went to hand Ali a bikini she'd found in the children's section – for a twelve-year-old. 'Here you go, Ali,' she said, handing it in. Ali pulled the curtain back a tiny bit and Sally caught a glimpse of her. When she turned back to me, her face was pale and she had tears in her eyes.

'I know,' I said. 'It's a million times worse when you see her with no clothes on.'

'Thank God you caught it before it got worse.'

'Check me out!' Sarah said, parading around in silver-sequined togs with a big hole cut out in the middle of the stomach.

'It's a bit Las Vegas for a family holiday,' I said.

'Come on, Sally, how cool is this?'

Sally laughed. 'Well, it certainly makes an impression.'

'Exactly. Who wants to blend into the background?'

'Clearly not you.' I smiled at her.

'Come on, Mum, all the other togs are so boring and conservative. I'm sixteen, not forty!'

'Don't say forty as if it's ancient,' Sally shook a finger at her. 'We forty-somethings are still hot.'

'Have you seen Mum's togs lately?'

'They do need updating,' I admitted.

'I'll be back in a jiffy.' Sally dashed off to find me a new improved swimsuit.

Ali came out of the dressing room in jeans and a sweatshirt, holding the twelve-year-old's bikini. 'It fits,' she said, looking pleased.

'Hey, Ali, whaddya think of my togs? Cool?'

'Wow, yeah, you look great. Really skinny.'

'Can I get it, Mum?' Sarah pleaded.

'Sure.' I was determined not to mess up Sarah's body image. If she felt good in that swimsuit, she could bloody well have it.

Sally came back with a red halter-neck model, simple, but sexy. I tried it on, and it looked good. I checked the price tag. Yikes! Sally really did have expensive taste.

I poked my head around the curtain. 'It's a bit pricy.'

'Show me it on you.' She looked into the dressing room. 'Ava, it's gorgeous and so flattering. You know Nadia's going to be parading about in a teeny-tiny bikini and you want to look your best. You're buying it. I bought a ridiculously expensive bikini yesterday because I want to look good beside Nadia, too.'

'Shouldn't we be comfortable in our bodies at this stage in our lives and not care what anyone else looks like?' I asked.

'Are you?'

'I'm buying the swimsuit.'

'Listen, are you absolutely sure you want me to tag along on your holiday?' Sally asked.

'For the zillionth time, yes. You'll be doing me a huge favour by coming out for a few days. It's hardly an intimate family holiday with Charlie and Nadia. And Paul's still in a grump because he doesn't want to be away from the pub on New Year's Eve, so it will be great to have you.'

'I'll book my flight for the thirtieth. You'll be well settled in by then and, hopefully, will have found a nice bar for us to get drunk in.'

When we got home I told Ali I wanted to weigh her. She started crying and begging me not to, but I insisted. Then she ran up to her bedroom and locked the door. I banged on the door and demanded that she come into the bathroom to be weighed. She reluctantly came out.

She stood on the scales. 'Seven stone. It's only two pounds but at least we're going the right way. Well done.' I smiled at her.

She actually seemed relieved. 'You see, Mum? I told you it wasn't a big deal.'

Two pounds. At this rate it would take months to get her weight back up. Please, God, may the holiday work.

We arrived in Tenerife after eight hours' travelling – I hadn't been able to book a direct flight so we had to change planes in Madrid and then there had been a two-hour delay. It was five o'clock in the afternoon and everyone was tired and grumpy. But once we stepped out into the warm sun, I knew I'd made the right decision. It was wonderful to feel the sun on my skin and gaze at a cloudless blue sky.

We piled into a taxi and I gave the driver the name of the hotel.

'Is it nice?' Sarah asked him.

'Yes, hotel is *muy bien*.'

'What does that mean?' Charlie wondered.

'It means it's very nice,' Ali explained.

'Why didn't you ask the driver in Spanish, Sarah? You've been studying it for three years. Surely you know how to ask if something is nice,' Paul said.

'For God's sake, Dad, we've just landed after travelling for, like, ten years. I don't feel up to practising my languages right now.'

'It is nice to try to speak other language. When peoples come to Poland we are happy when they are trying to speak Polish.'

Sarah leant over and said, '*Gracias, señor*,' loudly to the driver.

'So where are we going?' Charlie asked.

'The hotel is in a place called Los Cristianos. It's only fifteen kilometres from the airport. I booked it in a bit of a rush, but it looks nice. It's a small hotel with views of the harbour and beach.'

'Apparently Los Cristianos is mental. Milly said her sister came here last year with three friends and had a wild time. They never went to bed before nine a.m. The nightlife is supposed to be insane.'

Paul looked at me. 'Is she winding me up?'

'Well, no, actually. I made a last-minute booking so I had to Google the area afterwards. and it did mention a very lively nightlife.'

'Fantastic.' Charlie rubbed his hands together.

We drove past a pub called the Full Monty with a banner announcing Neil Down was performing that night. 'Maybe we should go there for dinner.' Paul grinned at me.

'I did the best I could under severe time pressure.'

'It's nice to be away,' Ali said.

'What's our curfew here?' asked Sarah. 'The Spanish don't go out till, like, midnight, so it should be four a.m.'

'In your dreams.' Paul laughed.

'When in Rome, Dad.'

'We're not in Rome.'

'Here we are.' Our driver pulled up to a small hotel, overlooking the beach. It was painted white and had red shutters and window-boxes overflowing with little purple and yellow flowers.

Everyone murmured their approval. 'It looks nice, but where's the pool?' Sarah wanted to know.

'Let's check in and find out.' I walked through the red door into a tiled reception area where we were greeted by Miguel, the manager. The hotel had thirty rooms and we were all on the third floor. The pool was on the roof. We arranged to meet up there in twenty minutes.

I walked out onto the balcony of my room and breathed in the fresh sea air. All I needed now was a sangria and some flamenco music. But instead I heard 'thump thump . . .'

I leant over the balcony to see where the music was coming from. To the left of the hotel, fifty yards from our balcony, there was a bar called Cock and Bull.

Paul came out. 'Tell me that's not Cher?'

'I'm afraid so. Look.' I pointed to the bar.

'Oh, shit – we're going to be listening to Eurotrash music all week.'

As if on cue, Rod Stewart's 'Do You Think I'm Sexy' blared out of the speakers.

'Stop – it's a form of torture.' Paul covered his ears.

'Don't worry. I brought ear plugs and there's always alcohol to numb the pain.'

'I like the sound of that. Come on – let's go for a swim and a beer.'

I put on my new red togs, which Paul whistled at – he hadn't whistled at me in a long time.

While he went for a swim, I lay on a sun-lounger and basked in the heat. I was feeling really good about myself until I saw Nadia strutting towards me in a teeny-tiny sparkly thong bikini. Her stomach was like a washboard. I tried not to let it bother me, but it did.

'Wow, look at Nadia. She looks hot,' Sarah said, lying down beside me. 'I must say, her boobs look really good. You can hardly see the scars. Maybe you should get yours done, Mum.'

'They look cheap. Parading around in a piece of string at thirty-eight is ridiculous.'

'Every guy here – even the younger ones – is staring at her.

189

Look, they're all drooling.' Sarah was impressed. 'Maybe I should get a thong too.'

I grabbed her arm. 'Don't even think about it. Your dad would hit the roof.'

Paul came over to dry himself. He looked pretty good in his togs, very toned from surfing. He plonked himself down beside us. 'The water's fantastic. Where are the others?'

'Ali's changing, and Charlie and Nadia are over there.' I pointed to the left where they were walking towards us with a tray of drinks.

'Jesus!' Paul said, when he saw Nadia. 'Doesn't leave much to the imagination, does it?'

'It's tarty.'

'She certainly makes an impression.'

'A bad one.'

Paul continued to stare at Nadia. I hit him on the arm. 'Stop gawking like a teenage boy.'

'I'm not. I'm just taking in the view.'

'Do you really think she looks good?'

'Careful, Dad,' Sarah warned. 'That's a loaded question.'

Paul finally turned his head away. 'No. I prefer my wife with her private parts covered and not on public display. And that goes for my daughters too,' he added, wagging a finger at Sarah.

'Well, you certainly don't have to worry about Ali exposing too much flesh,' Sarah said, as Ali walked towards us, huddled in her towelling robe.

'Drinks for everyone,' Charlie announced, setting down the tray. He was sporting togs with palm trees and coconuts on them. The same ones that most of the teenage boys were wearing.

While we drank our Cokes, Ali went for a swim. I kept an eye on her to make sure she wasn't exercising too much. But she was doing lap after lap. I asked Paul to tell her to stop. He bent down at the edge of the pool. 'Ali, you've done enough swimming. Why don't you come out and lie down for a bit? Get some sun. You could do with a bit of colour – you're very pale.'

'I'm not finished yet. I just need to do a few more laps.'

'Alison, this is not up for discussion. You are to get out now. No more swimming.'

'For God's sake,' she snapped, as she climbed out of the pool, quickly wrapping the robe around her so no one could see her emaciated frame.

But Paul had seen her. 'Jesus Christ, you're skin and bone. I knew you were thin but . . . Oh, Ali.' He turned to me. I just nodded. What was there to say? Now he had seen for himself how bad things had got. While I didn't like him to be upset, a part of me was glad. He'd back me up more now and not pass it off as a phase or a silly diet. He could see now how serious it really was.

Ali came over and sat beside me. Despite the heat she was shivering, so I wrapped an extra towel around her shoulders. 'The sun will warm you up in no time,' I said, rubbing her back. But it didn't. She continued to shiver and eventually went inside to get a jumper.

It was twenty-six degrees centigrade.

25

The next day after lunch, Ali went for a nap. Nadia had already gone to her room to lie down because she had burnt her bum – that's what sunbathing in thongs will do to you – and Paul was on his laptop as usual.

Charlie, Sarah and I decided to go to the beach. We got three sun-loungers side by side and a big umbrella for Charlie who couldn't really handle the heat. While Sarah and I soaked up the sun, Charlie treated us to cocktails from the beach bar. Sarah's was non-alcoholic, but mine was laced with rum and tasted great. Between keeping Ali out of the pool, supervising her at mealtimes and listening to Sarah moaning about how the hotel wasn't very cool, I hadn't really had any time to relax. Ali seemed to be eating, but she always ate the vegetables and hardly any meat. I had been arguing with her at every meal, trying to encourage her to eat more, but she just got angry or upset. It was draining and I was feeling the strain.

'Get that into you, Ava,' Charlie said, patting me on the back.

'Thanks. Cheers – to a good holiday,' I said.

Sarah snorted. 'Seriously, Mum, this place isn't exactly the Four Seasons. Bobby's family would never come here.'

'It's a four-star hotel in the sun. You should be thanking me for bringing you, not complaining.'

'Bobby was really worried I might go off with another guy, but I called him when we got here and I was, like, "Hello! You so don't have anything to worry about." He was all, "Oh, I bet you look really hot in your amazing sparkly togs," and I was, like, "Well, yeah, I do, but I wouldn't go near anyone here."'

'It's far from Buckingham Palace you were raised,' Charlie reminded her.

'Yeah, but that doesn't mean I can't marry a millionaire. Bobby's father is minted, so if we get married I'll be holidaying in the Four Seasons.'

'Where do you get these notions?' I marvelled at my daughter's warped mind.

'Look, Mum, I'm hot, I'm young and guys love me. Why shouldn't I go for a guy with money instead of a guy with none?'

'You should go out with someone because you like them, not because of the size of their wallet.'

'I love Bobby. I think he rocks. The fact that he's loaded is a bonus. Would I fall for a road-sweeper? No, because I wouldn't look at him in the first place.'

'Love works in mysterious ways,' Charlie assured her. 'Look at me falling for Nadia. Who would have thought it?'

'Wake up, Charlie, she saw you coming and set her sights on you. You're older, you have a few quid in the bank and you funded her plastic surgery. She chose you. You actually had nothing to do with it. Trust me, when a hot chick decides to go for a guy, he doesn't stand a chance. I decided at the beginning of the year that I was going to go out with Bobby and three weeks later I had him. It's a piece of cake, really. Men are very simple creatures. You laugh at their crappy jokes, you act like every story they tell you is the most amazing thing you've ever heard, you tell them how cool they are and do little things for them like helping them with their homework or making a fuss if they have a sports injury or a headache or whatever. Seriously, it's a no-brainer.'

'Hold on there a minute. Are you trying to tell me that I had nothing to do with getting Nadia to fall for me?'

'Nothing. She made you want to go out with her.'

'How?'

'Duh, Charlie, sex. She could see you were gagging for it. So she used the talents God blessed her with – her body. Even pre-boob job, she was pretty hot.'

'Where did we get you?' I wondered. 'If Ali had a tenth of your confidence she wouldn't be in the state she's in.'

Sarah shrugged. 'Ali's stunning and doesn't know it, which is a total waste. I know I'm gorgeous and I use it to my advantage. Besides, I'm miles more laid-back. I just don't get as stressed out as she does. I never did. Ali's always been a worrier. She used to worry about nuclear wars and stuff. I'm, like, why worry about that crap until it actually happens and then you'll be dead anyway, so who cares? Or if you and Dad had a fight she'd be all "Oh, no, they're going to get divorced," and I'm, like, "So what? It'd be quite cool if they do because then we'd get double the presents and attention." We're just different, thank God. Imagine two Alis!'

Imagine two Sarahs, I thought. The house couldn't fit two egos that size. She was right about Ali being a worrier, though: she always had been. I wondered if that had anything to do with her anorexia. I really hoped the psychologist would have some answers.

Sarah's phone rang. 'Hey, babe . . . I'm sitting here with two hot guys drinking margaritas and getting a serious tan . . . Duh, joking. I'm with my mum and Charlie drinking fruit juice. I told you, Bobby, there are no guys here I'd go near. This one guy came over yesterday and tried to chat me up by the pool, but he kept talking about football and lager and how cool he thought Justin Timberlake was . . . I know, he's so last year. Then he asked me what my favourite drink was so I told him it's a tall skim double-shot vanilla latte and he looked at me as if I was, like, foreign or something . . . I miss Starbucks . . . Ali? She's OK. She ate half a slice of toast this morning and we all had to do a Mexican wave. I suppose it's something . . . Yeah, my spray tan still looks good. You did a great job. How's yours? . . . Don't worry, I'll give you one as soon as I get back . . . I won't need one, I'll have a real tan! . . . Yeah, I know, I miss you too. Only five more days to go. Ciao.'

'Sarah, stop being such a snob. You weren't raised like that,' I scolded.

'What? The guy had clearly never been to Starbucks.'

'Starbucks is a coffee shop, nothing more.'

'Mum! Starbucks is a way of life. It does the best coffee in the world.'

'Stop talking rubbish and don't dismiss someone because they don't drink lattes.'

'Well, I'm not going to marry down, I'm going to marry up. I'm either going to be a famous actress or a trophy wife or a millionaire businesswoman.'

'Trophy wife?' I balked.

She shrugged. 'Why not marry someone with shedloads of cash and spend your days shopping and going for lunch and to glamorous parties every night? Look at Victoria Beckham – she has a great life.'

'She had a successful career before she got married,' I reminded my daughter.

'Have you heard her sing? She just got lucky and – fair play to her – she used it to her advantage. Maybe I should join a girl band. It seems like a cool way to meet really rich guys. Mind you, I'd have zero interest in marrying a footballer because you'd have to go to their matches and football's so boring. I'm think-ing a businessman with loads of offshore accounts, like Bobby's dad. That'd be cool.'

'Sarah, there will be no trophy wives in this family. Your father and I have spent a fortune on your education and you will have your own career and be self-sufficient. It's very impor-tant to have your own money. It gives you self-esteem. And if anything ever goes wrong with your marriage you'll be able to look after yourself and your children.'

'Thanks for the lecture, but I hadn't actually finished. After I marry the minted guy, I open my own boutique, which is a mas-sive success, and then I design my own brand of clothes – Haras Nellum – which is Sarah Mullen spelt backwards. How cool is that? The Haras brand goes global, gets bought out by, like, LMV or Armani or someone and I make zillions and that's how I become super-rich and famous.'

'It appears she has it all worked out,' Charlie said.

'Haras Nellum,' I said, laughing.

'It sounds like a Muslim greeting.' Charlie snorted.

'I don't know what you're laughing at,' Sarah huffed. 'I'm deadly serious. I know I'm going to be rich and famous. Some people just have it. Bobby says I totally have an X-factor about me. So, watch this space.'

The more she talked, the more hysterical we became and the grumpier she got. Eventually she stomped off. 'I'm going to call Bobby in private and tell him how lame my family is.'

When Sally arrived I was thrilled to see her. I had actually been feeling quite lonely – Ali spent most of her time in her room, but when she was with us, it was a constant struggle to get her to stop swimming and eat. Paul spent at least half the day on the phone to Johnny, his manager, or watching the pub on his laptop. Charlie and Nadia went off and did their own thing and Sarah was always texting Bobby.

'I am so glad you came,' I said, as we sat by the pool sipping a glass of wine.

'I'm thrilled to be here,' she said. 'It's cold and miserable at home, and being away for the dreaded New Year's Eve is such a relief. My sisters always feel they have to ask me over and it's difficult to come up with an excuse not to every year.'

'Do you think Ali looks any better? Does she look like she's put on any weight?' I asked my best friend.

'It's hard to tell with that big towelling robe wrapped around her,' Sally fudged. 'Is she eating more?'

'A little, but it's hard going. Every meal is an ordeal. I'm trying to be enthusiastic and upbeat and encouraging but sometimes I just want to get the food and stuff it down her throat. I know that's a shocking thing to admit but watching her chew every bite fifty times before she swallows is so frustrating. It's going to be a long road.'

'Hang in there. The beginning is bound to be the worst

part. I'm sure once she starts to feel better it'll be easier to manage.'

'I hope so.'

'Oh, my God,' Sally said, staring open-mouthed as Nadia sashayed towards us in bright pink high-heeled mules and a G-string bikini that consisted of three small pink fig leaves held together with thin gold straps. 'That's obscene.'

'Probably one of her work outfits.'

'I have to say she's in great shape for a thirty-eight-year-old. Maybe I should take up pole dancing.'

'You're fantastic as you are.'

'Her abs are amazing.'

'Believe me, I'm aware of how toned they are. I see them every day.'

We glanced at our own stomachs and took a gulp of our wine.

26

We all went out to dinner on New Year's Eve to a restaurant across the road from the hotel. Paul had spent most of the afternoon on the phone to the pub. I literally had to prise his mobile out of his hand before dinner. Everyone had dressed up, even Ali, although she was wearing a big cardigan over her dress. We sat down to dinner and I had the usual song and dance with Ali over what she ate. She'd say she was full, I'd tell her to have two more forkfuls. She'd say no, I'd plead and cajole . . . and on it went. It was like when they were toddlers and I'd try to get them to eat vegetables. They'd push their plates away and clamp their little mouths shut, and I'd have to pretend the spoon was a plane or a train, and if that didn't work I'd bribe them with the promise of sweets. Unfortunately there was no food I could bribe Ali with.

Sally, Paul and Sarah pitched in and we managed to get her to eat a little more. Once the main course was over, I ordered Ali some ice cream and watched her mash it up and play with it for ten minutes, only licking her spoon when she caught me glaring at her. I tried not to lose my temper. Keeping calm was important, but it was New Year's Eve and I was tired, emotionally drained and fed up.

Suddenly Charlie cleared his throat and stood up. 'I'm glad you're all here because I wanted you to be witnesses to what I'm about to do.'

With that, he got down on one knee, took Nadia's hand and said, 'Nadia, you have made me the happiest man in Ireland these last few months.'

'I think it's more like weeks,' Sarah said.

'Don't interrupting Charlie,' Nadia snapped.

'Charlie! What are you doing?' I asked, trying to pull him back into his chair. He swatted me away.

'Well, he's not breaking up with her,' Paul whispered.

'And so, I am asking you, Nadia, if you will do me the honour of being my wife.'

'Wait!' I interrupted. 'Charlie, listen to me, why can't you just live together? Why do you have to get married?'

'Ava, we've discussed this already. Stop trying to ruin my romantic moment,' Charlie grumbled, and took a ring out of his pocket.

'I does. I does. I does,' Nadia shrieked, grabbing it and clamping it on her finger.

'Is that Mum's ring?' I gasped. 'The one I asked you to keep for the girls?'

'Oh, shit,' Sally mumbled.

Charlie looked a bit sheepish.

'No girls' ring. My ring,' Nadia said, admiring my mother's diamond ring.

'Their boyfriends can buy them rings,' Charlie said.

'They'll have to now.' I was furious.

'It's cool, Mum, seriously,' Sarah said. 'It's way too small for me. My engagement ring is going to be three times the size of that or there won't be a wedding.'

'It's fine with me too,' Ali said. 'I'll probably never get married anyway.'

'Of course you will, you're a real catch,' Paul said, putting his arm around her. It looked enormous on her tiny shoulders.

'Right, well, that's sorted. Let's toast the bride-to-be,' Charlie said, and ordered a bottle of champagne while I tried, in vain, to look pleased at the idea that Nadia was going to be my new stepmother.

'Come on, Ava, you can do better than that,' Paul murmured in my ear.

'No, I bloody can't.'

'He's sixty-eight – you can't stop him,' Sally reminded me.

'He's making another huge mistake.'

'We all know that, but it's his big night so we just have to try to be happy for him,' Paul urged.

'Look on the bright side. Maybe it'll be third time lucky. Charlie married your Mum for love. The second time he married Catherine because she was good fun – far too much fun, as it turned out. This time he's marrying for pure lust. Who knows? It could work.' Sally was doing her best.

'She's a money-grabbing wench. Even Magda says so,' I hissed.

'He's happy,' Paul said. 'Look at him. He's the happiest he's been since he discovered Catherine was a roaring alcoholic.'

He had a point. Charlie did look happy. But the whole thing was insane. He had jumped into marriage with Catherine and look how that had turned out. This was headed in the same direction. Nadia didn't love him. How could he be so naïve? Why did he have to rush into marriage? I didn't want to see him get hurt again. 'But she's a gold-digger,' I mumbled.

'If that's how he wants to live out his twilight years, who are we to judge?' Paul said.

'I've had one awful stepmother. I don't want another. Why is he so clueless?'

'He's not clueless, he just doesn't care. He likes her.'

Charlie was sitting with his arm around Nadia, beaming. Nothing and no one would ever persuade me that this was a good idea, but I decided to make an effort for Charlie's sake. 'Well, cheers to you both.' I raised my glass.

'Well done.' Sally squeezed my arm.

'I'd like my granddaughters to be bridesmaids,' Charlie announced.

'As long as we can choose our own outfits,' Sarah said.

'No problem.'

'Congratulations, guys,' Ali said, going over to kiss them both. 'I'm heading off to bed now. Goodnight.'

I watched her walk into the hotel, pulling her cardigan around her – still thin, still cold, still unhappy.

The rest of us stayed in the restaurant to ring in the New Year. At half eleven Paul's phone buzzed. He took the call and then came over to me. 'Sorry, Ava, there's a problem in the pub. I have to go back to the room – I need my laptop. Hopefully it won't take too long to sort out.'

He was gone before I could respond. I sat back and sighed. Sarah said she wanted to go and call Bobby, then Charlie and Nadia got up and said they were going for a moonlight walk on the beach.

'Happy bloody new year,' I said, draining my glass.

'It's not that bad,' Sally said.

'Isn't it? My husband's holed up in our hotel room watching his pub on his computer! My father has just got engaged to a pole dancer and my daughter won't eat.'

'When you put it like that it doesn't sound so good.'

'Let's get really drunk.' I ordered a bottle of wine and twenty cigarettes. My family had driven me to drink and smoking.

One bottle led to another and then I insisted on going to a night-club. 'I'm not going back to my room until the sun comes up,' I announced. 'I need a blow-out. Come on, we're going dancing.'

'OK, but maybe you should have a bottle of water so you don't pass out.'

'To hell with water. Let's do shots.'

'Whatever you say.'

We went to Mambo, a local club, and sat up at the bar. I ordered tequila – I hadn't drunk it since I was in college and ended up with alcohol poisoning after consuming half a bottle at a twenty-first-birthday party. 'To a successful year at Happy Dayz,' I said, toasting Sally and knocking back the shot.

'To parents with pots of money, no sense and spoilt kids,' Sally said.

'To my best friend. I hope you meet Mr Right or, if not, then I hope you meet lots of gorgeous Mr Wrongs to have fun with,' I slurred.

'I'll drink to that.' Sally laughed. 'And here's to Ali getting better and to Paul working less.'

'Fat chance.' I drank anyway.

'Can I buy you ladies a drink?' the barman asked. I peered at him. He wasn't bad-looking. His deep tan was set off by a very white shirt, open to the navel to reveal a smooth, hairless chest. He had dark eyes and black hair with flecks of grey in it.

'Yes, you most certainly can. What's your name?' I asked.

'Carlos.'

'I'm Ava and this is my friend, Sally.' But Sally wasn't paying attention because she was being chatted up by an English guy who had just arrived at the bar.

'Ava is a beautiful name,' Carlos told me.

'Thank you. Your English is very good.'

'That's because ninety per cent of my customers are English.'

'Do you like working here?'

'I hope so – I own it.'

'Oops, sorry, I didn't realize.'

'No problem. Now, what can I get for you, beautiful Ava?'

'Surprise me!' I giggled like a schoolgirl. This was fun – I was having fun. I was still young and attractive. To hell with everyone, I deserved to have a good night out.

Carlos served me up some kind of cocktail that had smoke coming out of it. At this stage I would have drunk pond water. I knocked it back in three gulps.

'Slowly, Ava, there is a lot of alcohol in there.'

'I need it.'

'You are sad?'

'No, I'm demented.'

'Your husband is a bad man?'

'Not bad, neglectful. My father is a lunatic and my daughter won't eat.'

'You don't have a daughter! With a body like this, I can't believe it.'

'Oh, Carlos, you're good at this.'

'You have very beautiful eyes.'

I leant forward. 'Really?'

'Yes, they are like emeralds. And your mouth is like a rose.'

'And is my hair like woven silk?' I giggled.

'Yes, and your breasts are like two perfect melons.'

'And is my skin like satin?'

'*Exactamente!*' He took my hand and kissed the inside of my wrist. It was nice, and I felt all tingly.

'Let's dance, Carlos. I never dance any more. I used to love dancing. I was really good. My husband and I went to clubs all the time, but then we had kids and jobs and now we never go anywhere.'

'Come on, *mi amor*, I will dance with you all night.'

Carlos helped me down from the bar stool and led me onto the dance-floor, where I proceeded to shake, writhe and twirl like a mad person. Sally and her new friend, Fred, came to join us. Carlos went to talk to the DJ and suddenly a slow song came on. It was Céline Dion's 'My Heart Will Go On', which Sally and I proceeded to sing along to, screeching at each other while Fred and Carlos tried to prise us away to dance.

I found myself being swept around the dance-floor with Carlos pressed up against me, leaving me in no doubt that he wanted to have sex with me. Just in case I hadn't felt the enormity of his hard-on, he whispered into my ear, 'I want to make love to you all night long.'

Suddenly all the twirling was making me feel a bit queasy and his aftershave was very pungent. 'I just need to pop to the toilet,' I said, tapping Sally on the shoulder as I passed her. She followed hot on my heels.

'I think I'm going home with Carlos,' I announced, splashing water on my face.

'No, you're not. You're just having some fun and then you're going to your own bed and your husband.'

'Maybe I won't,' I said, flicking my hair. 'Carlos said I'm the sexiest woman he's ever met and he wants to make me scream with desire.' I started laughing.

'Fred's a lot more eloquent.' Sally giggled. 'He said I'm the best bit of Irish totty he's ever seen.'

'Oh, God, Sally, what are we like?'

'We're two friends having a bit of fun.'

We heard someone knocking on the door. 'Ava, *guapa*, I am waiting for you,' Carlos shouted.

'Coming, just one second,' I said, trying not to laugh. 'What are we going to do?' I slurred. 'Maybe I should just go for it.'

'No, no, no.' Sally wagged an unsteady finger in my face. 'Come on, I'm getting you out of temptation's way.' She grabbed my hand and pulled me towards the emergency door in the corner of the Ladies. We pushed it open, setting off a piercing alarm, and ran back to the hotel, laughing hysterically all the way.

Paul was awake when I stumbled in. 'Where the hell were you?'

'Out having a good time.'

'It's six in the morning. I was worried.'

'It was New Year's bloody Eve. You're supposed to go out and have a good time. We've never spent New Year together because of the pub and the one time I get you to come away you spend it in the hotel room on the phone.'

'Johnny needed my advice,' he snapped.

'Did he? Or did you just need to feel you were in charge?'

'There's no point talking to you – you're drunk.'

'Gee, I wonder why. Maybe it was because my life is pretty stressful right now and I could do with some bloody support,' I said, beginning to cry.

'I know I messed up tonight, but I am here for you, Ava.'

'It doesn't feel like it. I need more help with Ali.'

'Look, January's always quiet in the pub. I'll be around more, I promise.'

There he goes again, I thought, fitting us in around the pub. I lay down on the bed and passed out.

27

We arrived home on 2 January. Ali and I had an appointment with Mary Boland, the psychologist, for Monday morning. It was a relief to know that I'd be getting Ali seen by more professionals. I needed all the help I could get.

On the Sunday evening I phoned Sally to remind her that I'd be late into work the next day because I had to take Ali to the doctor. 'OK,' she croaked. 'No problem.'

'You sound exhausted. Were you out last night?'

'I certainly was.'

'I know that giggle, Sally Keene. Tell me everything.'

Sally started talking and didn't draw breath . . .

Her friend Judy, having woken up on New Year's Day feeling depressed at the thought of facing into yet another year alone, had decided to throw a post-New Year's Eve party for all the single people she knew. You just had to turn up with one single heterosexual male you were not dating and a bottle of booze. Sally had no plans for Saturday so she bribed her friend Mark to go with her. He had recently been dumped and was feeling very angry.

For the first hour or so everyone was very polite and made small-talk, while coyly eyeing up any talent in the room. But the drinks flowed and soon inhibition went out of the window. Unfortunately the alcohol fuelled Mark's bitterness towards women and he ended up abusing some poor girl. Sally could hear him roaring, 'You're all the same. Bitches, the whole lot of you.'

'Who brought that nutter?' Judy asked. Sally shrugged her shoulders and denied any knowledge of Mark.

She decided to hide behind the Christmas tree in case he saw her and came over. She was crouching down when she heard a noise. She was not alone in the hiding place. A very attractive man was huddled behind the other side of the tree, looking terrified.

'Who are you hiding from?' he asked.

'That lunatic is the male friend I brought to the party. I'm disowning him,' she whispered. 'What about you?'

'My ex-wife has just turned up and she has some serious anger issues. Maybe I should introduce her to your friend – they might hit it off.'

'Or kill each other.' Sally giggled. 'Why is your wife so angry? Did you cheat on her?'

'Why does everyone presume that men cheat on women?'

'Because they do.'

'OK, fair point, but in this case, she had an affair and when I left her and proceeded to move on with my life, she decided she wanted me back. Needless to say I told her to take a hike and she went doo-lally.'

'What did she do?'

'She set my car on fire.'

'Were you in it?'

'Are you joking? I'd be six feet under – she doused it in petrol.'

'Wow. I kind of admire that.'

'You do?'

'It's a very passionate thing to do.'

'And psychotic.'

'It's fiery.'

'And mad.'

'Sizzling.'

'And insane.'

'Hot.'

'So you're good at synonyms. Can I kiss you now?'

The last time someone had asked Sally if they could kiss her, she was sixteen years old at the local disco. There was something incredibly nice about being asked as opposed to being lunged at. 'Shouldn't we exchange names first?' She smiled at her fellow fugitive.

'Sorry, of course. Simon.'

'Sally,' she said, proffering a hand as he leant in and kissed her. Just as she was savouring the moment, she felt a sharp pain on the side of her head. 'Ouch.'

When she looked up, a very angry woman was wielding a wooden Santa Claus. She was smaller than Sally with shoulder-length black hair and a very straight fringe that gave her a French look. She was very pale, with a lot of dark eye-liner around her brown eyes and blood-red lipstick. The overall effect should have been sexy but she had overdone it and looked a bit like a vampire.

'Get off my husband, you dirty slapper.'

'Back off, Maura, we're not married any more,' Simon said, and made a grab for the Santa, but Maura was too quick for him. She belted him over the knuckles with it. 'Ouch!'

Then she lunged again at Sally, who panicked and gave the Christmas tree a big shove. It swayed briefly and fell down on top of the mad wife. All you could see were her shoes sticking out from under it, like the Wicked Witch of the East's – Sally kept expecting the Munchkins to appear singing 'Ding Dong The Witch Is Dead'.

She couldn't believe it. Why was she so unlucky? She had finally met a nice guy and now she'd gone and killed his wife in self-defence. How many years would the judge give her – ten? By the time she got out of prison she'd be fifty-three and would have no chance of meeting a man.

A loud screeching woke her from her reverie. 'Get this tree off me,' roared Maura.

'Run before she gets freed,' whispered Simon. He grabbed Sally's hand and sprinted out of the door.

They stopped running at the corner of the road to catch their breath. 'Do you think I did any permanent damage?' Sally puffed.

'God, I hope so,' he said, and they started laughing.

'Was she like that when you married her?'

'Put it this way, my stag turned into a kind of intervention with my mates telling me to dump her. They all said I was making a huge mistake.'

'And you ignored them.'

'I thought she was feisty and spontaneous. I liked that.'

'Feisty is different from certifiable.'

'I know that now. I was brought up by very strict Quaker parents. Emotional outbursts were not encouraged. I found Maura fascinating.'

'That's one word for her. I'd say life was never dull.'

'No, it was exhausting, and then she had the affair and I packed my bags and ran.'

'How long were you married?'

'Six years.'

'Kids?'

'Thankfully, no. We tried but it never happened. I'm glad now. Imagine having a mother like that.'

'They'd never have been normal with her DNA.'

'So . . .'

'So . . .'

'Can I invite you back to my place for coffee?' Simon asked.

'How about my apartment for sex?'

'Direct. I like it.'

'I'm forty-three. I don't have time to be coy.'

He pulled her close and kissed her. 'Happy Newish Year.'

She smiled. Maybe it actually would be.

'Oh, my God, Sally, that's fantastic.' I was absolutely thrilled for her. She sounded really excited and happy. 'So, what happened when you got back to your place?'

'We ripped each other's clothes off and had sex.'

'Was it fantastic? Go on, make me jealous.'

'Honestly? No. It was nice, it was comfortable, it was pleasant but it wasn't fantastic. We had so much chemistry I thought it was going to be amazing, but it really wasn't.'

'Well, maybe it was drink or nerves or something. Don't worry, it might be better the next time.'

'I'm not worried because I haven't told you the second part of the story yet . . .'

That morning, when Sally was making coffee, Simon came in. He was even cuter in daylight – except for his hair, which was weird. Maybe it was just bed-head, she thought. He shuffled about uncomfortably. 'Morning.'

'Hey there, would you like some coffee?'

'Great, thanks.'

'So, how'd you sleep?' Sally asked, trying to get the conversation going.

'Not very well.'

'Oh.'

'Look, Sally, about last night –'

Here we go, she thought. He's going to tell me he had a nice time but he's not ready for anything, he's just come out of a marriage, he needs space, I'm a nice girl but this is not going anywhere, blah, blah, blah.

'I don't feel that I, uhm, well, that I was, uhm, up to scratch as it were.'

'What?'

'It's just that, without blowing my own trumpet, I'm usually better than that and I just feel I'd like another chance to . . . I got stage fright or something and I don't want you to think that last night is a true reflection of –'

She leant in and kissed him. 'Before you talk me to death, I think we should go back to bed.'

Thankfully, this time it wasn't gentle or nice. It was passionate and energetic, with banging headboards and even a little spanking. It was fantastic. As they lay wrapped around each other, panting from their exertions, they heard shouting outside.

'WHORE! A WHORE LIVES IN THIS APARTMENT BLOCK. SALLY KEENE IS A PROSTITUTE.'

Simon groaned. 'I'm so sorry – it's Maura.'

'How the hell does she know where I live?'

'She must have asked someone at the party.'

'We have to get rid of her. I don't want my neighbours hearing this.'

'I'll go and talk to her,' he said, getting up.

'No, I'll deal with this,' she said, pulling on her dressing-gown. She looked out the window. Simon's ex was directly below, shouting her head off. Sally filled a bucket with cold water, opened the window and poured it on her head. 'Now fuck off home, you psycho, or I'll call the police.'

She slammed the window and turned around to find Simon gaping at her.

'What? You hardly thought I was going to invite her in for breakfast? She needed to cool down.'

He came over and kissed her. 'Maura may have met her match.'

28

Paul insisted on coming to the meeting with Mary Boland. He was still feeling guilty about New Year's Eve and was trying to make it up to me.

We arrived at the surgery with Ali, dressed in her usual baggy clothes, shivering. I was worried she'd caught some bug on the flight home.

Mary Boland came out to greet us. She was an attractive woman; small, short dark hair, smartly dressed, in her late fifties. She had a confident, assured way about her and didn't seem shocked by Ali's appearance.

We introduced ourselves and sat down.

'Welcome, all of you. Now, from what Dr Garner has told me, Alison, you've not been eating lately and your periods have stopped. Is that right?'

'No, I am eating now and I've put on weight, so I really don't need to be here at all.'

'All right. Well, let me be the judge of that. You look very pale. Are you feeling tired and a bit down in the dumps?'

'No, honestly, I'm fine. My parents are just overreacting. I feel great.' Despite her protestations, Ali began to cry. I handed her a tissue and rubbed her back.

'I can see you're very unhappy. A lovely young girl like you should be out playing sports and going to parties. I'm going to do everything I can to help you. So, let's start by weighing you to see if you put on any weight over the holidays.'

Ali stood up and walked over to the scales.

'Take off your big jumper and empty your pockets, please,' Mary said.

'There's nothing in my pockets.'

'Can you show me?'

Ali blushed. 'There's nothing to show.'

'Alison, I need you to empty your pockets.' Mary stood with her hands out.

Ali slowly took out two large stones and placed them in Mary's palms.

'Oh, Jesus!' I gasped.

'What's going on?' Paul was confused.

'Lots of patients try to hide their weight loss by filling their pockets with stones or wearing heavy jewellery or drinking litres of water before a weigh-in. I've seen all the tricks. All right, Alison, let's see what you really weigh.'

Ali reluctantly stood up on the scales.

'Six stone three.'

I stuffed my hand into my mouth to stop myself screaming.

Paul gasped. 'I thought she was seven stone when we went on holidays?'

'She was,' I croaked.

'But she ate on holidays – we watched her all the time. Jesus, we spent hours trying to encourage her to eat more. How could she lose all this weight?' Paul began to pace the room. Then, turning to Ali, he said, 'I don't understand – what the hell are you doing? What's going on here?'

'It's no big deal. It's just a few pounds.' Ali pulled her arms around herself protectively.

'Alison probably wasn't seven stone when you last weighed her,' Mary explained. 'Alison, did you have stones in your pockets when you were last weighed?'

Ali nodded.

'Oh, Ali, why did you lie to me?' I fought back tears. 'I was trying to help you.'

Mary walked Ali back to her chair and sat down beside her, holding her hand. 'Alison, do you understand that you are now dangerously underweight?' she said gently. 'Our bodies need food to survive. If we don't eat, we die. It's as simple as that.

You're a beautiful young girl who has her whole life ahead of her. But I can see you're struggling with this. So we're going to get you the help you need to get better.'

Ali began to cry.

Mary patted her back. 'It's all right – you're here now and we're going to help. I know how hard this is for you. But we've caught the anorexia early, which is very good news, and you have a supportive family, which is also very important to your recovery. Don't you worry, we'll have you smiling and laughing again soon.'

Ali was shaking. I went over to her. She didn't shrug me away. She rested her head on my shoulder and sobbed.

'It's OK, pet, we're all here to help,' I said, stroking her hair.

Paul was wearing a hole in the carpet.

'Why don't you sit down, Paul? I'd like to talk to you and Ava,' Mary said.

He collapsed into a chair and I managed to calm Ali down. Mary then asked her if she would wait outside. 'I want to talk to your parents for a minute and then we can have a group discussion on how to move forward with your treatment.'

The minute the door closed I couldn't hold back the tears. 'What do we do now? Is she going to die? I thought she was eating more – I watched her like a hawk. I don't understand how she could have lost so much weight.' My mouth had gone completely dry. I was in shock.

'People suffering from anorexia become very cunning. You can't watch Alison twenty-four hours a day. She was probably exercising all night while you were asleep and hiding food up her sleeves or in her napkin. An anorexic will always find ways to lose weight. The important thing here is that we act immediately.'

'Just tell us what we need to do. Please just help us make her better. Where is the best place for treatment?'

'Unfortunately the healthcare system here provides almost no assistance or funding for people with eating disorders. There are currently three public hospital beds and an estimated two hundred thousand sufferers.'

'But that's a joke. How can there only be three beds? It's a bloody disgrace,' Paul ranted. 'We're like a third-world nation when it comes to healthcare. How the hell is anyone supposed to get better? You look at the system in France, it's –'

'Will Ali be able to get one of the beds?' I cut across him. I didn't want to discuss the shagging state of the healthcare system. I just wanted to make my daughter better.

'Unfortunately they're only for the over-eighteens.'

'But how will she get better?' I was panicking. How could there be no help when hundreds of thousands of people were sick?

'The only way for you to make sure that Alison is treated straight away is to get her into the Gretta Lyndon Clinic, where I also work. It has an excellent eating-disorders unit with amazing results. I would recommend that Alison goes in as a full-time patient for a few weeks. I have to warn you it will be expensive.'

'I don't care how much it costs. Please just get her a place.' I would have sold my soul to the devil to make Ali better.

'Now, just hold on a minute here,' Paul interrupted. 'I'm not locking my daughter up in some nuthouse.'

'I can assure you the clinic is the furthest thing from a nuthouse. It's a warm, modern, open facility that cares deeply about its patients. I really think Alison would benefit from going there. Once she starts eating and gains weight, she'll be put on an outpatient programme. But for now I would urge you to admit her on a full-time basis for a few weeks to kick-start her recovery.'

'Whatever you say. Will she be OK? Will they cure her?' I was like a needy child. I wanted Mary to tell me that Ali was going to be fine, that I had nothing to worry about, that she and her team would fix her and that I'd have my daughter back – the old Ali, the wonderful Ali, not this stranger who lied and hid things and was angry all the time.

'They have a very high success rate, especially with teenage anorexia, and Alison should be fine. But the sooner she gets proper care the better her chances of a full recovery become.'

'So you don't think she's going to die.' I was desperate for reassurance.

'With the correct help, I'm confident she'll make a full recovery.'

'Ava,' Paul said, turning me by the shoulders to face him, 'we are not sending our seventeen-year-old to be locked up in this place. I don't care how good it is. She can come and have sessions with Mary and we'll watch her more closely at home.'

'We have been watching her,' I snapped, 'and she's got much worse. She's starving herself to death. We need help.'

'I'm not locking her up. There must be another way.' Paul dug his heels in.

I didn't want to argue in front of Mary, but I lost my temper. 'Jesus, Paul, I'm not happy about this either, but Ali could die. You need to get that into your thick head. It's not a diet or some silly teenage phase. Our daughter has a serious problem.'

Mary stepped in. 'It could take up to a week before I can get Alison admitted. In the meantime, why don't you see if you can persuade her to eat? If she does gain weight before she's due to go to the clinic, we can reassess the situation.'

'Excellent. We'll get her back on track this week,' Paul said, pleased.

I wanted to punch him. How could he be so naïve? Ali was beyond our help. She needed professional and experienced people who knew how to cure her.

Mary called Ali back in and gently explained to her that if she didn't start putting on weight immediately she would have to go to a clinic for a few weeks to get better. 'It's a very nice place, so don't worry if you do have to be admitted. But if you manage to put on weight by yourself, then we can look at an out-patient programme for you.'

'Forget the clinic. We'll sort you out, Ali.' Paul put his arm around her. 'You just need to get your appetite back.'

Mary took Ali's blood pressure. It was very low. 'Alison, you must rest as much as possible, no exercise at all, and try to eat small amounts of food regularly. OK?'

'OK,' Ali whispered.

'Come on, let's get you home.' Paul walked Ali out to the car.

Mary handed me an information leaflet about the clinic. I took it and tried to say thank you, but a strange noise came out of my mouth. She put her hand on my shoulder. 'You've had a shock today. It's impossible to process all the information at once. Go home and think about your options. I'll call you as soon as I have a bed for Alison in the clinic and you can decide what to do then. Stay strong, Ava.'

I walked to the car in silence. My hands were shaking violently and I couldn't get my seatbelt on. Ali was crying silently in the back seat. 'Why are you doing this to yourself? I don't understand?' I wailed. 'Why do you want to starve yourself like this? Why, Ali? Why?' I beat the dashboard with my fists.

'I'm sorry, Mum. Please don't send me away to that clinic. I'll eat, I promise.'

'Stop shouting at her. The poor girl's in a state.' Paul glared at me. 'Don't worry, Ali, you're not going to any clinic.'

'Are you deaf?' I shouted. 'She's really bad. You can't fix this with one bloody meal.'

'Calm down, you're upsetting Ali. I'll sort this mess out.'

'Thanks, Dad. I'll eat now, I promise,' Ali said.

'See?' Paul said to me. 'There's no need to panic.'

I gripped my bag and stared out of the window. There was no point arguing with him when he was like this. I knew Ali wouldn't eat, but he had to see it for himself. I'd let him take charge of her meals for a day or two so he could see first hand that he was dealing with a serious illness.

When we got to the house, Charlie, Nadia and Sarah were in

the lounge watching an old video of the kids that Charlie had taken years ago. In it, Ali was wearing a little nurse's uniform and she was carefully wrapping a bandage around Sarah's head. They were five and three and a half, so happy and carefree. My heart ached.

Charlie looked up and noticed my blotchy face. 'What happened?'

Everyone turned to us.

'Ali's very sick. She's lost more weight.'

Charlie went over to hug Ali, who was crying. Sarah sat open-mouthed on the couch with Nadia. Then she said, 'How much more?'

'Nearly a stone.'

'Oh, my God!' Sarah's eyes welled up.

'What did the psychologist say?' Charlie asked.

'Ali may need to go to a clinic for a while, to get help.'

'No, she won't, because we're going to make her better here at home,' Paul said. 'If Ali puts on weight in the next few days, she'll be staying with us.'

'I'll eat, I promise,' Ali said.

'Ali, I just want you to get the best help so you can get better quickly and put all this behind you,' I explained.

'But you'll eat now, won't you, Ali?' Sarah said. 'I mean, now that you understand you have anorexia and you've accepted it you can start eating. Right?'

'You ate a bit more when we were in Tenerife, didn't you?' Charlie asked her.

'Yeah, I did,' Ali said.

'It probably takes a few days for that weight to show up on the scales,' said Paul, 'so we all need to calm down.'

'She not eating in Tenerife. I see her putting the food into the napkin when you no looking,' Nadia announced.

'What?' I said.

'Only once and it was because I didn't like it,' Ali tried to explain.

217

'I saw her putting food into her napkin in Tenerife too and she was exercising in the bathroom every night,' Sarah said.

'Shut up, you bitch,' Ali shouted.

'I'm sorry, Ali.' Sarah's voice quivered. She looked at me. 'Ali was doing star jumps in the toilet for hours – I could hear her – and when I told her to stop she wouldn't and I could see it was hurting her to do them.'

Paul was staring at Ali. 'Why did you do that?' he asked.

'Because she's sick,' I reminded him, for the millionth time.

'I'm not *sick*,' Ali screamed. 'You're all overreacting. It's just a few pounds.'

My phone rang. It was Mary Boland. Ali had a place in the clinic, starting on Wednesday, or if we wanted to wait and see if she put on weight we could have a bed the following Monday.

I walked outside to speak to Mary. 'Book us in for Wednesday.'

'I think that's wise,' she said.

I knew Ali was beyond our help. I now had two days to convince my husband.

29

Later that day I tried talking to Paul alone to get him to consider the clinic. 'It's like this. If Ali had cancer, we'd send her to hospital for chemotherapy. If we don't treat it, the anorexia could kill her. We've tried and failed miserably to help her. We need professionals – more importantly, *she* needs them. We don't know what we're dealing with. Look how bad it's got in only a few months. I've been researching it on the Internet and the most important thing with anorexia is to treat it early with proper professional input. We have to make up for lost time. We have to act now.'

'We are acting. We'll continue taking her to doctors and psychologists and whoever else she needs to see, but I am *not* locking her up in a clinic and that's final. She promised me she'd eat a good dinner tonight.'

'Well, you can cook it and sit with her on your own and persuade her to eat it. And when you've succeeded, hell will have frozen over,' I said, and stormed out of the room.

Paul went to Ali's bedroom and told her to come down and have some dinner with him. They went into the kitchen and he cooked her a bacon sandwich. It had been one of her favourites.

I hovered outside, listening.

'What are you doing?' Charlie came up behind me.

'Listening to see how Paul's getting on.'

'Is he having any luck?'

'Not so far and he won't either.'

'You never know, he might get her to eat.'

'No, Charlie, he won't. Ali's too far gone. He just doesn't realize it yet. I've tried to explain it, but he is so stubborn.'

'Go easy on him. Men like to fix things. It's what we do – if something's broken, we fix it. Paul just wants to make Ali better.'

'But he can't and we can't waste any more time trying. She's really bad, Charlie,' my voice began to quiver, 'and she needs to get into that clinic as soon as possible. I want to fix her too – I'm just more realistic about it.'

Charlie hugged me as I cried quietly into his shoulder. 'I'll talk to Paul later, pet, and see if I can convince him. Let him try this first. He needs to do it.'

'Thanks, Charlie.' I kissed him on the cheek.

'I'm off out to meet George for a pint. I'll be back at eleven and I'll talk to Paul then.'

'OK.' I watched my father walk out of the house and then went back to listening at the kitchen door. I could hear Paul chatting to Ali, trying to cajole her into eating.

'Listen, Ali, men like women with flesh on their bones. Why do you think Sophia Loren and Marilyn Monroe and Halle Berry and Eva Mendes are considered sex symbols? Because curvy is sexy. No guy finds skinny girls attractive. Now come on, eat up.'

Half an hour went by.

'Is there something you want to talk about? You can tell me anything. If you're in trouble or upset about something, I'll help you. That's what dads are here for. We fix things.'

Then an hour.

'Ali, you have to eat up. If you don't you'll have to go to the clinic and I know you don't want to go there and I don't want to send you, but if you don't eat I won't be able to stop it happening. I'll tell you what, if you have a few small bites, I'll get you the new iPhone. Come on, Ali – for God's sake, it's just a bacon sandwich.'

An hour and a half. Suddenly I heard a raised voice.

'Just eat the sandwich . . . Do you want to go to that place? . . . Well, then, put it in your bloody mouth. It's just a sandwich . . .

What's the big deal? . . . You promised you'd eat . . . I don't want to send you there, but you have to eat . . . Jesus, Ali, don't do this . . . Please, Ali . . . Eat it or I swear I'll shove it down your throat . . . EAT!'

The door swung open. Ali ran out and up the stairs. I went in and Paul was sitting with his head in his hands.

'What happened?' I asked, rushing over to him.

'I hit her.' He had tears in his eyes. 'I spent nearly two hours trying to get her to eat one bite, but she just wouldn't. I begged her, I pleaded with her – I even tried bribing her – and then I lost my temper and slapped her. I slapped my daughter.' He buried his face in his hands. 'I've never hit the girls. Ever. I just lost it. She was sitting there looking like a flaming skeleton and she wouldn't eat even a tiny piece. It's like trying to get through to a brick wall. Where's our girl? Where's my Ali?'

'Look at me.' I pulled his hands down from his face. 'You're a brilliant dad. Ali loves you. You just lost your temper because you're scared. You're terrified of what could happen. I've wanted to hit her loads of times lately. I'm not saying it's a great idea, but it's just fear, Paul.'

'What's wrong with her? Why the bloody hell can't she eat?'

'She's sick, Paul. She's very sick.'

'But why?'

'That's what we need to find out. That's what Mary and the other professionals are going to help us figure out.'

He took my hand and squeezed it. 'I love you and I love our kids. This family is all I've ever wanted in life. I can't let anything happen to her. She can't die, Ava, she just can't. I won't let it happen.'

'That's why we're going to get the best professional help we can. Ali needs proper care, Paul, and we can't do it on our own. I'm devastated about the clinic too, but if it makes her better it's worth it. I Googled it and it has hundreds of letters from former patients who are completely cured. She's going to be fine.'

*

When I went to check on Ali she was in bed asleep – or pretending to be. I brushed her hair off her face, kissed her cheek and told her I loved her. She didn't move.

Later that night, Sarah came into my room. I was sitting in bed with my laptop, going through websites on how to treat anorexia.

'Where's Dad?' she asked, climbing up beside me.

'He's gone to work.'

'Is Ali going to be OK?'

'Yes, she is.'

'Then why are you sending her to a nuthouse?'

'Because she needs a lot of help and I can't do it on my own. And it's not a nuthouse, it's a clinic that specializes in eating disorders.'

'What if we all worked together to help her? I'll watch her at school, and Charlie could watch her at the weekends when you're working, and Dad could watch her on Mondays and we could do it that way so she wouldn't have to go away.'

I shook my head. 'It wouldn't work. None of us is equipped to deal with this. We don't have the tools. Look how bad it's got already. I don't want to send her away, Sarah, but I have to.'

'How long will she be gone?'

'Hopefully only a couple of weeks. We'll have her home as soon as possible. Now, give me a hug – I need one.'

'Oh, God, Mum, are you going all touchy-feely on me now? The odd hug is OK, but only if you're really desperate. I'm sixteen and it's just not cool to be hugging your mother.'

'OK, just the odd one, then.'

30

The next afternoon while Ali was having a nap and Paul and I were working out our finances, trying to figure out how much the clinic was going to cost, the doorbell rang. Sarah came thundering down the stairs to answer it. A very orange Bobby sauntered in. 'Hey, Mr and Mrs M,' he said.

'You've a better tan than any of us and we're only just back from the sun,' Paul noted.

'I hit the tanning salon over the holidays,' Bobby drawled. 'Couldn't have my girlfriend coming back browner than me.'

Sarah came in dragging Charlie behind her. 'Mum, Dad, Charlie, I need you all to come into the lounge. Bobby and me are going to perform some of our play and we need your feedback. I want to see if we're projecting our voices correctly. So you'll have to sit right at the back of the room and then you can tell me if you can hear properly. No talking while we're performing. I need you to concentrate so you can give us a proper review. It has to be perfect – who knows what this play could lead to?'

'I've no doubt it'll be entertaining anyway,' whispered Paul, 'and we could do with the distraction.'

Bobby didn't look too pleased about having to perform in front of an audience. 'Babe, we're not ready. I'm not totally comfortable with anyone seeing it yet.'

'We're doing it and that's that. Come on, we need the practice.'

Sarah rearranged the furniture, then dragged Bobby outside to get ready. Charlie grinned at me. 'I've a feeling this is going to be classic. Relax and enjoy it – it'll be good to get your mind off Ali.'

The door was thrown open and Sarah arrived, draped in a

sheet, like a Roman emperor. She climbed up onto the couch, crouched and waited . . .

'Bobby!' she hissed. 'Come on.'

The tangerine man came in, wearing a similar sheet over his jeans, Sarah's pink beret on his head and carrying a wooden spoon as a sword. I think he was blushing, although it was hard to tell under all the fake tan.

Sarah popped up, and leant over the edge of the couch. 'Ohmigod – aren't you, like, Romeo Montague? How did you get in here? Did you, like, climb over the electric gates and get past the killer dogs?'

'I jumped over the gate with, like, springs in my legs because of love and also the workouts I've been doing at the gym.'

'Hold on, time out,' Sarah announced. 'Bobby, why did you add that bit in about the gym?'

'Because I don't want the guys to think I'm a fag, shouting about being in love and stuff.'

'Hello! It's a play.'

'I know – it's just some of the stuff is embarrassing.'

'Can you please try to keep to the lines?' Sarah huffed.

'Fine.'

'Romeo, if my old man finds you in here, you are seriously dead. Your family is our total enemy.'

'A red card from you, Juliet, would be, like, way worse than death.'

'How did you know this was my bedroom window? Have you been stalking me or something?'

'Love, babe. Love showed me the way.' Bobby cringed as he said the lines. Paul, Charlie and I tried not to laugh.

'Ohmigod, I am so embarrassed right now,' Juliet said. 'Do you really love me? Don't mess me around. I've been really forward with you. I've come on strong, which is so not like me. But I'm really into you, so be straight with me.'

'Are you kidding me? I am totally into you. I swear on my Brian O'Driscoll Grand Slam signed jersey that –'

'That's your most favourite possession ever.'

'I know, babe. Listen, Juliet, I'm seriously into you.'

'This is mad. We need to slow things down. It could just be a bit of a flirt.'

'Hello! I just said I loved you. I don't say that to other girls.'

'OK, chill. I love you too.'

'I said it first.'

'Well, Romeo, I, like, really, really love you. I love you to infinity. Oh, no, someone's coming, I've got to go. Look, if you're really serious about me, text me tomorrow first thing.'

'OK, cool. Goodnight, and I'll totally be on to you in the a.m.'

'I'll marry you. Gotta fly.'

'That line is stupid – I haven't asked you to marry me yet,' Bobby grumbled. 'Juliet is way too pushy. I'd never go for her.'

'How many times do I have to explain? It's not real life, it's a play.'

'I know, but Romeo is a dork who gets bitch-slapped. I don't want to play him.'

Sarah tossed her hair. 'Fine. I'll ask Adrian Shandwick to do it. I know he'd be delighted to step in and take your place.'

'He's a tosser.'

'Actually, he's really cute. I'll go and ring him now.'

'There's no need to be like that. I'm just saying I think Romeo could be a bit more macho. No guy likes to be forced into marriage. She should give him the chance to ask first.'

'Well, that's the way Shakespeare wrote it.'

'Yeah, well, dudes nowadays are a lot more butch. They don't go around all day in culottes and stupid hats with feathers coming out of them, writing poems.'

'I'm calling Adrian.'

'Don't! I'll say the stupid lines. But I'm not wearing culottes in the play. I'm wearing jeans and that's it.'

'OK, whatever. Can we just get on with it?' Sarah barked, hiding behind the couch.

Bobby rearranged his pink beret and got back into character. 'Leaving you now is worse than losing the rugby school cup final, or missing the last episode of *24*. Farewell, Juliet, catch you tomorrow.' With that, Romeo walked towards the door.

Sarah came out from behind the couch. 'Ta-da. So, what did you think?'

Charlie set us off – he just couldn't hold it in. Having managed to control ourselves throughout the 'performance', we now just fell apart. Tears streamed down our faces and none of us could speak. It was such a welcome relief from worrying about Ali, there was a slight hysteria to it, a letting loose of emotions.

'It's not supposed to be a comedy.' Bobby seemed puzzled.

'I don't know what you're laughing at. They both die in the end. It's a really sad story, a tragedy. You're total ignorant-anuses or whatever,' said our very own Juliet, as she flounced out of the door followed by her star-crossed lover.

We were still laughing when Nadia arrived in, looking very pleased with herself. 'I haff news for you.'

'What news?' Charlie asked her.

'I knowing how to make Aleeson better. My friend tell me her daughter haff the same problem. She not eating, so my friend sit on top of her, tie her hands together and push the food into her mouth. Daughter crying and shouting, "No, no." Mother says, "Efery day you no eat, I do this." Now the daughter eating again. Aleeson don't need clinic, you need be stronger with her. You are too nice. I help you. I sit on her and you push food in.'

'Nadia, if you sat on Ali, she'd snap in two,' Paul pointed out. 'I'm not sure that tying our daughter up and force-feeding her is the answer to her problems, but thanks for the suggestion.'

'You needs to say no to your childrens.'

'Thank you, Nadia, but I don't appreciate being told how to raise my children by someone who has none,' I snapped. Who the hell did she think she was, coming in here and telling me how to be a mother? I felt bad enough about Ali as it was. I didn't need Nadia rubbing salt into the wound.

'Don't bite her head off,' Charlie interrupted. 'Nadia's only trying to help.'

'By suggesting I treat my daughter like a farmyard animal?'

'Calm down, pet. She was only making a suggestion.' Charlie defended his fiancée.

'It's a ridiculous one. It's barbaric.'

'She's just trying to help. She's very fond of Ali.'

'That true. Aleeson has always been fery nice to me. Making cakes and asking about my dancing. She is luffly girl. Sarah is fery different. She is hard. I thinks you will haff problems with her. You needs say no to her.'

'Mum and Dad say no to me all the bloody time, thank you very much,' Sarah said, coming back into the room as Bobby left. 'And I'm not hard, I just have very good self-esteem, which is probably why I'm down here talking to you and not eating one cornflake a day like perfect Ali who you're so mad about.'

'Sarah, there's no need to be rude,' Charlie said.

'She's entitled to defend herself,' Paul jumped in.

'In my town, childrens don't talk to adults like this.'

Would this stupid woman ever shut up? 'As I said, Nadia, someone without children should not be dishing out advice. I don't tell you how to pole dance so don't tell me how to discipline my children – and please feel free to move back to your village with the polite children any time you like.'

'Actually I do having the children,' Nadia announced.

'*What?*'

'I pregnant.'

31

'Jesus Christ!' Paul exclaimed.

'Jesus Christ!' I shouted.

'Jesus Christ! Are you serious? Is it true?' Charlie whooped.

'Jesus Christ! This family just gets weirder,' Sarah said.

'I'm going to be a daddy.' Charlie jumped up and hugged Nadia.

'Seriously, Charlie, you'll be, like, a hundred when the kid is fifteen,' Sarah pointed out, maths never being her strong point.

'There's life in the old dog yet.' Charlie grinned.

'My sixty-eight-year-old father is going to have a baby. Well, that's fan-fucking-tastic. Can this day get any better?'

'Why you no happy for me?' Nadia snapped. 'I make you daddy happy man. I giff him sex, luff and now a baby.'

'When is this baby due?' I asked. It could be a ploy to extract money from him. She could be lying.

'I not know. I only do test today. I go to doctor tomorrow. I fery happy.'

'So am I.' Charlie kissed her.

'I can't deal with this right now.' I got up to leave the room.

'A bit of enthusiasm wouldn't go amiss,' Charlie muttered. 'You always said you'd love a sister or brother.'

'WHEN I WAS SEVEN! I'm sorry, Charlie, but I'm finding it difficult to get excited about the prospect of my father siring a half-sister or -brother four decades younger than me. I've got a lot on my plate right now.'

'It'll give us all a lift to have a baby in the house,' Charlie replied.

'IT'S INSANE!' I shouted, grabbing my coat and keys and storming out of the door.

*

I drove straight to Sally's apartment. Thankfully she was in and alone. I sat down on her couch and put my head in my hands. 'Sally, you're not going to believe the time I've had.'

'I'm listening,' she said, pouring me a glass of wine and sitting down on the opposite couch curling her legs up. Her apartment was decorated in two key colours – cream and beige. Everything in it had a purpose and a place. There was no chaos; it was elegant and uncluttered. I felt calmer just being there.

I told her about the disastrous weigh-in with Mary Boland and how she had booked Ali into the Gretta Lyndon Clinic. I told her that Ali would be having very intense sessions with Mary for the first few days to try to get to the bottom of her anorexia. 'They said the first week is when the patients are most vulnerable and open to talking. It all sounds very full-on but I have to trust them – they have amazing success rates.'

'Poor you and poor Ali.'

'I always thought I was lucky with Ali because she was such an easy child – happy and good-natured. But now I think Sarah's the easy one, because she's self-sufficient and confident and sure of herself. Ali needs much more care, attention and nurturing. All the websites I've been on say that girls who develop anorexia suffer from low self-esteem. I know I've made mistakes as a mother, but I always made sure I told the girls how great they were and how proud I was of them. So, why is Ali's self-esteem so low?'

Sally put her glass down. 'Self-esteem comes and goes depending on what life throws at you. I used to be incredibly confident, a bit like Sarah, but then I met Jeremy. I knew he was married and what I was doing was wrong, but he said he was going to leave his wife and I was so mad about him I ignored all the warning bells in my head. After three years with him, my confidence and self-esteem were shattered. He had lied to me, manipulated me, used me and turned me into a clingy, possessive, paranoid wreck. It took me a long time to build myself back up.'

'Oh, Sally, it must have been awful. How did you do it?'

'One small step at a time.'

'Ali's going to the clinic in the morning. I feel sick every time I think about it. I'm putting my seventeen-year-old daughter into a clinic. She keeps begging me not to, but the doctor said it's vital she gets proper help.'

'Keep reminding yourself that you're doing this to help her, not harm her. The sooner she goes in, the sooner she'll come out.'

'How did everything get so messed up? We were sailing along and then, *bam*, this happens. And the irony is that I was just thinking my parenting days were nearly over. As far as I was concerned Ali was raised. I only had a couple of years left keeping an eye on Sarah and then that was it. I could kick back and relax. I'd done it. I'd raised two great kids. The hard part was over. Now I could enjoy having fun with them as adults. But the hard part is only beginning. Mary Boland said that Ali's recovery will be a slow and frustrating process.'

'Why don't you take a couple of months off from the business and just focus on Ali?'

'To be honest, Sally, I need to go to work – it'll be a welcome distraction. I'd go mad sitting at home, worrying. Besides, the clinic is costing a fortune so I could do with the money.'

'Well, any time you're feeling overwhelmed just let me know and take a few days off.'

'What I'd really like to do is take a one-way flight to Brazil – especially now, with Nadia pregnant on top of everything –'

'WHAT?'

'Yes! I forgot to tell you. Nadia has just announced she's expecting Charlie's baby.'

'Are you serious?'

'Would I joke about it?'

'What a mess.'

'Tell me about it. He's completely trapped now. She'll take him to the cleaner's.'

'Are you sure it's his baby?' Sally asked.

'It *could* be someone else's,' I said, perking up. 'She's a pole dancer. Why would she be faithful to an old man? But how can we find out?'

'DNA test.'

'But you can only do that after the baby's born, by which stage she'll have fleeced him.'

'Well, on *CSI* or *NYPD Blue* or one of those shows, there was an episode about this. Apparently at about thirteen weeks, if you get a blood sample from the pregnant woman, that blood carries the baby's DNA, which can then be compared to the father's blood.'

'OK, Sherlock – but how do you propose we ask Nadia for a blood sample without her becoming suspicious?'

'I haven't worked that bit out yet.'

'Maybe we could give her a sleeping tablet and then draw blood,' I suggested.

'I'm not sure that drugging a pregnant woman is a good idea, or that it's legal. If it's not Charlie's baby, she'll slip up eventually.'

'What if it is Charlie's child?'

Sally didn't have an answer for that.

'Maybe I should fly to Fiji instead. It's further than Brazil. No one would find me there. Oh, God, Sally, how did everything get so complicated?'

'You're having a rotten time, but it's all fixable. Just take it one day at a time. Ali will go to the clinic and get better. Charlie will find out soon enough if this baby is his or not. In the meantime, try to make sure he doesn't give Nadia lots of money. In a way, having her living with you is good, because you can keep a close eye on her.'

Suddenly I heard a loud voice shouting, 'Sally Keene is a whore. She's screwing my husband.'

'What the hell?' I stuttered.

'Simon's psycho ex-wife,' she explained. 'I now have a stalker.

I always quite fancied having a stalker – a man who was so obsessed with me that he'd hang around my house just to catch a glimpse of me in my car, go through my bins so he could have a chocolate wrapper of mine to keep, have my pictures plastered all over the walls of his house . . . and tell everyone who'd listen how incredible I was. But, no. My stalker is my new boyfriend's psychotic ex-wife who stands outside my apartment every night shouting, "Sally Keene is a whore." I called the police and they warned her off. So yesterday she put pictures of her wedding day through my letterbox with "home-wrecker" written across them. They should have freaked me out but actually they're quite reassuring because Simon looks miserable in all of them.'

'So how is he?'

'He's pretty great.' She smiled. 'It's only been a few days, but it's been really great.'

'So you've seen him a few times since Saturday?'

'He never really moved out after Saturday,' she said, beaming.

'That's fantastic. When can I meet him?'

'I'm not going to introduce him to anyone for a while. I just want to take this one really slowly.'

'I totally understand. But as soon as you're ready let me know.'

'I promise you'll be the first person he meets.'

'I'm thrilled for you. Enjoy every minute of it.'

'Sally Keene is a whore. She's screwing my husband,' we heard from below the window.

'What are you going to do about her?' I asked, peeking out. I could only see her silhouette.

'I'm hoping she'll get bored or catch pneumonia or something and piss off.'

'How long does she go on for?'

'Usually about an hour a night.'

'She really is a nut-job.'

'Total.'

'But he's worth it?'

'Hell, yes!'

'Is he staying tonight?'

She nodded. 'He should be back soon.'

'OK, I'll shoot off. Thanks for letting me ear-bash you about my woes – and I really am thrilled for you about Simon.'

'Good luck with bringing Ali to the clinic tomorrow. Call me after. I'll be thinking of you. Remember, it's for her own good.'

'Thanks, I will.'

'Sally Keene has Aids.'

'That's a new one.' Sally chortled.

'She's a real charmer, I can't imagine why he left her. Is she dangerous?'

'Not so far. I think she's all bark and no bite.' Sally stuck her head out of the window. 'That's enough, thanks, Maura. Everyone now knows I'm a whore with Aids. Your job is done. You can go home.'

32

After yet another sleepless night, tossing and turning about Ali, Charlie, Nadia, the baby and my general failure as a mother, I dragged myself out of bed feeling utterly wretched. I was dreading taking Ali to the clinic.

By the time I got downstairs she was sitting in the hall with her coat on and a small bag packed. She refused to look at me.

'Have you had breakfast?' I asked.

'What do you think?'

'Please eat something.'

'I'm not hungry.'

'Ali, please, I'm begging you. A small bowl of Special K.'

'I said I'm not hungry. But you don't have to worry. I'm sure they'll force-feed me in the nuthouse you're sending me to.'

'Come on, Ali, don't be like this. I'm doing my best to make you better.'

'Yeah, right.'

'That's enough,' Paul said, as he came down the stairs. 'This is as difficult for your mother and me as it is for you. The only reason you're going to this clinic is because you won't eat. We'd much rather keep you at home.'

'Come on, we'd better go,' I said, trying desperately not to cry.

'Wait!' Sarah shouted, thundering down the stairs. 'Here.' She thrust her iPod into Ali's hand. 'I downloaded all your favourite songs. It should keep you sane in there.'

'Thanks.' Ali put it into her pocket.

'I've a little something for you too,' Charlie said, shuffling over in his pyjamas. He handed Ali a photo album. 'I put in photos from when you were a newborn up to now. Hopefully it'll help if you're feeling lonely. I'll be in to see you as often as they let me.'

Ali's lip quivered. Charlie hugged her. 'There now, pet, you'll be back home to us in no time. We'll all miss you.'

'See you, sis. And if anyone famous is in there with you, make friends with them,' Sarah said, giving Ali an awkward hug.

Paul and I had decided that it was best if I took Ali alone. Less fuss and emotion.

Paul walked over and took his elder daughter in his arms. 'My beautiful Ali. My pride and joy. I know you can beat this. I know you'll come back to us in no time. Fight it, Ali, fight it.'

I walked out to the car to wipe the tears streaming down my face. I needed to compose myself for the drive.

Paul had to carry Ali to the car and lift her in. She was inconsolable. He wiped away her tears and kissed her cheek. 'I love you,' he croaked, and closed the door.

As we left, I heard Sarah say, 'If Ali's your pride and joy, what am I?'

We drove in silence, Ali crying while I tried hard not to. The clinic was housed in a lovely Georgian building covered with ivy and surrounded by well-tended grounds. I parked close to the entrance and took Ali's bag out of the boot.

As we walked towards Reception, Ali grabbed my sleeve. 'Please, Mum, please don't do this. I'll eat. I'll eat anything you want me to. I'm sorry, Mum, I'm sorry for putting you through such stress. I know it's been hard for you and Dad. But please don't leave me here. Please, Mum, *pleeeeeease.*'

I continued walking. I couldn't speak. My beautiful daughter, my first-born, my angel, followed behind, begging and pleading. I'm pretty sure I felt my heart break.

We sat in Reception, crying. I was out of words, out of explanations, out of excuses. I prayed I was doing the right thing.

Thankfully, within minutes a very nice nurse came to introduce herself. She said her name was Denise and she was the nurse in charge of the eating-disorders section of the clinic. She didn't seem remotely put out by our tears. 'Everyone feels emotional when they first come. It's totally normal. We'll take great care of you, Alison, don't you worry about a thing. We're here to help you get better and we'll have you home to your family in no time.' Then she handed me a tissue. 'Ava, you're not to worry either. The first day is always the hardest for everyone.'

I wanted to hug the woman. I felt immediately at ease with her. She seemed so sure that she could fix Ali. It was exactly what I needed to hear. As we were shown around, I noticed that the doors were kept locked and the windows could only open a certain amount. I later discovered that this was supposed to prevent the patients climbing out and running away.

Every bedroom was painted the same bland cream colour, but most people had put up posters or photos and tried to personalize their rooms. There was a kitchen that you were allowed use under supervision, a large dining hall, a TV lounge where people could meet up and chat, and a schoolroom. Outside the gardens were lovely. Although it was January, you could see how glorious they would be in springtime.

The clinic smelt of disinfectant, but there were bouquets of flowers sitting in bright vases and colourful paintings on the walls. The staff clearly made an effort to keep the place as cheerful as possible.

Denise took us into her office and asked Ali to strip down to her bra and pants to be weighed. She was six stone. She had lost more weight, and although I was upset, it reinforced my conviction that I had done the right thing. Ali needed proper help.

Denise told us that because Ali was so underweight she would be put on immediate bed-rest.

'What does that mean?' I asked, as Ali got dressed.

'It means that she cannot do any exercise at all, not even walking. She must lie in bed with her feet up.' Turning to Ali, she said, 'If you need to go to the bathroom, you must ask a

nurse to help you. For the moment you will be taken everywhere in a wheelchair. You'll be on five-minute observation
during the day – that means we'll check on you every five minutes to make sure you haven't left the bed. At night-time you'll
sleep with your door open so we can check regularly to make
sure you don't try to exercise. You will also have supervised
showers. A lot of the girls try to exercise in the showers and
bathrooms. We need to make sure that doesn't happen.'

Ali looked horrified.

'Isn't that a little extreme?' I asked.

Denise shook her head. 'Alison has lost over thirty per cent
of her bodyweight so she mustn't burn any essential calories by
walking or moving unnecessarily. She needs to be on full bed-
rest for the time being.'

'What about meals?' I asked, as Denise showed us to Ali's
room. It was small, with simple cream walls and a single bed, a
bedside locker and a small wardrobe.

'She'll have her meals brought to her on a tray and all meals
and snacks will be supervised to make sure she doesn't try to
hide her food. After each meal she will be on a sixty-minute
post-meal bed-rest. This means no visits to the toilet for a full
hour after eating.'

I tried not to look as shocked as I felt. It was like a prison.
They were all but tying Ali to the bed.

'I know it may seem rigid, but these rules work,' Denise
assured me. 'Alison is dangerously underweight. She needs to
put on weight as soon as possible. Even the slightest movement burns calories.' Then, turning back to Ali, she smiled.
'Don't worry, Alison, it's not as bad at it sounds. We're all here
to help you get better. The sooner you put on weight, the sooner
you can go home. You'll make lots of friends here – the other
girls are a nice bunch. You can get together and give out about
us nurses. Look, there's Emily.' Denise called a very frail girl
into the room and introduced us. 'Right, Ava, I'll leave you
to help Alison unpack and then you can say goodbye,' she

said. 'I think ten minutes should be plenty of time,' she added pointedly.

While Ali chatted to Emily, I hung her clothes in the wardrobe and placed her personal belongings on her bedside locker.

'Don't worry, the first day is always the worst,' Emily said. 'We know the new girls by their blotchy faces. It's really hard – we've all been there.'

As Emily talked, she kept hopping from one leg to the other.

'How long have you been in here?' Ali asked.

'This is my third time. The first time I was in for three months, the last time seven weeks and I've been back in a week now.' Emily hopped from side to side again. Five hops on the right leg, five on the left. I tried not to stare.

'Why do you keep coming back?' Ali asked, sounding panicky.

I willed myself not to shove Emily out of the door. I didn't want Ali hearing about repeat visits and relapses. She was not coming back here. This was a once-only stay. She would get better and come home.

Emily sighed. 'Because apparently I can't manage to maintain my food intake when I go home. I can't get control of my obsessive jumping and I started cutting myself again,' she said, pointing to her bandaged arms.

SELF-HARM! I needed her out of the room and away from Ali. Where were the girls who were putting on weight and getting better? Where were the success stories? Why the bloody hell did this girl have to be the first person Ali met? She must be really messed up. I didn't want Emily anywhere near my daughter. What if she put ideas into her head? I was struggling with a straightforward eating disorder – there was no way I could manage self-harm too.

'Were you put on bed-rest on the first day too?' Ali asked.

Emily nodded. 'Most of the girls are. It's a pain, but once you start putting on weight, they'll allow you to get up.'

'Well, that's good news,' I said. 'It was lovely to meet you,

238

Emily, but I'm just going to say goodbye to Ali now.' I showed her to the door. She hopped most of the way.

'See you later, Alison, good luck,' she called.

''Bye, Emily.'

I turned to Ali. 'It's going to be OK, love. That poor girl is very messed up. You are only going to be here for a week or two and then we'll have you home and everything will be back to normal. All you have to do is focus on eating and getting better.'

'Don't leave me, Mum.' Her body convulsed with sobs.

'Oh, Ali, please don't cry. I promise it's only for a little while. I hate this too. But I just want to make you better, pet.'

Denise came back into the room and told me it was time to go.

I took a deep breath and said goodbye. Ali clung to me like a terrified child.

I faltered.

Denise stepped in, peeled Ali's arms from me and gently nudged me out of the door. I could hear Ali's screams as I stumbled towards the exit.

I wandered around the car park, trying in vain to find my car, blinded by tears. I felt a hand on my shoulder. It was Paul. 'I dropped Sarah to school and I just couldn't face going to work, so I followed you here. I knew it'd be awful for you and I felt bad that you had to do it on your own. How is she?'

'Terrible. I feel as if I've put her in prison,' I cried, as I leant into him for comfort. He put his arms around me tightly.

'Is the place horrible? Is it full of nutters?'

'No, it's not that bad – and the staff seem really friendly and efficient. It's just that she was begging me not to leave her and I had to turn my back on her. Oh, God, I hope we're doing the right thing.'

'We are. The night I tried to get her to eat and hit her, I realized how bad things had got. Ali's strong – she's a fighter. She'll beat this, you'll see.'

I admired my husband's belief and tried to banish my fears.

I decided not to tell him about Emily. He didn't need to hear it and, to be honest, I needed to block it out of my mind. There was no room for thoughts of Ali not getting better or having relapses. I was determined to stay focused.

'When can we visit?' he asked.

'Not for five days. They want her to settle in first. But we can call her every day.'

'It *is* like prison.'

'We'll give it a week and see how she gets on. If it's too awful, we can always take her out.'

'Hey, Ava.'

'What?'

'Have I told you lately that I love you?'

'No.'

'Well, I do,' he said, hugging me.

'Thanks, I needed that.'

33

The next morning, when my alarm went off at seven, I threw it across the room – I had slept badly again. Paul offered to take Sarah to school and call Sally to tell her I'd be a bit late for work.

When I got up, I found Nadia lying on the couch watching daytime TV. She waved a remote control at me as I walked past her into the kitchen where Charlie was busy making a sandwich.

Magda was in the kitchen, too, tidying up. 'How you, Ava? Charlie tell me poor Aleeson is in hospital. I fery sorry. You OK?'

'Thanks, Magda. I'm very worried but I'm OK.'

'She be well soon. She haff nice family and she fery intelligent girl.'

'I hope so.'

'Mothers worry efery day. It our job.'

'Have you kids, Magda?' Charlie asked.

'She has two boys back home in Poland,' I filled him in.

'It must be hard for you, being away from them,' Charlie commented.

Magda stopped cleaning and leant back against the counter. 'Yes, it is. I miss boys fery much. But I Skyping efery two or three days.'

'How old are they?'

'Oldest boy is twenty-two and youngest boy is twenty. I working to pay for university. Only one more years and then I goes home.'

'I don't know how you do it, Magda. Ali's only been away for one night and I miss her terribly.'

'I haff no choice, I want my boys to haff better life than me.'

'You're an amazing mother. I hope they appreciate it,' I said.

Magda snorted. 'Childrens no appreciate nothing.'

'Speaking of children, did you hear I'm going to be a dad?' Charlie announced.

Magda looked at me. I nodded. 'Nadia is pregnant?' She was genuinely shocked.

'Yes, isn't that wonderful?' Charlie beamed.

'You crazy man!' Magda shook her fist in front of Charlie's face and then marched straight into the lounge and began to shout at Nadia in Polish.

I don't know what she was saying but it didn't sound like 'congratulations'. Nadia jumped up and started shouting right back. Charlie and I watched while they went at it like two alley cats. Magda poked Nadia in the chest. Nadia's face went red with rage and she pushed Magda backwards. Magda ran towards her and shoved Nadia back onto the couch. It was at that point that Charlie decided to break it up. 'Now, ladies, we all need to calm down here.'

Magda hissed one final sentence at Nadia and stormed back into the kitchen where I was pretending not to have witnessed anything.

'She a fery bad girl,' she proclaimed.

'What did she say?' I was hoping Nadia had admitted it wasn't Charlie's baby.

'She say it Charlie's baby, but she lie. Like you say here in Eyerland, she a "slapper",' Magda said.

'I agree with you, Magda, but what can I do? Charlie's in love with her and she says it's his baby.'

'I keeping eye on her. I getting my Polish friends to keeping eye on her. She not a nice girl. She from bad family in Poland. Her sister also a slapper. She haff three childrens from different fathers.'

So Nadia came from a long line of slappers. Charlie really was screwed.

Charlie came back in. 'Now, Magda, I don't want you upsetting Nadia. You really shouldn't have pushed her. It's not good for a pregnant woman to be stressed.'

Magda shook her head. 'I likes you, Charlie, but you fery silly man. You needs to be thinking with this,' she tapped his forehead, 'and not with this.' She pointed at his crotch, then walked out with her mop and bucket.

In one sentence Magda had summed up Charlie's problems. Succinct and to the point.

When Magda had left the room, Charlie said, 'Poor Magda's jealous.'

'Of what?'

'My relationship with Nadia.'

'Why on earth would you think that? You tried it on with Magda and she broke your nose, remember?'

'That was before she got to know me. I think she regrets that now.'

'She's happily married, Charlie.'

'So she says, but you saw the way she reacted when I told her Nadia was pregnant – that was pure jealousy. I definitely have a way with the Polish ladies.'

'I now know where Sarah gets her self-esteem from,' I muttered, as Charlie continued to pile ingredients into his sandwich. 'Is that for you?' I asked.

'No, it's for poor Nadia. She has very bad morning sickness.'

'It can't be that bad if she's able to eat that.'

'Ava, I know you're under a lot of pressure but I want you to be nice to Nadia. She's going to be the mother of my child – your little sister or brother.'

I put down my mug of tea. 'Seriously, Charlie, don't you think you're a bit old to be having children?'

'I feel as young as a teenager.'

'Well, you're certainly behaving like one.'

'There's no need to take your stress out on me or Nadia.'

'I'm not. I just think you're making a huge mistake.'

'I love her.'

'CHARLIE!' Nadia roared. 'Hurry up. The baby so hungry.'

'She's very easy to love.' I tried not to smile.

'She's just not feeling well today.'

'She's a joy to have around. The next thirty-six weeks of her pregnancy are sure to be great fun.'

'CHARLIE!' Nadia screeched.

Charlie rushed out with the sandwich and I headed off to work.

Later that evening when I got home, Paul was in the kitchen making dinner.

'Wow!' I was stunned.

'I thought I'd cook tonight, give you a break.'

'Fantastic. I'm thrilled.'

'How was work?'

'Actually, I enjoyed it. I feel bad admitting it, but it was nice to have a bit of mental time out from worrying about Ali.'

He nodded. 'I know what you mean. I've just been in the pub doing the wages and I didn't think about Ali for a whole hour.'

'I spoke to her earlier.'

'How was she?'

'Not great. She's still really angry about being put in the clinic. I explained yet again that we were just trying to help but she doesn't want to know. To be honest, she barely said two words to me.'

'I hope we're doing the right thing.'

'Me too. Hopefully Mary Boland will be able to reassure us when we see her in two days.'

'Did you get to talk to that nurse, Denise?' Paul asked.

'She says Ali's doing well, but it'll be slow. She thinks she'll be on bed-rest for at least another week or two.'

'I don't know, Ava, it seems very rigid.'

'We've been over this a million times. She needs their help, Paul. She was getting really bad at home.'

'You're right.' He turned back to stir the pot.

Sarah strolled in the door with her tangerine man in tow. 'Oh, my God – Dad, are you cooking?'

'Yes, I am.'

'Why?'

'I felt like giving your mother a break.'

'You must have done something really bad.'

'No, he didn't, and I'm delighted he's cooking so don't put him off,' I warned her.

'Every time I walk in the door something weird's going on in this family. First Ali going to the nuthouse, then Nadia and the baby and now Dad cooking –'

'Hi, Bobby.' I interrupted Sarah's sarcasm.

'Howzit going, Mrs M? I hear there's a pitter-patter of, like, tiny feet on its way.'

'The less said about that the better.'

'Can Bobby stay for dinner?' Sarah asked.

'Of course,' I said.

'His mum's away again and Mia, the housekeeper, is at her English class.'

'Well, Bobby, if you're ever stuck for dinner, feel free to call over here,' I said.

'Thanks, Mrs M, I appreciate that.'

'Yeah, tea-time is so much fun in our house. We all stare at Ali while she spits her food into her napkin.'

'Stop that, Sarah,' Paul said. 'Your sister's sick. Don't make fun of her.'

'How was school?' I changed the subject.

'Crap. Everyone kept following me around asking if it was true that my sister had been locked up in a loony bin. You should hear the rumours. One girl actually asked me if it was true that Ali ate nothing but her fingernails. Someone else asked me how Ali had lost all the weight and if I could give her a list of everything she'd cut out of her diet because she thought she looked great.'

'God, that's sick.' I was shocked.

'Some of the girls were giving Sarah a really hard time,' Bobby said.

'What did they say?'

Sarah shrugged. 'Jane Collins, who is a fat cow and has always been jealous of Ali, told everyone that Ali was in a straitjacket because she couldn't get over David and that when Bobby dumped me I'd end up there too.'

'The little bitch,' Paul raged.

'I'm going to call the headmistress first thing tomorrow,' I fumed.

'No, Mum, you're not. It's all fine now. Bobby and me dealt with it. Bobby told Jane he had no intention of breaking up with the coolest girlfriend ever and that she was just a fat loser who spread rumours about people because she had no life.'

'Good man, Bobby,' Paul said.

'Brilliant retort,' I added.

'You were amazing too, babe,' Bobby said. 'When the vultures were asking Sarah all these questions, trying to find out what was going on so they could gossip about Ali, she made it sound as if Ali being in a clinic was actually really cool.'

Sarah fiddled with her watch. 'I told everyone that Ali had mental exhaustion and was in a really exclusive top-secret rehab clinic with lots of celebrities. So now everyone's jealous of her. They think she's in the Priory.'

'Good for you. I'm proud of you defending your sister like that.' Paul smiled at her.

'There was no way I was going to let those bitches spread rumours about Ali.'

'I'm sorry you had to deal with all that. Girls can be very cruel.'

'I'm fine, Mum, it's no big deal.' I watched her blink back tears as Bobby took her hand and squeezed it.

'So, Paul, what's for dinner?'

'How does pasta with sauce sound?' He waved a jar of Loyd Grossman at us.

'A lot better than frozen pizza,' Bobby admitted.

'Do you often have dinner on your own?' I asked.

'Well, my dad lives in Spain most of the time and my mum visits him a lot so I suppose you could say I'm no stranger to frozen dinners.'

'But Mia cooks for him sometimes,' Sarah said.

'Yeah, Mia's, like, a really good cook, but she has English lessons two nights a week.'

'Where's Mia from?'

'China. She does great Chinese food, actually.'

'Does your mum ever cook?' I was curious to know what she did. Sarah had told me she didn't work and was a lady of leisure.

He smiled. 'Not really. She doesn't eat much apart from salads – she's always on a diet – so I kind of look after myself.'

'You should see her, Mum. She's super-slim, like Victoria Beckham.'

Hardly bloody surprising if all she eats is lettuce. 'I thought you hadn't met Bobby's mum.'

'I haven't yet, but I've seen pictures of her in the house. She's really glamorous.'

I now regretted having changed after work. I was in tracksuit bottoms and sweat-shirt – I looked more Sporty Spice than Posh Spice. 'Well, Bobby, you're always welcome to come to our house for dinner.'

'Thanks. I really like coming here – there's always loads of stuff going on. It's crazy and fun. It's a real family house. I guess because I'm an only child my house is way too quiet. And you're a very good cook, Mrs M.'

'That's very nice of you, Bobby. You must feel free to stay for dinner more often. There's always plenty.'

'Speaking of good cooks, who wants some pasta?' Paul asked.

'I'm starving,' Sarah said, as Paul and I rushed to serve her, thrilled that at least one of our daughters wanted to eat.

34

Two days later, Paul and I sat nervously in Mary Boland's office. I was pinning a lot of my hopes on Mary being able to reveal what was wrong with Ali. I was also praying that she'd tell us Ali was on the road to recovery and would be home soon.

'Paul, Ava, nice to see you again.' She shook our hands.

While Mary opened her file on Ali, I blurted out, 'So, how is she? Did you get to the bottom of it? Is she all right? Did something awful happen that we don't know about? Is she going to be cured?'

Mary waited for me to pause for breath. 'I've had several sessions with Alison over the last few days. She's a lovely, bright, intelligent girl who is trapped in a cycle of controlling her food because she feels out of control in other aspects of her life. The important thing to realize here is that Alison's problems are not about food and weight. She simply wants to distract herself from her real emotions.'

'So why is she starving herself?' I was desperate to get to the bottom of it.

'When you control hunger you feel better. It blocks everything else out. Alison's food control is keeping everything together. She feels that if she gives up this control, her life will fall apart. It is her "safe place". She doesn't want to be "fixed". Starvation is causing an emotional disconnection.'

'From what? Is this because of David breaking up with her?' I asked.

'There are many aspects to it,' Mary explained. 'Alison told me about the break-up and how heartbroken she was, and humiliated, when David immediately started going out with Tracy, but she also mentioned something more dramatic that had happened a long time ago when she was nine, something she hasn't been able to forget. An incident that had a very big impact on all your lives. She said it's something she has never felt able to discuss with you. Something you covered up. A taboo.'

Paul and I looked at each other. 'Oh, my God. I thought she believed the story I told her,' I said.

'I didn't think she'd seen anything,' Paul added.

'In fact, she saw the whole incident and was traumatized by it. This, plus the upset of David rejecting her for a thinner girl, made her decide to try to lose some weight. She realized that she liked the feeling of being in complete control so the downward spiral began. Alison also has extremely low self-esteem, which is very common in eating disorders. We need to build that back up.'

'She's a beautiful, bright, intelligent girl. Why would she have low self-esteem? I don't understand.' Paul was clearly feeling frustrated.

'A lot of creative, intelligent, articulate girls have low self-esteem. They tend to be very sensitive souls and can sense when something is not right at home and will always try to make it better. They put others first.'

'She does do that,' Paul agreed. 'She's always been the peacemaker in our house.'

'So, what do we do?' I begged.

'By seeking professional help and sending her to the clinic you are doing everything you can to help her recover. But Alison is still in denial that she has a problem. My job is to get her to accept that she is using control over food as a form of escape and suppression of emotions. But only she can fully make herself better. I've asked her to write a letter to the anorexia. It should help her to express how she feels. Recovery will be a slow process, but it is important to remember that she can be cured of this.'

'I may have made it worse. I hit her,' Paul blurted out. 'Did she tell you? I didn't want to send her away to the clinic but she refused to eat and I lost it and hit her. I have never hit my daughters – I'm not that kind of man. I still can't believe I did it.' His voice shook. He looked down at his hands. I put my arm round his shoulders.

'She did mention the incident,' said Mary. 'But I know you're a good father – Alison adores you. She told me how out of character it was. Just remember to control your anger the next time, because I have to warn you both, this is going to be a long, uphill and frustrating battle. Eating disorders like ano-rexia don't cure themselves overnight.'

'It will never happen again, I can promise you that,' Paul assured her.

'How can we help her?' I asked.

'You have sought the correct care for her and now you need to leave it up to the professionals. Obviously you will be instru-mental in supporting her recovery, but it's up to us and, more importantly, up to Alison now.'

'So there's nothing specific that we can do?'

'Your role for the next while will be to cheer her on and sup-port from the sidelines while we work our magic.'

'But there must be something I can do. I'm her mother – I know her better than anyone else.' I was finding it hard to let go. I wanted to be involved in my daughter's recovery. I hated not seeing her or what was going on. Since I was seventeen, I'd had to look after myself. I was used to being in control and liked to be in charge. I liked to be informed. I didn't want to leave Ali completely in the hands of the professionals. I wanted to work alongside them, not be pushed into the background. What if she needed me? What if they tried to get her to eat something she didn't like?

'There are things that only a mother knows – like the fact that Ali hates blueberries,' I persisted.

Mary leant forward. 'Ava, I understand this is difficult for you. Leaving your most precious possession in the hands of others is the hardest thing to do, but I can assure you that we know exactly what we're doing. You need to let go. Alison is the only person who can make Alison better. She's almost an adult now and she has to do this on her own, with help and support, of course, but if she doesn't heal herself, she will relapse.'

I tried not to get upset. A mother's job was to fix things when they went wrong but in this case I had to step back and watch her struggle through on her own. I suppose it was like when your child takes their first steps and every time they wobble you want to reach out and save them, but the only way they learn how to get back up is by falling down.

'This is a tough situation for any family so I want you to remember to take time for yourselves and your younger daughter. Continue with your jobs and your lives, otherwise it will consume you.'

'OK, Doc. Bottom line, is Ali going to get better?' Paul asked.

Mary paused. 'Yes, I believe she will.'

Sarah was waiting for us when we got home. 'So, what did the psychologist say? Are we all mad?'

'Don't joke about it. It's very serious,' I said.

'I'm just trying to cheer you up. It's nothing but bloody doom and gloom in this house.'

'You're right,' Paul observed. 'You are absolutely right. We can't all sit around being miserable. It's not going to help anyone.'

'Wow, Dad, you do realize that you have, like, actually agreed with me for the first time ever?' Sarah said.

'Miracles do happen.' He smiled.

'So is it because of David? Is that why she's not eating? Is she going to be OK?'

'They think she'll be fine. But we need to talk to you about something.' I led her to a chair and told her to sit down.

'Oh, God, what now?'

'Ali told the psychologist about something she witnessed when she was nine. It had a very bad effect on her and I –'

'Oh, please, are you talking about Dad being shot?'

Paul stared at her. 'You know about it too?'

'Come on, guys, it was like downtown LA, with all the gunfire and the shouting. I probably would have slept through it but I was sharing a room with Ali who was all freaked out and woke me up. She was crying and shouting, "Dad's dead." But when I looked out the window, I saw you waving your arms and roaring, so I knew you were all right. The next day Mum made up the story about the appendix and it was pretty obvious that you wanted us to play along, so that was that.'

'Weren't you affected by it?' I asked.

Sarah looked genuinely puzzled. 'No. Why would I be? Dad was totally fine and the guy went to prison. End of story.'

'Did you worry he might come back?' Paul asked her.

'No, because Mr Hardy across the road told me it was an accident waiting to happen. He said you were looking for trouble coming home from the pub with a big bag full of cash from the tills every night. He said every criminal in Dublin targeted businesses that dealt in cash. He said you were a total moron for trying to fight off Brendan Howlitt and hold on to the bag, and it was a good thing that you'd got shot, because now you were behaving responsibly and putting the money into a night safe after closing the pub, and the neighbourhood would be a much safer place because of it.'

'That interfering fucker! I'll kill him!' Paul hissed.

I couldn't believe that grumpy old busybody would say something like that to a child. It had been a really traumatic time. Paul had very nearly died on the operating table and I was a nervous wreck for months. It was only really when Howlitt was put away for fifteen years that we began to relax again and put it behind us. Our priority at the time had been to protect the girls from it. Charlie had been amazing: he had moved in and helped out with them while Paul was in hospital and been a rock of strength for me. I would have been lost without him.

'Dad, I wouldn't bother confronting Mr Hardy. He's got

Alzheimer's and the shooting happened, like, eight years ago, so I'd say the chances of him remembering are slim to none.'

'So you honestly don't think you were affected by it in a bad way?' I wanted to be sure she wasn't just being brave.

'Nope, not at all. Ali used to have nightmares about Howlitt getting out of prison and coming back to kill us all in our beds, but I never did.'

'I remember Ali's nightmares. She always said she was dreaming of ghosts. I should have guessed.'

'Come on, Mum, how were you supposed to know that Ali's ghost was actually a code-word for the freak who shot Dad?'

'I should have handled the whole thing differently. I just wanted to protect you. I was so terrified that Dad was going to die I couldn't think straight.'

'Don't sweat it.'

'Are you annoyed with us for pretending I was in hospital with appendicitis?' Paul asked her.

'No. Look, guys, I'm not throwing up after eating, I'm not taking drugs or cutting myself or leading a double life as a hooker because eight years ago you tried to protect us from the truth. I'm cool with it. Ali's always been way too sensitive.'

How could two daughters born of the same parents be so different? I was extremely relieved that Sarah wasn't angry with me, but I felt wretched that Ali had been so frightened, that I hadn't known and hadn't been there to comfort her. I had been so wrapped up in trying to get Paul better and keeping things 'normal' at home.

Parenthood was a non-stop learning curve. What worked with one child was the completely wrong thing to do with another. It was a minefield and after the session this morning I felt drained and unsure of myself. What other bad decisions had I made? What other damage had I unwittingly caused?

'Mum,' Sarah said, interrupting my thoughts, 'don't beat yourself up. With the psychologists and the nutritionists and the special treatment, Ali will be fine. She's too smart to die.

Besides, I don't fancy being an only child. Way too much focus.'

I reached out and squeezed her hand. 'Mary, the psychologist, said she'd like to have a couple of family sessions with Ali. Are you all right with that?'

'Are you kidding me? Come on, Mum, talking about myself is my idea of heaven. When can we start?'

Paul went over and put his arm around her. 'Sarah Mullen, you're a breath of fresh air. Don't ever change.'

'Steady on, you two, all this affection is freaking me out.'

Paul kissed the top of her head. 'I have to pop into the pub. I'll see you later.'

As he walked out, Charlie walked in. 'How did it go?' he asked, sitting down on the couch with me and Sarah.

'Ali's not eating because four zillion years ago Dad got shot.'

'You know about that?' Charlie was shocked.

'Apparently Ali saw it happen,' I explained.

'Oh, no, poor Ali.'

'Yeah, well, she woke me up so that I'd be traumatized too.'

'Are you?' Charlie asked Sarah.

'No.'

'I thought they believed all the stuff about Paul's appendix,' he said to me.

'So did I, but they've known all along.'

'Why didn't you say anything?' Charlie asked Sarah.

'Because you all kept going on about how it was just an operation and it was pretty obvious that you didn't want us to know what had really happened, so we just played along. To be honest, I kind of believed it after a few weeks. I almost forgot he was shot. It's one of the advantages of being shallow. Ali, on the other hand, has obviously been dragging it around for all these years.'

'Did the shrink find all this out?' Charlie wondered.

'It came up in the session today.'

'Is that why she's not eating?'

'It's the trigger, but there are lots of other reasons too. David, her sensitivity to others, her need to please, her perfectionism . . . Seemingly these are all reasons why she has developed anorexia. But the psychologist said that the most important thing to remember is that it's not about the food, it's about control.'

'What's she trying to control?'

'Her emotions, I think. I'm still learning,' I admitted. 'To be honest, Charlie, I'm reeling from it all.'

'She's always been a control freak,' Sarah piped up.

'No, she hasn't,' I defended Ali.

'I cannot believe you're saying that. You obviously never shared a room with her like I did for five years. She's a neat freak. She made me colour-code my clothes and I wasn't allowed to have anything on the floor. Not even my shoes – they had to be put away in the wardrobe every night. She drove me insane. I'd come in from playing outside and find my dolls' clothes had been washed and ironed, their hair washed and dried and their shoes polished! She used to line up my pencils on my desk at exactly the same angle and hoover every day – even under the bed. The best day of my life was when I got my own room.'

I'd forgotten how annoyed Ali used to get with Sarah's messiness. I never thought it was a big deal but Sarah was very untidy. Was it another symptom of her need to control things? It had never seemed extreme. 'She just likes order in her life. I don't think that's a negative.'

'Of course you don't because you're a total control freak too,' Sarah said.

'No, I'm not. I think I'm pretty laid-back.'

Sarah and Charlie laughed loudly at this statement.

'I have my father and his pregnant girlfriend living with me, a husband who is married to his job and two demanding teenage daughters. I think I'm very bloody laid-back actually.'

'Oh, yeah, you're practically horizontal.' Sarah giggled.

'Ava, you have many fantastic qualities, but you could never be described as easy-going.'

'I object strongly to that. I'm very relaxed about a lot of things. There is constant chaos in this house and I hardly ever complain.'

'You're always giving out about the mess,' Sarah said.

'Just because I don't like to have stuff lying around everywhere doesn't mean I'm obsessive.'

'You go mental if I leave wet towels on the bathroom floor.'

'It's disgusting.'

'You can't go to sleep unless the kitchen is completely tidy,' she added.

'I like to wake up to a clean house.'

'We never had animals because you didn't want animal hair on your couches.'

'Who does?'

'Loads of people.'

Charlie stepped in. 'Ava, love, no one is saying that there's anything wrong with liking things a certain way, but if you're wondering where Ali got her orderliness from, you don't need to look any further.'

'You're both being totally unfair. I'm very easy-going compared to most people. Now, Sarah, go and make your mad mother a cup of tea.'

Charlie stood up. 'I'll give you a hand.'

'Regular or herbal?' Sarah asked me.

'Herbal, please. Can you make me a green tea, but not the organic green tea, the one with jasmine? And can you make it the big spotty cup? And can you bring me a few biscuits as well – not the chocolate ones, the plain ones, thanks.'

'Yes, sir.' She grinned.

'That is not being controlling. It's called being precise,' I shouted after them, as their laughter filled the room.

35

Sally decided it was time to bring Simon out of the witness-protection programme and introduce him to Paul and me. She told me she didn't want to go for dinner because she thought it would be too formal, but that Simon had been very interested when he heard Paul was into surfing and said he'd love to try it.

Paul was lending Simon all the surf gear he needed, so on the morning of the double date, he laid it out on the hall floor and started sorting through it.

Sarah came downstairs. 'What are you doing?'

'He's getting a wetsuit and all the other stuff for Simon,' I told her.

'Has he ever surfed before?'

'No.'

'He does realize it's January?'

'He's a successful lawyer so I presume he can figure out what month it is,' I retorted.

The doorbell rang. 'It's them!' I froze. Paul and Sarah laughed at me.

'Maybe you should open the door and let them in,' Paul suggested.

'OK. Now, remember, act casual, like it's no big deal that Sally has a boyfriend,' I reminded them.

I opened the door and Sarah screeched, 'Oh, my God, Sally, what is that? Your boyfriend? I've never seen one before.'

Sally turned to Simon. 'That's Sarah, the one they're sending off to boarding school next year.'

'Ha ha.' Sarah walked over and proffered a hand. 'Nice to meet you, Simon. I'm Sarah, the sane sister.'

'I've heard all about you.' He winked at her.

'Just ignore her. I'm Ava, great to meet you. Come on in – try not to trip over the mess.'

'Hi, Simon, I'm Paul.' The two men shook hands.

'Nice to meet you both,' said Simon. Then, seeing the state of the hall, he added, 'Thanks for sorting me out with all the equipment. I'm really looking forward to this.'

'You must be mad,' Sarah said.

'I've always wanted to try it – it looks like fun.'

'Yeah, but you do realize you're going to die out there? It's, like, freezing.'

'I did point that out, but he's mad keen,' Sally said.

'Well, I think it's great. It shows a very adventurous spirit.' I smiled at Simon.

'No, Mum, it shows he's insane.'

'Maybe Maura rubbed off on him.' Sally grinned at Simon, who laughed good-naturedly.

'Oh, is Maura your mad wife? Mum told me she's a total nutter.'

I tried to suppress the urge to put a surfboard in Sarah's mouth.

'She definitely has a screw loose,' Simon admitted, 'but, thankfully, we're separated and Sally seems very sane.'

'That's what you think.' Sarah snorted.

'Less of your cheek, thank you.' Sally wagged a finger at her. 'How's the play going?'

'Very well, thanks. I reckon I'll be the hottest Juliet ever.'

'And how's Bobby?'

'Still cool.'

'Good for you.'

'OK.' Paul stood up. 'Before I start packing the car, Sally and Ava, are you sure you don't want to come surfing with us?'

'I've tried it and hated it,' I reminded him. To Simon, I explained, 'I spent the entire time falling under waves and being hit by the board. I was black and blue when we got home. I need to warn you that it can be pretty tough out there.'

Simon smiled. 'Thanks, Ava. I may not get up today, but I'm keen to give it a go. Even if it's just to tell the boys in the office that I did it.'

'Well, you can count me out. There's no way I'm getting into ice-cold water in a rubber suit to try to stand on a tray. Not even for you, babe.' Sally kissed Simon, who hadn't let go of her hand since they arrived.

'Wow, you guys really are in love,' Sarah said. 'Way to go, Sally.'

They were utterly besotted with each other. He couldn't take his eyes off her and she just glowed with happiness. It was lovely.

'Simon, it's going to be bloody cold out there, so I'm giving you a rash vest to put on underneath the wetsuit. It'll give you an extra layer of insulation. I've got boots and gloves and a hood for you too,' Paul said, showing Simon the gear. 'And I'm going to lend you my long board.' He produced a surfboard that was at least nine foot tall. 'It's better for beginners. I use it mostly for summer surf.'

'That all looks great.'

'It's good to have a partner in crime. Right then, let's hit the road.'

'Enjoy yourselves, you crazy people. I'm going to stay here in my warm house and watch movies.'

'See you later. Be good.' I kissed Sarah and climbed into the car.

Paul tied the surfboards to the roof and threw the rest of the gear into the boot. Sally and Simon climbed into the back. Even though I'd told Sally it would be freezing on the beach so she should wear really warm clothes and a windcheater, she had dressed up for the occasion. She was wearing black skinny jeans with high wedge-heeled boots, a black polo-neck and a fur-trimmed suede jacket. I was wearing an old pair of jeans, a long-sleeved thermal T-shirt, a polo-neck, a jumper, a fleece, a big wool-lined windcheater and wellingtons.

Every time I looked in the mirror, Simon and Sally were whispering to each other or kissing. They couldn't get enough of each other. Sally was like a young girl in love. I envied them. They seemed so carefree while I felt crushed under the weight of everything that was going on. When I glanced at Paul, the lines on his face seemed deeper. You could tell he was feeling the strain too. I longed for the days when we'd had no worries or responsibilities.

Sally and Simon giggled about something in the back and he kissed her neck. I remembered when Paul and I couldn't keep our hands off each other. I remembered when he used to look at me the way Simon looked at Sally – as if she was the most incredible person on the planet, pure adoration. We needed to get our mojo back. We were still young, but I felt old.

When we got to Magheramore Beach, Paul pulled up on the side of the road. 'Sorry, guys, I have to park here. They've put a gate up to stop cars driving down. It's only a five-minute walk to the beach and it's good for surfing.'

While Paul and Simon sat on the edge of the boot changing into their rash vests, wetsuits, boots, hoods and gloves, Sally and I sat in the back. Sally was shivering. It was sunny but bitterly cold.

'Look at Simon's body – isn't he hot?' Sally asked, admiring him.

'I don't want your boyfriend to catch me checking him out,' I whispered.

'Go on, he's not looking.'

I glanced over the top of the back seat to see Simon's stark naked back – and bum – and then he turned around. Shit! I jumped back down, cringing. 'Well, he thinks I'm a pervert now.'

'Did he see you?' She giggled.

'Yes, he bloody did. I'm so embarrassed.'

'Don't worry – he was married to a nutter so he thinks all women are mad. Did you see his bod?'

'I got a good look, more than I ever hoped to see, and, yes, he is in good shape,' I lied. Simon wasn't particularly fit. He was pale and round.

'I'm telling you, Ava, the sex is fantastic.' Sally sighed with satisfaction.

I sighed over the distant memory of amazing sex with Paul. My advice from Madame Sophie had gone out of the window with everything that was going on at home. Paul and I hadn't had sex in ages. He hadn't even looked interested. We were both too shattered. Sleep was a welcome relief, these days.

Sally got out to help Simon with his wetsuit. They kissed and hugged when she fitted the hood over his head. Paul pulled his on expertly, then took the boards down from the roof. He strode off down the lane as we trundled after him, Simon holding Sally's hand, me trailing behind, envying them their closeness, both physical and emotional.

'Argh!' Sally shouted, as she stumbled into an enormous pothole. Her foot was stuck in knee-deep water. Simon pulled her out.

'Bollox! I love these boots.' Her right foot was covered with muddy water.

'I told you to wear wellies,' I reminded her.

'Yeah, well, I wanted to look nice.'

'You'd look good in anything,' Simon assured her. They kissed, again, and Sally cheered up. She hobbled forward, her boot squelching along the path.

The beach, when we got there, was stunning. It was a small bay with cliffs on either side and you had to walk down steep steps to get to the sand.

There were two other surfers. Paul knew them so he went over to say hi, while Sally and I laid out the rug. I sat down while she hovered beside a shivering Simon.

'Simon, Sally tells me you're a lawyer. What do you specialize in?' I asked.

'Would you believe family law?' He grinned.

'You must see some sad cases.'

'I do, actually. It's always tough when there are kids involved. Thank God Maura and I didn't have any. It just makes everything so much more complicated.'

'And they'd have had her genes,' Sally added.

'Which would not be a good thing. Yours, on the other hand, are a different matter. Our kids will be great.' Simon kissed her.

Paul came back. 'Sorry about that. They're two guys I meet down here all the time. The smaller one is a professional surfer. They said the surf's really good today, up to eight feet.'

Simon didn't seem too thrilled by that.

'Simon, I just want to give you a few tips before we head into the water,' he continued. 'It's all about paddling and balance. You need to watch the board – it can, as Ava said, hit you and knock you over. When you're paddling out, if the nose of the board starts to dip forward into the water – it's called pearling – you just need to move back on it to readjust your weight. If you put too much weight on the back of the board – this is called corking – you need to shuffle forward until it's lying naturally in the water. When you're paddling out, do it like the front crawl, one arm at a time.'

'Right, excellent. How do I stand up on it?'

Paul laughed. 'It's very difficult to get up on your first go, but the best way to do it is like this.' He lay down on his board to demonstrate. 'Lie on your chest, head up, looking forward. Put your hands on the board beside your shoulders, palms down, like you were going to do a push-up. Push your upper body up while pulling your feet under you, laying them on the line down the middle of the board so your weight is centred.'

Simon copied him. Sally clapped. 'You're a natural.'

'Thanks.' He kissed her again.

'Sally, can you peel yourself off him for a minute?' Paul asked.

'I'm trying to be encouraging.'

'Just don't smother him before he's got into the water. Now, when you come up on the board, remember to keep low. If you stand up straight you'll fall. You have to crouch down like a sumo wrestler and grip the board with your feet. And always remember to look up. If you look at your feet, you'll fall down.'

'It's really hard so don't worry if you can't get up. I was hopeless.' I wanted to reassure Simon. He didn't look very sporty and the chances of him getting up were very slim. I also wanted to make polite conversation with him so he didn't think I was some kind of peeping Tom.

'Thanks, Ava. I'm a pretty good skier so I'm hoping to get the hang of it quickly.'

I didn't mention that I was a very good snowboarder and it had made shag-all difference to my surfing skills.

'Let's go for it,' he said, taking his glasses off and handing them to Sally.

The two men jogged down to the water's edge. Well, Paul jogged, Simon kind of panted along beside him, trying to balance the board under his arm. When they got to the edge, Paul said, 'I'm going to head out to catch the waves breaking. Why don't you stay here in the white water near the shore? Just be aware of the currents. They're pretty strong and tend to drag you to the left towards the rocks.'

'Go on, Simon, I know you'll be great,' Sally shouted.

'Let's do it,' Paul said, and ran straight into the icy sea.

Simon followed. After he'd gone three steps, we heard, 'FUCK! It's freezing.'

Paul looked back and laughed. 'Come on, you'll warm up soon.'

Simon followed him in, cursing all the way.

For the next half an hour we watched him trying to lie and balance on his surfboard and paddle, but it kept tipping over. We saw him swallow half the ocean. But he kept trying. Paul meanwhile had paddled far out and was standing up and riding waves like an old pro. I hadn't realized how good he'd got. It was pretty impressive to see him balancing on a wave . . . sexy.

'Do you think you should tell him to come in?' I asked Sally, as Simon disappeared under the water again.

'No point. He's a man. He'll stay out there until he gets up on that board or dies of hypothermia,' Sally said.

'FUCK!' we heard again, as the board smacked Simon on the shoulder.

We both began to laugh.

'Thank God he's crap at it because I have no intention of freezing my arse off while he surfs. I'm turning blue. No wonder you never come with Paul.' She pulled her jacket around her and tried to drink the coffee from the flask but her hands were shaking too much and she spilt it on her jeans. 'Shit. It's unbearably cold, my foot is wet and soggy, my boots are ruined and my hair is a mess with all this wind and sand. There is no way in hell I'm ever letting him do this again. He can stick to golf. This is not civilized. It's for teenagers looking for thrills. Paul is insane. How can he like it?'

'He loves it. He says he completely switches off and thinks of nothing but the next wave. It's a mental holiday.'

'FUCK IT!' we heard, as the board walloped Simon on the side of the head.

'Or in Simon's case a mental thumping.' She giggled.

'I think you're safe. It doesn't look like Simon's talents lie in surfing.'

'Thank God for that. I've lost all the sensation in my toes. Have you anything else in that basket, like alcohol?'

I handed her the second flask, which had brandy in it.

'At least this will help numb the pain.'

'Sally, does Simon want to have kids?' I asked gently. She put the flask down.

'I don't know. He's mentioned them a few times but only in general terms and I always change the subject.'

'Have you told him how you feel about it?'

She looked away. 'Not yet. I'll get around to it.'

'*Whoooooohoooo!*' Paul whooped, as he came in on a huge wave.

'FUCK THIS,' Simon roared, as he disappeared under the water again.

'Hey, boys, Ava and I are turning to ice. Have you had enough fun yet?' Sally shouted.

'Five more minutes,' Paul said, paddling back out.

We heard an unintelligible grunt from Simon.

'Paul's five minutes means half an hour,' I warned her.

'I can't take any more, I'm too cold.' She was shivering again.

'We could just head back to the car and drive to the nearest pub.'

'Tempting as that sounds, it has taken me forty-three years to find a good man and I ain't leaving him here to drown.'

'Looks like your surfer dude has had enough.' Simon was struggling out of the sea, dragging his board behind him.

'Piece of cake,' he said, flopping down on the rug as we laughed. 'Stop! Don't make me laugh – I think I've broken a rib. Everywhere hurts.'

'I'll kiss your face now and the other sore bits later,' Sally said, and they kissed.

I tried not to look as uncomfortable as I felt. I walked down to the edge of the sea and motioned for Paul to come in. He came out, smiling. 'God, that was fantastic. Is Simon all right? Not too battered and bruised?'

'I think he's recovering,' I said, as we watched the two love-birds smooching.

'Ah, young love,' Paul said, as he walked up to them. 'Come on, you two, we need to get this man into some warm clothes. I hope you haven't been put off for life – it was tough out there today.'

'I have to be honest with you, Paul.' Simon's teeth were chattering so badly, it was hard to make out what he was saying. 'I really don't think surfing's for me. I'm a Quaker, and we're better suited to golf and chess.'

'Fair enough. Let me at least buy you a well-deserved drink.'

'That I can handle.'

'Hear, hear,' Sally said, as she and Simon walked arm in arm up the lane.

'You looked good out there,' I said to Paul.

'I was showing off for you.'

'It was fun,' I admitted.

'It was nice having you there today.'

Sally had to help Simon out of his wetsuit because his hands were completely numb. I started the car and put the heat on full blast to help the men defrost while they were getting changed. I made sure not to look in Simon's direction. Paul, meanwhile, whipped his suit off and got dressed. When Simon finally got his clothes back on, he shuffled into the back seat with Sally, who blew on his hands and rubbed them to try to get his circulation going.

Paul hopped into the front seat and we headed off to the nearest pub for food and drink.

'Oh, thank you, God, I can feel my feet again,' Simon said, wriggling his toes in front of the log-fire.

'Here you go, this should help.' Paul came over with drinks, toasted sandwiches and chips. We devoured the lot.

'So, Simon, what are your intentions with young Sally here?' Paul asked.

Sally choked on her drink.

'Shag her and move on.' Simon smirked.

'Respect,' Paul said, and they high-fived each other.

'Stop, please, you're hilarious,' Sally said.

'She's not a bad catch, our Sally – easy on the eye, successful, owns her own place, no messy divorce, no snotty-nosed kids . . . not much baggage for an old bird.'

'He's the one with the baggage – a certifiable ex-wife who stalks me.' Sally bit into a chip.

'I had the pleasure of meeting Maura recently.' I smiled at Simon.

'I hope she didn't give you a hard time. She's just gone off the Richter scale since I met Sally. She can't handle me moving on.'

'And am I right in thinking she's the one who went offside when you were married?' Paul asked.

'With her boss, total cliché.'

'What is it with women? She cheats on you and then goes mental when you meet someone else. How does that logic work?'

'I don't think Simon's the one to ask – he married the psycho,' I said, as we laughed.

'From one extreme to the other, right, babe?' Sally said. 'From a fruitcake to a completely sane, reasonable woman.'

'Absolutely.' Simon kissed her palm.

'Will you two lay off?' Paul remonstrated. 'You're putting me off my food.'

'I put up with it for years from you two,' Sally reminded him. 'You used to be all over each other. It's my turn now, so suck it up.'

36

Visiting day came around. During my phone calls with Ali over the last few days she had either cried and begged me to come and get her or was monosyllabic. She'd answer every question with yes or no. She was punishing me for leaving her there. I always called her from my bedroom, so I could lock myself into the bathroom and cry in peace afterwards.

Donna called me to say that Ali had asked her to bring in some schoolwork. Ali had said she needed the distraction of studying while she was in the clinic. It would help keep her sane.

I was delighted to hear that and told Donna I'd check with clinic staff and get straight back to her. When I asked Denise and Mary they said that all the girls tried to keep up with schoolwork as much as possible. It was good for them and stopped them obsessing about food – even if only briefly.

I called the school and spoke to the headmistress, Mrs Wilkins, who said she'd ask all the teachers to give Donna the necessary notes and assignments to bring in to Ali.

I called Donna back to fill her in. 'How did Ali sound when you spoke to her?' I asked.

'Uhm, well, you know, OK, I guess.'

'It's all right, Donna, you can tell me the truth. It's important that we don't have any more secrets. We all want Ali to get better, so please be honest.'

'She cried a lot and she sounded kind of angry.'

'Did she talk about food? Did she say she was eating?'

'She said she's trying really hard but that they're feeding her massive portions. But, Ava, when I asked her what she had for lunch it was only a small bit of cheese, two crackers and a milkshake. It didn't sound like a lot. I guess it'll take a while for her to eat normally.'

'Unfortunately it's going to be a slow process. We're just going to have to be patient and encourage her. I really appreciate you bringing her in her work, Donna. It's very sweet of you. You're a good friend.'

'It's no big deal. I miss Ali. I was kind of relieved when I found out she had anorexia because I couldn't understand why she was being so weird all of a sudden. She changed so quickly and it was scary. She's my best friend and I really miss her.'

'Hopefully she'll be back to herself soon. Look, I'm going to visit her tomorrow. If you like I can pick you up and you can bring over the assignments.'

'That'd be great.'

'OK, I'll meet you after school,' I said, relieved that Donna was coming with me.

Initially we'd all planned to visit Ali, but Mary had suggested that I go on my own for the first visit, then build it up. She said Ali would probably still be angry and resentful and she wanted to make sure that the visit was as calm as possible. She thought Donna coming was a good idea as the girls were always pleased to see their friends: it reminded them of 'normal life' and often helped spur them on in their recovery. I knew Ali would be pleased to see Donna. She was not the 'enemy'. I was.

When we arrived at the clinic, Denise told us that Ali was in a session with Mary Boland and would be another fifteen minutes. We went and sat in Ali's room to wait. I saw Emily hopping down the corridor and prayed she wouldn't see us. She worried me. I didn't want Ali to befriend her – she was too messed up. I wanted Ali to become friendly with some girl who'd put on two stone and was about to go home. I was terrified Emily would be a bad influence on her.

'Why does that girl keep jumping up and down?' Donna

asked, as we watched Emily hop every few seconds from one foot to the other.

'She's got OCD.'

'That would wreck my head. It must be exhausting.'

Emily saw me through the door. Shit.

'Hi, Ava, are you here to see Alison?'

'Yes – hi, Emily. This is Donna, Ali's best friend.'

'Oh, yeah, she mentioned you. How's it going?' Emily smiled at Donna.

'Good, thanks. How are you?' Donna asked politely.

'Not great.' She pointed to the fresh bandages around both arms.

'What happened?' Donna asked.

'I was having a bad week and a friend brought me in flowers that were tied with wire so I cut myself open.'

'Oh, my God, it must have been agony.' Donna was appalled.

Emily shrugged. 'I'm kind of used to it.'

'How has Ali been?' I asked, wanting to get off the subject of self-harm.

'Not so good. She's been lurching between anger and tears, but I think she's beginning to get used to it.'

'How long have you been in here?' Donna asked.

'This is my third time. I'm not very good at coping on the outside.'

'Sorry to hear that,' Donna said.

'Why do you think you find it so difficult?' I asked.

'Well, when you're in here, all the food is weighed and measured and served to you. You know exactly what you're eating, how much and when. But when you leave you could find yourself in a restaurant panicking because you don't know what the portion sizes are or if the food was cooked in butter or oil or if when you ask for a coffee with skimmed milk you're actually getting skimmed milk. It totally freaks you out. Even when you're eating at home it takes ages to weigh and measure everything and you have to make sure you have a snack with you at all times to keep your calorie intake up. Sometimes you just don't feel like eating but once you skip a meal or snack it's a slippery slope.'

'Would it help if someone did all the weighing and measuring at home for you?' I asked, trying to work out how best to help Ali when she came back to us.

Emily shook her head. 'Not really, because you don't trust anyone. You need to do it yourself so you know that it's exactly the right amount and no extra has been added.'

'Is the cutting related to the anorexia too?' Donna pointed to Emily's bandages.

'No. My father was a drunk who abused all of us. Not physically but emotionally. You know the kind of stuff – "You're useless, you'll never amount to anything. You're ugly and stupid . . ." My two brothers went to America as soon as they left school and shortly after that my dad left us and went off with another woman, so it's just Mum and me at home now.'

'God, Emily, that's terrible,' I said, warming to the poor girl. 'If it's any consolation I think you're beautiful, clever and very brave.'

She blushed and hopped. 'Thanks. I'm not, though. But Ali is. She's really gorgeous.'

'And the seriously cool thing about Ali is that she doesn't know it,' Donna said.

'She's so modest,' Emily agreed. 'I'm glad she's in here – she's great to talk to. She's a really good listener.'

'She so is. I used to tell her all my problems,' Donna said, and then got embarrassed. 'I mean, not like I have any compared to you.'

Emily hopped up and down. 'When she heard about my screwed-up family, she said she felt lucky to have such a normal one.'

'That's nice to hear.' I smiled.

'Here she comes.' Emily hopped over to say hi to Ali, who was wheeled into the room by a nurse who helped her out of the wheelchair and up onto the bed.

'I'll leave you guys to it. Catch you later, Alison,' Emily said, hopping off.

'Hello, pet.' I went over to hug Ali.

She gave me a frosty reception. 'Hi, Donna.' She looked at her friend, who came and sat on the edge of the bed.

'Hey, Ali, how's it going? I've brought you loads of stuff. You're not going to believe how much work they're piling on now that the mock exams are coming up.'

The two girls talked about school and study, and Donna showed Ali the assignments she needed to hand in by the end of the week.

'Emily seems nice but, God, what a messed-up life she has,' Donna commented. 'You must feel really normal compared to her.'

'What's normal about being forced to lie down in bed all day and have people bringing in trays of food every five minutes and staring at you while you eat?'

'It doesn't sound too bad,' Donna said. 'I'd love to be waited on hand and foot in bed. Do you think I could book in for a week? I could do with the rest.'

Ali managed a weak smile.

Denise came in and I introduced her to Donna. She told us that Ali had put on two pounds so far. It was good progress, but she needed to eat more of her meals if she was to reach six stone six and come off bed-rest.

'Well done,' I said, trying to encourage Ali.

'That's brilliant,' Donna enthused.

'Well, I'll leave you to it,' said Denise. 'Ava, don't forget your family session this Saturday morning with Mary Boland.'

'I won't, thanks, Denise.'

'I'll leave you guys to catch up.' Donna got up and put her bag on her shoulder. 'I'll wait for you in Reception, Ava. See you, Ali, hang in there.' She hugged her friend and left us alone.

Silence.

'Everyone says hi. They're all dying to see you at the next visit.'

'Yippee! I can't wait.'

'Sarah's practising day and night for the big play.'

Ali rolled over and started to flick through her science book.

'Ali, can't you try to talk to me?' I pleaded. 'We all just want you to get better and come home. I know this is hard for you, pet, but please don't shut me out.'

'You're the one who shut me out. Putting me in this prison.'

'I had to do it to make you better.'

'You just wanted to get rid of me.'

'You know that's not true.'

'Do I?'

'Jesus, Ali, I'm doing the best I can,' I said, choking back tears.

She turned to look at me and started to cry. 'Please don't leave me here. Please, Mum. Don't make me stay. I'm begging you, take me home.'

'Ali,' I said, hugging her, 'I love you and I would walk through fire for you, but the only person who can make you better now is you. The only person who can eat for you is you. The only person who can deal with your anger is you. If I could eat for you I would. I'm sorry, pet, but you have to help yourself. It's breaking my heart to see you in here, but it's the best place for you right now. You need help – and, to be honest, so do I. We all need to understand why this has happened and how to prevent it ever happening again. All I want is for you to be happy. I miss you.' I kissed her forehead and hurried out before I completely broke down.

When I got home, Sarah and Bobby were arguing in the kitchen. It sounded very heated. I crept into the lounge, sat down and listened.

'Seriously, Bobby, it's not that long till the big performance and you really need to work on your lines.'

'I did work on them but you keep changing them.'

'That's because you keep going on about rugby and it's just not Shakespeare. It's OK when you say, "Juliet, I love you more

273

than my personally signed Brian O'Driscoll Grand Slam jersey," but you can't say, "Don't worry, Juliet, I'm not scared of your old man. I can run as fast as Luke Fitzgerald who's nearly as fast as Shane Williams."'

'Why not? It makes total sense – they've got some of the fastest legs in rugby.'

'That's the whole point. I just don't think the Montagues and Capulets played rugby back then in, like, ancient times. So you have to tone it down.'

I smiled to myself. Sarah was the most unwittingly funny person I'd ever met. If she ever became more self-aware, she'd make a good comedienne.

'Mr Goggin said it was OK to put in a few rugby references,' Bobby said. 'He said as long as it doesn't change the storyline he's fine with it. I've only dropped three in.'

'It's two too many.'

'This Romeo guy's a fag.'

'Romeo's not *gay*! He's in love with Juliet who, in case you missed it, is a *girl*!'

'Well, he's a geek, then.'

'The only geek here is you.'

'Why are you taking it so seriously? It's just a school play.'

'Because it's the only thing that's keeping me sane at the moment while my family is falling apart. And I think I have real talent as an actress and I want to prove it. I'm not intelligent like Ali so I want to make Mum and Dad proud of me this way.'

'OK, babe, I get it.'

I peeped out to see Bobby giving Sarah a hug. I was so glad she had him – especially now when she needed someone to lean on. He was very good to her and put up with all her bossiness. Paul and I were so distracted with Ali that Sarah was getting left out. I was going to make damn sure we were in the front row of the audience at the play, clapping loudly so she'd see how proud we were of her.

37

On Saturday morning at nine forty-five Paul, Sarah and I went to the clinic for our family session. Paul and I were really nervous while Sarah was as cool as a breeze.

When we drove up the drive, she whistled. 'Hello! This is amazing. It's like a really posh house that Prince William or someone would live in. I thought it was going to be grey and depressing like a mental institution. I wouldn't mind staying here myself.'

'It's not half as nice inside,' I said.

'Well, it's pretty fancy on the outside.'

As we walked towards Reception, we saw a very large girl going for a walk with a nurse.

'Ohmigod – is that what happens when you get better? Do you turn into a big lump of lard?' Sarah asked.

'Keep your voice down,' I hissed. 'Some of the people in here have overeating problems.'

'They shouldn't put the fatties in with the sticks. It'd hardly make you want to eat if you saw those ten chins staring you in the face,' she whispered. 'I presume they have to be in a different section or there'd be no food left for the anorexics.'

Thankfully, before she could voice any more opinions, Mary Boland came to meet us. She showed us to a small room with five chairs set up in a circle.

'Welcome, everyone, and thank you for coming. Now I know you're all probably nervous. This is a very important meeting. Alison is putting on weight, which is positive, but the nurses and I feel that we still haven't broken through to her. She's gaining weight simply because she is unable to exercise and is eating small amounts of food regularly. She's a very fragile, sensitive girl, who is struggling with life. Alison needs to build trust in the world before she can give up control of food and we need to build her self-esteem. She needs to value herself as a person. She needs to figure out who she is and what her place is in the world. She is a very lost soul at the moment.

'In today's session she must be allowed talk through her feelings and you must be prepared for her to be very angry. She's angry with the world, with you, with herself, with the situation she is in, and she's frightened of eating and letting go of the only thing she can control. She is absolutely terrified to give in and eat because then the feelings and emotions she has suppressed with hunger will come flooding back. Whatever happens today, try not to take anything she says personally.'

'That's easy for you to say. You're not on the receiving end of it,' Sarah said.

'I know this is difficult for you, but you must be patient. Recovery is a long and slow process. It will be very much one step forward and two steps back. It's important for you to vent your frustration before you see Alison so that you can be as calm as possible with her,' Mary warned us.

'Whatever we say, it's always the wrong thing. I'm terrified of saying something that'll make her worse. I feel as though I'm letting her down by not bringing her home like she begs me to every time I call,' I admitted, trying not to cry.

Mary nodded. 'These feelings are completely normal. All parents are afraid of saying the wrong thing. What's important is for you to look her in the eye and keep asking her how she feels. Ask her things like "How do you feel when you control the food? Does it make you feel better? Can you tell us why you're angry?" Plan what you're going to say to her so that it doesn't come out the wrong way. Allow yourself to be comfortable with gaps in the conversation. They can be positive, not negative. Maybe you could paraphrase what she says to you to show her you understand. That will encourage her to say more.'

'Easier said than done,' Paul interrupted. 'You can't have a conversation with someone who refuses to speak to you. She won't talk to me when I call. I can't get through to her.'

'Sometimes when conversation proves difficult, we suggest the parent writes a letter expressing how they feel. Tell her how much you want her to get better and how much you love and value her and how you want to help her in any way you can.'

'I suppose that's an idea,' Paul said.

'You must remember that recovery is going to take a lot of courage and energy on Alison's part. Eating is torture for her.'

'And watching her not eat is torture for us,' I commented.

'I understand this is a very trying time for all of you. Now, why don't we bring Alison in and have a chat?'

Ali was wheeled into the room. Paul and I went over to kiss her while Sarah waved from her chair.

'Welcome, everyone,' Mary said. 'What I'm hoping to achieve today is an open and honest conversation about how you're all feeling and to try to come up with some steps and plans to get Alison back on her feet. The key today is to listen without judgement. I need everyone to remember that. There may be some anger and some frustration, but we must be patient and non-judgemental. We are all here for a common goal – to help Alison get better.'

Paul and I nodded eagerly, Ali looked at the floor and Sarah yawned.

'Now, can you tell me a little about Alison's childhood?' Mary asked us.

'She had a very happy childhood,' Paul said. 'Before all of this started, she was a perfect child – bright, kind, considerate, happy. She's never given us a day's trouble. Always a straight-A student, never had any problems at school, just a really great daughter.'

'She had a very normal childhood,' I added. 'She always seemed, as Paul said, very happy and content. We're just a regular family. Nothing strange or unusual went on.'

'Except the shooting,' Mary reminded me.

'Oh, God, yes, except the shooting, which I think, in hindsight, we mishandled. We should have been honest with the girls and not tried to protect them. We thought we were doing the right thing. They were so young and I was worried they'd be traumatized, but I can see now that it was the wrong way to deal with it. I fully admit that we messed up there and I feel awful about it.'

'How do you feel about that, Alison?' Mary asked my daughter.

Ali said nothing.

'Come on, Alison, don't bottle your emotions up. It's all right to be angry. Whatever you're feeling, let it out.'

Ali's head snapped up and she stared at Mary, eyes blazing. 'I'M RAGING!' she shouted. 'I'm pissed off that my parents made up that stupid story about Dad having appendicitis when everyone knew he'd been shot. Why couldn't they tell me the truth? Why couldn't they talk to me about it? Why did I have to live with this ridiculous lie in the house? I was never able to say I was scared. I was terrified the man would come back and shoot us all. I only found out he went to prison when I eavesdropped on their conversation. No child should be shut out and lied to like that. They didn't protect me, they stifled me. They made me suppress how I felt. They stunted me. But I had to play their game. They were trying to pretend they weren't upset. When I found Mum crying, she'd say she had something in her eye. LIES, LIES, LIES. I was desperate for someone to reassure me, to hug me and tell me it was all right. I was nine, for God's sake. Instead I was constantly hugging my parents and trying to make them smile again by being the best child I could be. I was consoling them! It's ridiculous. I tried talking to Sarah about it, but she wasn't even eight and whenever I brought it up, she'd just say, "Who cares?"'

Paul and I looked at each other in shock. We'd never seen Ali like this before. She was shaking with pure fury. It was like looking at a stranger.

'I'm sorry, pet. I didn't want you to be frightened so I said Dad had his appendix out. I can see now it was silly. I'm sorry you were scared and had no one to talk to. I wish I'd done things differently. I had no idea you knew – it must have been awful for you.'

'I'm sorry too, Ali. We wanted to protect you. We thought we were doing the right thing,' Paul added.

'Well, you didn't protect me. You made it a million times worse. I felt so alone. I had no one to talk to,' she fumed.

'Excuse me,' Sarah said, sitting up straight. 'I'd like to say something to my sister.'

'Go ahead,' Mary encouraged her.

Sarah leant forward and roared, 'GET OVER IT! Dad got shot eight years ago. It happened. He survived. No one died. Why do you have to go around dragging the past behind you on a leash? MOVE ON. GET A LIFE. Jesus Christ, you don't hear me bitching and moaning about how you ruined my life by waking me up and telling me about the bloody shooting. I probably never would have found out about it if you hadn't dragged me over to the window to be a witness. Am I starving myself to death because of something that happened eight years ago? No, I bloody am not, because I like life, Ali. I like having fun and boyfriends and not sitting around whining about my past. Get over yourself. Mum and Dad are, like, totally stressed out. You're ruining their lives. They've aged ten years in the last few weeks – they look old now. So why don't you stop being so selfish and eat something? I'm sick of hearing how sensitive poor Ali is and how perfect she is. She's killing herself and we're all supposed to dance around and feel sorry for her. Well, you know what I think? I think you're a drama queen. Have you got enough attention now, Ali? Are you satisfied now that your family is totally miserable and too terrified to say boo to you in case you stop eating four cornflakes a day and die? You're being a selfish cow and I'm sick of your bullshit.'

There was silence in the room. Mary went to speak, but Alison jumped up and pointed a finger at Sarah. 'Fuck you!' she snarled. 'We weren't all born thinking we're God's gift to men. We don't all have your over-confidence and delusional idea that we're the best thing to happen to the earth. The only reason you don't have issues about the shooting is because you're so self-obsessed that anything that doesn't directly affect you goes over your head. You don't care about anyone but yourself. You've never worried about anyone else in your life. As long as Sarah's OK, then to hell with the rest of us. You don't care about studying or if Dad's pub is doing well or if Mum's company is making money or if Charlie is losing his mind. You think global warming is great because it means we'll get better weather. You're so shallow and selfish it makes me sick.'

'Oh, no, Ali. I think you'll find that starving yourself is what's making you sick. And as for not being sensitive, do you honestly think I want to be like you and end up in a loony bin with a bunch of anorexic, self-harming freaks? And if I'm so selfish then what the hell am I doing here, with my play coming up, listening to you crashing on about how difficult your childhood was? Do you honestly think I enjoy coming to this nuthouse? You're the one who's delusional.' Sarah sat back and crossed her arms.

I sank into my chair, stunned at both outbursts. The girls had always been very different, but they had got on well. Sarah made Ali laugh and Ali made Sarah think. Sure, they'd had their fights, but nothing like this – never, ever had they been so hurtful and personal. Paul looked equally shocked.

'Well, that was very revealing,' Mary said, as I cringed. What did she mean? That now she could see our family was completely dysfunctional? That both my daughters were messed up?

'Well done, girls, you both let go of a lot of suppressed anger, which is extremely healthy. Right, let's move on to another topic that Alison has brought up in our one-to-one sessions. She said she feels a lot of pressure from you, Paul, to do well in her finals and go on to study medicine. She finds this difficult to deal with at times.'

Paul bristled. 'I've never put pressure on her. I just encourage her like any good father would. She said she wanted to be a doctor. I was delighted and told her to go for it. Where's the harm in that?'

'Do you want to study medicine, Alison?' Mary probed.

Ali shook her head. 'I never said I wanted to be a doctor. I said I wasn't sure what I wanted to be and Dad said that because I was so clever I should study medicine. He said it'd make him so proud to have a daughter who was a doctor. He pushed me into the decision.'

'What would you like to study?' Mary asked her.

'I'm not sure yet, maybe journalism.'

Paul's mouth opened like a goldfish's. He closed it, then said, 'But you told me you wanted to be a doctor.'

'I only said it to make you happy. I knew that was what you wanted me to do. I didn't want to disappoint you, so I went along with it. But it's not what I want to be.'

'Well, why didn't you just say so?'

'Because every time you meet someone you tell them how proud you are that your daughter is going to be a doctor. I didn't want to let you down in front of everyone.'

Paul stared at his daughter. 'Ali, I've been proud of you your whole life. You could never let me down. I don't care what you study. I'd like you to go to college because you're smart, but as for what you become, that's up to you. I just want you to be happy. I'd love a doctor in the family, but if you want to be a journalist, that's fine with me. I never meant to put you under pressure. I can't believe you felt that way. I'm sorry.'

Ali cried into her handkerchief. Paul went over and gave her a hug. For the first time in months, she showed him affection and hugged him back. Mary smiled at me and mouthed, 'Excellent progress.'

'And now to the subject of David,' Mary continued. We were

clearly going to cover all the angles today. 'Alison has told me how heartbroken she felt and how humiliating it was to be in school every day seeing David with his new girlfriend.'

'I tried talking to her about it but she wouldn't talk to me,' I explained.

'I couldn't talk to you about it, Mum, because you were too emotional. You kept getting upset and saying he was an idiot and I was great and there were more guys out there. It wasn't what I wanted to hear.'

'What did you want to hear?'

'I just wanted you to listen. I didn't want you to fix it or tell me what to do. I just wanted you to let me talk.'

'I did listen.'

'Only for about a minute and then you'd tell me to move on and forget about him and that he wasn't worthy of me . . .'

'I was trying to build up your confidence.' I looked at Mary, confused. 'What did I do wrong?'

'Nothing,' she assured me. 'It's just that sometimes there is no need to say anything. Sometimes it's just best to let a person talk and get their troubles off their chest without providing any advice or solutions.'

'I was trying to make her feel better.'

'Of course you were. Now, Alison, did you find it difficult that your sister was in a relationship?'

'Yeah, I did. Sarah and Bobby were always all over each other and you could see how into her he was and that was hard.'

'Oh, so it's my fault now?' Sarah snapped. 'What am I supposed to do – dump Bobby to make you feel better?'

'That's not what Alison is saying,' Mary said. 'She's just explaining that it was difficult to see two people in love when her heart was broken.'

'Well, maybe if she'd taken my advice instead of moping around feeling sorry for herself, she wouldn't be in here.'

'Oh, please, are you talking about your stupid ten-step plan?' Ali retorted. 'It's so lame.'

'Well, in case you hadn't noticed, I'm the one with the boyfriend. And if I did get dumped, Ali, I'd get off my arse and find myself another. I wouldn't go around feeling sorry for myself, blame everyone else for my problems, stop eating and tell my mother to shut up and say nothing except "Listen to me moaning." You're pathetic.'

'No, you're pathetic because you never see how anything you do affects other people. You can't see how snogging Bobby in front of me the day after I got dumped might have been hard for me. Or that you constantly doing badly in exams puts more pressure on me to do well or that –'

'I cannot take another second of this bullshit.' Sarah got up and put her coat on. 'I refuse to listen to any more poor-me stories from my sister. She's given everyone in the family a good battering.'

'I'm sorry you feel that way, Sarah. Alison was just being honest. Why do you feel so defensive?' Mary asked.

Sarah shook her finger at Mary. 'Don't even think about trying your psychobabble on me. I'm the normal one in this family. I don't have "issues". I like my life just the way it is. And, as my sister so sweetly pointed out, I have no self-esteem problems. I know I rock. So you can save your analysis for the freaks who need it. I'm out of here.' Sarah walked out the door. Before closing it, she turned back to Ali: 'You used to be great. I don't know how you got so messed up, but I wish the normal Ali would come back. I miss her.'

38

'I just don't understand,' Paul said, for the zillionth time. 'Why did Ali say I was forcing her into medicine? Mary must think I'm some kind of tyrant. I never said Ali had to be a doctor. I just said I thought it'd be a great thing to do and she agreed with me. I'm afraid to say anything to her now. If I look at her sideways she'll probably accuse me of something else.'

'Calm down,' I soothed. 'She was just venting. She's angry at everyone and Mary said the more she lets out, the speedier her recovery will be. It's all that pent-up emotion that's causing her eating problems. She was pretty hard on me, too, and on Sarah. Mind you, Sarah didn't hold back either – I had no idea she was so furious with Ali. How did we manage to raise such angry kids?'

'I have to say I agreed with everything Sarah said,' Paul admitted. 'I've been wanting to tell Ali to get over herself for weeks. To think Sarah was the one I always worried about and now she's a rock of sense. I never in my life thought Ali would be the one to cause so much trouble. She seemed so sensible. Sarah was the wild one, the one we needed to watch. But look at them now. Jesus, Ava, it's so frustrating – I want to shake Ali. All this tiptoeing around is doing my head in. If I'd stopped eating and tried to blame it on my parents I'd have got an almighty kick up the arse.'

'Well, we've moved on from that and now we listen to our children and help them instead of brushing problems under the carpet. One of the main reasons Ali is sick is because we didn't talk about the shooting. We pretended it didn't happen and look at the result. Communication is vital.'

'Why didn't we have two sons? Two big strapping lads who'd

spend all day chasing a ball – none of this sitting around feeling hard done by and blaming their parents for everything.'

'Because if we had two boys, we wouldn't have Ali and Sarah. And despite your protestations you adore them. Look, I know this is really hard, but we have to be patient and we have to try to stay positive.'

'I'm trying, Ava, although I really don't understand what the hell is going on inside her head. But I'll do my best and bite my tongue.'

I decided not to tell Paul that in the research I had done, the average time for someone suffering with anorexia to recover fully and regain a healthy relationship with food was five years. Each case was different and early detection was the key to a speedier recovery, but there was no quick fix.

'Well, I'd better go and see how the pub is doing – I've been neglecting it a bit lately with everything that's going on.' Paul kissed me and went off to work.

As Paul left, Charlie came in. 'How did it go? How's my grand-daughter?'

'It was gruesome, actually. She tore strips off all of us. The psychologist must think I'm such a bad mother.' I sighed and Charlie came over to sit beside me. It was nice having him there. I didn't have to pretend with him. I felt I had to be positive in front of Paul and Sarah, but with Charlie I could be totally honest. 'She's so angry with all of us. It's really upsetting and humiliating to have our lives and our mistakes exposed in front of Mary. I keep going over and over the past and what I could have done differently, but I can't change it. It happened. I'm just hoping that now Ali has ranted and raged about it she'll be able to move on. It's her only hope. She has to let it go. It's killing her. You should see her, Charlie – she's so full of anger. I barely recognize her. And when she's not shouting at us and blaming us, she's crying.'

'Poor Ali,' Charlie said.

'I'm scared. I feel as if we're losing the battle. There's a girl in there Ali's befriended, Emily, who's been in and out of the clinic three times. What if Ali can't fight it? I just want this to be over. I want my family back. I want Ali to get better. Did I do this to her? Is it such a sin to try to protect your kids from knowing their father was shot? Doesn't every mother try to spare their children pain? Am I really such a monster?'

'Ah, less of that self-pity. It won't get you anywhere,' Charlie said. 'Hold on now, before you bite my head off, I do see that it's very hard for you. But being a parent is a thankless job so you might as well get used to it.'

'Excuse me! I never caused you any trouble. And in case you hadn't noticed you are currently living in my house with your pregnant girlfriend. I've been the adult in this relationship for as long as I can remember.'

'It's amazing how people's memories fade. Who was it that came in and entertained you every night when you were in hospital with jaundice for two months when you were ten? Who was it who drove you to hospital when you went into labour with Sarah and you couldn't get in touch with Paul? Who was it who held your hand and sat with you for two days while the doctors tried to save Paul's life after the shooting? Who moved in and looked after the girls while you nursed Paul better? Who –'

'OK. I get the point and you're right. You've always been there for me. I'm sorry, Charlie. It's obviously a never-ending cycle of children blaming parents that goes from generation to generation.'

'Ah, yes, but when you get to my age, you get your own back. You move in with your child and they feel obliged look after you.' He grinned.

Sarah's head popped around the door. 'Just so we're clear, Mum, you and Dad are not moving in with me when you're old and wrinkly. There is no way I'm having you cramping my style. It's an old folks' home for you.'

'Charming,' I said.

She came in and sat beside us on the couch. 'Seriously, Mum, I'm not being mean but once I get my own place, I'm not sharing it with you and Dad. We've lived together long enough. Space is a good thing.'

'I agree,' I said. 'Are you OK after this morning?'

'Yeah – and I don't regret anything I said. It was good for Ali and me to let loose. She needs someone to tell her what a pain in the arse she's being and she obviously had some things she needed to get off her chest.'

'Are you upset about anything she said?'

'I think her accusing me of being selfish was way over the top and I don't agree with it. But she was right about one thing. I shouldn't have snogged Bobby in front of her just after she got dumped. It was thoughtless.'

'Well, thanks for coming and I do think it was healthy that you both got so much out but I hope you're not going to stay angry. I hope you'll make up with her, because she needs you, Sarah.'

'Don't worry, Mum, I'm not going to get the hump and ignore her. But I'm not talking to her today. I'll call her tomorrow when she's calmed down.'

Nadia came in and flopped into a chair. 'Oh, my Gods, I so sick. This baby kill me.'

'It's just morning sickness. It'll pass,' I assured her.

'You no understand. I dying.'

'I've had two children, Nadia. I know what morning sickness feels like. It's not great, but it's temporary.'

'Must be a boy. Only man can give me so much pain,' she moaned, as she popped another chocolate biscuit into her mouth.

'Hey, Nadia, where's my dress? I need to try it on. The play is, like, six days away,' Sarah reminded her.

Nadia made a big song and dance of getting up off her chair to fetch the dress. She returned with a tiny spangly piece of material.

Sarah jumped up. 'It looks cool. I'm going to try it on.'

'It's very short,' I said.

'She say she wants to haff legs out, so I makes it short.'

Sarah came back in. The dress was essentially a pair of togs with lots of sequins and glittery stones sewn onto it. It had a little chiffon skirt that went down to mid-thigh and a piece of chiffon draped over one shoulder. She looked like a cross between a burlesque dancer and a Roman slave.

'Ohmigod, I am so hot!' she squealed. 'Nadia, you did a great job. It's amazing.'

'I tell you I fery good.'

'It's very revealing,' I said.

'Hello! It's practically down to my knees.'

'Your dad will go mad when he sees it,' I warned her. 'You know how he feels about very short skirts.'

'He's not going to see it until I'm on the stage, so it's not going to be a problem.'

'It needs to be longer.'

'Mum,' Sarah said, eyeballing me, 'this is a really important event for me. I've never worked so hard on anything before. I'm the lead role and I need to look incredible. Clare, who is, like, playing the Nurse – who is actually supposed to be a nanny but the Shakespeare guy obviously got mixed up and called her Nurse – anyway, Clare is wearing an actual nurse's uniform, but not like a real nurse. It's a sexy nurse's outfit she got on the Internet.'

'Surely your teacher won't allow that.'

'He hasn't seen it. None of the girls are showing him their costumes. They're all wearing really short minis and stuff. Mine will actually be the longest by miles.'

'What's Bobby wearing?' I asked.

'He wanted to wear his rugby kit but I said no way. So he's wearing a really tight white T-shirt that says "Romeo Rocks" on the front and shows off his muscles and his tan. And then he's wearing Lycra cycling leggings that make his bum look *so* hot.

And then he's got, like, this really cool studded belt with a sword around his waist.'

'That sounds really, uhm, really modern,' I said.

'It's going to be the best play ever. And me and Bobby are going to be the stars. I'd better go and learn my lines. "Parting is such sweet sorrow,"' she finished theatrically as she exited the room.

'Paul's going to flip when he sees that outfit.'

'Let her be. Isn't it great to see her so enthusiastic about something?' Charlie said.

'You're right. It is. I can't wait to see the play – how are we going to keep straight faces? Lycra leggings! Shakespeare will be turning in his grave.'

That evening my phone rang. 'Hi, Mum, it's me, Ali.' She sounded nervous.

'Hi, how are you doing? Are you OK after the session this morning?'

'Actually, that's what I'm calling about. I'm sorry if I hurt your feelings.'

'I'm just glad you got all that anger out.'

'I feel bad about some of the stuff I said. I just kind of went mad.'

'It's OK, Ali, I'm not upset.'

'Is Dad?'

'No, he's fine too.'

'What about Sarah?'

'You know Sarah – it's like water off a duck's back.'

'Are you sure?'

'Yes, pet, I am. I don't want you to worry about anything. The session was actually very helpful. It's important for us to know why you're angry and where we made mistakes. It'll help us all move forward.'

'Thanks, Mum,' she said, beginning to cry. 'You're so great. I was really worried that you'd all hate me.'

'Ali, we love you. We will always love you no matter what you say or do.'

'It's just that Emily only has her mother and she's not really able to cope with her. She says her mum only calls her once a week and sometimes she doesn't come to visit her for ages. And I was scared I might have alienated you all today.'

'Oh, Ali, you could never do that. I promise you I'll always be here for you – and so will your dad, Sarah and Charlie.'

'I uh . . . uh . . . uh . . .' she sobbed '. . . just feel really lucky to have a normal family and I don't want to push you away.'

'You haven't pushed anyone away. Now, please, there's nothing to cry about. We love you and we think you're wonderful and we're here for you all the time. We're going to get through this, Ali. Everything is going to be OK.'

'Thanks, Mum. I'd better go now – I love you all.'

I hung up and cried – not the usual desperate tears: these were tinged with hope.

39

A few days later, Donna phoned me. She had been to see Ali the evening before. 'I just wanted to tell you that I thought she was a bit better today.'

'Really? That's great.' I was thrilled to hear this. Any improvement made my hopes soar.

'I brought her in some stuff to decorate her room – you know, just some posters and photos.'

'Ah, Donna, you're very thoughtful.'

'It's no big deal. But she seemed pleased. We were looking through the photos and there were a few from our school trip to Paris. It was brilliant and Ali looks gorgeous in the pictures, so I thought they might remind her of when she was happy and healthy. I think it kind of worked because she perked up a bit. And then I told her about David.'

'What about him?' I didn't like the sound of this. I didn't want anyone mentioning David around Ali. I was afraid it would set her off again. I wanted her to forget him and his stupid skinny girlfriend.

'He's broken up with Tracy. He got bored with her because she's so thick and all she wanted to talk about was modelling or the calorie content in food.'

'Oh.' That sounded good. If Ali thought David had dumped his girlfriend because she was obsessed with food, maybe she'd stop her own obsessing. 'What did Ali say?'

'Not much, but I could see she was thrilled. She was just worried about David thinking she was in a loony bin, but I told her Sarah had done an amazing job in school telling everyone that Ali had nervous exhaustion from studying too much and that she'd gone to a top-secret clinic where all the celebrities go for a rest.'

'Do the other kids really believe it?'

'Some people have guessed it's anorexia, but Sarah's pretty convincing. Anyway, I told Ali about Stephen Green's eighteenth birthday party, which is in March. It's going to be mega, so I said that maybe she should focus on trying to get well for that. It'd be so cool if she could come to it. She seemed excited so maybe she'll eat more now.'

'Donna, you're a star. Thanks so much for doing that. You really are an amazing friend. I owe you.'

'It's no problem. I'm happy to help.'

I hung up on a high. Maybe this would prompt the breakthrough Ali needed. Good old Donna.

The day got even better when Ali called to tell me she had just eaten a small scoop of low-fat chocolate ice cream. It wasn't exactly steak and chips, but she was volunteering to eat food she'd liked before the anorexia had set in, which was a really positive step.

'That's fantastic, Ali, I'm thrilled. I'm so proud of you,' I said.

'Thanks, Mum. Thanks for supporting me,' she said, beginning to sob.

'Oh, Ali, don't cry, this is great news.'

'It's not that – I'm just so worried about Emily.'

'What do you mean?'

'She's really depressed and I'm scared she's going to hurt herself again.'

'That's for the nurses and doctors to deal with. You can't start worrying about that. You need to focus on yourself and your recovery.'

'I am, but Emily's my friend and she's really down.'

I suddenly remembered the family session when Mary had said, 'Sometimes you just need to listen.' I bit my tongue and didn't tell Ali to forget about Emily, to ignore Emily, to shut the door on Emily and focus on her own problems. I didn't say that taking on someone else's issues right now was not a good idea.

I didn't tell her to find a friend who was getting better and not one who was getting worse . . . I shut up and listened.

'I'm sorry to hear she's down. What happened today?'

Ali told me that Emily had stopped by her room for a chat, as she did every morning, but this time she'd seemed particularly blue.

'I've lost a pound and three-quarters so they're putting me back on bed-rest.' She wept as she hopped around Ali's room.

'Oh, Emily, I'm so sorry.'

'I can't bear it, Alison. I can't go back on bed-rest – I just can't. I'll never get out of here. I'm trying really hard, but the hopping is out of control. I wish I could stop. I'm so tired, my legs are in agony, but I just can't. I hate my life. I'll be stuck here for ever.'

'No, you won't – this is just a setback.'

'My whole life is made up of setbacks.'

'Come on, Emily. Look, I've put on weight. And if I can do it, so can you. Just eat a little more every day. Two good days' eating and you'll be OK again.'

She shook her head sadly. 'It's my third time back in here. I can't seem to survive outside the clinic. I've tried so hard, but I just can't do it. I get so scared when I'm making my own lunches. Everything looks so big and fattening. It's easier in here where everything is measured for you. It's so hard on your own and it's easy not to eat when no one is supervising you. I just can't do it.'

'I've got a great idea. Why don't we try to get out of here at the same time and then we can help each other when we're at home? Maybe we could have the same meal plan. That would work really well. We could call each other every night to check how we're doing.'

'I'd just drag you down. I'm a hopeless case.'

'No, you're not. You're a brilliant person who deserves a break. I know you don't have much support at home so I'd be glad to help.'

'Thanks. You're really nice to offer but I know you'll be out of here long before me and getting on with your life.'

'We both need to be out of here and getting on with our lives. Look at this photo.' Ali showed Emily one of her and Donna in Paris. 'That's what we need to get back to. Happy times when food didn't control our lives. Come on, we'll do it together. I'll help you.'

'You're a really sweet person and I know you want to help, but the only person who can save me is me, and I'm not strong enough.'

'Don't say that. You are strong – look at all the crap you've had to deal with in your life and how well you've done it.'

'I'm in a clinic with anorexia and OCD. I don't think I'm doing such a great job.'

'Emily, most people with abusive alcoholic fathers would be in loony bins. You're doing great.'

'I'm tired. I'm really, really tired. I just don't want to fight any more.'

'You need a good night's sleep. Ask Denise to give you a strong sleeping tablet and I bet everything will look less depressing in the morning.'

Emily smiled. 'Maybe you're right. Thanks, Alison, you're a really good friend.'

'Sleep well. I'll see you tomorrow.'

'You see, Mum,' Ali sobbed, 'that's when I realized how lucky I am. I only have to deal with food. Emily has to deal with OCD and self-harming. I think that maybe if I can show Emily there is life after the clinic, it'll inspire her to get better too.'

As sorry as I felt for Emily, I really wished Ali would stop worrying about her. Ali needed to focus on her own problems. I chose my words very carefully. 'That's great, Ali. I'm sure you getting better will inspire all the girls. It'll make us very happy, too.'

'I know, so that's why I asked Denise to get me the ice cream.

But it was so hard to eat it, Mum. I really had to fight to put every bit in my mouth, but I did it!'

'Good for you. Did it taste nice?'

'Amazing! I'd forgotten how much I loved it.'

I did a silent dance. 'That's brilliant, Ali. You're taking back control of your life.'

'In one way I feel like I've taken control, but in another really scary way I feel like I'm losing it.'

'Well, Mary said it would be an uphill battle. So this is your first big victory and that's always the hardest one. From now on it should get easier. I'm so proud of you, Ali. This is a real breakthrough.'

'Thanks, Mum. I'd better go.'

'Sleep well.'

When Paul came in from work I told him the good news. 'You're telling me that Ali ate a spoonful of low-fat ice cream?'

'Yes, isn't that brilliant?'

'I'm sorry, Ava, but I find it hard to jump around cheering about this. It's not exactly a Big Mac.'

'It's a start. And the fact that she asked for it is actually a huge deal, so get excited because Denise thinks this is a big break-through. And Mary rang – she said that Ali had written a very strong letter to anorexia and this was also a big step forward. So we have lots to be happy about.'

'I'll have to take your word for it.'

'The only fly in the ointment is her friend Emily.'

'What's up with her?'

'She's going backwards – she's on bed-rest again, and Ali seems hell-bent on saving her. She needs her energy for her own recovery.'

'Typical Ali, always trying to look after everyone else. Isn't that what landed her in there in the first place? That, and me forcing her to do medicine and you not listening to her properly.'

'Well, I nearly bit my bloody tongue in half tonight with all the listening. There were so many times I wanted to interrupt her and tell her not to be so bloody ridiculous trying to save other people, but I didn't. Mary would have been very proud of me. But it was very hard.'

'Well done. I don't have a medal handy, will a kiss do?'

'A kiss would do just fine,' I said. He leant across and delivered it.

'And you'll be pleased to hear I've done some homework of my own.'

'What homework?'

'Mary said we should all write letters to anorexia, so I wrote mine today.'

Paul pulled a piece of paper out of his coat pocket and handed it to me. 'It's a bit rough, I need to work on it, but . . . well, see for yourself.'

Listen closely, dickhead,
You are a bully and a coward. You hide in my daughter's head, messing with her mind. But I am stronger than you, louder than you, and I love my daughter more than anything in the world. I will crush you like the piece of shit you are. I will drown you out until you are nothing but a distant memory. You won't win this battle. It is my role in life to protect my family. You won't destroy my girl, so fuck off and leave her alone.
Paul

I swallowed the lump in my throat. 'It's perfect. Don't change a single word.'

40

I went to work early the next day to make up for all the time I'd been missing lately. I wanted to ring Helen, about the sweet-sixteen *Moulin Rouge*-themed bonanza that we had coming up. Paddy Collins's daughter, Annabelle, was turning sixteen and having the party to end all parties. Paddy was estimated to be worth more than two hundred million euros and the party had an open chequebook policy.

'Any ideas on *Moulin Rouge*-themed food, Helen?' I asked.

'I've come up with a few. For the canapés I was thinking mini-croissants stuffed with cheeses and hams, crackers in the shape of the Eiffel Tower and the Arc de Triomphe, mini quiches, crab claws, Brie and cranberry *croque monsieur*, tomato *tarte Tatin* and baked Camembert with focaccia croûtons.'

'That sounds fantastic – especially tomato *tarte Tatin*. Brilliant.'

'They look really good and taste even better – the onion relish gives them a lovely flavour. Now for dinner we're starting with *foie gras* –'

'*Foie gras* for teenagers is such a waste,' I said.

'I couldn't agree more, but you said it's what the Collinses ordered.'

'You're right. It just seems so completely over the top. Anyway, sorry for interrupting, go on.'

'For the main course, the kids get the choice of either beef fillet with tomato polenta and Armagnac sauce or fillet of pan-fried turbot with pepper and fennel purée on basil butter.'

'My mouth is watering just thinking about it. Dare I ask about dessert?'

'We're going to have chocolate cigars, chocolate high-heeled shoes, shortbread can-can girls with chocolate feathers, bodice-shaped sponge cakes with silver-icing laces and little white chocolate gift boxes with red fondant bows.'

'Wow, Helen! That sounds incredible. How about the cake? Are you going to be able to make a three-foot replica of the Moulin Rouge as requested by the charming Annabelle?'

'I'm still working on that. It's going to be expensive.'

'"Money no object", to quote Paddy Collins directly.'

'They should clone him.'

'If only all our clients were like that.'

'Who are you giving out about?' Sally asked, as she came in and took her coat off.

'I'm not giving out. I'm saying what a dream client Paddy Collins is. I'm just reminding Helen that his pockets are deep so she doesn't have to worry about her budget.'

'Be as creative as you like, Helen. This is your chance to really go all out,' Sally shouted over my shoulder. Helen laughed.

'I'll let you go, Helen. Thanks so much.' I hung up.

'You're in early,' Sally commented.

'Feeling guilty for being out so much lately.'

'Hey, you know I don't mind. How are things?'

'I'm almost afraid to say it but I think she's turned a corner. She ate a scoop of ice cream last night and she sounded stronger than before.'

'Oh, that's wonderful. Good old Ali.'

'Hopefully it's a turning-point. Anyway, that's enough about Ali. I ear-bashed you about her for over an hour yesterday. Tell me about Simon. Tell me how in love you are and how romantic it all is. Go on, make me sick.'

'Well, things are going really well, apart from the certifiable ex-wife. We had to get a barring order for her because she's still coming to my apartment every night to tell my neighbours that I'm the Scarlet Woman. Mrs O'Brien next door, who has never been particularly nice to me, actually threw holy water over me last week when I was leaving for work to cleanse me of my sins. Simon got doused as well, even though I explained to her that he was a Quaker and therefore a waste of her good water.'

'Do you think it scared him off?'

'He thought it was hilarious. That's the thing about Simon, it's all so easy. After years of bad relationships and crappy dates, I've finally met someone who just fits. I used to worry that because I'd been living on my own for so long I'd become set in my ways but I love sharing my apartment with him. I love having his clothes in my wardrobe and his shaving things in my bathroom. I love having another body in my bed, even though he does hog the duvet. It hasn't been the really difficult adjustment that I expected. It's been easy.'

'Oh, Sally, it sounds perfect.'

'Honestly, Ava, it kind of is and I can't believe it myself. I keep waiting for something awful to happen. Simon rings when he says he's going to – what guy ever does that? We never run out of things to talk about and I don't feel I have to hold my stomach in when I'm walking around in my underwear. I've never not done that, even after three years with Jeremy. He makes me feel so good about myself – he's constantly telling me I'm wonderful and sexy and witty.'

'Stop! This is too much. It's like *Love Story* or something!'

'I know – and it's happening to me, which is so weird. I never, ever thought it would. There is just one teeny thing that bothers me, though.'

'Thank God for that. What is it?'

'His hair.'

'It does look a bit strange,' I agreed.

'I know it's really shallow – I finally meet this amazing man and here I am obsessing about his hair. But I can't help it. The more I looked at it, the more it looked like a really bad wig. It was really beginning to bug me so last night after a few glasses of wine I just blurted it out.'

'Oh, God. What did you say? What did *he* say?'

Sally explained that she had asked him straight out . . .

'What's the deal with your hair?'

He bristled. 'What do you mean?'

'I'm sorry, Simon, but it looks really weird. I swore I wouldn't ask, because it doesn't matter – it makes no difference to the way I feel about you. But I just don't see how you could have been born like that.'

'I wasn't.'

'Is it a wig?'

'No, it's a transplant.'

Sally spluttered her wine back into the glass. 'What?'

He sighed. 'My hair started to fall out about two years ago. Maura freaked. She said I looked old and ugly and she didn't want to be with a bald man.'

'The shallow cow,' Sally said, trying to deflect attention from her own criticism of his mop.

'She kept going on about it. She said she couldn't stand seeing me looking so old with my receding hairline. She said I shouldn't let myself go, there were options, men didn't have to be bald any more, there were treatments available and on and on. Eventually I gave in and went for a consultation with this hair specialist.'

'What did he say?' Sally asked, although judging by the barnet Simon had, he must have proposed sticking a raccoon on his head.

'He suggested a transplant.'

'How many did you have?'

'Hilarious. Just one.'

'Really?'

'Yes, it was a big one.'

'You don't say.'

'Is it that bad?'

'No, it's just very full and springy.'

'I know it looks like a rug, but apparently it'll calm down over time.'

'When did you get it done?'

'About eight months ago, right around the time my wife was shagging someone else.'

'She's a piece of work.'

'And it was bloody painful.'

'What do they do? Where does the hair come from? Is it real or animal hair?'

'Jesus – does it look like animal hair?'

'No!' she lied. 'It doesn't. I just thought I read something about it somewhere . . .'

'They take hair from the back of your head that is genetically resistant to going bald and transplant it to the balding area.'

'How?'

'They trim the hair at the back that they're taking out and then they give you a local anaesthetic in that area and then they cut it out.'

'That sounds excruciating.'

'And then they sew it into the front of your head where you're going bald. And then you have bloody scabs for a week or so.'

'I think I'm going to be sick.'

'And after all that pain the bitch had an affair.'

'Are you happy with the transplant?'

'It's ridiculous. The clinic I went to was a joke. I've seen guys with good transplants and they don't look like this.'

'Why don't you get it cut really short? I think it'd look great.'

'Do you? To be honest, Maura really knocked my confidence and I don't know what to do. I feel like a total gobshite for having gone ahead with it. I look back now and think how could I have been so stupid? But when someone keeps going on and on at you, sometimes it's easier to give in.'

'Just so you know, I have no problem with baldness. So, if all your hair does eventually fall out, I won't start shagging someone else. But I would like to take you to my hairdresser to get it cut tomorrow.'

'Be honest, what does it look like?'

'Do you remember Davy Crockett's raccoon-fur hat?' Sally started giggling.

'You cow,' Simon said, wrestling her to the ground. 'Take that back.'

'WHORE, SLAPPER, PROSTITUTE.'

Sally couldn't believe it. They had had Maura barred from coming within a hundred yards of her apartment. She looked out of the window and there she was, across the green, with a megaphone.

'Right. That's it.' Sally stormed out of the door.

She strode across the green and grabbed the megaphone from Maura's hands. Digging her finger into the woman's chest, she hissed, 'Now, you listen to me, you fruitcake. I've had enough of you shouting abuse at me. You screwed around while you were married to him and you ruined your marriage so stop blaming me. If you want to shout at someone I suggest you look in the mirror. And by the way what the hell were you thinking with the hair transplant? It looks ridiculous.'

'It's a lot better than it was. He looked terrible with a receding hairline.'

'Give me bald any day.'

'I want him back.'

'He's not available. Listen closely, Loopy-Lu, I've waited forty-three long, lonely years to meet someone like Simon and nothing — least of all you and your mad ranting — is going to persuade me to give him up. So why don't you give your vocal cords a rest? If you think you're scaring me off, you're sadly mistaken. Let me put it in terms you can relate to. I'll have myself transplanted onto him if I have to. This one is a keeper, so piss off and find someone else to torment.'

'Way to go, Sally.' I was impressed with my friend's feistiness. 'Did she leave?'

'Damn right she did. She scurried off back to her car with her megaphone and I went back to my boyfriend with the big hair.' We roared laughing.

41

The next evening Paul came home early from work again for dinner. When we finished eating, Charlie left to drive Nadia to work and Sarah and Bobby went upstairs to rehearse their play. We lingered over a glass of wine in the kitchen.

'How was Ali today when you spoke to her?' Paul asked.

'Good – she really seems to be trying to eat more and she says she wants to get better so she can get off bed-rest and come home. She seems to have turned a corner and she's actually talking to me for the first time in ages.'

'That's a bonus.'

'Makes a nice change from the one-sided phone calls and monosyllabic answers.'

'How's her friend getting on?'

'I don't think Emily's doing too well. Ali said she's still on bed-rest, isn't eating and seems very down.'

'Poor kid – the dad must be some arsehole to have turned her into such a basket case.'

'Apparently he was a very abusive drunk. I think Ali appreciates you more now.'

'Alleluia. Maybe I'll be forgiven for forcing her to do medicine.'

'Paul, you need to let that go.'

'I know and I will. It just threw me. I thought I was encouraging her and she says I was pressurizing her. It's made me second-guess everything I say to her now and to Sarah too. Take tonight, for instance, when Sarah was talking about wanting to be an actress. I wanted to tell her to cop on and focus on having a real career but I stopped myself in case I damaged her or something.'

'We both need to censor ourselves for a while, until things settle down. Only positive comments and lots of listening without opinions or judgement.'

'That can be easier said than done. I've seen Sarah act and Hollywood will not be waiting for her with open arms.'

'I know, but the play has been a great distraction for her. She's very upset about Ali and sometimes she feels overshadowed by Ali's academic success. This is a really big deal for her and she wants to prove to us that she has talent.'

'Sure we've seen most of the play already and it's a shambles,' Paul said.

'That's a bit harsh.'

'Ava, Shakespeare is regarded as the greatest writer of the English language and they have taken his most famous and tragic play and turned it into a French farce.'

'It's not a farce. It's just different and a bit over-the-top. But I think it shows initiative and creativity to translate the text into modern teenage-speak.'

'The "teenage-speak", as you call it, does my head in.'

'All teenagers go through phases of talking strangely or in code or made-up languages.'

'I didn't.'

'Didn't you? When I was in school we made up a language where you left all the vowels out. It was fun actually.'

'It sounds like a riot.'

'There's no need to be sarcastic. What did you do when you were a teenager?'

'Played sport, chased girls, smoked behind the bicycle shed – normal things.'

'To each their own.'

'I just hope the play isn't a total car crash.'

'Whatever the reaction of the other parents, you and I will be in the front row cheering her on proudly.'

The kitchen door swung open. Sarah and Bobby barged into the kitchen arguing.

'It's just ridiculous, Bobby. Romeo would never do anything so lame.'

'The whole play is lame. I just want to do something to keep my street cred intact.'

'You are so not saying it. Why do you want to change the words now? Like, hello! The play is tomorrow. It's too bloody late.'

'Time out,' Paul said. 'What's going on?'

'Bobby is supposed to say, "Juliet, you're an awesome dancer. I'm not worthy to touch your hand." But instead he's decided to change it to "Juliet, you're an awesome dancer. Let me show you some cool moves," and he starts to dance. It's not about Romeo being a good dancer, it's about me – I mean Juliet – being a cool dancer.'

'Why don't you show us the scene and we'll tell you if we think it works?' I said, trying to calm things down. Sarah was up to ninety about the play. She had some deluded notion that a Hollywood talent spotter might turn up to a school play in the Dublin suburbs.

'OK. We need more space so we'll have to do it in the lounge,' Sarah said.

And so, once again, Paul and I found ourselves sitting in our front room, trying not to laugh as our daughter and her boy-friend modernized Shakespeare.

'This is the scene where Romeo and Juliet are totally flirting at the ball,' Sarah explained.

Juliet, in a luminous pink tracksuit and Ugg boots, danced around while Romeo, in his white Abercrombie hoody and saggy tracksuit bottoms, shuffled beside her.

'You're a really awesome dancer. Do you want to see some of my moves?' Romeo said, and with that he flung himself onto the floor and started twirling around on his shoulders and head with surprising agility.

'So that's where break-dancing originated,' Paul whispered, 'in Verona.' I willed myself to keep a straight face.

As Romeo twirled, Juliet looked decidedly fed up. 'OK, I get the picture – you like to dance.'

Romeo hopped up. 'Can I snog you?'

'You're a bit keen, aren't you?'

'Yeah, actually, I am, totally.'

'Well, I'm not going to snog you.'

'Fair enough. I'll make the first move.' He kissed her.

'Bobby! I said no tongues. It's a play,' Sarah screeched, pushing him away.

'Quite right. None of that, thank you,' Paul chimed in.

'Sorry, I was carried away with the role,' Bobby admitted.

'Come on, focus,' Sarah snapped.

'Fair enough. I'll make the first move,' Romeo said, kissing Juliet, more appropriately this time. 'I feel as if all my sins have been washed away now.'

'Dude, are you telling me you've passed them all on to me? What am I going to do now? I'm totally infected.'

'I'll just take them back,' he said, kissing her again.

'You're a really good kisser,' Juliet said. 'And that's it, because then the Nurse comes in and ruins the moment,' Sarah explained. 'So what do you think? Do you not see how Romeo break-dancing in the middle of the play is totally stupid?'

'Well,' I said, trying to choose my words carefully so as not to offend either party, 'Bobby, you certainly have a great talent for spinning on your head, but I do agree that it might not be the best place to demonstrate it.'

'The thing is, Mrs M, Romeo is kind of a loser. He spends the whole play chasing Juliet around and then, like, does himself in because he loves her so much. I'm just not that comfortable playing someone who's such a geek.'

'But Juliet did just say that you were an excellent kisser,' I reminded him. 'So that's good for your reputation.'

'Hello! Can you stop being such a child?' Sarah raged at her boyfriend. 'It's a play. You are performing a role, not playing yourself. It's called acting. Do you think Leonardo DiCaprio thought Romeo was lame when he played him? I don't think so. And f.y.i., Bobby, every girl in school fancies Leo DiCaprio. So why don't you get over yourself and just play the part like we practised? If you can't do that, then I'll call Adrian the under-study and get him to take your place. He'd love to play Romeo so he can kiss me.'

'I never said I had to dance. I just said I thought it might work. It's called improvisation – really good actors try it all the time. I thought you'd know that. So we tried it and we don't think it works. I'm cool with that.'

'There you go, all sorted out. Well done, you two, good team work. Is there anything else you want us to give our opinion on?' I asked.

'No, thanks, Mum, we're OK now. Come on, Bobby, we need to do our spray tan. We should probably do three coats. We want to look really hot.'

'Totally. The Italians have really dark skin and we want to look like the real thing,' Bobby agreed.

'What do you mean, Italians?' Sarah asked, puzzled.

'Babe, Verona is in Italy. Romeo and Juliet are Italian.'

'Seriously?' Sarah asked, looking to her father for confirmation.

'Last time I checked, Verona was still in northern Italy,' Paul assured her.

'Ohmigod. I thought they were English, like Shakespeare. I thought Verona was some little village in, like, the middle of nowhere. We should do four sprays each if we want everyone to think we're actual Italians.'

'Let's get to it,' Bobby said, taking her hand as they ran upstairs.

'Tell me again how much we're paying for her education.' Paul sighed.

'She's happy, self-assured and has a very positive body image. Right now, that's all I care about,' I said.

'She certainly doesn't lack confidence. She has that poor fella wrapped around her finger.'

'At least we don't have to worry about building up her self-esteem.'

'Jesus, if it was any higher, she'd be insufferable.'

'I wonder how the other parents are going to react to the play? Sarah's taking it all so seriously. I hope she doesn't get into a huff if people laugh.'

'If? Ava, they're going to be in hysterics. I'll say this, it's been a welcome distraction from Ali.'

'I'm almost sad it's going to be over tomorrow.'

'No doubt with Sarah there'll be a new drama soon enough.'

The next morning, when I went into the kitchen, Charlie was up making breakfast. Nadia was still in bed.

'Ava,' Charlie said, 'there's a Red Indian after coming into your kitchen.'

I turned. It was Sarah, behind a thick layer of orange tan. She looked like one of the Oompa-Loompas in *Willy Wonka and the Chocolate Factory*. Bobby had clearly outdone himself with the spray last night.

'Wow!' was all I could muster.

'I know! How amazing do I look?' Sarah beamed. 'I could totally pass for an Italian girl.'

'Italian!' Charlie said, roaring laughing. 'You look like someone's attacked you with an orange paintbrush.'

'Whatever, Charlie. In your day everyone thought being pale was cool. Well, it wasn't. People look much better with a tan.'

'You look lovely,' I said, determined to give out only positive physical feedback to everyone for the rest of my life.

'Are you nervous?' Charlie asked her.

'Are you nuts? No way. I can't wait to get on stage. I totally have the X-factor and I want everyone to see it. I've been waiting for this moment my whole life. Bring it on.'

'You'll knock 'em dead, pet,' Charlie said. 'Nadia and I'll be there early to get good seats.'

'OK, but can you ask Nadia to cover up a bit? Bobby's mum

is quite conservative – and don't forget to keep seats for Mum and Dad in case they're late.'

'We'll be there on time,' I told her.

'I'd better get ready. Bobby's collecting me in his dad's Ferrari. He got special permission to drive it to school today because of the play. How perfect is that? The stars arriving in style.'

'Make sure he doesn't drive too fast,' I warned.

'Chill, Mum, he drives at, like, ten miles an hour in it because his dad would kill him if he scratched it. I'd be quicker walking, but it's still the totally coolest way to arrive in school. Remember to be really nice to Bobby's mum and don't let Dad talk about bogger things like hurley and stuff. Bobby's mum is into golf.'

'Your father and I will talk about whatever we want to with Bobby's mother. Now, take a deep breath and calm down.'

'The next time you see me, I'll be a star,' she said, disappearing out of the door.

Later that day at work, when I was getting ready to leave to go to the play, Sally was on the phone to Simon. She was giggling like a schoolgirl.

'I've got to go, Ava's leaving. I'll see you at seven outside the cinema.' She hung up and smiled.

'How is he?' I asked, turning my computer off.

'Very, very, very good.' She leant back in her chair and stretched her arms over her head.

'You positively glow – it's sickening.' I smiled at her.

'I've turned into one of those women I used to hate. Those smug women in happy relationships, who walk down the street smiling to themselves and beaming at strangers. That's me!'

'You've gone over to the dark side.' I put my coat on.

'Yes, I have and it's pretty damn great.'

'Enjoy it all, you deserve every bit of it.'

'You're right, I do.' She laughed. 'So, are you looking forward to the play?'

'I am, actually. I just hope it goes well.'

'Well, she does have the starring role – it's a big deal.'

'You should have seen her and Bobby practising yesterday – it was priceless. He kept flinging himself on the floor and break-dancing.'

'What?'

'Yes, break-dancing – in Verona at the ball.' We both snorted.

'Please don't forget your camcorder. I have to see this.'

'I won't, I promise. See you tomorrow – enjoy your movie.'

As I was opening the car door to climb in, my phone rang. 'Ava, it's Denise from the clinic. We need you to come right away. Emily's dead.'

42

I rang Paul screaming down the phone and told him to meet me at the clinic.

When I arrived, he and Denise were waiting for me in Reception.

'What happened? Is Ali all right?' I was hysterical with worry.

'It's OK.' Paul put his arm around me. 'Ali's fine. But they had to sedate her.'

'Jesus – why?'

'She went mad when she found out about Emily,' Paul told me.

'Oh, God.' I collapsed into the nearest chair and put my head into my hands. He sat beside me and rubbed my back. When I looked up, I saw how red Denise's eyes were. 'What happened, Denise? What happened to Emily?'

Earlier that morning, Denise told us, Emily had gone for a supervised shower. The nurses always stood outside to make sure the girls on bed-rest didn't try to exercise. After a few minutes the nurse heard some grunting. She asked if Emily was all right. She heard nothing, so she went in and saw that Emily was gone. Because she was so small and emaciated, she had somehow managed to squeeze out of the narrow bathroom window and run away.

The nurse sounded the alarm, and they searched the grounds for her but Emily was nowhere to be found so they called the police for help. Six hours later two policemen found her hidden behind a hedge on the side of a road, three miles away. She was covered with just her bath towel and there were cuts all over her body.

'She had found a rusty old can and slit herself from head to toe,' Denise explained. 'By the time they got to her it was too late. She had bled to death.'

'That's horrific.'

'Yes, it is. We're all absolutely devastated.' Denise tried to remain composed. 'When Alison found out, she was, as you can imagine, completely distraught. The two girls had become close friends. She got very agitated and started throwing the furniture around her room. We had to sedate her to calm her down.'

Paul stood up. 'That's it. We're taking Ali home. There is no way she's staying in this place.'

'Now hold on, Paul, don't do anything rash,' Denise pleaded.

'Rash! We're talking about a dead child here.'

'In the twenty years I've worked here, Emily is the first and only teenager to run away and commit suicide. We're all broken-hearted.'

'She's one too many,' Paul replied. 'I do not want my daughter in this place for one more night.'

'I really think that's a bad idea,' Denise said. 'Alison has turned a corner. She's been doing so well. She's eating more, she's engaging with the nurses, she's happier, chattier and so wants to get better. She's just beginning to improve. Taking her out now would be very unwise.'

'At least at home I can protect her. How can it be good for her to be hanging around with girls who are killing themselves?' Paul asked.

Denise took a deep breath. 'Emily was a very sick girl who had a lot of personal problems and very little family support. She was incredibly fragile and troubled. But she was also a very sweet and kind girl. From Alison's first day here, Emily helped her. She encouraged her to eat and would often come and sit with Alison during mealtimes to keep her company. She kept your daughter going during her first week when Alison was really struggling. Emily kept telling her that she knew she was going to get better. So instead of being a hindrance to Alison's recovery, Emily was actually an asset.'

'None of that changes the fact that she's dead,' Paul reminded Denise.

'I'm aware of that. But I can guarantee that this terrible tragedy won't set Alison back. It'll drive her to get well and get on with her life.' Denise looked at me for support.

I stood up, my legs shaking. 'OK, guys, let's not make any decisions now. We're all too upset. We need to talk to Ali when she wakes up and see what she wants to do.'

'She'll probably be out for a while,' Denise said.

'That's OK. We've got all night. I want to see her now – I need to see her.'

Paul held my hand and we walked down to Ali's room. When we got to her door, I stopped. I leant against the wall and composed myself in case she was awake. I didn't want her to see me in this state. I needed to be calm.

Paul rested his head against the wall beside me. 'How the hell did we end up here?'

'I wish I knew.' I wiped my eyes and blew my nose.

'Are we ever going to be normal again?'

'I hope so.'

'I hate this,' he said, getting upset.

'Me too.' I held his hand and squeezed it. 'Come on, let's go in and see her.'

The nurse sitting beside Ali's bed stood up. 'She's still asleep,' she whispered. 'I'll leave you alone.' She left the room and closed the door.

Ali was lying on her side.

I sat down in the chair beside the bed and brushed the hair off her face. 'Oh, Ali, what are we going to do?'

'Get her the hell out of here.' Paul sat down at the end of the bed.

'But she's doing really well, Paul. She's a different person on the phone these last few days, so much more positive. She sounds much more like the old Ali. I don't want to do anything that could set her back.'

'She had to be sedated because she was throwing furniture around the room. I think she's already been set back.'

'Of course she freaked out! She'd just heard her friend was dead. When she wakes up she'll be more rational and we can ask her what she wants to do. We mustn't make any hasty decisions. We have to handle this very carefully and take Denise and Mary's advice. I'll talk to Mary first thing in the morning.'

'I'm so sick of all this shit,' Paul said, rubbing his eyes. 'It's just one thing after another. I want it to be over and Ali to be back to normal.'

'I know, I'm sick of it too, believe me, but this is our life right now and we have to deal with it.'

'Do you ever feel like just walking away?' Paul asked, looking down at his hands.

'Every single day.'

His head jerked up. 'Really?'

I nodded. 'I go to bed every night feeling sick with worry and wake up sick with worry. I dread having to call the clinic. I'm so scared they're going to tell me bad news. I hate that my life is now spent worrying about whether Ali eats enough calories to survive. I feel so tired and old. I feel tired in my bones.'

'Did we really fuck up? Is it our fault that she's in here? I always thought we were pretty good parents. We had fun with them. We told them they were great, they always knew we were there for them. We worked hard to give them a private education and a nice house, clothes, presents, all that stuff. So how the hell did Ali end up in a clinic? I don't understand where we went so wrong. Emily's father was a drunk who abused her, so I understand how she ended up in here, but we're not drunks, we're good people. We love our kids.'

'I think we made some bad decisions, like lying about the shooting.'

'Jesus,' Paul hissed, 'I'm so sick of that being thrown in our faces. All we were trying to do was protect two small girls from the violent truth. Where's the crime in that?'

'I agree with you, but it had a bad effect on Ali and we have to accept that. Look, in all the research I've done there are no concrete answers as to why someone develops anorexia. All parents are frustrated like us. Every case is different. Every family's different. This horrible disease just seems to take over your mind and forces you to stop eating.'

'How much research have you done?'

'I spend hours on the computer every night. I reckon the more I know about the disease, the better I'll be able to help Ali. But it's a minefield – I don't seem to be getting anywhere. There are no answers, only a long, uphill road to recovery and sometimes I . . . uh . . . uh . . .' I began to sob.

Paul came around and hugged me.

'I don't know if I can do it, Paul. I'm so tired all the time and it's going to take years for her to get better. I can't do it on my own.'

'You're not on your own. I'm here.'

I pulled back and looked him in the eyes. 'Are you? Are you going to come home every night for dinner? Are you going to leave the pub whenever I need help?'

'I'll do whatever you need me to do.'

'Do you promise?'

'Ava, I know I've been working too much and that I've pissed you off lately, particularly on New Year's Eve, and I'm sorry. The night I hit Ali, I realized I needed to spend more time at home. I really didn't understand how bad she'd got. I honestly thought it was just a phase she was going through. I had no idea it was so serious. If it wasn't for you she could have –' He stopped, too choked up to go on.

'It's OK.' I kissed his cheek.

'No, it's not OK. I can see how stressed you are and I promise I'm going to be around more to help you. I'd become obsessed with work but Ali being sick has shown me that success means nothing without a healthy, happy family. I'm sorry I've been so distracted but I'm going to change that. I'm hiring a second manager.'

'Really?'

'Yes.'

'Oh, Paul, that's brilliant.' I threw my arms around him and we kissed, a long, deep, needy, passionate kiss.

My phone beeped. I grabbed it out of my bag to turn it off so it wouldn't wake up Ali.

It was a message from Sarah: 'I officially disown you and Dad. YOU SUCK'.

'Oh, Jesus – the play!'

43

We hurried out of the clinic. I rang Sarah's phone. Bobby answered.

'Hi, Bobby, is Sarah there? Is she OK?'

'Yes, she is. She's here with me in my house.'

'Can you put her on, please?'

'I'm sorry, Mrs M, she's actually just fallen asleep. She was kind of upset when you were a no-show at the play, so I brought her here and she cried herself to sleep on the sofa.'

'We had an emergency with Ali. I never meant to miss the play. Is she very annoyed?'

'Uhm, on a scale of one to ten, I'd say eleven.'

'I don't blame her. How did the play go?'

'It was OK. To be honest, I'm just glad it's over. It was wrecking my head. Sarah was great, though, really professional.'

'I'm so sorry we missed it. I know how important it was to her.'

'Yeah, it was a really big deal, but I'm sure she'll be OK in the morning.'

'Can you give me your address? We'll come and collect her now.'

'Sure, but I really think you should leave her here for the night. I can look after her and I won't try anything on, I promise. I just don't think there's any point waking her up now.'

'Are your parents at home?'

'No. My mum made it to the play, which was, like, a total miracle, but then she went straight to the airport. Honestly, Mrs M, I'll take good care of Sarah and you can swing by in the morning to pick her up. If she wakes up later and wants to go home or talk to you, I'll call straight away.'

'OK, Bobby, I think you're right. I'll see you first thing tomorrow. And thanks.'

'It's no problem, I like looking after her. She makes out like she's so tough all the time but she isn't.'

'Sometimes we forget that. Thanks, Bobby.'

Early the next morning, Paul and I drove over to Bobby's house. The driveway was a mile long and the house was a mansion. Large white marble columns framed the huge double front door. We rang the bell and Mia, the Chinese housekeeper, let us into the vast hall, which was the same size as the whole downstairs of our house.

'Wow,' I said, gazing at the ornate cornicing and parquet floors.

'It's a bit over the top,' Paul muttered.

'I agree, but still . . . wow.'

Bobby came into the hall. 'Hi.'

'How is she?'

'Definitely more chilled, but still kind of angry.'

We followed him into a huge kitchen. It had wall-to-ceiling windows across the back, looking onto a beautiful garden with fountains and lawns, a tennis court and swimming-pool. The walls were painted duck-egg blue with a beige tiled floor and a big cream Aga sitting alongside a huge black range oven. Three enormous crystal chandeliers hung from the ceiling. The whole thing was spectacular but it looked like a show-house, not somewhere that people actually lived. It felt cold and impersonal.

Sarah was curled up on a couch in the corner, looking decidedly pissed off. Bobby went over, kissed her and told her he was going to leave us in private, but he'd be upstairs if she needed him. Then he tactfully left us alone.

I walked over to her. 'Sarah, I'm so sorry. I know how much the play meant to you. We got an urgent call from the clinic and –'

She cut straight across me, eyes blazing: 'Blah, blah, blah. Let me guess, Ali ate a slice of apple and all the freaks threw a party for her. You know what, Mum? I really don't give a shit. I'm so sick of Ali and her eating/not-eating bullshit. It's all about her. You barely notice my existence any more. And f.y.i., I'm the normal one. I'm the daughter who isn't in a loony bin – so don't you think you should be high-fiving me, and not the anorexic? But, oh, no – when Ali says, "Jump," you two say, "How high?" It's pathetic. She has you running around in circles while she sits on her stupid bed and moans about her past. Well, you'll have all the time in the world now, because I'm out of your lives. I'm moving in with Bobby.'

'Now hold on a minute,' Paul said. 'Sarah, I'm really sorry we missed your play but your sister had an emergency. We didn't have a choice.'

She jumped up and screamed at him, 'You *always* have a choice. Wasn't one of you enough to go and hold Ali's hand? Did you both have to go? Couldn't one of you have bothered to turn up to the most important day of my life? Charlie's girl-friend cares more about me than you do. And what an impression she made on Bobby's mother. Oh, it was fan-fucking-tastic. She really thinks her son hit the jackpot with a girlfriend whose grandfather goes out with a pole dancer. She actually took a step backwards when she saw Nadia – who, by the way, was wearing her favourite leopard-print Lycra dress so the whole school could see her tits.

'Seriously, it could not have gone any worse. I'd say Bobby's mother will force him to dump me in the next week. Why would she want her son going out with a girl from a family that would blend right in on *The Jerry Springer Show*? When *everyone* kept ask-ing me where my parents were, I kept saying, "They'll be here in a minute," and then when you didn't bother to turn up or even call or text me to tell me where you were, I prayed you'd been killed in a car crash, because that was the only excuse that would have been good enough.'

'OK,' I said. 'You've had your rant and now I'd like you to listen to us. We were on our way to your play when we got a call from the clinic to say that Ali's friend Emily had committed suicide and Ali had completely freaked out. They had to pin her down and sedate her. She was in a really bad way. I'm sorry, Sarah, but we had to go.'

'So now I'm not just competing with Ali for attention, I have to deal with all the loopers topping themselves too. Don't you see? There's always going to be something. One of the fruit-cakes topping themselves today, tomorrow it'll be one of the fatties exploding from overeating. Well, congratulations, you totally humiliated me in front of my whole school.'

'We didn't mean to let you down, pet. We were really looking forward to seeing you perform. Now, come on, tell us how it went,' I said. 'Charlie told me you were fantastic.'

'Actually, it didn't go all that well. Obviously when I first turned up on stage, everyone, like, gasped because I looked so amazing and totally Italian. But I was so upset that my parents hadn't bothered to turn up I kept forgetting my lines. Then, the Nurse – as in Juliet's supposed nanny – walked on stage in her PVC Internet nurse's uniform and her dad – who did actually bother to turn up – freaked out and jumped onto the stage to cover her with his coat. They had this big tug-of-war and even-tually, our English teacher, Mr Goggin, had to drag them both off the stage. So then I had no one to say my lines to, so Mr Goggin came on stage in his suit and this really stupid wig and pretended he was the Nurse.

'Then when Bobby came on stage, his whole rugby team started whistling and jeering at his Lycra cycling pants, and he got all hassled and started ad-libbing and saying all these really inappropriate things that Shakespeare would so not have wanted Romeo to say. Like at one point when Romeo's under my balcony and he's supposed to say, "Oh, Juliet, you're so stunning and beautiful like the stars . . ." Bobby just glanced up and said, "Hey, Juliet, do you fancy a ride?" It was so pathetic and all his stupid team mates laughed, which just made him worse. In a way it's a blessing in disguise that there were no talent scouts there because it wasn't the performance I'd planned to give. So, my big day pretty much sucked.'

'I'm sure you were wonderful. The scenes you performed for me and your dad were really impressive,' I soothed.

'Yeah, well, you weren't there so you can't say.' Sarah looked out of the window, her bottom lip quivering. 'I don't want to live with you any more. You don't give a shit about me, it's all about Ali, and I've had enough. I want to live with Bobby. I'll come and visit you but I'm not living with you.'

'Sarah,' Paul said, sitting down beside her, 'I honestly can't tell you how sorry we are. Believe me I'd much rather have been at your play than in that bloody clinic finding out some poor girl had killed herself with a tin can. Sometimes as a parent you have to make very difficult choices. Last night was one of those times. I know you feel left out and I promise to make it up to you.'

'How?'

'By being around more and being more involved in your life.'

'Are you kidding me? The last thing I want is you sticking your nose into my life. You've already tried to scare Bobby off for snogging me.'

'But I thought –'

'Dad, I want you to turn up to things when I ask you. I do not want you suffocating me with your guilt. That would be way worse than being neglected.'

Paul looked at me helplessly. 'Sarah,' I said firmly. 'We know you're upset but you're going to come home now and have some breakfast. I'll call school and tell them you'll be in late. You can have the morning off. We know we really let you down yesterday. We're exhausted and we're stressed out from trying to juggle everything at the moment, but we were only trying to do the right thing. I know it's hard on you with Ali being sick, but we're having a tough time too, so please cut us some slack.'

'Well . . . you do look wrecked . . .'

Bobby popped his head around the door. 'Is everything OK?' he asked.

'Come in,' Sarah told him.

He sat down beside her. 'My mum just called. She said she thought you were really cool.'

'Did she?' I could see Sarah was thrilled.

'Totally.'

'Of course she liked you – you're one in a million,' I said.

'You're a very lucky boy, Bobby,' Paul added.

'Spare me your guilty compliments,' Sarah hissed. Then, to her boyfriend: 'So she doesn't think I'm a freak from a really weird family?'

'No. I told her about Alison and her anorexia and she was very sympathetic. She said she used to have bulimia, so she can totally relate to eating disorders. She said the Gretta Lyndon Clinic is really good. She went there about ten years ago and they cured her. She only takes laxatives now before really big parties so she can fit into her dress.'

'I cannot believe I never knew that about your mother. How could you not tell me?'

'To be honest, babe, I was only six so I didn't know what was wrong with her.'

It was nice to hear she'd been cured and thought highly of the clinic. I smiled at Bobby. 'I'm really glad your mum got better. Hopefully Ali will too.'

'She'll pull through, Mrs M. We're doing our best for her.'

'What do you mean?'

'Every lunchtime at school Sarah drags me into the chapel to light candles for Alison. We do positive visualization too, which is supposed to cure anything.'

Sarah was blushing. 'Do you really do that?' I asked.

She flicked her hair back and glared at Bobby. 'It was supposed to be a private thing. It's no big deal, Mum. Don't get all soppy about it. The sooner Ali gets better, the sooner this family can go back to normal.'

I resisted the urge to kiss her cross face. 'Thanks for all your help, Bobby.'

'Yes, thanks for looking after her for us.' Paul shook his hand.

'Come on, pet, let's get you home. Have you had breakfast?'

'No – Mia forgot to do a shop yesterday, so there's nothing to eat but frozen pizza,' she said.

'Well, let's go home and I'll cook you whatever you want. Bobby, come with us – you must be starving.'

'That'd be great.'

'OK, come on, then.'

We piled into Paul's car and drove away from the stunning, but sterile, mansion.

When we got home Charlie was in the kitchen having toast. I set about making breakfast for all of us.

'There she is, our very own Elizabeth Taylor,' Charlie said.

'Isn't she the wrinkly old woman in the wheelchair?' Sarah snorted. 'I sincerely hope I don't look like her!'

'Ah, you kids today, you've no sense of history. She was the most stunning film star of her day. Men fell at her feet.'

'She didn't age well. I guess she was pre-Botox.'

'And what about Romeo himself? Well done, son. You were like a young Richard Burton.'

Bobby looked blank. 'I don't know who that dude is, but I'm guessing it's a compliment, so thanks – but I'll stick to the rugby from now on. That's where my real talent lies. Sarah's the star,' he said, as she basked in his praise.

'You were pretty good too. Everyone was totally jealous of us, even if we did forget some of our lines.'

'You were the hottest Juliet ever.'

'We so rock,' Sarah said, kissing him.

'Although I've no idea what language they're speaking, it'd warm your heart to see young love like that,' Charlie said, as we tucked into our breakfast.

*

After breakfast, Paul gave Bobby a lift to school and was going to pick me up on the way back to go and visit Ali. Sarah waved her boyfriend off and came back into the kitchen.

'Bobby's a really nice guy,' I said to her.

'Hello! I know. I'm the one going out with him. He totally saved my life yesterday. And just so you know, you're not forgiven and I'm still furious. And if anything like this happens again, I'm leaving home and you won't be able to stop me. You are so lucky that Bobby's mother had bulimia and is all understanding about eating disorders and clinics, because if she was a normal mother she would have made Bobby dump me to get away from my freaky family. And if he had broken up with me, I would have blamed you for the rest of my life and probably ended up in the bed beside Ali, bitching to some shrink about my crappy parents.'

'Well, thankfully, that didn't happen and she likes you, as well she might. You are fantastic.'

Sarah rolled her eyes and then yawned. 'I'm exhausted. I didn't sleep well at all last night. I'm going for a nap.'

'Have a nice rest,' I said, hugging her as she squirmed.

'Muuuum, get off me – I told you you're not forgiven yet.'

I kissed her cheek. 'OK, but I want you to know that I'm really proud of you.'

'It's a pity you couldn't say that to me on a day when you hadn't totally let me down. But I'll take it all the same. It's about time you realized just how amazing I am.'

'Have a nice rest. Dad and I are going to see Ali now. I don't know how long we'll be. I'll call you when we're on the way back and give you a lift to school.'

She turned at the door. 'Actually I'll come with you.'

'Are you sure you're up to it?'

'Yeah. I want to see if she's OK,' Sarah said, and went to get her coat.

44

When we arrived at the clinic Denise told us that Ali was in her room and had just come from a session with Mary Boland that had gone well. She was much calmer. Denise looked better too – less traumatized.

We found Ali sitting up on the bed, looking tired, pale and very red around the eyes from crying.

I hugged her. 'How are you, pet?'

'I'm OK. Sorry I gave you a fright last night. I just completely lost it.'

'So you're not going to try and kill yourself?' Sarah asked.

'No. I was just upset when I found out about Emily. She was a really good friend. I still can't believe it.'

'It's terrible,' Paul said. 'The poor girl.'

'Everyone's in shock. It's never happened here before. It's just so awful.' Ali was trying not to cry.

'It's horrendous. Poor Emily,' I said.

Sarah's phone beeped for the millionth time that morning. 'Turn it off,' I snapped.

'I can't help it if everyone wants congratulate me on my performance.'

'Oh, was the play yesterday? How did it go?' Ali asked.

'Well, your little room-trashing episode meant Mum and Dad missed it because they were here playing nursemaid to you.'

'I'm sorry they missed it but my good friend died so of course I reacted badly.'

'I can see that from the state of your room.' Sarah looked around at the ripped posters and broken chair. 'I can't imagine you smashing up furniture. It's very rock and roll.'

'I just couldn't believe Emily was gone.'

'Well, she was pretty messed up. With the shitty father and the mother who couldn't cope with it all and then the hopping and the self-harm. She had no family and no quality of life. Who's going to fancy someone who jumps like a lunatic and has scars all over her? I don't blame her for topping herself – I would have.'

'She just couldn't see a life after here.'

'Well, you're lucky because you have zillions of people wanting you to get better and supporting you and waiting for you to come home.'

Ali nodded. 'I know I'm lucky.'

'Guess what?' Sarah changed direction.

'What?'

'Bobby's mother was in here, like, years ago. She had bulimia but they totally cured her. You should see her – she looks amazing. Maybe I could introduce you to her when you get out of here. She's really cool and super-glamorous. I met her last night and she thinks I rock.'

'She sounds great. I'd love to meet her.'

Sarah's phone beeped again. 'I need to go and answer these calls. Everyone wants to talk to me about the play. They all think I totally nailed the part.' She bent over to give Ali a kiss. It was the first time she'd done that in ages. 'I'm glad you're feeling better. Hang in there.'

'Thanks for coming in and I'm sorry Mum and Dad missed your play.'

'Yeah, well, hopefully none of the other freaks in here will top themselves. I'll call you later. Dad, can you give me the keys? I'll wait for you in the car.'

Paul handed them to her and she left. Then he said, 'Listen, Ali, after what happened yesterday I want you to know that you can come home if you like. You don't have to stay here.'

I held my breath and prayed she'd say no. I really wanted her to stay and continue getting better.

'To be honest, Dad, when I woke up this morning I wanted

to run as far away from here as I could, but after talking to Mary I know that would be the worst thing to do. I have to stay here, face this, deal with it and make sure I don't end up like Emily.' She began to sob. I climbed onto the bed and held her. 'We were going to help each other get better. We were going to support each other on the outside.'

'I know, Ali.' I tried to soothe her. 'I'm so sorry. It's such a terrible thing to happen – but, you know, as Sarah said, Emily had very little support and you have lots. We're all here to help you.'

Ali sniffled. 'I know Mum and I do feel very lucky. I just can't believe she killed herself. I feel that I let her down. I tried talking to her but I couldn't lift her out of her depression. She just kept saying, "I can't do it, Ali, I can't make it in the real world." I told her she could lean on me. I told her I'd help her, but it wasn't enough. If only I'd seen the signs maybe I could have stopped her. I should have seen this coming.'

'Ali, you could never have prevented this. You have to remember that Emily was very damaged. She had an incredibly difficult childhood where she was told she was worthless every day. She had no self-esteem or confidence whatsoever. She was extremely sensitive and fragile.'

'If only she'd seen a way out, a future. I tried to get her to think about life after the clinic, when she was cured and we could have fun together, but she didn't believe me. Now I'm scared I'll find it hard too on the outside.'

'Ali, Emily didn't have any foundations to lean on or any support group. You're different. You have a mother and father who adore you, a sister who loves you, and a grandfather who thinks you're the best thing in the world. You're bright, beautiful and a lovely person inside and out. You have everything to live for. You mustn't let this set you back. You have to use it to drive you to get better and get your life back. Emily didn't make it because she didn't see a future. You have a glorious future ahead of you. I'm here to hold your hand every step of the way. You must keep fighting, Ali.'

'I felt so strong yesterday, but now it's as though I've been punched in the stomach. It's such a struggle all the time, Mum.'

'I know it is, pet. But every recovery takes lots and lots of small steps. You just have to keep putting one foot in front of the other, and on the days when you want to give up, you grit your teeth and keep going. Look at your dad. After he was shot, everyone said he'd die from loss of blood. When he survived after eight pints of transfused blood and ten hours on the operating table, they said he'd never have full use of his legs again because of where the bullet had touched his spine. But he went to rehab and physio and he did his exercises every day, even when he was almost fainting with pain, and he got better and now he surfs ten-foot waves. You have a choice, Ali, sink or swim. Do you want to end up like Emily or do you want to live a life full of love and laughter? If I could make you better I would, but I can only prop you up. You have to choose to get better and fight for your life back.'

'I'm trying, Mum, I really am. I want to make you proud of me and I'm sorry to put you through all this. You lost your own mum when you were my age and then Dad got shot and now I'm causing you all this pain and I never meant to – I never meant to hurt you. I saw Emily's mother this morning walking out of Emily's room. She was bent over, wailing with grief, clutching Emily's sweatshirt. It was horrible. I went over to tell her what an amazing daughter she had and she just said, "They've taken my soul, there's nothing left."'

I gulped back tears.

'And it made me realize how awful it must be for you and Dad to see me in here and be so worried and I uh . . . uh . . . uh . . .' she sobbed '. . . I just really want to get better. I want to come home and be a daughter and a sister and friend again, not a sick and miserable human being.'

I hugged her. 'You don't have to be sorry. We made some really bad decisions when you were small. You've made us proud every day of your life. We love you more than words could ever express. You are not to worry about us because we're fine.'

Paul came over to the bed, his eyes glistening with unshed tears. 'I want to show you something.' He rolled his shirt up to show Ali the big scar where the bullet had gone through. 'Every time I look at this I smile because it reminds me of how lucky I am. I survived. I got better. I have a great life. I have a wife and two beautiful daughters. There was a moment just before the operation when I thought I was going to die, but something in me said, "No way. I'm not ready to go. I want to live for fifty more years. There's so much I want to do, so much I want to see and experience." I still feel that way. I know you're a fighter, because you're my daughter, and we Mullens never give up.'

'I l-lo-love you guys so much.' Ali put her head in my lap and bawled. I held her tight and Paul wrapped his arms around both of us. We all cried, tears of grief, tears of love and tears of hope.

45

When I told Sally about missing the play and Sarah being upset and feeling left out, she offered to take her out for lunch and make a fuss of her. I thought it was a brilliant idea and I knew Sarah'd be thrilled.

She flounced into the kitchen with the phone in her hand. 'That was Sally calling to invite me out for lunch. Just me, on my own. She's taking me to the cool new Japanese restaurant, Dashi. It's supposed to be incredible, like Nobu.'

'Wow! Lucky you.'

'Mum, I know it's a pity lunch because you and Dad humiliated me in front of the whole school, but I'm cool with that.'

On the day of the lunch, Sarah changed six times, eventually deciding on a very tight pink dress with black tights and sky-high heels. I thought the dress was far too short but I bit my tongue and told her she looked lovely.

'You'll knock them dead in that.' Charlie whistled.

'Thanks, Charlie. Apparently all the celebs go to this restaurant, so I want to look my best.'

'Well, you look great,' I lied.

'You so skinny.' Nadia stared at Sarah's teenage waist. 'You lucky girl. I getting big now. Customers will be noticing soon. I haff to gife up working.'

'You're not even two months pregnant, Nadia. You don't need to give up anything except maybe moaning,' I commented.

'Maybe if you stopped eating so much you wouldn't be getting fat – I saw you scoff down a whole box of Milk Tray last night after three helpings of apple crumble and ice cream,' Sarah said.

'I eating for two now. I haff big hungry baby in here. I thinks it a boy. Boys are hungry babies. I fery tired too. I go for rest now.' Nadia slunk off for yet another nap.

'She's eating for more than two.' Sarah snorted. 'There must be a football team in there – or Arnold Schwarzenegger's love child.'

'Leave Nadia alone. She's having a difficult first trimester,' Charlie said. He'd been reading *What To Expect When You're Expecting* and was now an expert on pregnancy.

'How many trimesters are there?' Sarah wanted to know.

'Three.'

'You'd better order a crane to take her to hospital at the rate she's eating – she won't be able to get out the front door.'

'Actually I was thinking of having a home birth. I think it would be nice to have the baby in a warm, friendly environment with everyone around to witness it. We'll need to get a birthing pool.'

'Charlie, are you seriously suggesting that we all stand around and watch Nadia push a kid out of her? You've really lost it this time,' Sarah told him.

'It's the miracle of life.'

'Charlie,' I snapped, 'if you want to have a home birth in your apartment, go ahead, but don't expect us to turn up.'

'Ava, my kitchen will be too small for a pool, so I'll need to borrow yours.'

'No way.' I wanted him to get the insane notion out of his head.

Completely ignoring me, he continued, 'The standard pool size is seventy-six inches by sixty-five. That fits two people comfortably, so I'd be able to get in with her.'

'Charlie, there will be no water birth in this house, and I can tell you right now that neither I nor my children will be witnessing Nadia's labour.'

'I was thinking of inviting Sally, too. Sure she's practically family . . .' he continued, oblivious to the steam coming out of my ears. I walked out before I strangled him and gave Sarah a lift to the restaurant to meet Sally.

As we were driving, she asked, 'Is Charlie serious about Nadia having the baby at home?'

'The scary thing about Charlie is that he's always serious.'

'You have to stop him, Mum. It's obscene.'

'I've never been able to stop Charlie doing anything. He's a law unto himself.'

'Well, I'm not going to any birthing freak show, so you can count me out. Besides, I've decided not to have kids.'

I couldn't hide my surprise. 'Why?'

'All they do is cause hassle even when they seem to be perfect, like Ali. Look at you and Dad. You're both physical and emotional wrecks. Where's the fun? It's just worry and stress. No thanks, it's not for me. And if when I get old I suddenly decide I do want one, I'll adopt.'

'It's up to you but I wouldn't rule out having children just yet. I admit it can be very stressful at times, but being a mum is the best thing about my life. You forget all the bad times when you experience those moments when you're so proud you can't breathe.'

'Are there many of those?' Sarah seemed doubtful.

I smiled at her. 'Lots.'

'Really?'

I nodded. We pulled up outside the restaurant.

'See you, Mum – and don't worry if I'm not home tonight. I'll probably just jet off to LA with Colin Farrell or some other celebrity I meet in here.'

I watched my beautiful sixteen-year-old strut into Dashi, flicking her hair as she went.

Much to my relief, Sarah didn't end up flying to LA to hang out by a guitar-shaped swimming-pool with a bunch of rock stars or actors: she went to Bobby's after the lunch. I was dying to know how it had gone, so I called Sally to get the lowdown. I was eager to find out if Sarah had opened up about feeling neglected and how she felt about Ali being in the clinic.

'Brace yourself, Ava, it was an eventful afternoon.' Sally proceeded to give me a blow-by-blow account . . .

Sarah plonked herself down at the table and looked around. 'Where are all the celebs? I thought it'd be full of famous people. I don't recognize anyone here.'

'The writer June Goodhall is over there.'

'Writer? That's hardly exciting. I'm looking for movie stars and rock bands – even a soap star would do.' Sarah scanned the room again.

'Why don't we order? Maybe someone "cool" will arrive later.'

They ordered their food and a bottle of wine, then Sally asked Sarah how things were going.

'The usual – sister in a nuthouse and grandfather who wants to have his pole-dancer girlfriend give birth in a paddling-pool in our kitchen. Just a regular day in our house.'

Sally laughed. 'Well, it's good to see you haven't lost your sense of humour.'

'It's the only thing keeping me sane. It's a madhouse.'

'Does it bother you?'

'It bothered me when Mum and Dad missed my play.'

'Your mum felt really awful about it and, to be fair, she did have a genuine excuse with Emily dying.'

Their food and wine arrived. Sally said Sarah could have two small glasses but no more: she didn't want her going home drunk.

'Look, I love my sister but it's always about her, these days, and I'm getting sick of it. Even when she's not living in the same house it's still all about Ali. I just wish she'd eat and be normal and come home.'

'It's hard for your mum and dad – they're really upset.'

'Hello? I am aware of that. I live with them and their sadness. I have to look at their tortured faces every day and try to think

333

of ways to cheer them up or distract them. Thank God for Charlie. Honestly, if he wasn't there I'd have left home.'

'It must be hard for you seeing Ali so sick.'

Sarah shrugged. 'I just don't understand why she's doing it. I knew about the shooting and I didn't freak out. I get that David dumping her for Tracy was embarrassing but not enough to starve yourself to death over.'

'Some people are more sensitive and fragile than others.'

Sarah crossed her arms. 'I'm fed up of hearing how sensitive Ali is and how we all have to watch what we say in front of her in case she goes off the deep end again. I'm fed up of seeing Mum crying all the time and Dad trying not to cry all the time. It's doing my head in. I'm sixteen, for God's sake. I'm supposed to be enjoying myself, having carefree teenage years. Instead my sister's in lock-down, my parents are on the verge of nervous breakdowns and my granddad is about to have a baby with a pole dancer. It doesn't get more messed-up than that.'

'I agree that this is a hard time for your family,' Sally said, 'but if you look at it a different way you're actually very lucky. You have a mother and father who love you, plus a granddad who dotes on you and a sister you're very close to. I have two sisters I don't get on well with – we've nothing in common.'

'Ali and I used to be close but now we're like strangers. I don't know how to talk to her any more. I miss her – the old Ali was great. Being the only child in the house sucks – it's way too much pressure. Bobby is the only thing keeping me sane.'

'He sounds like a great guy.'

Sarah twirled her wine glass. 'He's amazing. He's had to listen to me bitching and moaning about everything for months and he never gets pissed off.'

'He's a keeper.' Sally smiled at her.

'So, what about Simon?'

'So far so very good,' Sally admitted.

'Mum said she's never seen you this happy and that she totally hopes it works out because you deserve it.'

'Your mum is a very special lady.'

'She's OK.'

'She's a lot more than that, Sarah. She's a really amazing person. She hasn't had it easy with her mum dying when she was only seventeen and then Charlie going off the deep end and marrying Catherine. Poor Ava was left heartbroken, living in an apartment on her own with no support. But instead of feeling sorry for herself, she got on with her life, did well in college, met your dad and had a family. She always puts you guys first – she's a very selfless mother.'

'I know it must have been hard for her when her mum died. She doesn't really talk about it, though. I just want Mum and Dad to be happy again and not stressed all the time. I miss the way we were. How did everything get so serious and depressing? We never laugh now. I want my family back the way it was. We used to have fun slagging each other at dinner or going to the movies on Sundays and Dad moaning if it was a chick-flick and us moaning if it was a war movie, and just the stuff that families do. Now it's all just tension and tears.'

'It must be hard for you, but Ali seems to be on the mend now so, hopefully, you'll get back to normal before too long,' Sally said, trying to be reassuring, but Sarah wasn't listening. She was looking over her shoulder.

Then she leant in and whispered, 'There's a really weird lady sitting at the bar staring at you. She looks a bit psycho.'

When Sally turned Maura was glaring at her across the restaurant. 'For God's sake!' she exclaimed. Then, turning back to face Sarah, she explained, 'That's Simon's ex-wife. She's mad as a brush. She had an affair but now that he's left her and moved on, she wants him back. She's been stalking me but I thought I'd got rid of her.'

'You have a stalker? How cool is that?'

'It's not cool at all. It's actually a pain in the arse. I can't believe she followed me here. I really thought she'd stopped.'

'I saw this thing on TV and it said you should confront your stalkers. Apparently it freaks them out.'

'I did confront her.'

'What did you say?'

'I told her to piss off.'

'You obviously weren't scary enough. Let me try.' Without waiting for Sally's response, Sarah shouted over to Maura, 'Hey, stalker lady, why don't you leave my friend alone?'

Maura looked taken aback.

'Come on over here, if you're so brave,' Sarah goaded her. The people at the tables beside them were staring at her now.

Maura clambered down from her bar stool and strode over. 'How dare you speak to me like that, you little brat? Judging by that dress you're barely wearing, you're obviously a slut as well.'

Sarah snorted. 'Dude, if you had my legs instead of those fat stumps you'd be wearing this dress. And f.y.i., your ex, Simon, is way into Sally. He went surfing in January to impress her. I mean, come on, game over. She's a top chick and, let's face it, he's never going to go back to you. Like, hello? You can't screw around and expect your husband to stay with you. If Bobby cheated on me I'd dump him like a hot potato and screw his best friend. You got away very lightly. So, why don't you, like, get some therapy, deal with your shit and move on with your life?'

'You little –'

'Hello! I am so not finished. In case you missed it, your ex is in love with Sally. Seriously, you need to sort yourself out or you'll end up like my sister in a clinic full of wackos. What are you going to do? Stalk Sally for another few months and watch your ex fall more in love with her?'

'How dare you?'

'Lips moving, still talking!' Sarah said. 'You need to find yourself a new man. You're not bad-looking, and if you tone down the psycho behaviour I'm sure you'll meet someone. My grand-dad is, like, a hundred and twenty and he's going out with a thirty-eight-year-old. So it's never too late. But you need to start pumping your energy into meeting a new man, not stalking women. There's bound to be some dude out there who likes crazy women.'

The manager came over. 'Ladies, I'm going to have to ask you to leave. You're disturbing the other customers.'

'We're going.' Sally put cash on the table and picked up her bag.

'You haven't heard the last of me,' Maura shouted, blocking their way.

'What's wrong with you? You're just like my sister. He's not into you. It's over, accept it, get over it and MOVE ON!' Sarah shouted into Maura's face. Then, to the other lunchers, she added, 'And for anyone else out there who's hanging on to some pathetic fantasy of getting back with an ex-boyfriend who is seeing someone else – let me save you months of psychotic behaviour. HE'S NOT COMING BACK. FORGET ABOUT HIM BECAUSE, BELIEVE ME, LADIES, HE'S NOT THINKING ABOUT YOU.'

'That's enough advice for one day.' Sally pushed past Maura and hauled Sarah out of the restaurant.

46

Ali was due to have a weigh-in a few days after Emily's death. I was worried sick that she'd have regressed and lost weight. On the morning of her assessment, I paced up and down. When the phone rang, I was almost afraid to pick it up.

'Hello.'

'Mum!' Ali sounded breathless. 'I did it, Mum! I did it. I'm six stone six. I'm off bed-rest. I just walked back to my room all by myself. God, it feels brilliant. I don't need to be wheeled around any more and I can eat with the other girls in the canteen now.'

My knees buckled. Thank God. She sounded so excited. I hadn't heard her so animated in a long time. I wanted to weep with relief. 'Ali, that's the best news I've ever heard. Well done.'

'I know. I can't believe it,' Ali said, and then added sadly, 'I wish Emily was here – she's the first person I wanted to tell.'

'I'm sure she's cheering you on wherever she is.'

'I hope so.'

'Hang on, your dad wants a word,' I said, handing the phone to Paul.

'Did I hear correctly? You're off that bloody bed? Brilliant. Well done, Ali. Your mum's on cloud nine. We're so pleased for you. You'll be out of there and back home in no time. Keep it up – we can't wait to have you with us again.'

While Paul continued to congratulate Ali, I filled Sarah in. Paul then handed her the phone. 'Seriously, you'd think they'd just won the bloody lotto. I got so excited when I walked into the room to find Mum actually looking happy for the first time in for ever. I was sure we'd won the Euro millions, but she told me she was thrilled because you'd put on, like, two pounds or

338

something and now you can walk instead of being wheeled around and stuck in bed like an old person. And there I was thinking we were going to be travelling by private jet and spending our summers in St Tropez with all the other loaded people. Anyway, I'm glad for you – it must be nice to be able to move around without being escorted everywhere like someone on Death Row.'

Then, whispering, she added, 'You should see Mum and Dad – they are so over the moon. I've never seen them like this. So, keep it up, because it's actually really nice to see them happy again. I totally milked it and just asked Mum if I could go to a slumber party in Tia's house and she said yes! You know what she's like normally – she never lets us stay the night in other people's houses. Hang on, Charlie wants to talk to you so I'd better go. Don't let the freaks in there get you down. Ciao!'

'She's going to a sleepover?' Paul asked.

'She deserves a break. All this has affected her, too. Let her have some fun.'

'OK, but it'd better not be a mixed slumber party,' Paul warned.

'She swore it's only girls.'

We could hear Charlie on the phone telling Ali he hadn't seen Paul and me so happy since the day she was born, but Sarah overheard him.

'I have feelings too, Charlie,' she shouted. 'What about when I was born?'

'All right,' Charlie said to her. 'It's the happiest I've seen your parents since both you and Ali were born. Jesus, you've been very touchy since the play.'

'I'm tired of being relegated to second position,' Sarah grumbled. 'I'm standing my ground from now on.'

'God help us all.' Paul sighed.

'Sorry about that, Ali.' Charlie walked out of the room with the phone. 'It's impossible to get any privacy in this house – there's always someone lurking behind you. Anyway, we're all thrilled here about your great news. It must feel wonderful to be off that bloody bed and walking around. Keep eating your meals and we'll have you home before you know it. I miss you. You're the only sane one in this house. All right, pet, 'bye for now.'

After Ali's call, I felt genuinely positive about her recovery for the first time. A weight had lifted off my shoulders. Not the whole weight, but a chunk of it, and it felt wonderful.

The next morning I bounded into work full of enthusiasm and focus, ready for Annabelle Collins's sweet-sixteen extravaganza. The party was our biggest commission to date and her father, Paddy, had given us an unlimited budget to create a party his daughter would never forget.

Annabelle had demanded the *Moulin Rouge* theme. But, as she had explained to us, 'I'm not talking about a few feathers and some guys on stilts, I'm talking can-can dancers, trapeze artists, chandeliers, red velvet curtains and a really hot outfit for me to wear for my grand entrance. I have to look incredible. I want everyone to be blown away. I want a choreographer to teach me the can-can, but the dancers have to make me look good, so they'll have to be in the background. The spotlight has to be on me, not them.'

'Do you dance much?' I asked, somehow doubting that this chubby girl did anything but sit on a couch. She could have been quite attractive but it was hard to tell under all the add-ons. Her hair was dyed white-blonde with lots of long extensions. She was an orange shade of dark brown from too much fake tan. She had long acrylic nails and very heavy black eye makeup. The overall effect was startling.

'Oh, yeah, I'm a really good dancer – all my friends are always saying I'm like Beyoncé when I dance.' Annabelle stood up and shook her hips to demonstrate her agility.

It looked more like a wobble than a shake, but we weren't going to tell her that. 'With natural talent like that you'll have no problem doing the can-can. I know a very good choreographer who can help you,' Sally lied. In all our years of business we had never been asked to teach anyone how to dance.

'Annabelle is very keen to have a corset-style dress made. Can you recommend a good dressmaker?' Wendy Collins asked. 'Someone who specializes in corsetry.'

'Absolutely, no problem. I have an excellent lady who has helped us in the past.' I reckoned Madame Sophie would find something suitably sexy for Annabelle.

'I don't want some old woman who thinks sexy is a skirt to the knee. I want a corset and hot pants,' Annabelle told us.

'Darling, I think hot pants are too much. Why don't you get a little ra-ra skirt to go with the corset?' Wendy suggested.

'That sounds like a good idea,' I said, looking at Annabelle's chunky legs. Hot pants were not created for girls like her.

'Mum! I said I want hot pants and Dad said I could have whatever I wanted.'

'Fine.' Wendy gave in. Her daughter was clearly used to getting her own way all the time. She didn't seem to have the energy to put up a fight.

'Would you like a band or a DJ? Or both?' Sally asked.

'Duh, both, obviously. I want a big orchestra-type band at first for my entrance, and then I want DJ Rock Thejoint.'

Sally jotted down these details.

'We'd like to have the party at home in the garden, so could you organize for a marquee? Something with real glass windows and doors – not the plastic ones,' Wendy said. 'And nice toilets with someone to keep them clean throughout the night.'

'And a makeup artist and hairdresser to fix us up whenever we need it,' Annabelle added.

'Of course, no problem.' I tried not to smile. This party was going to provide us with a big pay cheque.

'And I don't want some crappy little marquee – I want a two-tiered one. I want a stage for me to dance on and stairs to make my entrance down so everyone can see me.'

Sally noted all of this in her book – with a large 'PITA' down the side of the page – our code for 'Pain In The Arse'.

Over the last few weeks, while I was busy with Ali, Sally had sourced the marquee, which was being imported from England, a choreographer, can-can dancers, aerial artists and all the trimmings and supplies we needed to dress the tables and marquee. The invitations had been hand-delivered to each of the hundred and thirty guests by two acrobats on stilts. They were little windmills that opened up to the music of Lady Marmalade and invited the guests to an unforgettable night at the Moulin Rouge. We enclosed a copy of the menu, which we had expanded so that everyone could choose a beef, fish, vegetarian, vegan, or coeliac option and enclose it with their RSVP.

Apparently no one was unable to attend.

We ran into a problem when the DJ refused to play a sixteen-year-old birthday party. He said it was demeaning to his artistry. We begged, pleaded and tried bribing him but he wouldn't budge. Eventually we got another DJ who was supposed to be almost as good. But Annabelle freaked when we broke the news to her.

'That's it, the party's ruined. I'm cancelling it. It's over. I've told *everyone* that DJ Rock Thejoint is playing. I'm not being humiliated. You said you could get him. You're crap party planners – I knew I should have gone with Partypeople. They did Zoe's party and it was amazing.'

'Annabelle, I can assure you we did everything to get him to come but he won't budge.' Sally tried not to lose her temper.

'The other DJ, Rhapsodie, is supposed to be brilliant. My sixteen-year-old loves him,' I said. Sarah had said he was cool, and I knew she had a good handle on what was cool and what was not.

'Are you deaf? I don't want him. I want DJ Rock Thejoint,' she screeched. 'You've ruined my life.' She stormed out as we sat in silence with her mother.

'There must be something you can do,' Wendy said. 'We have to get this DJ. He's all she's talked about for months.'

'Honestly, Wendy, we've tried everything,' I assured her.

'Let me call Paddy and see if he has any ideas,' Wendy said, dialling his number and filling him in. Paddy came on the loudspeaker. 'It's like this, ladies, if Annabelle wants this guy she gets him or I'm going to have to listen to her moaning for six months. What's his fee?'

'Six thousand for three hours,' Sally informed him.

'To spin a few records? Jesus, I'll take it up myself.' Paddy snorted.

'He's considered one of the best in the world,' Wendy piped up. 'And Annabelle is distraught.'

'Fine, double his rate. Tell him we'll pick him up in my private jet from wherever he is and drop him back in the morning. Set him up in the presidential suite at the Four Seasons and throw in a couple of bottles of Cristal – isn't that what all these guys drink? If he still says no, triple his fee.'

Amazingly, DJ Rock Thejoint decided that twelve thousand euros for three hours' work wasn't so demeaning after all.

With only a few days to go the choreographer had called to say that Annabelle, a.k.a. Beyoncé, had two left feet and was impossible to teach. Sally voted that I go down and try to help sort it out. 'You've got teenagers, you know how to handle them. I'll stay here and finalize the food with Helen.'

I had to pick Sarah up from school on the way to the dance studio. 'I just have to pop in here to sort out a problem with work. Do you want to stay in the car or come in?' I asked her.

'What's the problem?'

'Annabelle Collins is trying to learn a dance routine for her grand entrance and apparently it's not going very well.'

'Oh, God, what a loser. Everyone who knows her says she's a total pain. She loves herself and thinks just because her dad is loaded that makes her cool. Bobby sees her at Christmas parties and stuff because their dads are friendly. Even he said she's a pain and he never gives out about people. He lost the invitation, so he told me to tell you he's not going. He can't stand her.'

'Well, he's the only person who isn't. I agree, she does seem to be very spoilt but remember that she's a client, so no comments – even under your breath. OK?'

'As if.'

Sarah and I arrived in to see Annabelle thumping around the place, out of time with everyone else.

'She's the worst case I've seen,' Janice, the choreographer, whispered. 'I've simplified the dance to six moves but she still can't get it. Along with being a spoilt brat, she's thick too.'

Sarah grinned. 'I can't wait to tell Bobby about this.'

'Go over there, sit down and don't open your mouth,' I warned her.

Wendy Collins was sitting in the corner of the studio, encouraging Annabelle.

'You nearly had it there. That was much better,' she lied to her daughter.

The can-can dancers went one way and Annabelle went the other. She stomped over to Janice. 'I'm sick of this stupid dance. You're making it too hard for me. Your steps are really difficult, I can't remember them all. Why can't you make it easy?'

'There are six simple steps to remember and then repeat. It doesn't get any easier than this. You just need to stop staring at yourself in the mirror and concentrate,' Janice snapped.

'That's it. You're fired. How dare you speak to me like that? Mum! I want a new dance teacher.'

'Hold on a minute,' I said firmly. 'Janice is the top choreographer in the country. You're lucky to have her. Now, why don't you take a break and cool down?'

Annabelle went over to her mother and took out a bottle of Coke. Looking up, she saw Sarah. 'What are you doing here?'

I walked over. 'This is my daughter Sarah, Sarah, this is Annabelle.'

'Hi, how are you?' Sarah was at her most polite.

'That's a Hodder College uniform, right?' Annabelle asked.

'Yeah.'

'Do you know Bobby Masterson-Brown?'

'I do, actually.'

Annabelle flicked her hair. 'I know him really well. Our dads are, like, best friends. He's always over in the house.'

'Really? Wow. He's kind of cute.' Sarah reeled her in.

'Kind of? He's totally gorgeous. Apparently he's going out with this girl in his class who's not even that good-looking but thinks she's a goddess.'

'I actually know her and she's really hot. Loads of guys in school fancy her.' Sarah flicked her hair and eyeballed Annabelle, who remained oblivious.

'Well, my friend Amber saw them together and said she wasn't good-looking and that she was all over Bobby like a rash and he was, like, trying to get away from her.'

'Where was this?'

'After one of his rugby matches.'

'OK – we need to get back to practice now,' I said, knowing Sarah was about to reach boiling point.

Ignoring me completely, Sarah said, 'I see them together every day and he is all over her. He's totally into her.'

'I don't think so.' Annabelle took a sip of her Coke. 'Anyway, nothing will come of it. My dad and Bobby's dad always said we'd end up marrying each other because then the two fortunes would be combined and we'd be, like, the richest people in the country.'

'Do you honestly think he fancies you?'

Annabelle smiled. 'Well, yeah, but he's too shy to do anything about it. I'm going to have to make the first move. I've invited him to my party so you never know, it could be, like, fate.'

'Oh, really? Is he actually going to your party?'

'Hello! Everyone's coming. No one would miss it. It's going to be incredible. I have loads of people in school following me around begging me to invite them.'

'I heard he's not going.'

'Who told you that?'

'Bobby did. He said he'd –'

'OK!' I stood between them and glared at Sarah. 'We really need to get back to the dance.'

'Hold on – are you telling me Bobby told you he's not coming to my party?'

'That's exactly what I'm telling you. And, f.y.i., he hates blondes.'

'Liar.'

'Excuse me?'

'You're obviously jealous because you fancy him and you want to come to my party like everyone else in this country.'

Sarah stepped closer. 'I'd rather stick a hot needle in my eye than –'

'That's enough.' I grabbed Sarah and frog-marched her to the opposite side of the room, where Janice was talking to the dancers.

'What the hell are you doing?' I hissed. 'This is my job you're messing with.'

'She's a bitch. Did you hear what she said?'

'Yes, she is and I did, but this party is going to provide a huge pay cheque for Sally and me, so just be quiet and say nothing.'

'Fine.' Sarah sat down, took out her phone and started texting.

I turned to Janice. 'What can we do here? Can you reduce Annabelle's moves to four or even three and let the other dancers do the complicated stuff around her?'

'It'll look ridiculous. She can't even lift her leg beyond knee height – the other girls' legs lift right up to their shoulders.'

'And that's in a tracksuit – imagine how bad she's going to be in a corset and skin-tight hot pants.'

Janice started to laugh.

'Is there any way the dancers could all link arms and kind of pull her along with them?'

'They could, but it'll look awful and what do we do when they kick and do the splits?'

'Well, could she do some kind of twirl and stay standing?'

'Yes, she could, but I don't want my name on this. I don't want people knowing I taught this girl.'

'I understand where you're coming from, but Annabelle is only going to do a short entrance dance for thirty seconds, then the can-can girls will do a proper ten-minute routine and you can really show your talent with that.'

'OK – but if you're ever looking for a choreographer for a sixteenth birthday again, count me out. It's taking all my powers of restraint not to slap her.'

'I know how you feel,' Sarah piped up.

'Janice, if you focus on the footwork I'll deal with Annabelle.'

I went over and told Annabelle the plan. She pouted. 'I don't want the dancers showing me up. I'm the star here, not them.'

'The spotlight will be on you all the time and they'll be in the background,' I assured her.

Janice proceeded to teach Annabelle three simple moves that she just about managed, but she was still out of synch with the music.

'It's definitely going to be an unforgettable entrance.' Sarah giggled.

'It's like teaching an elephant ballet,' Janice whispered, as we tried not to laugh.

'If she wants to humiliate herself, there's nothing we can do,' I said. 'I reckon she'll split the hot pants doing the high kick, though. I'll need to warn Madame Sophie.'

Half an hour later, Annabelle was still dancing completely out of time but we had to leave the studio because we had an appointment with Madame Sophie for a final fitting of her outfit. I decided to drop Sarah home on the way. It was safer.

'Seriously, Mum, how can you work with that bitch?'

'Sometimes you have to work with difficult people. It's the same in all jobs. Your dad has to deal with drunks in the pub being abusive and I have to deal with difficult children. Most kids are nice, but you do get the odd one like Annabelle who's not so easy.'

'Did you hear her saying that she and Bobby were going to get married? I mean, where does she get off? She's, like, totally delusional. I texted him straight away and look what he sent back.' Sarah shoved her phone in front of me.

**Babe, A is frk. Wldn't
tch hr nvr mnd
mrry hr! I luv u. Wldn't
g 2 pty f u pyd me.
Yr rght, sh ft & gly
& u ht**

'Can you read that in English?'

' "Babe, Annabelle is a freak. I wouldn't touch her never mind marry her. I love you. I wouldn't go to the party if you paid me. You're right, she is fat and ugly and you're hot." '

'Well, I'm glad that's cleared up.'

'I wasn't exactly worried. She's hardly competition. I don't understand how she can think she's hot when she looks like that. Do these people not have mirrors?' Sarah examined herself admiringly in the car mirror. 'You either have it or you don't.'

After dropping Sarah home I drove to meet Annabelle and Wendy at the fitting. I hadn't seen the outfit before, but Sally had been to the two previous fittings. She had warned me that Annabelle was a sight to behold.

Madame Sophie greeted me like an old friend. 'Ava, *ma belle*, 'ow are you?'

'Good, thanks.'

'Did your 'usband enjoy ze lingerie?' she whispered.

'Very much, thanks. It was a big help.'

'It 'elps wiz ze sex, no?'

'Yes, it did. Now, let's see Annabelle, shall we?' I changed the subject, not wanting to get the third degree from Sophie about my sex life, which had been neglected again lately, with all the drama over Ali.

'We 'ave a problem,' Sophie told me. 'Annabelle ees too fat for ze 'ot pants. But she insists to wear zem. I tell Sally eet ees not a good idea, but she says zere ees nozzing she can do. Ze girl will look ridiculous.'

'I know, but Sally's right – this girl gets whatever this girl wants.'

'You Irish are much too nice to your childrens. In France we say, "*Non*," and zat ees zat. In Hireland, ze childrens dictate to ze parents. Zis ees very bad. Annabelle needs some slaps to ze behind.'

'Yes, she does, but disciplining her is not our problem. All we need to do is keep her happy until Saturday.'

'OK, I will say nozzing. But eef eet was my daughter –'

'Excellent, thanks.' I cut her off. I didn't have the time or patience to listen to Sophie's views on child-rearing. I just wanted to get Annabelle's outfit sorted before I lost my temper and slapped the bolshy teenager myself.

Sophie went into the dressing room to tie Annabelle into her corset. I could hear grunting, and '*Ah, non, ce n'est pas possible!*' and 'Ouch, you're hurting me, you witch . . .'

When Annabelle finally came out of the dressing room, I was speechless.

The corset was made of red satin and black lace and her significant cleavage was spilling over the top. You could almost see her nipples. The hot pants were covered with black sequins and were so tight they made her thighs look bigger than they were. She looked like an underage, overweight hooker.

'I look so hot.' She beamed into the mirror.

'I still think the shorts are a mistake. They're too tight and they don't flatter you,' Wendy said to her daughter.

'What are you saying, Mum? That my legs are fat? Are you? Are you telling me I have fat thighs?'

'Yes, you do 'ave fat legs,' Sophie put in. 'Zey are very fat, so why are you inseesting on showing them? Eet's ridiculous. Eef you 'ave fat legs you don't wear 'ot pants.'

'She does not have fat legs.' I jumped in. If there was one thing I knew about, it was the importance of a positive body image in teenagers. 'She has lovely legs. Look, Annabelle, all we're saying is that maybe they're a bit short. You're only sixteen and you are showing a lot of your body in that outfit. You have a wonderful figure, but maybe it's a bit too much exposure. It's nice to leave something to the imagination.'

She snorted. 'I don't think so. If you have it, flaunt it. When I'm, like, thirty and old and wrinkly, I'll regret not having shown off my legs. This is what I'm wearing, end of story.'

I bit my tongue. It wasn't for me to tell her how to dress. I wasn't her mother – thank God.

'OK – but I don't think Dad will approve,' Wendy said, playing her ace card.

'Dad said as long as I'm happy he's happy. And this is the outfit that makes me happy,' Annabelle countered.

Wendy caved. 'All right, we'll take it.' With that she got out her black American Express card and spent another fortune on her daughter.

Sophie shrugged and charged an extortionate amount of money for the outfit.

I called Sally on the way home. 'I need a stiff drink – the girl is a nightmare.'

Sally roared laughing. 'Aren't you supposed to be able to handle teenagers? You have two.'

'Yes, and I'm beginning to really appreciate them. Seriously, that Annabelle needs a good slap. Will you meet me at the Drift Inn in ten minutes? We need to go over some final details with Paul about the cocktail bar anyway, so we can work and drink.'

'My idea of heaven. See you in ten.'

I hung up and drove to the pub. This was the first time Sally and I had been asked to set up a cocktail bar at a kids' party, and when I'd asked Paul's advice on how to organize it, he'd offered to do it himself. He said he wanted to help: he knew the party was a big deal for me and he was glad to be a part of it. He'd been a great help, it was lovely to have him around.

I sat up at the bar and Paul brought me a mojito. 'You look stressed,' he said.

'Honestly, Paul, our girls are angels compared to Annabelle Collins. She is a salutary lesson in why you should never spoil your kids.'

'Just think, only three more days to go and she'll be out of your hair and her father's large cheque will be in your hand.'

'That part I'm looking forward to.'

'What part?' Sally sat down beside me.

'Getting paid,' I said.

'I'll drink to that.'

'Speaking of drinks,' Paul said, 'I have the specially created *Moulin Rouge* cocktail here for you to taste.' He brought over two glasses.

Annabelle wanted champagne cocktails and her parents had agreed but then asked us to make sure they were very weak. They didn't want the kids getting drunk.

'Yum – what's in it?' I asked.

'Cranberry juice, red grapefruit juice, a dash of grenadine and a splash of champagne.'

'It tastes great, Paul, well done.' Sally was impressed.

'And they're weak as requested so the kids won't be in a heap going home.'

'Perfect. Now can I have something stronger?' Sally asked.

'Mojito?'

'Lovely.'

Paul made Sally her drink, then went to sort out some problem in the kitchen. I filled Sally in about Annabelle's dancing.

'How bad are we talking?'

'Imagine the worst dancer you've ever seen and triple it.'

'She's going to humiliate herself.'

'I know, but she's adamant about making her grand entrance. At least the dancers can kind of carry her along so maybe it won't be a total car crash.'

'Can you imagine what the other kids are going to say? There's no way all one hundred and thirty of them are her friends – she'll be slated.'

I shuddered. Teenagers were a cruel bunch – poor Annabelle would indeed be savaged.

'How did it go with Sophie?' Sally asked.

'Worse – the outfit's a joke. The corset's beautiful, but she's falling out of it and the shorts are far too tight. She is literally peeled into them. It's a good thing she can't do high kicks because the seams wouldn't take the pressure.'

We giggled into our drinks.

'What did Sophie say?' Sally asked.

'You know Sophie – subtlety isn't her strong point. She told Annabelle she had fat legs and shouldn't be exposing them.'

Sally laughed. 'Good old Sophie. I like her directness.'

'She's direct, all right. I had to dodge her questions about my sex life, or lack thereof. Being there surrounded by lingerie reminded me that I've been neglecting my wifely duties – again.'

'The once-a-week sex that prevents your husband straying.'

'Exactly, and with all that's been happening with Ali, sex really hasn't been a priority.'

'Of course not. You've had so much on your plate. But if you don't mind my saying, I think you should try to set aside some time for yourselves, for your sanity. You both look worn out. You need to have some fun together.'

'You're right. Even Mary Boland told us we had to make time

for each other, but there never seems to be any time. All we talk about is Ali, all we think about is Ali.'

'That's not healthy, Ava. You have to remember that you're a person, too. Both you and Paul need to spend some time together as a couple, not as parents. Go out for dinner, get drunk, have fun and shag each other senseless. You need a blow-out. It'll do you the world of good.'

'You're absolutely right, I know, but I feel selfish if I'm not thinking or worrying about Ali. It's as if I'm letting her down or something.'

Sally put her hands on my shoulders. 'Ava, you're allowed to have a life. Yes, Ali's sick, but she's getting the best help there is. Worrying every second of the day will not help her. You need to focus on yourself – and Paul and Sarah, too. In the next week I want you to tell me you've been out on a date with Paul and had some fun. You deserve it. It's not going to harm Ali if her parents have a night out. It will harm her if her parents neglect each other and their relationship. OK?'

I nodded. Paul and I did need some time together as a couple . . . urgently.

47

Three days later it was D Day. Sally and I met out at the Collinses' house at eight in the morning. The marquee had been set up over the past five days. It was incredible. It had a large entrance hall with a cloakroom and lots of space for a big bar. This led into a huge dining room with a stage and a mirrored dance-floor. Then there was a mezzanine filled with *chaise-longues* and couches. There were five loos for the girls and three for the boys. The windows and doors were all glass, and a rich red carpet covered the entire floor. Twenty crystal chandeliers hung from the ceiling. It was like a ballroom.

Sally and I were spending the day overseeing the decorating of the marquee – we helped hang red and black velvet drapes across the room and over each window and door. We dressed the chairs in white crushed velvet covers with big red bows tied at the back. The table centrepieces were six-foot vases, filled with enormous red and black feathers. There was a *Moulin Rouge* backdrop at one end of the marquee and the movie was to run on a loop all night on a huge screen at the other end. The chandeliers were lit with red bulbs, giving a real boudoir feel.

The bathrooms also had red carpets and were stocked with every product imaginable – hair spray, deodorant, ten different types of perfume, an array of hairbrushes and hairdryers, hair straighteners, curling tongs, instant fake-tan sprays, nail varnish, hand creams, body creams, cleansers, toners, moisturizers, lipsticks, mascaras, eyeliners, eyeshadows, blushers, false eyelashes . . . Everything was provided.

Paul arrived after lunch with a team of four. They set up a bar on three long trestle tables, which they draped in red velvet. They lined up the red and black cocktail glasses. Each one had a mini feather swizzle stick in it. Paul filled a glass and handed it to me to taste.

'Yum,' I said, knocking it back.

'Easy there, it's only three o'clock. I don't want you falling down before the guests arrive.' He laughed.

'It's not very potent. I think I'm safe enough.'

'Do you need a stronger one?'

'Not yet, but I definitely will later on.'

'I'll make it extra strong.'

'You have my full permission to get me drunk and take advantage of me.'

'Really? Fantastic.' He beamed. I leant over and kissed him.

'Get a room!' Sally came up behind us. 'Paul, you are not allowed distract Ava until the party is over. After that she's all yours. Come on, Ava, I need your help. The acrobats have arrived.'

We walked over to meet them. I glanced back at Paul – he was staring at my bum. I smiled to myself. He hadn't done that in a long time.

Sally had flown the aerial artists over from the UK. They had specified that the ceiling had to be seven metres high and they needed at least two rigging points. We helped them get organized and then went to sort out the place names for the tables.

The entrance to the marquee was a huge wooden door with *Moulin Rouge* across the top, lit by bright bulbs. A red carpet led up to it with two security men dressed like circus ringmasters in red tailcoats manning it.

At seven o'clock, Annabelle and her parents came down to check out the marquee.

'Wow!' Annabelle said. Sally and I breathed a sigh of relief. 'Everyone is going to be so jealous of me. Oh, my God, these cocktails are amazing.' She gulped one down. 'This is so cool. Mum!' She dragged Wendy over to watch the trapeze artists rehearsing.

I introduced Paul to Paddy Collins. 'Very nice to meet you. Well done on the cocktails – they look good and taste weak.'

'You'll be happy to hear that there's barely a quarter of a glass of champagne in each one so you shouldn't have any kids falling around drunk, unless they sneak the drink in themselves.'

'They're being frisked at the door to stop that happening, but there's bound to be one or two that manage to get some in,' Paddy said. Then, to Sally and me, he added, 'Ladies, I don't know how you did it, but you've made Annabelle happy, which is almost impossible, these days. Well done, I'm impressed. I'll be recommending you to all my friends.'

'Thanks very much. You have a very nice family,' I said.

'I have a wife who can't say boo to our daughter. And a sixteen-year-old who is spoilt rotten and takes everything for granted. It's not how I thought things were going to turn out. I always thought I'd have a rake of sons who'd take over the business. But there you go. We were only able to have one child, our little princess, and I'm absolutely mad about her. She has me wrapped around her little finger. I can't say no to her even though I should.'

'I know that feeling,' Paul said.

'Nothing ever turns out the way you planned it,' I mused. 'You just do your best. We have two teenage daughters and they never stop surprising us.'

'Or shocking us, but it's worth it all the same.' Paul put his arm around me.

Wendy came back, beaming. 'It's a miracle – she's happy! Thank you.'

'You're very welcome,' Sally said.

'What do you think of this?' Paddy asked, producing a diamond-encrusted Rolex watch from his pocket.

'It's bling-tastic.' Sally admired it.

'She's been begging for it for six months but we pretended we couldn't source one,' Paddy said. 'It's the first watch of its kind sold in Ireland – she'll be over the moon when she sees it.'

'I'm sure she will,' I said, almost blinded by the diamonds.

'Quick, hide it, here she comes,' Wendy warned her husband.

'We have a problem.' Annabelle was hyperventilating. 'Where's my throne? I specifically asked for my chair to be a throne, so everyone knows where I'm sitting.'

'It's behind the stage,' I told her. 'You said you wanted to be carried down the stairs in it after your dance, remember?'

'Oh, yes! How could I forget? That was such an amazing idea of mine. India Murray's going to be sick with jealousy. She had a throne at her party but it was only a small one and no one really saw it. Everyone is going to see mine. OK, panic over. Come on, Mum, I need to go and put my costume on.'

They all went off to get ready.

'Jesus, I thought Sarah was high-maintenance. This girl's a joke.' Paul couldn't believe it. 'It just shows you that you can really ruin a kid by spoiling them.'

'I dunno – I think that one was born with "666" on her head,' Sally said.

'She's difficult all right,' I agreed.

'She needs a good kick up the arse. Did you see the watch? It cost about thirty grand,' Paul told us.

'Pity I'm no longer single, because despite the fact that Paddy Collins is no Matthew McConaughey I'd sleep with him for the gifts. Could you imagine? You'd be dripping in diamonds.'

'What about the small issue of a wife?' I reminded her.

'Come on, she'd be easy to get rid of. She's a total doormat.'

'What about the psycho stepdaughter you'd inherit?' Paul grinned.

'That's what boarding schools are for.'

'You've thought this through.' He was impressed.

'If it wasn't going to be love it was definitely going to be money. But then Simon came along.'

'And you got both.' I smiled at her.

'He's no millionaire.'

'I've never met a poor lawyer,' Paul pointed out.

'True. Can you believe I ended up falling for a Quaker lawyer? I always thought I'd end up with a ball-breaking City banker.'

'Love works in mysterious ways – look at Charlie,' I said.

'Look at this!' Paul said. We turned to see five coaches pulling up at the end of the driveway.

One hundred and thirty screaming, over-excited teenagers charged towards the door. All you could hear was 'Oh, my God . . . this is awesome . . . amazing . . . so incredible . . . so, like, authentic . . . You could so be in Paris right now . . . I wonder what she's wearing . . . She has such fat thighs and always shows them off, someone should, like, seriously talk to her . . . Look, she's put Dylan on one side of her and Mark on the other, she's so into both of them, it's a bit desperate . . . Do you think he'll go for her? . . . No way . . . maybe because she's, like, queen for the night . . . Oh, my God, they're serving cocktails . . . Wow, this is *soooooo* cool . . .'

At eight thirty, the orchestra started up and everyone was ushered to the front of the stage. The lights went down and twenty spectacular can-can girls in ruffled red dresses danced out, arms linked, half carrying a small chubby girl in hot pants. Once they were lined up, the spotlight went onto Annabelle, leaving the other dancers in semi-darkness. While they kicked their legs, she kind of skipped beside them, while they did handstands, she spun around in a circle, and when they did the splits, she stayed standing and threw her hands in the air in a theatrical 'ta-da'.

'I don't know much about dancing but that was shocking,' Paul whispered in my ear.

'You can't make a silk purse out of a sow's ear,' I murmured back. 'We did our best.'

'You did a great job – the place looks incredible. I'm very impressed.'

'That's really nice to hear. And thanks for helping out with the bar. It's brilliant.'

'We make a good team.' Paul smiled at me, and I kissed him.

'Mmmmm, more of that later, please,' he said, and reluctantly headed back to the bar where kids were fighting each other to get cocktails.

All you could hear among them was 'That dancing was *soooo* embarrassing . . . poor Annabelle . . . two left feet . . . So lame . . . Oh, my God, what was that? . . . I'm dying inside for her . . . Money can't buy you rhythm . . . What is she wearing? . . . The corset is like way hot, but the hot pants? Hello, thunder thighs . . .'

Annabelle left the stage and now that the can-can dancers were set free from trying to make her look good, they did an incredible set – high-kicking, cart-wheeling, back-flipping and doing the splits over and over again to the enthusiastic screams of the teenagers. Janice had done an amazing job on the choreography: they were fantastic.

Sally and I went backstage to make sure Annabelle's second entrance was set up. Six male models, naked to the waist, were going to carry her down the stairs and out among the guests.

'Come on, hurry up, I want to get out there – I want them to see me.' Annabelle was wearing a feather and diamond tiara to go with her throne.

The models lifted the chair onto their shoulders and carried her out. The band played 'Don't You Wish Your Girlfriend Was Hot Like Me' and the other teenagers ran up and cheered, although I definitely heard some jeering too.

Annabelle waved like a royal princess, loving every minute of it. But when the chair was set down she stood up to take a bow and a loud rip rang out. Annabelle froze.

'She's split her hot pants,' Sally gasped.

'Oh, shit. Tell the band to keep playing.' I ran over, pushed Annabelle back into the chair and told the men to carry her backstage.

'Wave,' I hissed. 'Behave as if this is all part of the plan.'

She stared at me, her lip quivering.

'Smile and wave,' I barked.

She waved weakly and tried to smile as we hustled her backstage.

Sally came running in after us. 'It's OK, a couple of the kids heard it and started saying you'd split your hot pants, and I told them that was bullshit, you were coming right back out now and they'd see you hadn't.'

'Why did you say that? Are you a total moron? I can't go back out there with my arse hanging out,' Annabelle screeched.

Sally pushed her face into Annabelle's. 'Listen to me, you spoilt brat. We knew you were going to split your hot pants – they were far too tight for your fat arse – so we had a spare pair made. Shut up and put them on.'

I produced them and helped her squeeze into them. 'You don't have a fat bum, Sally was just joking,' I whispered.

'Hello! I'm not blind – I know I have a great arse.' She rolled her eyes.

'Go on, get out there and show them all your hot pants aren't ripped,' Sally told her.

We peeked out from behind the curtain and watched Annabelle twirling around to show any doubters her non-ripped hot pants.

I felt a tap on the shoulder and spun around. 'Excuse me, I'm looking for the loo,' a boy slurred, but before I could give him directions, he threw up all over Sally's shoes.

She covered her face with her hands. 'I will never ever do a sixteenth-birthday party again. I don't care how much profit we make. It's not bloody worth it. Give me screaming toddlers any day.'

I put my arm around her. 'Come on, partner, let's go and get Paul to make us a very strong cocktail.'

'It'd better be bloody rocket fuel – I loved these shoes.' We looked down at the vomit-stained shoes and began to laugh.

We found Paul, who made us very potent cocktails. At one o'clock the coaches arrived to take the guests home. We helped usher the kids onto them and waved them off.

By the time we had cleaned up it was three o'clock in the

morning. We were all bleary-eyed. The barmen left, then Paul and I dropped Sally back to her apartment and went home.

'Thanks for tonight,' I said, kissing him in the hall as he took his coat off.

'You're very welcome. I enjoyed working with you. It's nice to see you in kick-arse organizing mode. Very impressive.'

'How do you fancy me kicking your arse around the bed-room?' I nuzzled his neck.

Paul whooped, hoisted me over his shoulder and hurried up the stairs where we had passionate, needy, emotional and long-overdue sex.

48

Three days later Sally didn't turn up for work. I called her phone but it was switched off. I called her apartment but it just kept going into answering-machine. By ten o'clock I was getting really worried so I drove over to see if she was all right. I buzzed her intercom. No answer. I buzzed again and again until finally she picked up.

'What?'

'Sally, it's me – are you OK?'

'I hate men,' she shouted.

'Fair enough. Can you buzz me in so we can discuss it face-to-face?'

I ran up the stairs two at a time. When I got to her apartment, the door was open and she was standing in the kitchen drinking wine straight from the bottle.

'Sally, it's ten in the morning. Put that down and talk to me.' I gently removed the bottle from her hand and led her to the couch. She sat down, put her head in her hands and groaned.

'Talk to me, Sally. What happened?'

'Simon proposed.'

'WHAT?' I jumped up. 'But that's brilliant news.'

'Is it?' She glared at me.

'Isn't it?'

'He wants kids.'

'Oh.' I sat back down. 'What did you say?'

'I told him how I felt about children.'

'Hadn't it ever come up before?'

She sighed. 'Every time it did I changed the subject. I was too scared to have the conversation because I knew what he'd say. But when he proposed it all came up and . . . well . . .'

'Tell me everything.'

Sally took a deep breath and explained . . .

When she'd arrived home from work the night before, Simon was waiting for her. The apartment was lit with candles and there was a bottle of champagne and two glasses on the table. Before she had taken her coat off, Simon threw himself down on one knee. 'Sally, I love you, will you marry me?' he blurted out.

'Jesus, are you serious?'

'Of course I'm serious.'

'Have you forgotten you're already married?'

'OK, well, will you marry me when my divorce comes through?'

'That's so romantic.' Sally giggled.

'Come on, Sally, my knee's killing me.'

'Yes, I'd love to marry you when your divorce comes through.' She helped him up.

'Shit, I forgot the ring,' he said, fishing around in his pocket.

'I would have thought you'd be better at this having done it before.'

'Actually, smartarse, this is my first time. Maura proposed to me.' He pulled a box out of his jacket. 'Here you go.'

Sally opened it. Inside she found a beautiful solitaire diamond. 'Wow, it's gorgeous,' she said, choked up.

'Here, let me.' Simon took the ring out and tried to put it on her finger but it was too small.

'Ouch.' She winced as he tried to push it down.

'Oh, for fuck sake, this is the worst proposal ever.'

'What were you thinking? It's tiny, it wouldn't fit a midget.'

'It was my mother's.'

'Really?'

'Yes, she was very slight.'

'Are you saying I'm not?'

'No, you're perfect. You obviously just have big fingers.'

'No, I don't, I have normal fingers but big knuckles.'

'Can they make rings bigger?'

'I'm sure they can.'

'I'll get it sized properly and propose again.'

'So are we engaged now or do I have to wait for round two? I'm confused.'

'Yes, we are, despite it being the worst proposal in history. Sorry.'

Sally kissed him. 'For a girl who never expected to get engaged it was just fine. Can we have some champagne now or do I have to wait for the next proposal?'

'I need a drink.' Simon popped the cork and they giggled.

'You know,' Sally said, snuggling up to him on the couch, 'you could probably get your marriage annulled.'

'On what grounds?'

'On the grounds that your wife's insane and a slapper and a stalker.'

'You have a point there.'

'Can we get married abroad with just a handful of people? I'm too old to do the big family wedding. Besides, I don't like most of my family, and I'm definitely not wearing white.'

'Abroad and small sounds great.'

'Are you sure you want to get married again? Because I'm fine if you don't. Living together is OK with me.'

Simon sat up and looked at Sally. 'I want to marry you. I love you and I want to have kids with you.'

Sally's heart sank. She took a gulp of champagne. 'Simon, there's something I need to talk to you about.'

'I knew it – you can't have kids. I thought that was why you kept changing the subject every time I brought it up. It's OK, don't worry, we'll adopt.'

Sally looked down at her hands and took a deep breath. 'I'm forty-three so the chances of me having children naturally are slim and we probably would have to adopt, but that's not the problem. The thing is, I don't want children.'

'What do you mean?'

'I mean, I don't want children. I've never wanted to be a mother. It's not for me. I'm not maternal.'

'That's totally normal. Most people don't feel maternal or paternal until they have their own babies. When it's your own child you'll feel –'

'Different,' Sally finished his sentence. 'No, I won't.'

'Of course you will. You're a very loving, kind, generous person – you'd be an amazing mother.'

'No, I wouldn't, because I wouldn't want the child I had. Simon, you're not listening to me – I do not want to have children.'

Simon stared at her. 'But I do.'

Sally held her breath. 'How badly?'

'I've always wanted them. I've always wanted to be a dad.'

'Shit,' she whispered.

'Don't you want us to be parents together?' Simon asked. 'We'd make a great team. I'd be really hands-on, I wouldn't leave you to look after the baby on your own.'

'That's not it. I don't like babies, I don't think they're cute. I think they're a pain. I like my life. I don't want to give it all up for a kid. Once you have a child that's it – twenty-four hours a day, seven days a week, fifty-two weeks a year for the rest of your life. I don't want that responsibility.'

'But I'll be here with you to share it all.'

'That doesn't matter. I don't want a baby.'

'But you're great with Ava's girls.'

'Yes, I like teenagers, but I don't want one of my own. I love taking the girls for lunch or treating them to a day's shopping on their birthdays but I also like dropping them home. Have you seen Ava and Paul lately? They're stressed out of their heads. I don't want that. I don't want another human being completely dependent on me for ever. It freaks me out. I like my life the way it is. I love you and I love being with you and I want to marry you but I won't change my mind about this, Simon. I'm just not cut out to be a mother.'

'Sally, I had a cousin who was the same as you but then she got pregnant and when she had the baby she said she couldn't believe how amazing it was and how different she felt about her own child. She's had two more since then.'

'Simon, you have to listen to me. I'm not your cousin and I'm not going to change my mind. If we had a baby it would break us up because I'd be miserable. I can't do it.'

'Not even for me?'

'Don't do that. Don't ask me to do something for you that you know I don't want to.'

'What about what I want?'

'If you really want children then I'm not the person you should be with.' Sally began to cry.

'I don't think I can give up my dream of being a dad for any-one,' Simon said quietly.

Sally blinked back the tears. He stood up. 'I'm going to go now. I'll call you in the morning.'

Sally nodded – she couldn't speak.

She drank two bottles of wine and passed out on the couch.

'Oh, Sally,' I hugged her, 'I'm so sorry. You guys are great together. I'm sure you can work this out.'

'How? One of us has to give up something they really want. Him having children, me not having children. We'll never find a compromise.'

'Maybe he'll change his mind. He'll realize on reflection that you're enough.'

'Would you have married Paul if he didn't want children?' Sally asked.

I winced. 'I don't know.'

'Don't lie, Ava. You always wanted kids. You wouldn't have married someone who didn't.'

There was nothing I could say. She was right. I was going to have children by hook or by crook and nothing and no one would have stopped me. Thankfully Paul wanted them too.

'You need to find a middle ground,' I said, trying in vain to find a solution.

'There is no middle ground. Maybe I should change my mind,' Sally said softly.

'Do you think you could have kids with Simon?'

She shook her head. 'No. But I don't want to lose him. He's the best thing that's ever happened to me and I don't want to give it all up, but I know having kids is the wrong thing for me. Oh, God, Ava, what am I going to do?'

I held her hand. 'All I can say is that you have to be true to yourself. Ever since I've known you you've been adamant about not having children. When Simon came along I did wonder if you'd change your mind, but you didn't and you haven't. Children, in my experience, are wonderful but they're also bloody hard work and if you didn't want them in the first place I think they could break a marriage and a person.'

'But what if I have a baby and fall in love with it like Simon's cousin?'

'That could happen, and if it did it would be wonderful, but you have to trust your instinct. I love being a mum, I really do, but I always wanted children. If you decide to have a child it has to be for yourself and not for Simon. You can't live a lie with kids. You'll be found out. They can sense if they're loved and wanted or not. They are incredibly sensitive, fragile human beings, as we've seen with Ali. Seriously, Sally, you can't have a Band-aid baby, it won't work. I've seen so many people have babies to save their marriages – and that's the last thing a baby is going to do. It puts a huge strain on relationships. Yes, it's amazing and wonderful and miraculous and utterly joyful, but it's also no sleep, shitty nappies, crying, worrying and stress.'

'That's why I don't want kids. But does that make me a selfish person?'

'No! It makes you very sane and clear-minded. You've never wanted children and, even though you've met a wonderful man, you still don't want them. And to be honest, Sally, if you had a child just to make Simon happy you might end up resenting the baby and him.'

'Why do I have to choose between a baby and Simon? It's not fair. Why do I have to lose Simon because I don't want a baby? Jesus, Ava, I've waited so long to meet someone and now . . .'

'OK. What if you did have a baby? What if you just decided to go for it?'

'The thought terrifies me. I can't do it.'

'Well, then, you have to trust those feelings. Talk to Simon, be totally honest. Tell him how much you love him and don't want to lose him. Tell him you think the two of you is enough and that changing who you are is the same as living a lie. I bet you he'll come round – he adores you.'

'I'm scared, Ava. What if he doesn't come round?'

I hugged my best friend tight. There was no answer to that question.

49

A few days later, Paul and I had a session with Mary Boland. I thought it was going to be a family session with Ali, but it turned out to be just me and Paul. Mary said she was delighted with Ali's progress and that if she continued to put on weight in the next week or so, she'd be allowed home for half a day as a treat.

'That's fantastic.' I beamed at Paul, who squeezed my hand.

'Yes, I thought you'd be pleased,' said Mary. 'Putting on six pounds in four weeks is really excellent. You should be very proud. This was probably the most difficult thing Alison has ever done. But I don't want you to think she's better just yet. There is still a long road ahead. She still feels sick after eating – bloated and uncomfortable. She still counts the calorie and fat content of every morsel she puts into her mouth. She still has the urge to exercise after every meal. But the important thing is that she's fighting it.'

Once again my excitement was reined in. Every time I thought Ali was cured, the experts assured me she wasn't. Anorexia seemed to be a life sentence. Did you ever break free of it? Food was always going to be a part of Ali's life – you have to eat to live. Would she ever be able to sit down and enjoy a meal again? Would food always be a battleground? I felt as if we were constantly taking one step forward and half a step back. But it was vital that I understood everything about the illness if I was to help Ali cope when she came home. I was terrified of making a mistake and having her end up back in the clinic, like Emily.

'Will the anorexia ever go away?' I asked Mary.

'Yes, it can, but not for a long time. It tends to re-emerge at times of stress. Alison's negative thoughts will be the very last thing to go. For a long time to come she will have thoughts about being too fat. She must ignore these.'

'Are you saying it's like a voice inside her head?' Paul asked.

'That's exactly what it's like. The anorexia takes the form of a voice that starts out like a friend. It tells Alison that it wants to help her look better and feel better, but the minute she fights back, the voice turns very nasty and aggressive. At the moment Alison has told me that the voice is shouting at her not to eat. Telling her she's fat and ugly and repulsive. So far, through sheer force of will, she is managing to fight back.'

'Do all the girls hear voices? Is this normal or has the starving made her go a bit mad?' Paul asked, very concerned.

'The anorexia manifests itself in different ways. But most people hear an inner voice that helps them to control their eating. Alison is perfectly sane and is a very strong girl underneath it all. If you look at it this way, it takes an enormous amount of determination and willpower not to eat, so we know that Alison has incredible strength of mind, which will be the very thing that helps her to get better. But for a long time to come, her first thought every day will be "What will I not eat today?" and her last thought at night will be "What shouldn't I have eaten today?" Mealtimes will be a battleground for her. They must be made as stress-free as possible. When she does come home, you must listen to her concerns and talk through her feelings about the food in front of her. It's also best not to praise her too much when she eats. This can lead to panic – "Why am I being praised? I've lost complete control of my eating . . ." The less focus on the actual food and eating, the better. Gentle encouragement is best.'

Paul sighed. 'You'd need a degree to deal with this. I think I'll just avoid mentioning food at all.'

'All parents feel the same way. Just listen to Alison, tread slowly and carefully and you'll find the right words.'

Mary handed us a sheet of paper.

'What's this?' I asked.

'It's a letter Alison wrote to her anorexia. I think it'll help you understand what's going on in her head and also show you how determined she is to get better. I don't want you to go away from this meeting feeling deflated. Alison is doing really well.'

I unfolded the letter. Paul leant in and we read it together in silence.

Dear Anorexia,

You have been my friend for months now. You guide me and help me keep thin. But my life is such a struggle. I'm tired all the time. I'm cold all the time. I'm sad all the time. When I look at my future I feel afraid. Am I ever going to get out of here?

I like having you in my life because you help me organize my days around not eating and exercise. I like routine. It makes me feel safe. But everyone says I'm sick and I have to let you go. They say I'll never get better if I continue to listen to you. If I don't start to eat they'll force-feed me by tube. I couldn't bear that. The doctors and nurses say that I have to choose between you and life.

I want my life back. I want to be happy again. I'm seventeen. I shouldn't be locked in a clinic.

Because I listen to you I am stuck here on my bed being watched all the time. I'm getting angry with you now. I need you to go away from me. I need you to get out of my head and leave me alone. I need to find the old Alison. I'm destroying my family, the people I love most in the world.

Because of you I can't eat what I want. Because of you I can't walk to the bathroom. Because of you my friend died. I hate it. I hate my life. I hate you.

Leave me alone.

I WILL NOT LISTEN TO YOU ANY MORE.

Alison

'Jesus,' Paul finally said, filling the silence.

Mary nodded. 'It's very powerful.'

'Poor Ali. Will the voice stop?' I asked.

'The more she fights it, the weaker it becomes, and eventually as she gets better and stronger it'll peter out. But it may well come back from time to time, as I said, when she's stressed or over-tired or worried.'

'It does seem positive, though – she does seem to want to get better and to be almost saying goodbye to the voice, doesn't she?' I looked at Mary for confirmation.

'Yes, Ava, it's a very positive step forward.'

'Come on, let's go and see her.' Paul pulled me up from my chair. We thanked Mary and went to find Ali.

She was sitting at the desk in her room with Donna, studying. I could have kissed Donna: she was such a loyal friend. Ali looked happy for the first time in months. It was wonderful. We chatted for a few minutes and then left the friends to their books.

As we walked towards the car, Paul said, 'When Ali comes home, I'm going to let you do the talking at mealtimes. I'll be the strong silent one in the corner.'

'Thanks a lot!'

'No, honestly, Ava, I'm worried about saying the wrong thing. I'm no good at this. I don't understand what's going on with voices in her head and all the rest of it. You're better at talking about feelings and emotions, so I'll leave that side to you. I've decided to just nod and smile – it's safer. I'm afraid I'll say something that might set her off again.'

'Paul,' I said, turning him around to face me, 'you're a wonderful dad. Ali adores you. We all have to try to be as normal as possible around her. If you suddenly become mute, she'll wonder what's going on. Just be yourself. I have no idea how to handle this either. It's the steepest learning curve I've ever experienced. We'll just have to work it out as we go – and the most important thing is that she knows we love her and we're here for her. She wants to get better and that's all that matters.'

'What if she comes home and starts hiding her food and all that? I don't think I can face seeing her in here again.'

'We just have to hope she won't. Come on, we should be celebrating – Ali's getting better.'

'You're right, I'm sorry. I just worry.'

'So do I. It's our job to worry.'

'How about I buy you lunch?'

'Sounds great.'

As we were driving to the restaurant, my phone beeped. I checked my message. 'Damn,' I muttered.

'Sally?'

'Yes. She said they still can't sort it out. She met Simon last night and they ended up having the same argument again.'

'Maybe she should just have a kid with him.'

'But she doesn't want children.'

'Yeah, but loads of guys think like that and when they do have kids they think they're brilliant.'

'Women are different. It's kind of an inbuilt thing. You yearn for children when you want them and if you really don't have any kind of maternal feelings or yearnings then you probably shouldn't have them.'

'But if she doesn't have a child Simon will leave her, and if she does, she gets to stay with Simon and possibly have a baby she's mad about.'

'Or she has a baby she's not mad about and resents Simon for making her have it, breaks up with him and has a child who feels their mother doesn't love them.'

'All women love babies.'

'No, they don't. Sally's never wanted kids, and I'm worried that if she does have one to keep Simon it'll be a disaster.'

'Isn't it better for her to try than end up on her own?'

'I don't know . . . You could be right. Children are very fragile, as we know only too well. They need to feel loved and secure and wanted.'

'That's true,' Paul agreed. 'It's a tough decision. But he's a good bloke.'

'That's the bloody problem. He's perfect for her.'

When we got home, Nadia was in her usual position, lying prostrate on the couch, TV remote control in hand. Sarah was curled up in the armchair beside her. They were watching some documentary on Princess Diana. Paul and I snuck by them and went into the kitchen, but we could hear their running commentary.

'Oh, that Dodi so good-looking,' Nadia said.

'*Puuurlease*, he looks like a greasy chipper. You couldn't pay me to sleep with him. What was she thinking?'

'You crazy! Look at boat. He millionaire. You haff good life with this man. He buy you diamonds and beautiful clothes. I sleep with him, no problem.'

'Hello! You're not exactly fussy. You're currently shagging an old-age pensioner.'

Paul and I stifled our laughter.

'You fery rude girl.'

'Yeah, well, at least I'm not a gold-digger.'

'You Bobby haff money.'

'That's just a bonus. I was totally into him anyway.'

'I luff Charlie.'

'Yeah, right, and Diana loved Dodi.'

'She look happy.'

'She just wanted a free holiday surrounded by luxury. I bet she didn't even have sex with him.'

'They was lovers for sure. You not say no to man like this. He can haff any womans he wants.'

'Well, she never would have married him – she was just using him for his cash.'

'Lot of beautiful womans go with rich mens for money. Not means they bad peoples.'

'Hello! It's called prostitution.' Sarah snorted.

'If you beautiful young girl from Poland and you in London and haff no money and a rich man wants to be with you and he buying you diamonds and you taking and selling diamonds and sending money back to you mummy and daddy, why this so bad?'

'Because you're being paid for sex. There is such a thing as getting a job, you know.'

'*Pffff!* What job for Polish girl with no English? Only cleaning jobs. You want to cleaning toilet or on big boat drinking the champagne and helping you family? Peoples do things they not always proud of when they needing money.'

I looked at Paul. 'Do you think she's going to confess the baby isn't Charlie's?' I whispered.

'I doubt it. She's hardly going to confide in Sarah.'

'You never know, she may have got her at a weak moment.'

Sarah drawled, 'If the Polish girl is that beautiful why couldn't she be a model?'

'You no understanding. You haff eferything you want, you not knowing hard times. Life not simple.'

'Excuse me! I saw my father being shot and my sister's currently holed up in a loony bin, I think I know that life isn't simple. But it doesn't mean you have to sleep with men for money. Mum always told us that it's important to earn your own money and have your own bank account. I fully intend to marry a millionaire, but I'm going to be rich and famous myself too. Look at Posh and Becks! When you're both loaded and successful the relationship works much better.'

'How you becomes millionaire?'

'Duh, were you asleep during the play? Acting, of course.'

Paul choked on his coffee. 'That child is delusional. She needs to focus on her studies and less on this acting lark.'

'She's happy, she's eating, and she has good self-esteem. Let's leave her be for the moment.'

'You're right. I'll say nothing. Jesus, it's like walking on egg shells with all these women around. I'm telling you, Ava, I'm better off staying quiet – that way I can't say the wrong thing.'

Sarah flounced into the kitchen. 'Hey, you're back. How was therapy? What did Mary tell you this week? Let me guess – we all need to sit around and hold hands and tell each other we *luuuuurve* each other?'

'No, actually, she told us how well Ali was doing and how she might be able to come home for an afternoon soon,' I told her.

'Oh, wow, that's cool. Mind you, we'd better hide the chocolate biscuits – they might push her over the edge.'

'Hey, you're to be very careful what you say to your sister. She still has a lot of issues with food and they won't go away in a hurry. So, no smart remarks about calories or eating. We have to be supportive and listen to Ali and help her work through her fear of food,' I scolded.

'So, like, when is this all actually going to be over? When can we be normal again?'

'It'll take a while. There's no quick cure for this.'

'Well, I hope she doesn't stare at me when I'm eating like she used to, as if I was some kind of greedy pig. And do I still have to watch her in case she hides her food in her napkin?'

'Hopefully she won't do that any more, but if you do see her hiding food or throwing it out, I need you to tell me.'

'Does she eat normally now?'

'Not exactly. She has specially designed meals that are weighed and measured. It helps take the fear away,' I explained.

'Are you serious? She weighs her cornflakes?'

'Yes. It's all part of her recovery and, so far, it's working. So I'll be buying a set of scales for the house.'

'Well, f.y.i., if she ends up on bed-rest at home, I'm not bringing her food up to her on a tray and sitting with her for two hours while she eats half a yogurt.'

'Sarah,' Paul interrupted, 'I know it all seems a bit mad – believe me, I can't get my head around a lot of it either. If I didn't eat what was on my plate my mother would have walloped me. But this is what Mary told us we have to do to help Ali, and so far she's gaining weight and even getting a little bit of her personality back. So, if this is what it takes, then this is what we'll do. And we'll all pitch in and do our bit. I know this has been hard for you but just hang in there and hopefully it'll all be over soon.'

'OK, fine. But I'm not going to any more group-therapy sessions. I'm the only sane one in this family and I'm not having that Mary woman asking me stupid questions and trying to make me cry about stuff that happened a million years ago. Why can't these therapists just get a life? No wonder they all look so miserable and talk in whispery voices. They spend their whole lives listening to people bitching and moaning about their childhoods and blaming everyone else for their problems. Seriously, it's so boring. Get over it, you freaks.'

'Sarah, if I promise not to make you go to any more family sessions, will you please promise to keep your opinions on the clinic, food, eating disorders and therapy to yourself when Ali is around,' I bargained.

'What happened to, like, freedom to speak?'

'It's actually freedom of speech. Look, just keep your thoughts to yourself in front of Ali for the moment.'

'Fine, I won't say a word.'

'That'll make two of us.' Paul smiled at her.

I was over the moon. Ali was coming home on Saturday for half a day. Although she'd only put on another half-pound, Denise and Mary felt she was doing very well and deserved a home visit.

Denise had warned me that it might not be easy. She said Ali was nervous about eating with us and that I was not to expect too much from her. 'She can take up to an hour to eat a small meal. You'll need to be very patient. And you may need to encourage her if she's finding it difficult to eat in front of the family.'

'What should I say?' I was terrified of getting it wrong.

'Something like, "That's right, take another forkful. There you go, and another one . . ." Or if that doesn't work, sometimes it's best to distract her with stories about when she was young or funny things that happened when she was growing up. You'll need to plan a good hour for dinner. Ali eats slowly and if she feels rushed she might react badly. A good thing to do is to plan something nice afterwards. She can have a fifteen-minute walk, but no more. So maybe you can tell her that after she finishes her food you're going for a nice walk. It'll encourage her to eat.'

'OK, I'll do exactly that. I'm so pleased she's coming out. Will she be able to come home for good soon, do you think?'

'One step at a time, Ava. Your daughter is doing really well, but she has a long way to go yet.'

'I know, I know,' I said, frustrated at constantly being reminded that Ali wasn't cured yet. Couldn't these nurses and doctors ever be really positive? They were always warning us not to get ahead of ourselves, not to get too excited, not to expect too much. It seemed pretty obvious to me that Ali was getting better.

'Anyway, I hope you all have a lovely day,' Denise said.

I felt guilty for thinking badly of her. 'Thanks for your help and advice – and most of all, for being so nice to Ali.'

I cleaned Ali's room and bought fresh linen for her bed and flowers for her bedside locker. I bought a new tablecloth and napkins in her favourite colour – pale pink. I stocked up with the food that Denise had told me she was eating in the clinic: fruit juice, skimmed milk, brown bread, low-fat butter, bananas, vegetables, oat cakes, baking potatoes, cottage cheese, chicken breasts, lean meat, fish, yogurt, Müller rice and some high-calorie snack bars. The fridge was jammed. Ali would have plenty of choice.

'Is good to see you happy,' Magda said, as she helped me change Ali's bed.

'Honestly, Magda, I feel ten years younger. I'm so excited that she's coming home, even if it's just for a few hours. It's all progress.'

'I tells you she get better. She fery intelligent girl. Too intelligents for stop eating. This over now. You cans relax and be happy.'

'I hope so, Magda. I've been too scared to get my hopes up, but now I really think we're over the worst. It's just great.'

Magda patted my arm. 'You luffly lady. You family fery good to Magda. No more sad face, Aleeson will be fine. No problems.'

'Thanks, Magda, and you've been very good to us. We're going to miss you when you go home. Although I'll be really happy for you to get to see your boys.'

'I missing the boys now – I been away too long. Skype OK, but not same as to see faces.'

'It must be so hard.'

'Sometimes fery hard, sometimes not so hard. When I coming

here to work, I happy. You fery nice family. That why I so angry with Nadia. She bad girl. I knows this baby not Charlie baby.'

'Do you have proof?'

'No, but I asking Polish friends. I still looking for proof.'

'Well, if you find any, let me know.'

Two days later I went to pick Ali up. Charlie, Paul, Sarah and Nadia were at home tying balloons to the gate and the front door. I wanted her to feel really special.

When I arrived at the clinic she was sitting in her room with her coat on. She beamed up at me and we spontaneously hugged. It was wonderful. She looked really happy and excited, like a little girl at Christmas.

'Come on, let's get you out of here,' I said, leading the way.

When we got outside, she breathed in deeply. 'This is the first time I've been out in weeks. It feels fantastic.'

I smiled at her. 'I'm so proud of you. You're doing so well. I reckon you'll be out of here in no time. Now let's go home – the others are all waiting.'

Ali chatted non-stop. It was like having my old daughter back. She'd found her voice and her enthusiasm. I wanted to weep with relief.

When we got home, the gate and front door were tied with multicoloured balloons. It looked really festive. Ali was thrilled. 'Is this all for me?' she asked, as we pulled up.

'Yes, pet, we wanted to make a fuss. It's a great day for us.'

'Oh, Mum,' she said, and hugged me again. Then she jumped out of the car and ran over to the others and threw her arms around them one by one. Paul's face lit up – his daughter was back.

We went inside and Ali went up to her room to look around, then came down and said she loved her new sheets – she couldn't wait to come home and sleep in her own bed. We sat around drinking tea – with skimmed milk, no biscuits – and chatted. Paul had lit a big cosy fire in the lounge and it was like old times.

I had decided to have tea at four. I wanted it to be early so that Ali would have plenty of time to eat and go for a short walk before I had to take her back. I asked her to come into the kitchen with me and tell me what she'd like to eat.

When she opened the fridge she froze. 'Mum, there's so much here.'

'Well, I wasn't sure what you'd want, so I bought all the different food you've been having at the clinic. Just tell me what you'd like and I'll make it for you.'

'Uhm, I don't know. I, uhm . . .'

She was struggling. Shit, I shouldn't have bought so much. Obviously she wasn't used to choice and the large quantities of food staring out at her were overwhelming. 'Why don't I do chicken breasts and steamed vegetables, with yogurt for dessert? How does that sound?'

'That sounds fine,' she said, closing the fridge and looking relieved.

'You go back in to the others and I'll get this ready.'

As she walked out I was staring at her tiny frame. Six pounds wasn't much on a bag of bones. Perhaps the next six would make her look healthier. I busied myself with dinner, making sure not to put too much food on Ali's plate. Denise had said to make the amount of food look small so it didn't frighten her.

Thirty minutes later, I called the family in for tea. They had been warned not to comment that we were eating at four in the afternoon. Everyone had been told to say nothing about food and to keep the conversation light.

Sarah stared at her plate of steamed chicken and vegetables, but for once held her tongue. 'Can you pass the gravy, please?' she asked.

'There is no gravy,' I said. I'd decided we should all eat the same thing and I knew that gravy would not be on Ali's list.

'OK, then, can I have some butter or something to put on these dry vegetables?' I glared at her.

'Just stay quiet and eat up,' Paul said, chewing a cauliflower floret.

'Lovely dinner,' said Charlie. 'Well done, Ava. Very nice. I like plain food myself. Those heavy sauces they put on everything nowadays are no good for an old stomach like mine.'

'You saying you no likes my cooking?' Nadia asked. 'I cooking sauces. This food haff no flavour,' she said, waving a stem of broccoli in the air to prove her point.

My blood began to boil: what the hell was wrong with everyone? I had specifically warned them not to discuss food.

'Mum,' Sarah hissed, 'I can't eat this. I need gravy. It's too dry.'

I got up from the table, made some instant gravy and slapped it down on the table. 'Now, can you all please be quiet and eat up?'

Sarah, Nadia and Paul poured large quantities of gravy over their dinner. Charlie and I stayed without in solidarity with Ali. Ali was studiously cutting her food into tiny pieces. I looked around the table – everyone was watching her. She picked up a piece of chicken, and as she was about to put it into her mouth, she looked up. We all pulled our eyes away, but it was too late: she had seen us. She put the food into her mouth, began to chew . . . and gagged.

'It's OK, pet, take your time. Don't rush,' I said, desperately trying to keep calm.

'Take as long as you need,' Paul added.

'It's better to eat slowly,' Charlie said. 'We all eat too quickly nowadays and that's why so many people have problems with their digestive systems.'

'During the war, many Polish peoples haff no food. It good to take time to enjoy,' Nadia piped up.

'I'm starving, what's for dessert?' Sarah asked, but when Paul frowned at her she quickly shut up.

'That's right, Ali, one more forkful, good girl,' I encouraged her, but she continued to cough and gag. I froze. I didn't know what to do.

Ali spat the food into her napkin. 'I'm sorry,' she said, looking upset.

'Don't worry – try another piece.' I forced myself to remain calm.

I watched her attempt to eat a small piece of broccoli but the same thing happened. She just couldn't swallow it. I could see Paul's fists clenching around his knife and fork.

'I'm so sorry, I just can't,' she said. She ran out of the kitchen and up to her bedroom.

'Jesus Christ, I thought she was better,' Paul cursed.

'So did I!'

'So, like, what is actually for dessert?' Sarah asked.

Charlie went up to talk to Ali. I dumped the plates in the sink and ran upstairs to my bedroom. I needed to be alone.

As I was passing Ali's door, I heard Charlie soothing her. 'There, there now, don't be getting yourself into a state. It's all right, love.'

'It's not all right, I'm a failure.'

'You are not. You're the most wonderful girl in the world. You just have a problem that you're working out. These things don't right themselves overnight. Coming home was a big deal. You hadn't been here in weeks, the longest you've ever been away. It's emotional and, to be honest, it was a bit tense down there. Sure I could feel it myself. It was all a bit too much for you.'

'I wanted to eat it all up. I wanted to show you how I'm better now, to make you proud of me. I'm such a loser, Charlie. I just want to be well again,' she sobbed.

'Now, listen to me, you are getting better and stronger by the day. Problems with food, drink, drugs and depression – all these things take time to sort out. Some people don't have the strength to get better but you do. Your step-grandmother Catherine was an alcoholic for twenty years and I tried everything to get her well but it didn't work. The reason she didn't was because she never really wanted to. She preferred drink to life. You on the other hand are fighting to get better with every ounce of energy you have. You want to get well and that, my darling girl, is what's going to get you through. You've done brilliantly. I have no doubt in my mind that you'll beat this. You're a wonderful person, Ali. You have your whole life ahead of you and I know you're going to achieve great things. When you were born and I held you for the first time, do you know what I said to your mother?'

'No.'

'I said, "This girl is going to be really special." And you are.'

It was true – he had said that. Charlie had always thought there was something special about Ali. I leant my head against the wall and cried silent tears for that baby who had grown up and was now struggling to survive.

'I just want my life back. I want to be normal again. I want to be happy.'

'You will be. Sure weren't you happy this afternoon? When you bounced out of the car and came over to hug us, it was the old Ali back again.'

'I don't want to go back to the clinic, Charlie. I want to come home and go to school and college next year.'

'And you will. But you'll have to stay in the clinic for a bit longer. It's making you better, Ali. And when you're a little bit stronger, you'll come home to us again for good. Now what you need to do is focus on the future and not the past. What would you like to do next year in college?'

'Actually, I want to study psychology so I can help girls like me.'

'That's the best idea I've ever heard. When you're feeling a bit down, focus on that. Say to yourself, "I'm going to eat and get better so that I can help girls like me." I promise you, if you focus on that, you'll be well in no time – and think of all the girls you'll save.'

'So you really think I can do it?'

'I believe you can do anything you want. You're a really special girl. Don't forget that. Now, I brought a yogurt up with me. I'll leave it here on your desk and if you feel like eating it you can, but if you don't, that's fine too.'

I hurried out of sight as Charlie came out of the bedroom. I was too upset to talk to anyone. I felt as if we were back at the beginning when Ali was at her worst. I went into my bedroom, put my pillow over my face and screamed.

Paul drove Ali back to the clinic.

I sat up all evening sobbing. Charlie came in to talk to me, but I was too distraught to listen. I had genuinely believed my beautiful daughter was better. I had stupidly allowed myself to get excited. How wrong I was. It had been a disaster. Was it my fault? Had I frightened her by buying all that food? Did I cook the wrong thing? Say the wrong thing? Do the wrong thing? It was torture.

Paul was as upset as I was, but his feelings translated into anger. He ranted and raged about paying a fortune to the clinic when clearly it wasn't working and why were they telling us how well she was doing when she was obviously still a basket case? He shouted that it was ruining our family, that he couldn't concentrate on work, that he couldn't stand to see the strain it was putting on me. Then, worst of all, he began to cry. It's heartbreaking to see your husband racked with grief. He sat beside me on the bed and we both cried for our daughter, our first-born, our baby. Where had she gone? Was she ever coming back?

Eventually, Paul said he had to go to work to check on the pub, he needed the distraction. I nodded, incapable of saying anything reassuring to him. Five minutes after he left, the phone rang. It was Denise.

'Hi, Ava, I heard it didn't go so well,' she said gently.

I couldn't speak, just cried down the phone.

'I know it won't seem like much consolation now,' she said, 'but this always happens. With anorexia there is always a relapse of some kind. But the important thing to remember is that Ali is getting better.'

'NO, SHE ISN'T!' I shouted. 'She couldn't even eat a tiny amount of chicken. How can she be better?'

'I've spoken to her,' said a very calm Denise. 'She is absolutely gutted. She feels she's let you all down. The pressure of coming home and eating in front of everyone just got to her and she panicked.'

'We're her family, for God's sake. We're not a bunch of strangers. Why the hell can't she eat in front of us? All we want is the best for her.'

'I understand your frustration, but everything new that relates to food is terrifying for Alison. It was her first family meal in a month and she just froze. She wanted so much to eat everything on her plate and make you proud, but she was overwhelmed. The good news is that she ate the yogurt her grandfather gave her and she asked me for a high-calorie snack bar. It was a really difficult thing for her to do. She overcame a huge hurdle today. She didn't let the disappointment of the day take over, she fought back and ate. She is still determined not to lose weight. This is really fantastic news.'

'You'll have to excuse me if I don't get out my pom-poms. A snack bar? Is that really so bloody great?'

'Yes, Ava, it is. Alison could have fallen apart and withdrawn after failing to eat with you. But instead she has chosen to carry on eating and putting on weight. It's a huge deal that she asked for food when she came in from such a disappointment. You should be very proud of her for bouncing back so quickly.'

'Denise, do you have any idea what it's like as a mother to watch your anorexic daughter have a total melt-down over a tiny piece of chicken? I was so excited about today. I really thought the old Ali was back. I don't know how much more I can take. Paul's in a state too. It's killing us.'

'I know this must be extremely difficult for you but please listen to me when I tell you that I've seen hundreds of girls coming through this clinic and Alison is one of the strongest and most determined to get better. You must have faith in her. You mustn't give up hope. She needs your support and encouragement, now more than ever. This is a crucial time in her recovery. If she overcomes this setback, then I really think she'll thrive.'

I sighed. I felt old, tired, strung out, depleted and depressed. 'I'll try to be as supportive as I can.'

'That's all she needs. Now, why don't you pour yourself a glass of wine and try to get some rest? You sound exhausted,' she kindly suggested.

'Thanks, I'll do that. I'm sorry for snapping at you. I really appreciate the call and all your help. I'll talk to you tomorrow,' I said, and hung up.

I couldn't stop replaying the day in my head so I decided to try to write my letter to anorexia. Maybe it would help me get rid of some of my anger. The words flew onto the page:

Dear Anorexia,

I hate you. You have come into our home like a violent criminal and brutally stolen our daughter, our happiness and our sanity. Before you appeared, we were a happy family, a family that laughed a lot and loved each other.

But then you came and ripped us apart. You took our beautiful Ali away and left a scared, sick, unhappy girl behind. You sucked all the joy out of her life and filled her with negative thoughts.

Our angel is now in a clinic because of you, but she's going to get better. You will not win this war. You're messing with the wrong family. I will use every ounce of strength in my body to crush you. You will not ruin my daughter's life. I will not let you hurt Alison any more. I will hunt you down and banish you from her life.

A mother's role is to protect her children and that's what I intend to do. I know that the mistakes I made have allowed you to come into our lives, but I will not let you control us any more. You will leave Alison alone. She's going to lead a full, happy and beautiful life and you will burn in hell.

So farewell, evil voice, you will be replaced with my voice, telling Alison every day that she is wonderful, gorgeous, clever, kind, caring, special . . . I will tell her how proud *we are of her. I will tell her how on the day she was born I knew that my life was going to be enriched beyond my wildest dreams. She was the most perfect baby I'd ever seen and every day of her life has been a joy. I love her more now than ever and I will not let you hurt her any more.*

Go to hell where you belong.

Ava

I folded the letter and put it in my pocket. I lit the fire and sank back into the couch, sipping wine until Paul came home. He snuggled up beside me, sharing my drink, while I told him about my phone call with Denise and how she had said we were not to feel depleted, that Ali was still on the road to recovery.

'Well, that's good to hear – although hard to believe after today's fiasco,' he said. 'So I guess we just keep telling her we love her and we think she's wonderful and hope for the best. That's our job, right? To support our kids and, no matter when they fall, to catch them.'

'You're very philosophical all of a sudden,' I said.

'I was talking to one of the guys in the pub. His son was in a car crash and suffered from depression afterwards. He didn't speak or get out of bed for a year. John just said he sat beside his son every evening, told him he loved him and read him books. Eventually one day the boy got out of bed and got on with his life. So I suppose what I've realized is I have to be more patient. I want this to be over now, I want Ali to be better yesterday, but I can see after today that there's no quick fix. So I've decided to try to stay calm and let her get well at her own pace. I'm sorry it's taken me so long to understand what you've been telling me for months.'

'Wow, I'm impressed,' I said, smiling at my husband. 'I like this new Zen approach. I need to take some of my own advice. I've been sitting here furious with Ali when really I should be feeling sorry for her. The day started so well – it's just so disappointing.'

'Tell me about it! Look,' Paul said, showing me his hand. His knuckles were all bloodied.

'Oh, my God – what happened?'

'After dropping her back, I was so frustrated that I punched the wall outside the clinic. Intelligent move! It's killing me.'

'Here, let me get some ice for it. God, Paul, we're turning into lunatics. We'll all end up in the clinic soon.'

51

As I got up to get the ice, the front door flew open and Sarah and Bobby came rushing in.

'Oh, my God! You are so not going to believe what we've just found out,' Sarah said, tripping over her words.

'You've used up all the false tan in Ireland.' Paul found himself very amusing.

'Hilarious,' Sarah drawled.

I looked at my watch. It was one o'clock in the morning. 'I thought you were supposed to be at Tia's sleepover.'

'Yeah, well, we ended up going to Sapphire –'

'Sapphire?' Paul exclaimed.

'Yes, Dad, it's a nightclub – you know, where young people go to have fun.'

'That nightclub is not a place for young girls.'

'Like you'd know.'

'One of my barmen used to work there. He said it's full of people off their heads on cocaine. If I ever find out you've gone there again, you'll be grounded until you're thirty.'

'Hello! We're not living in Afghanistan! You can't lock me up for having a good time. What are you? The freaking Taliban? I have rights, you know.'

'Don't be rude to your dad, not tonight,' I warned her.

'Oh, why? Because we're all upset about Ali for a change? So we're back to bloody square one again. Can't eat. Voices in her head. Won't eat. Too much food. Gagging on food. Hiding food. Spitting food out. Why can't she just be normal? I'm sick of it.'

'We're all fed up,' I said, feeling sorry for her. She'd had to put up with a lot lately. 'But Denise thinks Ali will really get better now.'

'How did she figure that out? Was the clue when Ali couldn't even eat a sprig of dry broccoli without throwing up? We all know I'm not the smart one in the family, but it looked to me like she was a total basket case.'

'Sarah, I know this is hard for you too, but you need to calm down and be nice about your sister. Why are you so wound up?'

'Because, Mum, if you ever listened to me, you'd have heard me say that Bobby and me found out something unbelievable tonight.'

'We were like professional detectives,' Bobby added.

'What in God's name are you talking about?' Paul asked.

Sarah told us to brace ourselves and began to explain. 'So I went to Tia's sleepover, which was really a free house and an excuse to go to Sapphire, which is actually not all that cool so I won't be going back anyway, before you have a freak attack. Anyway, Bobby and I were there and most of the people we were with were, like, so drunk they were falling around, bumping into the walls and throwing up in the loos. The bouncers were getting really pissed off, so we pretended we didn't know them and left before we all got thrown out.'

'Don't think I won't be coming back to the fact that you lied to me about Tia's parents being at home and went to a nightclub without our permission,' I informed my younger daughter.

'Whatever, Mum. So Bobby and me are standing on the footpath trying to get a taxi but there are a million people and, like, four taxis and a rickshaw. The guy with the rickshaw was nearly as thin as Ali, so I doubted he'd be able to pedal me and Bobby the four miles home without collapsing and dying. So we looked around for somewhere to go for food while we waited for more taxis to arrive. I was still starving after the plate of grass you served us for dinner. But then I saw a sign for Zuzi's, which is where Nadia works, so I said to Bobby, "Let's go in and see if she can help us get home."'

'You went to a pole-dancing club?' Paul asked, looking crosser by the minute.

'We were totally not there for the girls, Mr M, we just wanted to get help with a taxi,' Bobby assured him.

'So we go in and it's all dark and full of dirty old men your age,' Sarah said, pointing to Paul. 'This foreign girl comes over who is basically naked.'

'Babe, she did have some clothes on,' Bobby reminded her.

'Hello! She was wearing a tiny G-string and had two tassels covering her nipples. She wasn't exactly in a freaking *burqa*. Anyway, she totally ignores me and is all over Bobby like a rash.'

'She just wanted to know what we were having to drink,' Bobby pointed out.

'She actually shoved her boobs in your face and you went bright red.'

'I did not. I was cool with it.'

'I know you were enjoying it. I could see that from the stupid grin on your face. So I pushed the waitress back and ordered two beers, but she said they only had wine and champagne, so Bobby decided to try to impress her and ordered a bottle of Moët.'

'I wasn't trying to impress her, babe, I bought it for you,' he claimed.

'You were staring at her boobs when you ordered it,' Sarah retorted. 'So the waitress goes off and gets the champagne and brings it back and hands Bobby the bill. It's a hundred and fifty euros! Bobby tries to pretend that he's not shocked and takes out his wallet but he only has sixty and I only have thirty, so we can't pay.'

'I should have brought my old man's credit card out. I'm only supposed to use it in life-and-death situations, but this was a major emergency. I was mortified,' said the big spender.

'So the waitress who was all over Bobby is now totally disgusted, because she can see we're not high-rollers. She starts getting stroppy and saying she's opened the champagne now and we owe her a hundred and fifty euros and she's going to call the manager. So then, out of the corner of my eye, I see Nadia strutting onto the stage and swinging out of a pole and I say to the waitress, "Chill out, you narky tart, we know Nadia, she'll lend us the money." So she looks over to where I'm pointing at Nadia upside-down on this pole – I have to say she's so bendy for her age it's seriously impressive – and the naked waitress starts going mental. She's shouting, "That Nadia is a bitch," and all that kind of stuff, but it was hard to understand because her English wasn't great and the music was really loud.'

'I found her quite easy to understand, I must say,' Bobby disagreed.

'Well, that's because she only spoke to you and ignored me. Anyway, the waitress is going mad shouting about Nadia being a whore. I'm, like, "Hey, I know, I could have told you that myself." But she's ignoring me and ranting on.'

'So I ask the lady, "Why are you so pissed off with Nadia?"' Bobby explains.

'And she says,' Sarah pauses for dramatic effect, '"I hate her because she stole my boyfriend." So I say, "Now, hold on a minute, who is your boyfriend?" And she points to this really big muscly guy at the bar who looks like the Incredible Hulk.'

'He was well ripped,' Bobby agreed. 'I'd say he spends minimum three hours a day in the gym just doing weights.'

'OK, the man had muscles. Can you get on with the story? I'd like to get to the end of it before sunrise.' Paul hustled them along.

'Patience, Dad,' Sarah reminded him. 'So I ask the waitress how long ago Nadia stole her boyfriend. And she says four months, and then she starts to cry and Bobby is all handing her tissues and rubbing her back and ogling her boobs.'

'I can assure you, Mr M, I was not looking at her knockers. I felt sorry for her, that's all,' Bobby said.

Sarah ignored him and continued with the story: 'Obviously I wasn't going to let that go, so I told her that Nadia was engaged to my grandfather and that she was pregnant with his baby. And then the waitress started to laugh and said the baby wasn't Charlie's, it's her ex-boyfriend's.'

'Hold on!' I interrupted. 'Did you just tell me that it's not Charlie's baby?'

'According to this waitress, Nadia has been using Charlie for money. She's been shagging this other guy for months and is pretending it's Charlie's baby so he'll give her more money. The boyfriend knows all about it and has been encouraging her to squeeze as much out of Charlie as possible.'

'That little bitch,' I raged.

'I always knew Nadia was a slut,' Sarah said. 'So I went over to her and pulled her off the stage and I was screaming, "You're a whore, I know it's not Charlie's baby – how could you do that to Charlie? He's been so good to you . . ."'

'What did she say?'

'She knew she was sussed. She didn't even deny it. She said she hadn't done anything wrong, that Charlie had had a good time with her and she hadn't got much money from him at all and she'd been planning to tell him the baby wasn't his . . . and then I got so angry I pulled her hair and told her she was a cheap whore, but her big beefy boyfriend came over and picked me up and tried to throw me out of the club. Bobby jumped on him from behind but he was way too strong for us.'

'Hold on there, babe. I had him in a head-lock. It was only a matter of time before he hit the deck,' Bobby objected.

Sarah rolled her eyes. 'Babe, he was twice your size. Anyway, the naked waitress came over and hit her ex-boyfriend over the head with the champagne bottle and the Hulk fell down, so me and Bobby ran out of there as fast as we could.'

'Jesus Christ, you could have been killed. A lot of the guys running these joints are ex-IRA,' Paul scolded. 'You're not bloody US Navy Seals. What the hell were you thinking?'

'Excuse me! We just saved Charlie's life and you're giving out to us?' Sarah was incredulous.

'Poor Charlie, how am I going to tell him? He's mad about Nadia,' I said.

'I dunno, Mum – but since Nadia said she was pregnant and started being so narky, I think she lost some of her charm for Charlie.'

'He was very excited about having a baby. Oh, God, what a mess,' I groaned.

'He's better off finding out now before she fleeced him,' Paul said.

'I know, but you're all forgetting that he's in love. After twenty miserable years with Catherine he deserved a break. How am I going to explain this to him?'

'You won't have to. I heard it all,' Charlie said, appearing from behind the door in his pyjamas. 'I woke up when Sarah slammed the front door and heard a commotion so I got out of bed to see if something had happened to Ali and then I got caught up in Sarah's adventures. Our own little Indiana Jones.'

Paul and I looked at each other.

'I'm sorry, Charlie,' I said, getting up.

'Don't worry, pet, I'll be grand. There's plenty more fish in the sea – isn't that right, Sarah?' He smiled over at his grand-daughter.

'Totally. She was never good enough for you. I pulled her hair really hard,' Sarah said. 'And I told her that she'd better not darken our door again or my dad would kneecap her.'

'Jesus, you'll get me arrested,' Paul said.

'I was protecting Charlie,' Sarah protested.

'That's enough detective work from you two,' I said. 'Now, Bobby, I think it's time you went home and Sarah went to bed.'

'I'll give you a lift,' Paul said. 'I'd like to have a word with you anyway about bringing my underage daughter to nightclubs.'

'Leave Bobby alone,' Sarah told him. 'It was my idea.'

'I've no doubt it was, but he needs to learn to say no to you,' Paul replied.

'The relationship works very well the way it is, thank you, Dad, so can you please leave it alone and not stick your oar in? I'm the normal daughter, remember?'

'Normal?' Paul sputtered. 'Accosting pole dancers and fighting bouncers is not normal behaviour for a sixteen-year-old girl.'

'Whatever happened to, "Well done, Sarah, nice work, Sarah. Congratulations, Sarah. Despite your sister freaking out at dinner and upsetting everyone in the family yet again, you managed to keep a cool head and help your grandfather"?'

'I'm very proud of you, pet,' Charlie said.

'We're just worried about you,' I reassured her. 'What you did was brave but extremely dangerous. We couldn't bear anything to happen to you.'

'Well, it didn't. And I saved the day. You can think of a suitable reward while I get my beauty sleep.' Turning to Bobby, she said, 'Babe, ignore everything my dad says. You were great tonight.'

'You rocked too. You had a total *Charlie's Angels* vibe. So hot.'

'Easy there, tiger, take yourself and your hormones and get into my car.' Paul ushered Bobby out of the house and Sarah went upstairs to bed.

I went over to put my arm around my father. 'Hey, Charlie, are you all right?'

He sank into the couch. 'Oh, Ava, I'm some gobshite. I was totally taken in by her. I actually thought she loved me. I was lonely and I wanted some fun – I was an easy target and she must have seen me coming a mile away. God, I'm an awful idiot. You were right, Ava, I never learn – out of the frying pan into the fire.'

'You're not an idiot. You're just trusting and generous and kind. I'm sorry it didn't work out.' I poured him a whiskey from the drinks cabinet in the corner and handed it to him. 'Here, drink this – you've had a shock.'

'I just feel so stupid. It looks like I'll always be the orphan boy desperate for love. Will I ever learn?'

'But that's what makes you so special. Despite having had no love when you were small and being dumped in an orphanage, you somehow managed to come out full of life and love and warmth. You're one in a million. Don't ever change, Charlie. Even if you have made mistakes the wonderful thing about you is that you never give up on love and happiness. I've really seen over the last few months how important that is.'

'I suppose as mistakes go it wasn't so bad. It was fun for the first few months and the sex was fantastic. As for the money, she didn't get much out of me.'

'What about the baby?'

'Ah, I'm too old to be having children. I can barely look after myself. I tried to convince myself it would be fine, that it was a new start, but I'm past being a dad. I've been blessed with a wonderful daughter and two fantastic granddaughters. That's enough for any man.'

I kissed his cheek. 'And I've been blessed with an amazing father and the girls with an incredible grandfather.'

'I'm not exactly a great example to them, marrying an alcoholic and then being conned by a pole dancer.'

'You're a great example to them of how to be generous and kind, and how important it is to have fun and not take life too seriously. I've allowed myself to get bogged down in mortgages and school fees and work and exams . . . And I stopped taking time to appreciate everything. But you've always been grateful for what you have and you live every day like it's your last – and that's right, Charlie, because you never know what's around the corner, as we've seen with Ali.'

'I have the orphanage to thank for that. I saw so many kids with broken hearts and broken spirits and I said, "No way am I ending up like that. I'm going to be happy." In some ways starting life with nothing is good because you never take things for granted. And when you get to my age, every day's a bonus.'

397

'I wish I could be more carefree like you. I'm always worrying about something, and if there's nothing to worry about, I worry about that. I wish I could relax more.'

'It's not your fault. You've had to be responsible from a young age with your mum dying so young and me going off the rails. I'm sorry you had to grow up so fast. You should have had more fun when you were younger. I should have been a better dad.'

I took his hand. 'Charlie, you were a great dad, unconventional maybe, but you've always been there when I needed you, and you're an even better granddad. I heard you talking to Ali earlier and you were brilliant. You said all the right things. I don't know what I'd do without you.'

'You'd be just fine. You've done a great job bringing up those girls. They're a credit to you. Don't worry about Ali, she'll get through this.'

'And what about you? Will you be OK?'

'Of course I will. You need to stop worrying about everyone else and take some time for yourself. Enjoy life, Ava. It goes by very quickly. Now, off to bed with you, you need some sleep – you're shattered.'

'OK. Goodnight, Charlie, and thanks.'

'For what?'

'For being your unique self.'

52

Sarah insisted on calling Ali first thing the next morning to fill her in on the Nadia saga.

'It'll distract her from counting the cornflakes in her bowl,' she assured me.

I snuck upstairs and listened in on the extension.

'Hey, Ali.'

'Hi, Sarah.'

'Are you better today?'

'I'm fine.'

'So what was with all that choking drama yesterday?'

'I just got nervous with everyone staring at me.'

'Well, the food was awful. I could barely eat it myself. Seriously, dry vegetables, come on. I'll be anorexic soon if Mum keeps cooking that crap.'

I couldn't believe Sarah was mentioning anorexia and criticizing my food. I'd kill her.

Ali didn't respond, so Sarah kept talking.

'So, anyway, you're not going to believe what happened last night. I found out that Nadia is a lying, cheating whore.'

'What do you mean?' Ali sounded shocked.

'It's not Charlie's baby. She's going out with this massive big bouncer and it's his kid. She was lying to Charlie to get money out of him.'

'Oh, my God – seriously?'

'Totally. Bobby and I went to her pole-dancing club and found out that she's been seeing this other guy the whole time and he's in on the scam too. They've been taking Charlie for a total ride.'

'Poor Charlie. Is he OK?'

'Hello! He's just escaped from the clutches of a gold-digging bitch, he's fine.'

'But he seemed to really like her.'

'What would you know? The whole time he's been with her, you've either been doing star jumps in the loo, counting corn-flakes or locked up.'

I had to put my hand over my mouth to stop myself shouting down the phone at Sarah.

'Shut up, Sarah,' Ali snapped.

'What? It's true.'

'I don't appreciate you slagging me about my anorexia. It's a bloody disease and I'm dealing with it. The last thing I need is you taking the piss out of me, so stop.'

'Fine, keep your hair on.'

I silently cheered Ali on.

'So, is Charlie really all right about Nadia?' Ali asked.

'He's a bit embarrassed about being taken for a ride, but other than that he's fine.'

'Has she moved out?'

'We threw all her tarty clothes into bin liners this morning and Dad dumped them outside the nightclub. There's no way she'll come back to the house – she wouldn't have the nerve.'

'What does Mum think? I bet she's relieved.'

'She seemed pleased, but it's hard to tell. She was really down when you came home and didn't eat.'

I winced and held my breath.

'I ate when I got back here. I'm getting better – it was just a little glitch.'

'Well, the next time you come home you'd better eat a Big Mac and large fries because I can't take any more of this misery.'

'You've made your point.'

'So, do you think they'll let you out again soon?'

'It depends if I put on more weight. I'm doing my best.'

'It was nice having you back – it sucks living here on my own.

Do you think you can come home and eat like a normal person the next time?'

'Yes – but it's hard, Sarah. It's unbelievably hard.'

'Do you still have the mad voice in your head?'

'Sometimes.'

'Can't you just tell it to fuck off?'

'It's not that easy.'

'Well, if you need any help, you can just tell me when it's talking to you and I can shout, "Fuck off," into your ear. It's worth a shot.'

Ali laughed. 'Thanks. I'll let you know.'

'Cool. Well, I'd better go. Bobby's coming over with this amazing new fake tan from the States. All the celebrities wear it. I can't wait to try it. If you want I can bring some in and spray you. You're way too pale. In fact, all the skeletons in there look like ghosts. Hey, why don't you spread the word that your sister does spray tans for, like, thirty euros? I could make good money. Ask around and see what the other sticks say and let me know.'

'Goodbye, Sarah.' Ali hung up.

Sarah was no diplomat and I could have strangled her for some of her comments, but it was nice to hear them talking like sisters again – and Ali had sounded much stronger. She'd pulled Sarah up on a few things, which was good: it was a sign of strength and self-belief.

While Sarah and Bobby tried out their new fake tan I called Sally. She'd been really down in the dumps and I was worried about her. I was so worn out from the disappointment of Ali's home visit that I'd barely had the energy to talk. But Sally had been such a rock of support to me that I wanted to be there for her no matter what.

'Hey, it's me – how are you?' I asked.

'Shite,' she said.

'Have you spoken to him?'

'We had the same fucking argument again last night on the phone. I can't take any more, Ava, I'm drained. I'm so miserable and lonely I think I'm just going to give in and have a bloody baby. I love Simon, he's perfect. I can't stand to lose him. No one has ever made me this happy or made me feel so good about myself. I can't let him go. I just can't.'

'OK, but it's really important that you make the decision with a clear head. If you decide to have a baby it has to be because you want to have a baby with Simon. Don't have it just to keep him. Children are with you every day for the rest of your life and they're very needy.'

'I know, I get it. But what can I do, Ava? If I don't have a baby I lose him. I don't want to live my life thinking, What if?'

'Nor do you want to spend your life looking at a baby and thinking you made a mistake. Look, Sally, I'm not trying to put you off having a child, it's just that you have to be sure it's the right decision for you.'

'I don't want to have a baby. I really don't. But I want Simon more than I don't want a child, so he wins.'

'I just don't think that's the best way to make such a monumental decision.'

'He said he'll be really hands on. He said he'll change the nappies and do all the night feeds and basically raise the kid.'

'Sally, a baby needs its mother. No matter how great Simon is, the baby needs you to feed and love it too. You can't have a child and disengage from raising it.'

'What about all those kids who went to boarding school at five years old?'

'That was years ago and a lot of them turned out to be very dysfunctional. If you decide to have a baby with Simon, I'll support you all the way, but think it through. Motherhood is a job for life and it's wonderful, but you have to want it.'

'What if after all this soul-searching I decide to have a baby and find out I can't have one because I'm so bloody old and then we have to go through the whole adoption thing? God, I don't know if I could do that. Adopt a baby who's already been abandoned and then find I don't bond with it. How badly would that mess the kid up?'

'Hold on, take it one step at a time. The decision you need to make is whether you want to be a mother or not. Whether the child is biological or adopted really doesn't matter.'

'Argh, my head is melted. I change my mind every five minutes. And the thing is that Simon's saying he'll pretty much raise the baby and he'll never be one of those guys who goes for drinks after work, that he'll always rush straight home to his family but all I can think is that *I'll* want to go for drinks after work and I won't want to rush home to a screaming child.'

'Well, then, maybe you need to tell him that.'

'I can't! He'll think I'm a cold-hearted bitch. He's so great, Ava. He's such a good person and I really love him. The bottom line is that I can't bear to lose him and I don't want to be on my own. I'll just have to give him what he wants and hopefully it won't be that bad. Maybe I will fall in love with the baby, like all those stories you hear.'

'Maybe you will,' I agreed.

'Or maybe I'll feel nothing. Why, oh, why does life have to be so complicated?'

'I wish I knew.'

'Tell me what to do, Ava, please, just tell me.'

'I'm sorry, but I can't. You have to do this on your own, but whatever you decide I'll support you a hundred per cent and I'll do everything I can to help you.'

'If I do have a baby, at least I'll have two handy babysitters in Sarah and Ali.'

'That's true,' I said, not having the heart to tell her that after the fiasco yesterday, it was quite possible that Ali would still be in the clinic when Sally gave birth.

'*Muuuuuuuuuuuuuuuuum,*' Sarah roared, 'come and check this new tan out. It's so cool.'

'I take it Sarah needs you,' Sally said.

'Sorry – I'd better go. Look, keep me posted and call me anytime, day or night, to discuss it. And, remember, go with your gut.'

'I'll try. Thanks.'

53

Sally called over to the house on Monday morning. I'd said I'd cook breakfast for her and fill her in on the Nadia saga before we went to work. She still hadn't come to a decision and said she couldn't bear to talk about it any more but that she was desperate for distraction and wanted all the juicy details of Nadia's betrayal.

I gave her a brief run-down.

'The conniving bitch. Poor Charlie,' she said.

'I know, and he's being really good about it, pretending he doesn't care, but I can see he's upset.'

'He'll bounce back – Charlie always does. God, though, I can't believe she was conning him while living here with the whole family. She's a piece of work.'

'I always knew she was after his money, but I didn't think she'd go to such lengths to get it. Lying about the baby was really shitty.'

'It's the lowest of the low. What about Sarah, though? She's a riot. I can't believe she and Bobby confronted Nadia. Fair play to them, they completely caught her out.'

'I didn't know whether to kiss her or shout at her. What they did was brave but incredibly stupid. They could have been in real trouble. Paul said some of the guys involved in these clubs are ex-IRA. And there's my sixteen-year-old daughter wrestling bouncers.'

Sally laughed. 'I'm sorry but it's hilarious.'

'I'd find it a lot funnier if it wasn't my daughter and my father.'

'It's – Jesus, what was that?' Sally asked, as we heard a big bang from upstairs.

'It's Magda. I told her about Nadia when she came in this morning and she went mad. She was cursing Nadia for giving Polish women a bad name and ranting about what a cheap tart she is and that her sister is the same – it runs in the family – and how she warned me about Nadia months ago and I should have got rid of her . . . She's been bashing around the house for the last half an hour.'

'I'm surprised she hasn't broken anything,' Sally said.

The door opened and Magda stormed in, waving her phone. 'I calls my friends and I telling them about Nadia and they all so angry. She not going do this any more. Nadia in big trouble with the Polish peoples. Nadia a fery bad girl. She giffing Polish girls bad name. You daddy fery lucky she gone.'

'You're right, Magda, he is better off,' I agreed. 'Don't worry. I know Nadia is just one bad egg, not a reflection of all Polish women.'

'God, yes, absolutely. There are plenty Irish Nadias out there too,' Sally assured Magda.

'Polish girls normally good girls. OK, Nadia not girl, she woman, but she bad woman . . .'

As we were happily slating Nadia, the doorbell went. As I was walking towards the door, something about the silhouette in the glass made me look through the peephole. I couldn't believe my eyes.

'Sally! Magda! It's *her*. It's Nadia!' I hissed.

Sally and Magda raced out to the hall. I opened the door and before us stood a defiant-looking Nadia. Magda started roaring at her in Polish and Nadia shouted back. The argument went on for quite some time. Judging by the tone, I think Magda had the upper hand, but Nadia certainly didn't seem to be apologizing. Eventually I interrupted them: 'What are you doing here?' I demanded.

'Is Charlie in?' asked the scarlet woman.

'No, he isn't. What do you want?'

'I wants to get my things.'

'Paul left your belongings at the club this morning.'

'I haff money here. I hide it under the bed.'

'Why would you do that?'

'I don't wants my boyfriend to get it. He wants to buy new car, but it's my money for when I am going back to Poland. It's for looking after baby.' She touched her stomach protectively.

'Are you sure it's not Charlie's money?' I asked.

'It's my money from working.' She looked upset. 'I working fery hard and this is eferything I am safing.'

'What about the money you owe Charlie?' Sally asked.

'I giffs Charlie sex. He happy man. I not owing Charlie money. He no giff me money.'

'I know he gave you some money – he told me.' I glared at her.

'Only for appointment to see doctor.'

'For the baby that isn't his?'

'You bad girl.' Magda shook a fist in Nadia's face.

'I not leafing without my money. I needs money for baby.' Nadia tried to push past us. We blocked her way.

'Now, just hold on there,' Sally said. 'Ava treated you really well and welcomed you into her home. You even went on holidays with them, for God's sake. This family has been through a really hard time lately. How dare you make it worse by lying to them about a baby? Do you have any idea how mean that was? Do you know what having a baby means to some men? Some men would give up everything, including true love, for a bloody baby.' Sally began to shout: 'Some men are obsessed with having babies. What kind of person are you? You should be on your knees begging for forgiveness.'

'I am sorry Aleeson is sick. She fery nice girl. But I haff baby now and I needs my money.'

I could tell we were going to be there all day – Nadia wasn't going to leave without her money and I didn't want it in my house. I just wanted her to get all her things and go away.

'Come in,' I said, allowing her inside.

407

Nadia, Sally, Magda and I went into the bedroom she had shared with Charlie. Nadia heaved the mattress up and lying underneath was a plastic bag, stuffed full of ten-, twenty- and fifty-euro notes. There were hundreds in the bag.

'Bloody hell!' I exclaimed.

'I not cleaning any more. I doing the dancing now, money is better.' Magda's eyes were out on sticks, looking at all the cash.

'I'm not sure how realistic Magda pole dancing is,' Sally whispered, as I tried not to laugh. 'She doesn't look very nimble.'

Nadia hugged the bag to her chest. 'These my tips from customers. I safe all. I going back to Poland to buy apartment and look after baby. You tells Charlie I say goodbye. He nice man. He fery good granddaddy.'

'I know how great Charlie is, thank you, and nice people deserve to be treated with respect and not used.'

'I giff Charlie good time. He happy with me,' Nadia objected.

'I think you got the better end of the deal – free lodgings, free food –'

'Don't forget the free boobs,' Sally said.

'Free boobs, free alcohol, free everything. Just take your money and leave and don't come anywhere near my house again.'

Magda started shouting at her in Polish. Nadia hurried towards the front door. Before she walked out, she turned to me. 'I hopes Aleeson get better soon. Here,' she said, handing me a CD. 'I make this for Aleeson. Music will help her.'

'Thank you,' I mumbled, taken completely by surprise. As she turned to go, I remembered something. 'Hold on.'

'What?'

'My mother's ring.'

'That is present from Charlie.' She covered it with her hand.

'It's one of the only things I have of my mother's. Charlie should never have given it to you. Give it back to me now or I'll call the police and have you arrested.'

Nadia reluctantly pulled the diamond ring off her finger and handed it to me. 'You fery lucky, Ava, you haff nice husband and daughters and house.'

'I know I'm lucky, Nadia, but I've made my luck. I didn't go around taking money from old men under false pretences. I worked my arse off for everything I have. Maybe you should try doing the same.'

'Now sod off and don't darken this door again.' Sally nudged Nadia out the door.

We watched as Magda shooed her fellow Pole down the driveway, shaking her fist in her face.

'I wouldn't want to get on the wrong side of Magda.' Sally laughed.

'Yeah, she's pretty scary – mind you, you were pretty scary yourself.'

Sally grimaced. 'The whole lying-about-having-a-baby thing touched a nerve.'

I hugged her. 'Of course it did.'

'Did you see all that cash?' Sally changed the subject. 'I'd no idea pole dancing was so lucrative.'

'Maybe we should take classes and get a job. Seriously, I'd say she makes more in one night than we do in a week.'

'And it's all cash.'

'No tax,' I mused.

'No paper trail.'

'Be hard work, though, all that swinging and hanging upside-down.'

'I'm sure we'd get used to it.'

'I'm not sure it's the kind of example I'd want to set for the girls, though. I don't think "pole dancer" would go down well as a career aspiration in their school.' I grinned.

Magda came back in. 'You no needing to worry about Nadia no more. She nefer coming back. Eferything is OK now. She not bothering you, she going back to Poland. I tells her that if any Polish peoples see her in Eyerland again, she in big trouble.'

'Thanks, Magda. You've been a great help.'

'No problem. I cleaning now.' She left the room and we heard her banging around in the kitchen.

'I wonder what's on the CD Nadia gave you for Ali?' Sally said.

'Let's find out.' We went into the lounge and put on the CD. It was a compilation of classical pieces that were, I must confess, very uplifting. A small corner of my heart thawed towards Nadia.

Ali was due for her weekly weigh-in. I had spoken to her on the phone and she had sounded very determined and positive. So, I tried to be hopeful too, but it was hard to muster up the enthusiasm. I had been so sure she was well until she had come home and hadn't been able to eat anything. I was afraid to build my hopes up again. I tried to be as supportive as I could, but I still felt really down about the visit.

Ali called to say that she had put on another half-pound. She sounded really excited. It meant she could stay off bed-rest. I congratulated her and tried to sound enthusiastic. But when I hung up I didn't feel particularly pleased. Half a pound was nothing. It was useless. At this rate she'd be in there for months. Half a pound on a stick body wasn't going to make any difference at all.

Mary Boland called to see how I was doing and to say how pleased they all were with Ali's progress.

'I'm sorry, Mary, but is half a pound really something to cheer about?'

'I know it seems very little to you, but what Alison achieved this week is actually monumental. You must focus on that and forget about the home visit. Alison has been finishing all her meals and doing as little walking as possible and has even asked for her meal plan to be increased next week. She has overcome the setback and is making fantastic progress. She has not let it get her down, or lost her focus. You have a very special daughter and you should be very proud. She's on the real road to recovery now. So please keep supporting and encouraging her. She needs you.'

'I'm not going anywhere. I told her I was pleased – I'm just a lot more wary of getting my hopes up again. Everyone keeps saying how long it takes for the eating disorder to go and how it's one step forward, one step back. So I've decided to be more cautious. I have to be. I need to protect myself. I completely fell apart when she wouldn't eat at home. I was too optimistic, too hopeful. So from now on I'm not going to allow myself to get excited. I'll just take each day as it comes. It's better for me and for my family.'

'OK, that's fine, but don't let one bad experience make you forget all the positive progress Alison has made. Being cautious is understandable, but try not to hold back too much. She's a very sensitive girl and she adores you and craves your approval.'

'I'm doing the best I can but I'm not super-human and I'm sick of this whole anorexia saga taking over my family's life. It's exhausting. We want the old Ali back,' I said, trying not to get upset.

'Ava, you must understand that the old Alison is gone. She's never coming back and you should be glad of that, because underneath her happy exterior lay a very confused, frightened, angry girl. What you are going to discover is a new Alison. A more open and honest Alison, who doesn't bury her fears and emotions.'

'I have one daughter who never hides her emotions. I'm not sure I can handle two!'

'Sarah does seem well able to express herself,' Mary chuckled, 'but it's important that Alison learns to do that too. Anyway, I just wanted to let you know that the dinner at home was actually the beginning of Alison's real progress. Watch this space.'

I wanted to believe her, but I was too nervous of being disappointed, so I took each day as it came and waited to see what would happen next.

In the meantime, Ali was studying hard for her mock final exams that were coming up. I wasn't sure she should do them. I didn't want her to be put under any pressure, but she insisted that she wanted to and that studying helped keep her mind occupied. So the following Monday I went to the school to collect the exam papers and drove them to the hospital where a nurse would supervise Ali to make sure she didn't cheat. We did this every day for five days while she completed all her exams.

On the last day, after dropping the completed exam paper back to the school, I got a call from Ali.

'Mum, you're not going to believe it,' she said, sounding ecstatic. 'I've just had my weigh-in and I've put on two pounds this week! Isn't that amazing? Two more pounds. They're going to let me go for two walks a week after lunch now. Isn't that brilliant?'

Two pounds was great – it was real progress. I tried not to let myself get too excited. 'That's amazing, pet. I'm so proud of you. Well done. We'll have to celebrate when we come to visit. What would you like me to bring in?'

Normally when I asked this question, Ali always asked for a book or a DVD or magazines, but this time she said, 'Actually, Mum, I'd love some chocolate-covered raisins.'

'That's a wonderful idea,' I said, hanging up before I started crying as my hopes soared anew.

54

The next day we all went to visit Ali in a show of moral support. When I gave her the small box of chocolate raisins, she took a deep breath and proceeded to eat the whole lot, while looking into my eyes. I held my breath.

When she took the last bite Paul, Charlie and I cheered and whooped. Ali basked in our praise.

'Seriously, this is getting out of control. Ali gets a bloody brass band because she ate a few raisins and all I get is grief. Even when I saved Charlie from the evil claws of Nadia, the crook, I got given out to. Talk about favourite child. You wouldn't want to be sensitive around here,' Sarah grumbled.

'You get plenty of attention and praise,' I said. 'If you need more, we'll try to give you more, but I think you get quite enough.'

'Yeah, from Bobby. It's a good thing I have a boyfriend who worships the ground I walk on. You should be thanking him and not trying to scare him away,' she said, glaring at Paul.

'I just told him he should learn to say no to you sometimes.'

'Yeah, well, he tried it and I told him he had a choice – to continue the relationship the way it was going or else we could break up. So we're back to the way it was, no thanks to you.'

'All the false tan must have fried his brain. Poor fella.' Paul laughed.

'Speaking of fake tan, did you ask the other skeletons if they want spray tans done?' Sarah asked her sister.

'I mentioned it to one or two, but they weren't very enthusiastic.'

'Hello! They must be mad – they so need it. Have they seen themselves in the mirror lately? They look like shit.'

'That's why they're in here,' Charlie said. 'Because when they look in the mirror they see a distorted image of themselves. Am I right?' he asked Ali.

'Yes. When you look in the mirror, you see huge, blubbery thighs and a face that's so fat you can only see two tiny pin-pricks for eyes.'

'Really?' Sarah asked. 'So as well as hearing voices you also have hallucinations? You're all mad.'

'It's just a distorted body image,' Ali explained.

'We need to get you out of here,' Sarah said. 'It can't be good to be surrounded by girls who are so fucked up.'

'Language,' I said.

'So when can you come back out? How much do you have to weigh?' Sarah asked, ignoring me completely.

'If I can get to six stone twelve and maintain it for a few weeks, they'll let me go home for good.'

'So what are you now? Like four stone?'

'No, I'm six stone nine, actually.' Ali glared at her sister. 'So I've only got three more pounds to go.'

'Well, the chocolate raisins should be worth a couple.'

'Sarah!' I hissed. 'I told you not to talk about food.'

'Keep your hair on. All they do is talk about calories and weight in here.'

'She's right – it's OK, Mum,' Ali said.

'So you could be out in a few weeks,' Charlie said.

'I hope so. I'd love to be home by the end of March because there's a big eighteenth-birthday party that I'd like to go to.'

'Ohmigod – do you mean Stephen Green's?' Sarah asked. She nodded.

'Everyone's talking about it at school. It's going to be amaz-ing. His dad is, like, *soooo* minted, it'll be super-posh.'

'That sounds great. When is it exactly?' I asked.

'Twenty-seventh of March.'

'Well, that's something good to aim towards. We'll have to get you a special outfit.'

'I'd like that.' Ali smiled.

'You see?' Sarah shouted. 'It's all, let's get Ali a new dress, spoil Ali, treat Ali. What about *me*?'

'If you behave yourself over the next few weeks, the three of us will go shopping together and I'll get you something nice too.'

'Can I get Rock & Republic jeans?' Sarah asked.

'We'll see.'

'Actually, Ali, I wanted to give you these.' Paul handed her a pile of university prospectuses. 'I thought you might like to look through them and pick the one you'd like to apply for. There are lots of choices.'

'Wow, thanks, Dad.' Ali was thrilled. 'I'll have a look tonight and maybe we can talk about it tomorrow.'

'You don't need to run it by me, pet. You decide yourself – whatever you want to do is fine by me. I'll be happy with any decision you make.'

'I'd like to discuss it with you. It'd be nice to have some input.' Ali smiled at her father, who looked chuffed.

I think I loved him more at that moment than ever before. He'd given up his dream of Ali becoming a doctor and was now only concerned with what she wanted, what would make her happy.

'How the hell did you do that, Ali?' Sarah was incredulous. 'Dad's just done a three-hundred-and-sixty-degree turn. Maybe I should stop eating too and he'll tell me that I can be an actress.'

'Dream on.' Paul grinned at her.

'I've got some news,' Charlie announced.

I froze.

'Don't tell us you've met another "refugee"?' Sarah asked.

'No, but you're not far off. I've joined Asylum Seekers SOS.'

'Why?' Sarah asked.

'I've decided that although I got duped by Nadia there are lots of genuinely unfortunate people out there, women and children especially, who need help. They flee their war-torn countries and arrive here with nothing but the clothes on their backs. I want to do something.'

'What will your role be exactly?' I asked, worried that Charlie might get taken advantage of again.

'I'm going to start off at the shelter helping to cook meals and keep the kids entertained.'

'You could do your Indiana Jones impression.' Sarah giggled.

'I was planning on it!'

'You might need to get a new hat – Mum's straw sun-hat wasn't very macho.' Ali laughed.

'Good for you, Charlie,' Paul said.

'Just be careful, Dad. Some of the refugees may not be as genuine as others.'

'Don't worry, Ava, I won't be asking any of them to move in with me. I've learnt my lesson.'

'And don't go out with them,' Sarah advised.

'I won't, although Noreen who runs the agency is a good-looking woman and I didn't see any wedding ring.'

We all laughed.

When visiting time was up, for the first time ever Ali didn't get upset. Neither did I. It was as if something had shifted. I think she finally believed she was going to get better and I was allowing myself to hope again.

On the way out to the car my phone beeped with a text from Sally. I'd been calling her all morning but she'd had her phone switched off. I read it and smiled with relief.

We're still bloody talking but finally getting somewhere. Things looking brighter!

*

416

Five days later Ali called with great news. She had got four As and two Bs in her exams and she had put on a pound and a half. I was genuinely speechless on the phone. My Ali was coming back to life.

Denise and Mary agreed that she could come home that Sunday for another afternoon visit. At first I was terrified. What if it went wrong again? What if it set her back? It was vital that I get it right this time, so I went to the clinic and spoke to Denise about exactly how to handle it.

She advised keeping everything very calm and low-key. No balloons, no welcoming committee, no big family dinner. She suggested that Ali eat with just me this time and gave me an exact copy of one of Ali's meal plans. She told me to have the scales out, so Ali could check the food if she wanted, to make her feel more relaxed.

'The most important thing is that Alison feels secure. She mustn't feel rushed or pressurized. Take everything nice and slowly and involve her in preparing the meal so she sees exactly what her dinner consists of.'

I took her advice and followed it exactly. The difference was miraculous. Ali was much more relaxed and so was I. This time it wasn't a big celebration, it was just my daughter coming home for a casual meal.

I brought Ali straight into the kitchen where I had laid out her food and I asked her to reweigh it to make sure I had got it all exactly right. She did so, and I could see her visibly relax when she realized that the amounts were exactly the same as the ones on her meal plan in the clinic. I had spent ages making sure there was not an ounce more.

Ali ate with just me so there was minimum focus and pressure. I chatted away as she slowly ate the meal. Although it took her forty minutes to get through a small piece of fish with some steamed vegetables and two baby potatoes, she ate it all. Inside I was jumping for joy, but I remained calm on the outside, not making any fuss.

When she had finished I used the line I'd practised with Denise: 'I'm glad you enjoyed that. Would you like a break now, or will you have your Müller rice straight away?'

'I'll have it now, thanks,' she said, and ate almost all of it.

When the meal was finished, Paul, Sarah and Charlie came in and we all had coffee together. I felt a weight lift off my shoulders. I had done it. I had managed to get my daughter to eat a proper meal.

Paul whispered to me at the sink, 'Did she eat it all?'

'Yes, she was wonderful.' I fought back tears.

'Thank God,' he said. He had tears in his eyes too.

I drove Ali back to the clinic. As I was leaving her I said, 'I had a great day.'

'Me too,' she said, and we gave each other a watery smile.

55

A week after the successful home visit, Ali had put on another pound and a half and had reached her target weight for being discharged. If she could maintain this weight – or put on more weight – she would soon be coming home for good.

She would still attend the clinic once a week for counselling and dietary advice, but she'd be able to go back to school and a normal life.

However, we were warned that if her weight fell back to six and a half stone, she'd have to go back in. We all held our breath.

In the meantime, Ali came home for two more afternoons and we continued with the same routine, just me and her eating alone with her weighing her food and everyone else coming in for coffee when the meal was over.

Her weight stabilized. She only put on another half a pound, but Denise and Mary felt that her progress was sufficient that she could come home on a trial basis. Before that could happen, Paul and I were called in for a long session with Mary where she gave us some basic rules for coping.

'I'd love to tell you that it will be smooth sailing from now on, but I think you both know at this stage that it won't be. Alison will have good days and bad days. It is very important that you as parents are singing off the same hymn sheet. You need to co-operate with each other and make sure that you are united in your decisions on how to deal with Alison's eating disorder. Remember to support each other and spend time together. You have a long road ahead and you need to be able to lean on one another in times of stress.

'It is important that you respect Alison and encourage her to become more independent. She must learn to look after herself, feed herself, take all her snacks and watch that her weight doesn't fall. The tendency with parents is to want to control and supervise all their children's meals to make sure their weight doesn't drop, but Alison must learn to take control of her own body and be responsible for her weight gain. Obviously you need to keep an eye on her and watch out for warning signs that she's not eating.'

'Should I keep having dinner with her on my own? Or should we start having family meals again?' I asked.

'I would say stick with just the two of you while she's first home, and then as she grows in confidence you can think about introducing her to full family meals again. But go slowly and take your cue from her. If you feel that eating alone with her every night is getting too much for you, maybe Paul could do it every second night, so you both have a break. You don't want to get worn out. As I've said to you before, anorexia nervosa can be a very frustrating illness and recovery is slow. You must avoid criticism and try to express positive sentiments as often as possible. But you must also set limits, and if Alison is behaving badly and refusing to eat, you must tackle it head on. Choose your words very carefully.'

'Can you give us an example?' Paul asked. 'I'm worried about saying the wrong thing.'

'If Alison is refusing to eat or talk to you, sit her down, look her in the eye and tell her why you're upset: "Alison, I'm upset because you're refusing to talk to me and eat your dinner. Can we please sit down and discuss it so that we can help each other understand what's going on?"' Mary suggested.

'Jesus, you'd need a degree in political negotiation for this,' Paul said.

'Patience will be your best friend. If you can try to remain calm, you'll be OK. Just remember to separate Alison from her eating disorder. Your anger should not be directed at your daughter, but towards her illness. If things are getting on top of you and you feel yourself getting angry, leave the room and go for a short walk or something to cool down.'

'I'd say I'll be doing a lot of laps of the block,' Paul admitted.

'We'll be OK,' I said, holding his hand. 'We can do this.'

'So far you've done a great job,' Mary told us. 'I wish that all the parents of the girls in here were so committed and supportive. I have no doubt that Alison will thrive. There will be occasional hiccups along the way, but if you can weather these, she'll continue to get better. Now, all I can say is the very best of luck and if you need to see me to talk anything else through, just make an appointment and I'll help you in any way I can.'

I stood up and gave her a hug. Previously we had only ever shaken hands. 'Thank you so much for helping us understand this cursed disease, for showing us how to put right the mistakes we made, but most of all for helping our daughter and saving her life. You've been wonderful.'

'I second that,' Paul said. 'We owe you a deep debt of gratitude.'

'Not at all. I'm just doing my job,' Mary said, embarrassed. 'It's been a pleasure – you're a lovely family. I wish you every success.'

After that we spent an hour with Denise going through Ali's meal plan for the next two weeks. It would be controlled and changed every fortnight until she had put on another half-stone and she felt able to manage all her decisions about food herself.

'We have no way of knowing how long it will take for Alison to reach independence. Some of the girls leave here and are managing their own meals within six weeks, but most take longer – some a lot longer. Alison is still very nervous about food, so we'll keep a close eye on her for the moment. Any questions or problems, just call me.'

We thanked Denise profusely for all her help too. Then we went to get Ali and bring her home.

She was perched on the edge of her bed with her coat on, looking nervous.

'Well, pet, it's finally here, you're coming home.' I sat beside her and put my arm around her. 'How do you feel?'

'I'm really excited but a little scared.'

'Of course you are, it's a big day, but we're going to be here for you every step of the way,' Paul said.

'Thanks.'

'Now, come on, let's get the hell out of here.' Paul picked Ali's suitcase up and held out his other hand. She stood up and took it. 'Have a last look, Ali, because you're never coming back here again.'

'Let's go,' she said, and we walked out. None of us looked back.

56

Ali came home on 13 March. For the next two weeks she was going to stay at home and get used to being out of the clinic before she went back to school. I took two weeks off work to help her readjust. Sally was very understanding, as always. If Ali could manage at school, I'd be able to continue working. Otherwise, I'd have to give it up, which I really didn't want to do because it was my sanctuary from the madness at home.

It was a game of wait and see. The first week went quite well. She ate all her meals with me, and although there were some days when she didn't finish what she was supposed to, she generally stuck to her meal plan. Each meal took an hour and there were times when I wanted to shout at her to hurry up, but I remembered what Mary had said about remaining calm.

In the second week, Paul offered to sit with Ali at dinner. I could see he was really nervous, but when I heard laughter coming from the kitchen, I knew things were all right. When Charlie offered to have two dinners with her a week, we began to get a rhythm going and I felt less burdened. Even Sarah was being nice and offered to give Ali a spray tan so that she'd look good going back to school.

I drove Ali to the clinic every Friday for her weigh-in, her session with Mary and her meeting with the dietician. She put on no weight the first week and half a pound the second, which they seemed happy with. As long as she wasn't losing weight it was OK.

The weekend before she was due back in school, I took the two girls shopping. I wanted to buy Ali something really nice for Stephen Green's party. I could see it was a big deal for her to go and I wanted to make sure she looked her best.

All the dresses she tried on were too big. I tried not to get upset when size eight looked huge on her tiny frame. Eventually we found one that looked lovely on her – it was aquamarine with silver beading and it really brought out the colour of her eyes. The woman in the shop pinned it back so we could see what it would look like when it was taken in. She was still painfully thin. The shop assistant kindly promised to have it ready for Friday. Ali seemed really pleased. It was only when we left the shop that I realized how nervous I had been. I was terrified that we wouldn't be able to find Ali something to wear and she'd have a melt-down and stop eating again. I breathed a silent sigh of relief and felt my shoulders relax.

'Can we get my jeans now?' Sarah begged.

'I need a cup of coffee first,' I said, feeling weary.

'Typical,' Sarah fumed. 'We've been to ten shops with Ali and tried on a zillion dresses but now you're too tired to get my jeans.'

'Is it too much to ask that you give me ten minutes?'

'Forget it – just give me the money and I'll get them myself. I know exactly which ones I want. I'm not a freaking beanpole, so they'll fit me and I won't need to get them taken in.'

'Sarah!' I hissed. 'I said I'd get you the jeans and I will. What difference does ten minutes make?'

'I always have to play second to Ali and I'm sick of it. She's home now, she seems to be normal, so why do we still have to tiptoe around to make sure that she's happy before anyone else gets a look-in?' she ranted.

Before I had a chance to tell her off, Ali jumped in. 'OK, enough fighting. Mum, go and sit down and have a coffee. I'll go with Sarah to get her jeans.' Then, to Sarah, she said firmly, 'Sarah, if you make any more comments about my weight or whether I seem "normal" or not, I'll wallop you.'

Sarah looked shocked. I silently cheered for my elder daughter. She was taking control and expressing her emotions – fantastic!

Sarah found her voice. 'Jesus, Ali, relax. I was only joking.'

'Sometimes your jokes are hurtful and someone needs to tell you.'

'Did they teach you to be all bossy in the loony bin?'

'The clinic taught me to stand up for myself and express how I feel,' Ali snapped.

'Keep your hair on – there's no need to get huffy about little things.'

'Describing the clinic as a loony bin is not a little thing. It's insulting and degrading to me and the other patients in there,' Ali stated.

Sarah stared at her. 'I didn't mean to insult you, Ali. I'm sorry.'

'It's OK – come on, let's get those jeans. I'm dying to see them.'

I sat back and watched my two daughters walking down the street to the next shop, and grinned. I was thrilled to see Ali standing up for herself. She had never done that before. She really was a different person, but in a good way – in a way that would make her stronger, more confident and improve her life. It was going to take Sarah a while to adjust to this new assertive sister, I thought, smiling to myself.

I sat down and sipped my coffee. Something felt different. What was it? I suddenly realized that this was the first time I could remember in so long that I didn't have a knot in my stomach. I didn't feel sick. I felt calm, hopeful. Even – dare I say it? – happy. I sank back in my chair and savoured the moment.

A few days later there was another milestone. Charlie's apartment was ready and he was moving in. His furniture had been taken out of storage and delivered the day before. We all drove over with him, helped him unpack his clothes and hang up pictures and photos. When we were finished and the place looked more homely, I opened a bottle of champagne to toast him.

'To Charlie, wishing you all the happiness in the world in

your new home, and if you ever get lonely, come back and stay. We'll really miss you. You've been brilliant – I don't know what I would have done without you.' I began to get emotional.

'Good luck, Charlie, and thanks for everything over the last few months. You've been a huge help to all of us,' Paul said.

'I hope you'll be really happy here, Charlie,' Ali said. 'You deserve it. Thanks for being so great to me while I was in the clinic.'

'Charlie,' Sarah said, raising her glass, 'it's not going to be the same without you. You've been my granddad and my surrogate sibling while Ali was in the clinic and my fill-in parent at the school play and my best friend. It's going to be really boring without you around. You totally rock.'

'Stop now or you'll start me off,' Charlie said. 'It's all of you I want to thank. Paul, for welcoming me into his home and not minding the chaos I caused. Ali, for making me realize how precious life is and how we need to look out for each other and mind each other. Sarah, for always making me laugh, for being my partner in crime, my right-hand girl, and for saving me from myself – and Nadia. But most of all you, Ava, my baby girl, for inviting me to live with you, for looking after me, looking out for me, worrying about me, feeding me, clothing me, putting up with my antics and house-guests and for being so good to me while your own life was being turned upside-down. You're one in a million.'

I went over and hugged him. My father – the maverick, the trail-blazer, the lunatic, the sweetest man, the kindest heart, the maddest notions.

57

As we drove home from Charlie's apartment, my phone beeped. It was a text from Sally:

Decision made. So relieved. No more soul searching. Will fill you in 2mrw at lunch.

'Sally said she's sorted it out,' I said quietly to Paul – the girls were chatting in the back of the car.

'Well, that's great. What did she decide?'

'I don't know. She said she'll fill me in tomorrow. But I'm guessing she's given in and agreed to try for a baby. I really think it's the wrong decision.'

Paul shrugged. 'Maybe there is no wrong decision. Maybe it's just what you make of your decision and how you deal with it that counts.'

'I never thought of it like that.'

'Impressed, huh?'

'Very.' I grinned.

'What are you two whispering about?' Sarah demanded.

'None of your business,' Paul said.

'Is Sally going to have Simon's kid?' she asked me.

'I don't know. I'll find out tomorrow.'

'I don't think she should,' Ali piped up.

'Why not?' I was curious.

'Because if you just do things to please other people you won't necessarily make yourself happy and that can lead to problems.'

'Duh, I figured that out when I was three,' Sarah drawled.

When we got home the girls went upstairs. Sarah was helping Ali to get ready for Stephen Green's party. She was doing her makeup.

Paul and I sat in the lounge, having a glass of wine, reading the papers. We could hear squealing from the bathroom.

'It's great to hear them having fun,' Paul said.

I smiled at him. 'It's a sound that's been missing for a while.'

'Are you OK about Charlie moving out?' he asked.

'Yeah, I'm fine. I'll really miss him but I'm also glad to have the house to ourselves. I'm keen to get normality and structure back to our lives. It's been so mad for the last few months that I'm craving peace and calm. Besides, he's only a ten-minute drive away.'

'That's true and he'll actually be moving back in next weekend to keep an eye on things.'

'What do you mean?' I asked.

Paul handed me an envelope. It contained a return ticket to Paris. 'I'm taking you on a long-overdue weekend away. We're going to Paris for two nights and we're staying in the Hôtel de Verger – do you remember it? It's the one in the converted abbey near the Luxembourg Gardens. I've booked the same room with the balcony. If the weather's nice, we can have breakfast there looking across the city.'

I stared at him.

'Say something.'

I shook my head.

'Are you pleased? I thought it was a good idea, kind of like a full circle. Ali was conceived there and now she's back home after being so sick and I figured that it'd be a good place to celebrate.'

I put my head in my hands and bawled.

'Jesus, Ava, I didn't mean to upset you. Look, I'll cancel it – we can go at a later date. Maybe it's too soon after Ali coming home.'

'*Nooooo*,' I sobbed. 'It's . . . it's . . . it's my favourite place. It's . . . it's . . . my favourite memory. It's perfect.'

'Thank God for that. You gave me a fright,' he said, taking me in his arms. 'I thought I'd really upset you.'

'Not sad tears, happy tears,' I muttered into his jumper. 'It's just wonderful.'

'I love you, Ava,' he whispered into my ear.

'Ditto,' I said, wiping my eyes and kissing him.

'Oh, *puuurlease*, get a room.' Sarah came in as we were mid-kiss.

'Get used to it. There's going to be a lot more of it going on.' Paul winked at me.

'Teenagers do not want to see their parents snogging – it's gross.'

'Well, then, you'd better learn to knock before barging in.' I laughed.

'Whatever. Now, are you ready to see Ali's incredible transformation?'

'Absolutely,' I said.

'Prepare to be blown away. I'm a genius at make-overs.'

Sarah led us out to the hall and called Ali. She came out of the bathroom and walked down the stairs.

Paul wolf-whistled. She looked so pretty, young and excited. Sarah had actually done a great job with the makeup. Ali didn't look washed out, she looked healthy. Her eyes sparkled for the first time in months.

'Isn't she totally hot?' Sarah asked.

'You're a vision of loveliness,' Paul gushed.

'Beautiful,' I agreed.

'Stop – you'll make me cry and I can't ruin my makeup.' Ali laughed.

'Don't you dare cry – it took me ages to get your eye-shadow right,' Sarah warned.

The doorbell rang. It was Bobby. He stopped in his tracks when he saw Ali. 'Dude, you look amazing,' he enthused.

'Thanks,' Ali said, blushing at all the attention.

'Your hot wheels are here, ladies,' Bobby said, swinging his car keys.

'What do you mean?' Ali asked.

'I knew this was a really big deal for you, so I asked Bobby to borrow his dad's Ferrari so you could arrive at the party in total style. Everyone is going to be so jealous.' Sarah beamed.

'Are you sure that's OK?' Ali asked Bobby.

'Totally. I'm happy to do it. Sarah told me she wanted it, and you know how hard she is to say no to,' he said. Then, to Paul, he added, 'Although I'm working on saying no to her more often, Mr M.'

'Good lad. It gets easier with practice,' Paul told him.

'Have a lovely time, pet,' I said, kissing Ali on the cheek. 'Enjoy yourself. You deserve it.'

She put her arms around me and whispered in my ear, 'Thanks, Mum, for everything. I would never have made it without you. I love you.'

I choked back tears as my beautiful first-born walked out of the door back into the real world to embrace the life she could have lost.

58

The next day, I went to meet Sally for lunch. I had booked her favourite restaurant – Le Petit Loup. When she arrived I had a bottle of champagne waiting on ice.

'What's all this in aid of?' she asked, delighted.

'It's for two reasons. It's to thank you for being such an amazing friend to me over the last few months and allowing me to ear-bash you about my woes on a daily basis. And I wanted to congratulate you properly on being engaged.'

She grinned. 'I'll drink to that.'

'So, how are things?'

'Brilliant! We spent hours together yesterday just talking and crying and baring our souls. It was the most incredibly raw and draining conversation I've ever had. We put all our cards on the table, complete honesty. He told me his hopes, dreams and wishes and I told him mine. He said he didn't want to lose me, but he did want children. I said I didn't want to lose him, but I couldn't bring a child I didn't want into the world for anyone. It was cruel and unfair. As usual we went around in circles for hours. I don't think I've ever cried so much. I actually felt dehydrated.'

'How did you resolve it?'

'The one thing we agreed on was how much we loved each other. That was set in stone. But he also wants to be a dad and I don't want to be a mum. So we have finally come to an agreement.'

'What?' I was nervous about the answer.

Sally played with her fork. 'It's going to sound a bit unconventional. I need you to brace yourself.'

I sat up and paid full attention. 'I'm all ears.'

431

'We're going to get married as soon as his divorce comes through and then Simon's going to adopt a baby on his own. I'll have no legal rights to it. I'll just be its stepmother or surrogate mother or whatever the term is, if there even is a term.'

'Wow.' I wasn't sure what else to say. It was certainly an unusual arrangement.

'We're going to live beside each other – Simon's going to buy the apartment across from me that's for sale. He'll be the baby's primary parent, but I'll be there to help him out. I know I'll love the child and I know I can help to bring it up, I just don't want the responsibility of being its actual mother. Does that sound really weird?'

I cleared my throat. 'It *is* unconventional, but knowing you and him, I think it's inspired. You're both getting what you want and he'll be a great dad and you'll make a fantastic stepmum, so the baby will be much loved. For you guys, it's the perfect solution.'

'I'm glad you think so. We really looked at every single angle and this was the only way we felt we could both be truly happy and fulfilled. I get to stay with Simon and I'm really happy to be a stepmum. I'm not sure how we'll work out the sleeping arrangements – I guess I'll sleep there a few nights a week – but we're committed to staying together and moving forward.'

'That's great. Isn't there some movie star who lives in a separate house from his wife and kids?'

'Yeah, Woody Allen and Mia Farrow lived in separate houses, but the less said about that the better. They're not exactly a shining example of success.'

'Sorry,' I said.

'Some bloody comfort you are.' Sally began to laugh. Within seconds we were both in hysterics.

'I've got it!' I shouted. 'Helena Bonham Carter and Tim Burton live in adjoining houses in London. They seem really happy.'

Sally waved her glass in the air. 'Hurrah! Yes, they do seem happy, and if it can work for them, it can work for Simon and me.'

We drank to that. I then broached with Sally the prospect that I might have to give up work for a while if Ali didn't manage to eat properly. If I had to hold her hand I would – anything to stop her going back into the clinic. 'You know how proud I am of Happy Dayz, I love coming to work with you every day, but if Ali can't manage her food on her own, I'll have to give up for a while to focus on her.'

'Hold on a minute. If, and it's only an if, Ali can't manage her food intake, you can go home and help her with her meals, and while she's in school or studying you can work. Didn't the psychologist say you needed to keep your own life? Besides, I thought Donna said she'd eat lunch with her and let you know if anything started to slip.'

'Yes, she did, bless her. But a lot of girls find it difficult to maintain their meal plans once they get out of the clinic. Look, with luck, Ali will be fine and there won't be any problems, but I just wanted to mention it in case.'

'OK, fine. Whatever happens we'll work around it. I'm not losing my work partner. How's Ali getting on so far?'

'Really well, actually, she hasn't lost any weight. It's so nice having her home. She's back to her new self – a more assertive, but still sweet Ali.'

'It's been a rough few months, hasn't it?' Sally squeezed my hand.

'I feel as if I've lived a lifetime since September. And I used to think I had it all figured out. I was a working mother with two great children. No problems with drugs, alcohol, teenage pregnancies . . . Well, that bubble was certainly burst. I'm just like every other parent out there. I have no idea what I'm doing. I'm trying my best to deal with each crisis as it comes along and hoping against hope that I make the right decisions.'

'You're doing a great job, you're a great mum.'

I put my fork down, chewed slowly and swallowed. 'You know, Sally, I really thought I was, but I'm not. I'm just a mum. I make mistakes, big ones, and I have to deal with the consequences.

433

This experience has crushed any notions I had about having good parenting skills.'

'Everyone goes through rough patches with their kids. I was a nightmare to my poor mother, but I turned out OK. You're doing the best you can and that's all anyone can ask. You can't control the way your children react to things – it's in their DNA. There was no way you could have predicted Ali's anorexia. You really have to stop being so hard on yourself. You're a wonderful mother and Paul's a brilliant dad. You're a great team.'

'Thanks. Speaking of teams, did I tell you Paul's taking me to Paris next weekend?'

'No!'

'He's booked the same hotel we stayed in eighteen years ago, where Ali was conceived. I can't believe he remembered. It's such a lovely surprise – well, it was a shock actually. Paul's never organized anything in his life. I'm thrilled.'

'Good for Paul . . . and good for you. You guys deserve a break. Do you want me to look in on the girls?'

'Thanks for offering, but Charlie's moving back in for the weekend.'

'How is he?'

'He's really good. He comes over every day for his dinner – he has dinner with Ali on their own two nights a week, which is just brilliant as it gives Paul and me a break. He's also started working at the refuge and so far hasn't invited anyone to live with him. Although he seems a bit keen on Noreen who runs it, so God only knows what'll happen there.'

'Any word on Nadia?'

'According to Magda, she's gone back to Poland with her suitcase full of money to have her baby. Good riddance to her. Speaking of mad women, have you seen your stalker Maura lately?'

'Not since Sarah scared her off.'

'Oh, God, don't remind me – she's a liability.'

434

'No, she's just completely fearless, which is a fantastic way to be.'

'Fearless is one way of putting it. It's strange, you know. This journey we've been on with Ali's anorexia has made us all closer. Sarah and Ali are getting on really well, but it's more equal now. Ali is being more assertive and giving out to Sarah when she starts going off on tangents or being sarcastic about the clinic or food. Paul's home four nights a week for dinner. He eats alone with Ali two nights and then with me and Sarah the other two. He's just so much more involved with the girls now. His relationship with Sarah is so much better. Instead of fighting all the time they have great banter. And he's closer to Ali too – he doesn't have her up on this unnatural pedestal as the perfect child. He realizes that she's just a normal teenager with problems and insecurities, that she's going to make mistakes and he needs to be there for her.'

'That must be a relief for Ali. Being stuck with the perfect-child label is impossible to live up to.'

'You're so right. I think Ali feels a weight off her shoulders, to be honest. And as for Paul and me, things are just so much better. It was scary – we were really drifting apart, but because we've had to cling to each other through this rollercoaster ride, we've found each other again. Honestly, I feel as if we've fallen in love for the second time. It's amazing.'

'So maybe Ali's crisis wasn't all bad.'

'I hate the fact that she's been so sick and that she won't fully recover for a long time, but I now believe that in life you get dealt a hand of cards and you just have to struggle through and make the most of what you have. We're battered and bruised but, as a family, we're closer, more honest and caring.'

'I'm all about being honest. It's worked out for me.' Sally smiled.

'Which is so fantastic. So, any idea when the wedding will be?'

'We're thinking late June, when Ali's exams are over. I want the girls to be my bridesmaids.'

'Oh, Sally, that's so nice. They'll be thrilled.'

'It's probably going to be in Tuscany – I'm working on the location. But it's literally going to be you guys and us. I'm not inviting any family because if I invite one I have to invite all of them, and Simon's parents are dead and his brother lives in an ashram in India, so he probably won't come anyway.'

'What is the blushing bride planning on wearing?'

'Definitely not white. Maybe a scarlet dress, seeing as I'm marrying a divorcee and I'm refusing to procreate.'

'And you're not exactly a vestal virgin.'

'Not exactly.'

We giggled.

I leant back in my chair. 'Tuscany in June sounds like heaven. I can't wait.'

'Speaking of which, I'm really sorry, Ava, but I have to go. I'm meeting Simon to pick up the ring. He's had it enlarged from midget size to big-knuckle size.'

'Off you go. That's a very important date. I'll see you tomorrow bright and early.'

'Thanks for a lovely lunch and for your invaluable friendship.' She kissed me and rushed off to meet Simon.

I finished my drink, paid the bill, put my coat on and walked down the street feeling the warmth of the spring air as I went.

Acknowledgements

I had a lot of help researching this book and I'd especially like to thank:

Harriet Parsons from Bodywhys for her patience, kindness and generosity in educating me about eating disorders; Dr Valerie Freeman, consultant clinical nutritionist, for helping me understand the potential causes of anorexia and how to heal it; Patricia Deevy, my editor, who was instrumental as always in this book being completed; Rachel Pierce, who held my hand through the numerous rewrites and played a big part in making the book better; Michael McLoughlin, Cliona Lewis, Patricia McVeigh, Brian Walker and all the team at Penguin Ireland for making the publishing process so enjoyable; all in the Penguin UK office, especially Helen Fraser, Tom Weldon, Joanna Prior, Naomi Fidler, Clare Pollock and the fantastic sales, marketing and creative teams; Hazel Orme, as always, for her incredible copy-editing; my agent Gillon Aitken and Kate Shaw and all at the agency for their hard work; Marianne Gunn O'Connor – my new partner in crime; Mick Drumm for his insight into surfing.

Thanks to my friends for their warmth, humour and most of all their loyalty. Good friends are a very precious commodity. To Sue and Mike for always being there. To Mum and Dad for always cheering me on. To Hugo, Geordy and our beautiful little Amy, for allowing me to experience the joy of unconditional love. And to Troy, for putting up with me and encouraging me as I tore my hair out over this book and, most of all, for being the best person in the world to go through life with.

This book was difficult to write. I felt such a strong sense of responsibility to honour the many incredible women I met who helped with my research. I have tried to portray eating disorders in an honest and candid way. Unfortunately the clinic described in the book is fictional. There are no such clinics in Ireland for sufferers of eating disorders. This is something that needs to be changed. Bodywhys and other voluntary organizations like it are doing incredible work to help sufferers of eating disorders and their families. But it's not enough: we need government funding and we need to increase awareness of this potentially fatal illness.